MYRA, BEYOND SADDLEWORTH

Jean Rafferty

Give me back my broken night
my mirrored room, my secret life
it's lonely here,
there's no one left to torture
Give me absolute control
over every living soul
And lie beside me, baby,
that's an order!

Leonard Cohen, *The Future*

A Wild Wolf Publication

Published by Wild Wolf Publishing in 2012

Copyright © 2012 Jean Rafferty

First print

ISBN: 978-1-907954-25-2

www.wildwolfpublishing.com

This book is for my brother, Peter, who died before he should have.
I loved him very much and miss him terribly.

Author Foreword

Many people have questioned the morality of writing a fictional novel about Myra Hindley when the families of her victims are still alive, and when the surviving Moors Murderer, Ian Brady, refuses to reveal the location of the body of their last known victim, Keith Bennett.

I find this strange when there have been so many non-fictional representations of Myra Hindley and Ian Brady and indeed, broadcast dramatisations of their lives.

As a former journalist, I am well aware of the power of factual writing, but fiction is a more exploratory form. Like many people, I have often wondered what kind of person commits such atrocities. *Myra, Beyond Saddleworth* is an honest attempt to find out.

I do not wish to add to the pain of the families who have lost their children. I can only assure them that the book is not sympathetic to the people who caused them such suffering.

Acknowledgements

I once heard someone saying books were written not by writers but by committees. While most of the writers in the room were aghast, it is nevertheless true that few books are written without a huge backup team. My team have been generous with their time, their opinions and their emotional support. I love and thank them all: The great South African novelist, Zoë Wicomb, gave me not only her friendship but new ways of thinking. Any imprecisions or lapses of taste in this novel are entirely the result of my own imperfect judgement.

My family and friends helped me throughout the difficult personal circumstances in which the novel was written: my sister Mary and my late mother Mollie supported me in everything and kept the laughs coming; my brother Andrew and sister Kate believed in me when I feared the novel would never be published; my brother David's affection extended even to reading the critical commentary that accompanied it for my doctorate; and my brother Peter thought the novel was a page-turner but died before he could reach the end. I miss him all the time.

My friends gave me emotional and practical support and the astuteness of their perceptions: Margaret Wells, Zen Brayley, Val Black, Katie Grant, Maggie Anderson, Habie Schwarz, Ian Cotton, Dennis Hackett, Pat Hagan, Gwyneth Hughes, Simon Hamilton and Elizabeth Marriott, the last of whom even found me my publishers, Wild Wolf, whose support for 'dark, edgy fiction' is unusual and brave in the world of publishing today.
My agent Guy Rose had the nerve to take me on when other agents liked the style but were afraid of the subject.

Dr Rachel Douglas and Karin Livingstone were kind enough to read and make thoughtful comments on the manuscript.

Ian Brady's willingness to correspond with me gave me insight into the insight into the way he thinks, despite his unwillingness to discuss the murders themselves.

Last but not least, I thank Alex Brown and Squeaky, who sparked the idea off in the first place.

PART I

RELEASE

1 RELEASE

From Manchester the road begins its climb towards the moors, stretching ahead on a colossal scale, three lanes up the hill and three lanes down, like a road built by the Nazis. M feels her stomach griping with something like fear. In less than an hour she will be on her own, properly on her own for the first time in forty years—no bells punctuating her day, no warders telling her what to do, no locks turning in the door. Free.

There is so much traffic that the taxi moves very slowly. A line of massive lamps, rearing back like flat-headed snakes ready to strike, stakes out the division between the two directions. It's raining and the moisture softens the light, splaying it outwards like spotlights at the night soccer matches the lads in their street went to. Beyond the road on either side is blackness. She knows the moors are there but she can see nothing.

'Give us a fag, will you, driver?' she asks.

He turns, nettled by the rough rasp of her voice, the peremptory tone. 'Haven't you got your own, love?'

'I'm supposed to be giving up. I've got terminal lung cancer.'

He is silenced for a moment, but what can he do, faced with such insane need? He flips his pack back to her. She smiles in the dark—silly sod, believing that. Carefully she slips two cigarettes on to her lap.

'Have you a light?'

He sighs and hands his lighter back. The flame flickers for a second and he sees her fresh skin and soft haircut. Not bad looking for a big lass, but he's not keen on posh birds.

'Look, there's the sign for Saddleworth,' she says. 'That's where the Moors Murders were committed, wasn't it?'

'It gives me a funny feeling just driving past it, to tell you t' truth. Makes your skin crawl.'

The rain is driving against the windscreen now, so she can hardly see. She still looks, scouring the space ahead in case she can glimpse something, catch a whisper of what happened here. Nothing. Nothing.

Up and up the road climbs. All she can hear is the whining and grinding of car engines stopping and starting as the traffic slows and moves on. The rain bounces off the bonnet and windscreen like beats on a steel drum. Near the top the road flattens out and divides into two to bypass a farm plumb in the centre. She can't believe what she's seeing. 'Do people live there? How do they get in and out?'

'Daft buggers. Held out for too much money so they just built t'road around 'em.'

She sniggers. 'They'd be skin and bone now, never able to get out for something to eat. Mouldering old skeletons.'

The driver laughs, but glances back in his mirror, startled by the blackness of her humour. The car turns off the motorway shortly afterwards and they're in country roads that climb and turn. She begins to feel sick. It's different when it's you that's driving. She used to love the whole business of it, the one thing she could do that Brady couldn't. Being in your own portable world where no-one else could get at you or get in your way—she was good at it. The driving instructor told her she had very quick reflexes. 'You never panic, do you?' he said. 'A cool head in a crisis, that's you.' She can't believe the numbers of people who have cars now. In the old days you were unusual, special, if you could drive. Now it seems everyone can do it. No way she'll get the chance now—the money they give her will never stretch to a car, that's for sure. Bastards. They've given her the least they decently could. She was better off in the bloody jail, with Lord Astor giving her two hundred and fifty quid a month for her 'expenses.'

They plunge downhill now, into a large mill town, its buildings made of local grey stone. A group of teenagers hang around next to the chip shop. Bunch of twats. The heavy rain has them all crowded into a doorway, swigging what looks like home brew from a lemonade bottle. They'll probably poison themselves with it and good riddance. Louts. Some things never change. It's been nearly forty years since she's had chips from the chippie. Loads of salt and sauce. Mushy peas. Chips aren't the same inside. As for those oven ones they brought in, what's the point of them? If you're going to eat chips you want the fat.

The driver pulls up at the end of a terrace of small red brick houses. 'Here you are, love. Want a hand wi' that bag?' She decides against it and pays him, then regrets it a moment later—the rain soaks her almost immediately and her case is heavy. Why did she bring all those books? She has the key ready in her pocket, though, has been fingering it for miles.

Inside, the hallway is pitch black, but she can smell the house, smell fresh paint, emptiness. She searches for the light switch, sniffing her way forward like a cat, sidling, catlike, along the wall till she feels an inner door and then the switch against her shoulder. The hall suddenly gleams with light. She can't believe how elegant it is, all yellow and gold stripes with a lovely frieze about halfway up.

In the living room the wallpaper is pale yellow with gold writing in Latin or something and the ceiling is studded with lots of funny little lights, like stars. It's beautiful. She sits down on the sofa and stares at the blank television, her hands shaking. This can't all be for her, can it? How come they've cut her some slack after all these years? Just shows you what willpower can do. If she hadn't kept on at the European court they'd never have let her out. She pulls out the taxi driver's lighter and lights the second cigarette. Just a cheap plastic lighter, unfortunately. She tosses it on to the coffee table and draws the smoke into her lungs, half closing her eyes as she feels its narcotic reassurance.

The whole cigarette is gone before she's calm enough to move again. The kitchen is on the other side of the hall and has a circular table that you can eat at. Will she ever have guests? She's never been much of a cook—Mam used to bring food over for them when she and Brady were living together. They paid her for it of course. He liked mushy stuff, like macaroni cheese and creamed rice. Slop, not fit for an adult to eat.

7

On the table is a little note with a phone number, from her landlady, probably. 'Tea and coffee in cupboard above kettle. Bread, butter, milk and bacon in the fridge—your brother told me you had a long way to come. I hope you enjoy living here. Call me if you need anything.' M crumples it up and throws it into the plastic bin in the corner. She doesn't want any busybodies nosing around here.

Upstairs there's a large bedroom with strange, ruched curtains, peach-coloured and made of some shiny material. She's never seen anything like them before; they look really posh. The bed is a double one and has a matching duvet. The first time she ever saw one of those was that trip to the moors five years ago to find Pauline Reade and Keith Bennett. Well, their bodies anyway. There were duvets at the police training place they stuck her in at night. She likes the way they settle round you when you sleep, much cosier than the scratchy old blankets they used to give you inside.

In the bathroom she plays at lifting the fancy taps up and watching the water trickle away down the plughole. It's all so pretty, white and blue tiles with a dolphin frieze round the middle and a shower with a glass screen at the end of the bath, the sort of bathroom she's seen in films, though she never dreamt ordinary people had them. A tin tub on Saturday nights and an outside privy, that was what she grew up with.

M wanders through to the last room, looks round at the white wildflower-patterned wallpaper and curtains, the matching bedspread. Suddenly she takes off at a run, across the landing to the other bedroom, flying at the double bed. 'It's mine,' she screams, bouncing up and down on it. 'Mine, mine, mine.' She's never had a double bed to herself and rolls around on it, sinking into its softness, splaying her legs out to reach the edges. It seems suddenly a limitless space, hers to occupy, to fill with whoever or whatever she wants. No more quickies on a quilt under the bed, with someone else keeping watch outside the door. No more hiding.

She can do what she wants.

Oops, what time is it? Mustn't miss the news, best to know what the bastards are saying about you. Five to ten, according to her watch. It's a good one, gold-plated and diamond-set with a mother-of-pearl face, cost over a hundred pounds. A girlfriend gave her it on leaving Holloway, sort of a fuck-off present because the bitch didn't want to make herself useful on the outside.

M would like to eat something but is exhausted. Instead she makes a cup of tea, wishing she'd nicked a third fag. When is it bloody coming on? Nothing but stupid ads. Get a move on, for goodness sake.

Finally the chimes announce the News at Ten. Thank goodness. A nerve in her neck is pulsing. M can't wait to see what they say about her. She watches with the avidity of one seeing into her own future.

For fuck's sake, not that bloody mugshot again. She wants to put her fist right through the television screen. Forty years that picture's been following her around, like a malign twin, someone who's related to her but is not her. It's like staring into a mirror and seeing someone else look back at

8

you. The woman in the photo bears no resemblance to who M is today. Don't they understand, she's like Dorian Gray in reverse? She may have started out looking ugly but she's different now. She's not that woman any more, doesn't look even a little bit like that, not now they've given her the nose job and all the nips and tucks.

At least her death is the first thing on, though that's par for the course—they love banging on about the wicked Moors Murderers, makes their ratings go up, the hypocritical creeps. If she had a penny for every word written or said about her she'd be a millionaire by now.

Good grief, they had the funeral at seven thirty in the evening, when it was completely dark. Smart, no-one would expect it to happen at night. They were probably afraid the hearse would be attacked or something. How people have the nerve to look down on her when they'd tear her limb from limb if they ever got hold of her. There's a hell of a lot of folk capable of murder out there.

Just eleven mourners. There's her brief, Andrew. And Lady Astor. Who'd have thought she'd have a member of the aristocracy at her funeral? And Lara, beautiful Lara. How cock-a-hoop she was, getting a famous criminologist to fall in love with her. Lara's looking good. Oh, that time in the garden …

Now they're saying the hospital she 'died' in has already had her room painted. Out of courtesy for other patients? How ridiculous! What do they think's going to happen to them? Do they think they'll absorb evil through breathing the same air as her, like passive smoking? that evil is embedded in the paint? Do they think they can catch it off her? It was fun being smuggled out of there, though, with that red wig and the nurse's uniform. Pity she couldn't have kept it. You never know when a disguise will come in handy.

Anger and tea revive her and she decides she will unpack after all. Upstairs, there's a built-in wardrobe in the master bedroom, or should that be the mistress bedroom? A fine word, mistress. Mistress … the word rolls round her head. Form mistress, Brady's mistress, Mistress Quickly … mistress of all she surveys. She stacks her blouses and jumpers on the wardobe shelves, slides her lilac suit out of the case, holding it up against her. How good she always felt in it, the jacket skimming her waist, the trousers generous but elegant. Any time she met the press she wore it.

By the time she's put her jewellery box and makeup on the dressing table and her toiletries in the bathroom, she's beginning to flag again. Just the books. She lugs them into the small room. Her office? Well, why not? She's always been good at writing, why shouldn't she have her own office? Maybe she could get a book published, like Brady, bring in a bit of brass.

When she finally slips into the big double bed she feels she would like to sleep for a year. She can hardly believe she is here, she is free. *She can do what she wants.* Best leave the light in the hall on—she's always hated the dark, too scary. That was one thing about prison, it's never totally black. The door casts a grotesque shadow into the room but she doesn't care, for once slips into sleep without chemical assistance.

Under the surface of her eyelids cars whizz up the motorway, their drivers standing up in the front seat, arms stiffly held in front of them like Hitler inspecting a rally of his troops. Lights probe and arc across the road, irradiating the whole night sky. *She* is Hitler. She is standing up in the front seat of the car and the other drivers become soldiers, marching in procession up the glorious path to … to what? To power? godhead? honour? Heil Hessie! Heil Hessie! Heil Hessie!

She's twisting with sweat when the sound penetrates her sleep. It's eerie, a strange, raucous barking at once urgent and unearthly, like a dog, but not like a dog. She has never heard such a sound before. She's afraid at first to move, thinks she's still in the dream. The hound of Hell is pursuing her, crazed, driven, his rank breath scorching her cheek.

At last M realises that the sound is real and goes to the window to raise the ruched blind. Something—is it a dog?—is streaking round the corner to the back of the house. The barking goes on, relentless, driving her mad, and she races through to the back bedroom. The security light is on and the yard all lit up. There, just feet away from her, is a fox, standing guard over what looks like a half-eaten pie. Some bastard must have chucked it into her yard. But a wild animal there, how strange. It reminds her of a picture she once saw, of a fox sitting on a chair in someone's living room, a bright spotlight shining on it. Her fox is a handsome creature, his coat gingery red, his eyes bright with greed, but why is he not afraid of her? What's he doing living in a town at all?

Wait, wasn't there a television documentary years ago about a family of foxes living beside a railway, surviving from pickings out of people's dustbins, half-eaten hamburgers, bits of biscuit? Urban foxes, they were called. This bold dog-fox in the night must be one of them.

He stares up at her, eyes warning her not to come near. As she watches, his dainty little vixen trots up to join him. Ah, that was who he was calling with his hoarse, unsettling cry. The female looks up at her inquisitively, but is not interested. Her head goes down to the food and she bites at it with exquisite teeth.

The vixen is pretty but it's the dog-fox who enthrals her. He continues to stare up at her, willing her to silence … to submission? If M were down there, if she were to drive away his vicious little vixen, would he attack her? Would he fly at her neck and puncture the skin? tear at her flesh with feral fury? She shivers, but not with the cold. Rather she is hot, her blood fired by how beautiful he is, and how cruel. She loved her dog Puppet but this animal has no need of her, she could never tame him.

He is still, watchful, ready to defend his partner. As M stares back at him she admires his powerful haunches and shoulders, his staunch maleness, his capacity for ferocity. A whisper of memory stirs in her mind and is swiftly pushed away. She drags her eyes away from him. Down below the vixen has finished eating and draws her tongue across her teeth in satisfaction. The dog-

10

fox, now that the strange bond between human and animal is broken, opens his mouth in a huge yawn. Together, with no apparent signal between them, the two foxes turn together and run off, bellies close to the ground.

They streak across the back lane and through a gap in the railings to the park beyond. Slowly M lets the blind down again. She gets back into bed, knowing her chance of sleep is gone tonight, though she settles back on the pillows and closes her eyes. The fox and vixen are running still behind her eyelids, faster and faster across a wide expanse of grass. The fox has a goose in his mouth. His chops drip with blood and feathers fly around his feet as he runs. Silly goose. Silly, silly goose …

Brady knows they're watching him. All of them, the psychotic retards they call patients and the even more psychotic and larcenous morons who are the officers. The television room is crowded tonight as her image flashes on to the screen. The pack's lust for blood throbs in the stale air. This place stinks like a pig pen.

He knows she's dead, knew she'd go as soon as they started talking about chest infections and angina. Not a flicker, he will not give them even a flicker of emotion to take away and feast upon, bloodsucking ghouls. He stares expressionlessly at the screen as the announcer says it. So that's it, then. She's gone, gone.

He tries not to think of the moment when she died. Did death rattle in her throat? Or did she just sigh and slip away, her eyes rolling up in her head?

Things weren't the way people thought between them. Most of the time they had laughs together, like any normal couple. There were days, months of days when there was no blood, no death. Days when they went up to the moors and drank cold white wine, watching the wind shiver through the tussocky grass; days when they ate their tea at the kitchen table and then held hands on the sofa, listening to tapes of The Goons when her gran was at the bingo. Why on earth did everybody think 'Monty Python' was so subversive? The Goons were the ones who really showed the absurdity of human behaviour, the pomposity of the powerful.

His mind keeps sliding back to her last moments. He knows what happened. Of course he knows. It was cigarettes and a heart worn out by forty years of captivity, forty years of being treated like a performing seal in the circus, flipped this way and that in the name of public opinion. But he needs to *know*. Everyone does. That's why the mothers wrote to him. They wanted to know where their children's bodies were. Ridiculous really. Pointless to hanker after old bones, picked clean now by everything that creeps in the earth.

He thinks the officers are speaking to him but he can't be bothered listening. He rarely answers them anyway. Probably just the usual sneering slop from the zombies who run this place, this cold-storage room for dead meat. How dare these cretinous thieves set themselves up as better than he is? They sneak and snoop, thieving from the inmates in the name of authority, inflicting their petty punishments in the name of order. Huh, the only order here is the corrupt one that these swines wallow in.

He's very tired. That's what happens after a death, even if it's someone you don't know that well. And he knew her, knew her to the core. They were more than lovers—what was between them was solid and impregnable as the flinty rocks on the moor, as enduring as the hills. It will last forever, what they made between them. They said she'd given him up but that was for appearance's sake. They stayed the course. She said in public that

12

she hated him, but gate fever corrupts the spirit, extorts weasel words from even the strongest.

People are moving off to bed now, vacant-eyed and shuffling, their minds and legs shackled by antidepressants. His hot water bottle is going cold. He needs to heat it up again, is shivering as usual. How, despite his strongest efforts, has his body refused to die? Fifty years of smoking, three years of force feeding and here he is hanging on, still alive—after a fashion, you couldn't call this life.

He holds the warm bottle against his stomach and lies down on the bed. Why did they have to take away his chair? He preferred to sleep in it, sitting upright so he could see if any of the Ash-witz Gestapo came sidling in to pilfer what few belongings he has. No wonder the village shopkeepers despise them and refuse to serve them when they lumber in, knuckles dragging along the floor. They'd pull the rings from the fingers of dead men, that lot. Greedy, grasping hypocrites.

He half-closes his eyes. She swims in front of his lids, smiling, but is he remembering her or her photograph? She's in one of the books on his shelf, hair bright blonde in the sun, looking healthy and relaxed, the sort of girl you were proud to be with. He doesn't care that few would agree with that. Why should either of them be defined solely by eighteen months out of their lives? an ad lib existential exercise born of frustration?

If he'd been educated, none of it would have happened. He would have found more lucrative and legally acceptable ways to channel his energies, as the ruling classes do. Like Bush and Blair, sending young men to fight the battles they don't dare to. No wonder the Muslims blew up the Twin Towers. The only question is, why are there not more September 11s? They deserve it, these politicians. They compare what he did to the Holocaust, but they have more blood on their hands than he has.

He can't summon up the energy to agonise over M's death, as so many bereaved people do. They're thinking about themselves, not the dead person, asserting the uniqueness of their loss when people are dying all around, every day. It makes him laugh, the way they think in their bloody song titles. *My Way, Simply the Best,* or that Celine Dion one about the heart going on, as if it could. The people who choose that one for funerals have never seen a dead person up close, never felt that moment when the breath suddenly leaves the body and there is nothing left—no spirit, no mind, nothing.

The death of another human being is no more meaningful than the death of a maggot. Hers matters only to him. Nothing is changed. He was never going to see her again anyway, but tonight he feels it most acutely. No-one will ever touch his body again, no soft woman's hand will ever stroke his skin.

They touch him when they force feed him, but that's not the same thing. He'd rather they didn't lay their pustulating paws on him, would rather they let him die too. God, it's cold tonight. One day he'll just freeze to death, a solid block they'll have to chip off the bed. Penguins could die of exposure here. They've got the fucking heating turned off again. Indolent swine, too lazy to do their jobs and stay awake at night. They can't sleep when it's clanking away, so they leave the inmates freezing. Fucking arseholes.

Would M have had it easier in the women's prison? They probably titivate the place more there. Need to, with all those women on the rag together. Not that he ever put up with that stuff from her, not appropriate somehow. It was imperative that their project not be compromised by normal considerations of the flesh, one of the prices you pay for living at the extreme end of human endeavour. You don't have the right to give in to the petty ailments that ordinary people whine on about.

M was pretty good about that sort of stuff really. She was more likely to explode in rage when she had her period than mope about the place. Whoosh, the temper she had on her. Never seen anything like it—that day she smashed all of Granny Maybury's dinner plates, just because the old lady got fish in for the dinner. 'You know I hate fish,' she shouted, though she'd had rock salmon from the chippie only the week before. She'd hesitated, torn between smashing the dinner plates and tearing up the photos in his album. Then she'd seen his face—and sense. Just as well for her that she chose the plates.

It would be nice to have her strong legs wrapped round him now, to warm him up, but it's not the sex he misses so much as the companionship. He liked the lunchtimes best in a way, just the two of them locked in his office, keeping the rest of the world out. They studied their German in there, read books together, Hitler's speeches or bits from the books he bought in a brown paper bag from that wee shop round the back of the Dilly in Manchester. De Sade, especially *Justine*—not what people think. More philosophising than sex. Witty, though. *What does the virtue of women profit us? It is their wantonness which serves and amuses us; but their chastity could not interest us less.* He had a way with words, the old Marquis.

M seemed shy at first, modest. When they lived at Bannock Street they had the usual tin bath and she'd shut the door and tell everyone to keep out when she had her bath on a Saturday. Her sister Maureen used to tease her about it. 'Do you think any of us care about your fat arse?' What a cow, not the sweet little thing she's always portrayed as. Why do people want to make it simple, good girl/bad girl?

Cant.

Cunt.

He closes his eyes. He can smell the rough male smell of his own hospital blanket, the stench of the wings, institution stench of too many communal meals, too many under-washed men, too many shitty bogs. She used to wear Coty *L'Aimant* perfume. He remembers buying it for her one Christmas. All the girls thought it was *the* best perfume on the market, goodness knows why. It smelt cheap, though it was very potent. For him it was sex—that heavy smell, mingling with her cigarette breath as she ran her hands over his body. It didn't take her long to stop being shy. 'Is that it?' she said the first time, too guileless to fake it. 'Am I supposed to feel guilty about that?'

14

'Don't you?'

'No, it were lovely.'

Someone on the wing is singing, tonelessly. A toilet flushes somewhere. He can hear the flipping of cards as the screws play poker in the corridor outside. There is no space to think in this sinkhole.

They did love each other, to the end.

So many mistakes.

'She's dead.' The voice at the other end of the line is so excited that Beth Hunter, the former Betty Higginbottom, takes some moments to recognise the voice of her friend, Pat Shields.

    'Is that you, Pat?'

    'Croaked tonight in the hospital.'

    'Who?'

    'That black-hearted bitch won't be able to hurt anyone now.'

    'Who?'

    'Myra Hindley, of course.'

    'Are you sure?'

    'Yes, of course. The governor told me herself.' Her friend's voice is rough with anger. 'Would you believe it? Some of the other officers were upset.'

    Beth puts down the pupil's essay she's been marking. For all that she knows Myra Hindley has been ill for some time, the news is a shock. She feels her stomach drop, as if someone she loved has died, though you couldn't call what she felt love. She was too young in those days, all swept up in the passion of a teenage crush. The other girls in her class were mooning over Johnny Taylor, who swept his hair up in a Billy Fury quiff and wore a Teddy boy jacket, but she always wanted to be different from the rest of them. It was as if she knew already that she wouldn't be staying in those mean little houses where you heard every thump of love or loathing through the wall; as if she knew already that those mean little streets could not contain her.

    She told no-one what she felt, of course. They'd have humiliated her, with the careless cruelty of those who consider themselves to be the norm. Myra herself might even have teased her. *Hey, Betty Bigbottom! So you like girls?* For a moment Beth feels as though the sooty smell of Gorton is sweeping through her elegant Georgian townhouse. Pat is still banging on at the other end of the line. *How could you do that to a child? Scum. Perverted.* Beth touches the photo of her Will for luck. How *could* you do that to a child?

    'Pat, we'll definitely raise a glass in thanks when we have our Christmas lunch.'

    'I can't believe she's finally gone, that loathsome, putrid piece of shit,' says Pat.

    Beth sits for a long time after coming off the phone, heedless of the pupils' essays and the fact that she should be starting dinner. It's only Charles and her, now that Will is in the Army. They could have an omelette, or bacon and eggs. The weekly menu list stuck to the fridge says Pork with Chanterelles in a Madeira Sauce, but she can't face tackling that. She finds herself curiously upset. Ridiculous to be sad at the passing of a child murderer—or is she simply sad at the passing of her youth?

    She should be relieved. No-one will ever know now about her months as Hindley's stalker, the winter evenings when she hung about at the corner of the street, hoping to see Myra come in from work before Mam called her in for her tea. Beth would be frozen sometimes, damp incarnate from the wet fog, but she never wanted to go home before her idol arrived. 'Want me to get yer the paper, Myra?' she'd say, though Myra rarely did. She wasn't unkind, just a little distant, though the newly teenage Betty thought that was as it should be. On the days when Myra shrugged and gave her threepence to fetch the Manchester Evening News she was ecstatic.

That was before Brady came on the scene. He was a good looking man then, tall and always stylish in his black shirts and coat. He looked different from the other men round Gorton. 'He's a Jock, i'n't he?' her Dad said. 'Bound to be a bit odd.'

'He i'n't odd—he's handsome,' her mother said.

'That long slick of dripping? Rubbish.'

Beth gets up to clear away her papers. Charles hates disorder; his office at the university is almost anally tidy, with students' essays stacked up in neat piles according to their year of study and his books arranged alphabetically on the shelves. Beth plumps up the needlepoint cushions on the sofa, running her hand over the luxuriant rose pattern with its thick, fleshy leaves. Moquette, that's what you called the material the armchairs in their living room were made of, a horrible, stubbly beige stuff that was rough to the touch. They didn't have a sofa in those days, only got one when HP came in.

Why did she never tell Charles about her crush on Hindley? He'd surely just have laughed. There was nothing for her to feel ashamed of. She never did anything about her feelings, other than run a few errands and gaze in wonder. In those days Myra was an exotic creature, with her jutting face and cheekbones, her hair bleached startlingly blonde, her fishnet tights and white winklepicker shoes. 'She's a hard ticket, that one,' her mam said, but Beth thought she looked like nobody else. She has never liked a woman in that way since. Well, she didn't then either; it was just a schoolgirl crush and after the murders she didn't want to think about her ever again.

Isn't there a bag of mixed leaves in the fridge? A salad with warm poached eggs and some croutons, she thinks. She's running the leaves under the tap when the phone goes again. 'Guess where I am?'

'Hey Jude.'

'Very funny. Guess.'

'Up some murky alleyway in Peshawar? On top of the Eiffel Tower?'

'I wish. I'm standing in freezing rain outside the hospital Myra Hindley's just died in.'

'Why are my friends obsessed with Myra Hindley tonight?'

'Didn't you once say you came from somewhere round where she lived?'

'Ye-es.'

'Oh go on, Beth. You must have some little bit of local colour for me.'

'She was a few years older than me. You never know people the same when there's that age gap.'

'I know, but you must have known the family.'

17

'Don't you ever leave your journalist's hat at home?'

'No, course not. More than my job's worth. How are you anyway, darling?'

'Don't bother trying to suck up to me now. Why don't you try Pat? She worked at the prison when Hindley was there. Oh silly me, you've tried her already.'

'Of course I have, sweetie. Pat really hates her, doesn't she?'

'I think she hated the glamour that got attached to her in prison.'

'I suppose so. She's a bit chilling though, isn't she?'

'Pat? She doesn't mean half the things she says really.'

'Look, I'd best go, darling. The snapper's making faces at me so I think we're about to move. When are we having our Christmas lunch?'

'Soon. And don't you be late.'

'As if.'

She is gone, in her usual abrupt way. Beth doesn't know how she can live like that, rushing all the time, meeting deadlines, never still. No wonder she couldn't keep her husbands. It's a mystery to Beth how she ever stopped long enough to find three of them in the first place, but no doubt being gorgeous shortened the process. She pours herself a glass of white wine, wondering if she can restrict herself to two glasses tonight, and does a half bottle a day make you an alcoholic? Maybe she'll add some ice from the spiffy new fridge that Will insisted she buy, a big stainless steel sarcophagous he thought was the coolest thing. He loves making cocktails for his lady friends just so he can show the damn thing off. The ice thingy is very handy; now she can dilute her wine and feel virtuous.

'All right, your turn next,' she says to the cat, which is insinuating itself around the table leg in preparation for a full-blown attack on Beth's own leg. Not for the first time she wonders if cats are Darwin's missing link, the species which made the leap from one to another. There's something serpentine, boneless about their movements. 'And how is my darling Squeaky?' she coos, stroking her chin. 'How is Princess Squeaky Blossom La La? Hmm, none the better for some idiot calling you funny names, poppet, are you?' The creature stares at her, its yellow eyes indecipherable, though it purrs incessantly. 'Yes, you love your mummy, don't you?'

She hesitates between some cold chicken and one of the little foil sachets. How spoiled they are now. Their cat at Benster Street had only scraps to eat, bits of rejected mince or potato off everyone's plates. Tom was scrawny compared to Squeaky, his fur matted in comparison to her sleek coat. 'Here, you finish this off,' she says, cutting the chicken into small chunks. Those old houses were cold and damp. Her poor mother thought this place was a palace, with its central heating, its electric shower, the Aga cooker that keeps the kitchen warm and cosy even when they're not there. God, they didn't even have an inside toilet in that house. It was so cold, stumbling outside at night. Your pee was the warmest thing about it.

She feels as though someone else lived there, not her. But then she was someone else in those days. She was Betty, whose name appalled her.

18

Higginbottom, how mortifying. She changed it by deed poll as soon as she went to university, didn't want anyone to glimpse the shameful name on her student card. No-one else from round there went so she was never afraid of being found out. Her Dad was mad at first. 'My name not good enough for you, is it?' he said. But Beth's mother calmed him down. 'She's a young lass. It's embarrassing for her.' Mam always had her way in the end.

'There's a suspicious lack of cooking smells around here.' Charles, her husband, lets himself in the back door and leans over to kiss the top of her head.

'Sorry, darling. Are you starving?' He always is, despite his slender build.

'Ah, you're on the white?'

'Would you prefer red?'

'There's that nice Fleurie I was rather looking forward to, the one from *The Sunday Telegraph* wine club.'

'Well, you just open it, my love.'

He beams, pleased to be given permission. 'Would you like some?'

'Just a little to try, then.'

He brings out two of the fine wine glasses they bought on a weekend break to Stockholm last year. Gosh, he loves his rituals. She watches with affection as he fiddles about in the drawer for the little gadget to take the foil off the bottle. Then his special corkscrew, a classic shape but in polished Italian glass that looks like blue enamel. He pours a little into each glass and raises his towards her. 'Well, let's see,' he says. 'Let's jolly well see.'

She rolls the wine round her throat, enjoying its warmth, the spicy sensation of it melting into her veins.

'Ah,' says Charles. 'Now this is the one that Hugh Johnston called silky and racy. Quite an achievement, to be both those things, don't you think?'

'I don't know,' says Beth. 'Most of the undergarments in Jude's possession would fit that description.' She busies herself frying the croutons, watching the slick of olive oil curdle and swirl in the pan. 'That is nice. I think I'll forget the white. Very ordinary compared to that.'

'Mmm ...' He makes little smacking noises with his lips as he drinks, as if making a precise calibration of each sip. In reality he is simply extending each tiny moment of pleasure. If he is undeniably a sensualist, it is sensualism in a Puritan form, controlled not just in order to heighten pleasure, but to preserve his own image of himself as a person of distinction and discrimination, a person who is not simply greedy. He scoops a neat handful of salted peanuts from the dish on the counter, his wrist turning gracefully to ensure that he takes just so much and no more.

'Did you finish your marking then?' he asks.

'Not quite. Too much excitement, I'm afraid. First of all Pat phoned me to tell me Myra Hindley had died, then Jude phoned from the hospital where they were keeping Hindley.'

'Didn't Pat have a bit of a bee in her bonnet about Hindley?'

19

'Oh yes. Don't you remember all that nonsense at the prison, when Hindley threw a complete flaky? She banged her head in rage, then said a warder had hit her. Nearly caused a riot. The governor was furious at Pat, said she should have been watching Hindley more closely.'

'So she should,' he says briskly. 'A woman like that always has a following. You can't ever let your guard drop with these people.'

Beth moves around him, laying two table mats, setting the cutlery neatly beyond the mats, just the way he prefers, filling up his glass. 'Shall we have some Mozart?' he says, rising from the table to rifle through the pile of CDs at the side of the mini-system. 'The Divertimenti, perhaps?'

'Jude says Pat was really chilling talking about Hindley.'

'What did she say?'

She knows he is being polite. He looks too beatific to care about anything beyond his red wine and the fresh sound of the strings.

'I don't know. You know what she's like. She thinks Hindley should have hanged. Or better still, be chopped up into little pieces while alive and boiling oil poured over her.'

'Yes, not the most moderate of your friends, darling.'

Beth fishes the poached eggs out of the boiling water and lays two carefully on each plate. She doesn't want to think about the houses where children are never coming back; doesn't want to think of the police dragging the dark moors for bodies or the mothers' screams when they heard the news; and she especially doesn't want to think of the children's last moments. How could God allow people like Myra Hindley and Ian Brady to go on living when they did such monstrous things?

She pierces one of her eggs with her fork, watches the golden yolk bleed into her rocket leaves. She wants *this*, this quiet kitchen with its heat cocooning her, its expensive appliances that will never break down. She wants this music, none other, this Mozart stuff tinkling away in the background, jolly and ordered and sunny, as if the foulness of the world does not exist. She wants this, her sweet, safe husband who will put his arms round her in bed tonight and help her sleep, help her keep out the dark.

4 WHAT THEY GOING TO DO TO ME?

She looks so old. She was always elegant but now she's shrunken, tiny, a miniature version of herself. M picks her out instantly from across the room but she shows no sign of recognising her own daughter. Huh, if she'd visited in prison more often she'd have kept up with how M looked. Just as well really, don't want her to blow the gaff.

The matron leans down to speak in the old lady's ear. 'Your niece has come to see you, Nellie.'

Nellie looks baffled. 'My niece?'

M steps forward. 'It's me, Auntie, Maria.'

At the sound of M's voice, her mother's eyes widen in astonishment. 'I thought …'

'I know, Auntie. But I'm better now.'

'Let's wheel her into the conservatory and then you can have some peace,' says the matron. 'I'll bring some tea and biscuits, shall I?'

'That would be lovely,' says M.

The matron tucks Nellie's blanket more firmly around her. 'It can be a bit cold in there at first but don't worry, love—I'll put the radiator on.'

Inside, the conservatory smells of earth and greenery. There are potted ferns and parlour palms and a row of little cactuses struggling along the window sill. Beyond the glass is a large garden, its shrubbery dank with rain, water dripping down from the bare branches of the trees. 'It's lovely here in the summer,' says the matron, with a shrug at the weather. 'But at least you'll have some privacy.'

'And no telly, thank goodness,' says Nellie. 'I'm fed up to the back teeth of cookery programmes. All that fuss. It's only food, i'n't it?'

M is relieved to be away from the smell. That combination of stale pee and clothes flecked with yesterday's porridge is worse than the nick ever smelt. She flops down in a wicker armchair, waits till the matron has gone. 'Well, aren't you pleased to see me?'

Up close, Nellie seems even frailer, her arms skinny as pipe cleaners, her skin pale. Her voice, when at last she speaks, sounds ancient and wavery. 'I thought you were dead, our Myra.'

'I might as well be to you. You never came to see me anyway.'

'I'm not well.'

'No, not now. But you haven't always been this old, have you?'

'Let's not go over all that again, will we?' Tentatively she touches M's hand. 'It's good to see you, love.'

There's a bustling at the door and a girl comes in with a tea tray. 'There you are, Nellie. Try and eat something today, won't you, honey? Got to keep your strength up.'

'Aye, I'll never be able to run the marathon next week if I don't have a custard cream, will I?'

21

The girl sniggers and hands the tea round. Once she's gone Myra takes out a cigarette. 'The look on your face was a scream. As if you'd seen a ghost.'

'I thought I had,' says her mother quietly. 'You're not supposed to smoke in here, love.'

'What they going to do—put me in prison?'

M draws smoke deep into her lungs as she contemplates her mother's brown trousers and beige cardigan. Nellie's slippers are pink and furry, not like anything she'd have chosen for herself in the old days. She was always elegant then, slim and petite and dressed in the latest fashions. 'We'd best get you some decent stuff to wear now I'm around,' says Myra. 'You won't want tat like that when you're out with me.'

Nellie leans back in her chair, eyes closed. 'I don't go out much now, our Myra.'

'You've got to stop calling me that, Mam. I'm Maria now. Or call me M. That way you won't get mixed up.'

'M? Very modern.' Her mother sounds mocking. Some things never change.

'Actually, Ian used to call me that, years ago.'

'That pervert. I'd have thought that's the last thing you'd want anyone to call you.'

'There's a nice little pub not far from here, the matron said. I could take you there for lunch if you like. Or maybe we could go on holiday—to Greece or Italy, get you a bit of sun on those old bones.'

'And I suppose I'd pay?'

'You know, I don't know why I bother. I'll probably get into trouble for coming here and you just give me grief.'

Nellie takes a sip of her tea, her movements dainty, self-controlled. She has a ladylike quality M has never managed to achieve. 'Trouble?' she says. 'Why?'

'Because they don't trust you, of course. They think you'll blab to someone.'

'I weren't brought up to blab. *Oh yes, my daughter the serial killer is out of prison now.* Do me a favour.'

'Well, I know what you're like, Mam, but I suppose they just think you're an old lady who's probably not quite the full shilling.'

'What a cheek. I'll give them not the full shilling.'

M laughs. 'I know—you could eat them for breakfast.'

'There isn't even anyone here to tell. My friend May died and Nancy Higginbottom lost her marbles years ago.'

'Betty's mum? I'd forgotten she was here. What a pity she's gone gaga—it'd be nice for you to have someone to talk to about the old days.'

'Aye, they were so good, weren't they?'

'Well, some of it was.'

'I suppose it weren't all bad,' sighs her mother.

Myra hands the plate of biscuits to her. 'Aren't you going to have a custard cream?' she asks.

'I've never liked them, love.'

'They're a bit plain, aren't they? Give me a luscious big cream cake any day.'

Nellie is silent, her mind drifting back to a summer's day, long ago. Was it August? That bastard Brady had been arrested but the police hadn't put two and two together about Myra. Still, people were talking already. They always do. *She must have known, mustn't she?* Whispering behind their hands in the queue at the shops. Nellie sent Myra in for bread while she went to the butcher's. When she came out, there was her daughter, standing eating a cream bun. It seemed so undignified somehow. Your boyfriend's been accused of murder and you're stuffing your face in public. It were callous, that's what it were. But then that's Myra all over. She's had to accept that a long time ago. There's a lack there. Something wanting.

'You should have died in prison, love.'

'Thanks for the maternal support, Mam.'

'So they weren't going to tell me that my own daughter was still alive?'

'They give you a new life, Mam. I'm in the country now, in Yorkshire. The governor said they'd have preferred to send me somewhere down south but they were afraid I knew too many criminals down there. I spent a lot of time in Holloway and that last one in Kent, Highpoint. In the end they reckoned I'd stand out less in the north.'

'Well, they've done a good job on you when your own mother can't recognise you.'

'I don't recognise myself when I look in the mirror.'

Just as well. If Myra really saw what she was she couldn't live with herself. What is it she wants? Money probably, or maybe just the thrill of disobeying the authorities. Never had the sense she was born with, that one. 'My handbag's on the back of the chair,' she says. 'Hand it to me, will you?'

Myra passes the bag to her. 'I won't be able to come very often, Mam. It's a bit dangerous for me.'

'I know, love.' Nellie hands her five tenners. That should keep her happy for a bit. 'This has been enough excitement to last me a while.'

'You don't need to give me this.'

'It's all right. There's nowt to spend it on in here, is there?'

'You look tired. I'll leave you to it. Want me to get someone?'

'I'll just have a little nap here. It'll be nice to be on my own for a bit without them girls calling me 'sweetie' and 'lovey' as if I was ten years old.'

M bends down to kiss her mother, wrinkling her nose at the smell of her hair. It's coarse now and goodness knows how often they wash it. It used to be so nice and soft and blonde. Nellie's eyes are closed by the time M slips out of the conservatory into the garden. Her Mam can get a bit of time on her own and *she* won't have to talk to the matron. She fingers the notes in her anorak pocket. Fifty quid, not bad. She'll get a taxi to the station this end and

23

then another one when she gets back home—none of this three buses lark. She was made for better.

5 DARK ALTARS

The church is surprisingly full. She thought there would be nobody else here at a mid-week Mass. Aren't congregations supposed to be falling off these days? There are a few young mums with kids, some middle-aged couples and the usual geriatric groupies, all twittering round the priest and twitching at the flowers.

She remembers their sort from years ago. Her neighbours, Mrs O'Reilly and Mrs Hagerty, went down the chapel every Friday night, their pinnies in their bags and their hair all primped up. God knows what Mr O'Reilly and Mr Hagerty thought of their wives' passion for a middle-aged celibate who drank too much and stuffed himself stupid like a big fat capon.

Today's priest drags himself away from some old duck to go to the sacristy and put his robes on. Hordes of schoolchildren start filing in at the back of the church. Just her luck. They're quite well-behaved now, while their teachers are watching, but just wait till they get up for communion. Is there no peace anywhere?

She's disappointed by this church. It's whitewashed and modern, with no atmosphere. She wants gilt statues of the Sacred Heart, altars hidden in dark corners. She wants carved stone angels and pillars like they had in the church in Gorton. She wants mystery, the fragrance of incense and sanctity, the blood of sacrifice. Here there is only cleanliness and light and a kind of brisk piety that seems pointless to her. It isn't what she signed up to the Catholic Church for. It won't do.

Her mother seemed awfully fragile yesterday. Thin and pale as an earthworm. They probably aren't feeding her properly in that home. You read about it all the time. They give the old people the wrong clothes, the wrong nighties, even the wrong teeth. Shocking really.

Still hard as nails, old Nellie, though. 'You should have died in prison, Myra.' After all these years ... Who does she think she is, to judge? Has she never made a mistake? Why didn't she stop it when Dad was ladling into them with his belt? If ever there was child abuse, that was. Pushing them over the table and yanking their knickers down. Disgusting pervert. Right in full view of the street. Anyone could have looked in them windows and seen. Well, she got her own back in the end, when he was too weak to fight back. Used to crack him across the back with his own walking stick. Served him right.

The priest makes his entrance and the congregation rise. He's wearing ordinary green vestments, another disappointment. She prefers the purple ones they wear for Lent—royal purple, the purple of witchcraft and sorcery; the Ride of the Valkyrie, purple music, goddesses riding through the purple night sky. Duh de re duh duh, duh de re duh duh ... for heaven's sake, what now? A young man walks down to the front of the church and starts strumming away at a guitar. He's wearing a woolly jumper and an earnest expression. Excruciating. Lord of the fucking dance, for christssake. She'd better find somewhere more appealing than this godforsaken church.

25

The children in front of her are sniggering. She doesn't blame the little blighters but is just about to lean forward anyway and tell them to behave when she sees the woman at the end of their bench, so small and slight that you'd take her for a child herself at first. She's pale and exquisite, with a Botticelli face, a nymph emerging from the pew like Venus from the sea. No, not that one, the other one, the girl in the flowery dress, the Primavera. Her eyes are such a light grey you'd think they'd been stonewashed, like denim. Long legs, small breasts, but firm. Pity you can't see her bum.

The woman is staring at the children beside her with the avidity of the childless. Huh, another thirty-something who forgot to notice her biological clock was ticking. Poor chick, she looks lost, as if life eludes her. What a fidget, sighing, propping her chin on her hands. Although she appears to be watching the Mass, she isn't. She's watching the children. Poor, sad little chick.

Hey little chickie, come to Momma.

The priest gets up for his sermon. He's droning on about forgiveness and M suddenly realises he's talking about her. 'She's at peace now,' he says. 'And so must we be. We cannot pursue Myra Hindley beyond the grave. The time has come to let her go.'

Some of the teachers stir, uneasy at the mention of a notorious child-killer when children are present. The kids chew gum and kick each other's ankles, unconcerned. One old duck in front of her snorts. 'She doesn't deserve to be at peace. God'll never let her rest,' she says to her neighbour, who nods in agreement. So much for Christian compassion. The sad little chick looks disapproving, though. That's a good sign.

More happy clappy stuff as Ernest Jumperino comes back with his guitar to sing some other godawful cheery hymn. Thank goodness they can never do away with the ritual, though it's hard to hear the priest's chanted words with that racket going on. *Blessed are you, Lord, God of all creation. Through your goodness we have this bread to offer, which earth has given and human hands have made. It will become for us the bread of life.* The priest raises the host, the white wafer hardly visible from this distance. The body of Jesus. They're made by nuns, those things. Nuns like her Pat. It was bonkers really to think they could ever escape from prison, but wouldn't it have been great if they had? They'd be living in the sun by now, maybe with a little farm or something. Or would they? Might have been hard to make money without having to work at some tosspot job.

As the sun breaks through the high windows the golden spikes of the monstrance at the side altar are irradiated, sending a hundred little light shards into the atmosphere. Next, the chalice with the wine is raised aloft, its gleaming surface solid testimony to the wealth and power of the church that M loves. Within the gold-lined cup, the dark red wine is changing into blood, molecules whirling, liquid churning, transforming itself into the blood of Our Lord. She closes her eyes, ecstatic in the radiance and the gold and the blood.

The congregation make their response. *May the Lord accept the sacrifice at your hands, for the praise and glory of his name, for our good, and the good of all his*

26

Church. There must always be a sacrifice. She knows that better than most, all those years atoning for someone else's sin. The children start clattering out for Communion. M waits till the blonde slides to her end of the seat, then stands abruptly herself, almost bumping into her. They exchange smiles as they walk to the front to receive the host. She lets the other woman go ahead on the way back. Delicious firm bum. Everything about her is firm except her soul, which is clearly mush.

Instead of going back to her own seat, she stays at that end of the pew, knowing the little chick will turn round to shake her hand in the Kiss of Peace. M is ready with a shy smile when she does. At the end of the Mass she stands quickly. 'Well, a challenging sermon.'

'People are dying to make monsters, aren't they?' Her voice is silvery and surprisingly crisp, ringing with the clarity of centuries of good breeding. They walk together to the exit.

'Are there always so many people here?'

'Oh, that's a new initiative by the local Catholic school,' she says. 'Every week a different class comes in on Thursdays.'

'What a good idea. It's always nice to have children around, isn't it?'

'You're not from here, then?'

'No, I'm from the other side of the Pennines, Manchester originally.' She extends her hand. 'I'm Maria, like the Sound of Music, y'know? though I'm not sure how many hills I could climb nowadays.'

She laughs. 'You don't look much like the governess type either. I'm Sophie Ferrers.'

They're delving into their purses to find money for the St Vincent de Paul collection when the priest approaches them. 'Good morning, ladies,' he says. 'We're having a little bunfight in the church hall to celebrate the children taking part. Would you care to join us.'

'A cup of tea would be marvellous,' says Myra. 'It's a bit chilly round here.'

'I don't recognise you as one of my parishioners,' says the priest.

'No, I've just come to the area, though I'm not sure how long I'm going to be here. I'm Maria Spencer.'

'Welcome to St Stephen's. Always good to have new members of the flock, however temporary. I trust you'll come too, Miss Ferrers. Or should I say Ms these days?'

'Yes on both counts, Father.'

They go into the church hall together, their shoes clattering on the bare wooden boards.

'Pompous old twit,' says Sophie. 'You grab us a seat and I'll bring the tea over.'

Myra sits at a small table at the side, ignoring the long trestles where the schoolchildren are shoving egg mayonnaise baps down their throats. Their teachers bury their heads in their tea, concentrating on not seeing.

Sophie brings two mugs over and a pile of sandwiches. 'Don't know about you, but I'm starving.'

27

Myra pulls out her fags. 'I'm watching my waistline these days,' she says. She is about to light up when one of the geriatric groupies scurries over. 'You can't smoke in here, dear. This is a public place.'

'There's hardly anywhere you can smoke these days, is there?' says Sophie sympathetically.

'Are you a smoker too?'

'No, I've never smoked. Our family was always too busy being sporty for that. Papa likes the odd cigar with his port, though.'

Papa, not *Dad?* Sophie must be really posh. She sits there eating a mountain of sandwiches with casual disregard for the conventions of feminine eating that can only come from being upper class. How does she stay so slim? Isn't she beautiful though, with her rough-chopped blonde hair and her lovely little breasts, hard and round as conkers?

'Don't you like it round here, Maria, that you're not staying long?'

'Oh, that was just to put him off. I'm not sure I'll stay with his church.'

'There aren't very many Catholic ones round here, I'm afraid. You don't like our Father Murphy then?'

'I just don't like the music much. It's very important, isn't it, for worship?'

'I bet you like the old hymns, don't you? *Oh mother, I could weep for mirth*,' trills Sophie.

Oh mother, right enough.

'Come on, join in. Let's start a new trend.'

The kids at the next table start sniggering and mimicking Sophie's high, pure voice. Myra embarks on a lengthy cough. How the fuck is she supposed to know what comes next? She's only a convert, not a dyed-in-the-wool, cradle to grave Catholic.

'Oh, you poor thing. That sounds a dreadful cough.'

'Emphysema. All my own fault, I'm afraid. Too many fags. I'd still love one right now.'

Sophie looks shocked. 'I'm so sorry.'

'Don't worry about me. I'm just glad to be here at all.' She takes her cigarettes out of her bag, then remembers and puts them back. 'So, Sophie, what do you do? Have you a day off work that you can come to Mass on a weekday?'

'Not exactly. I'm a social worker and get to work flexitime. I'm a Mass junkie, I'm afraid.'

'Me too. It's such a comfort, isn't it? I'd be dead without my religion.'

'Dead?' Sophie knows better than to laugh the word off. She's probably quite a good social worker.

'You've no idea what I've been through, Sophie. I could write a book about the things that have happened to me.'

'Really?'

'Don't worry, I wouldn't burden you, though somehow I feel I could tell you anything. You'd probably run a mile if I did.'

Two boys are now wrestling by the side of their table and four little girls are running round and round the room. One of the teachers lifts himself from the general torpor to deal with the noise. Sophie stirs her tea, a moment of suspense. Slowly she says, 'I'm sure I wouldn't.'

'You're kind.' M leans over and pats her hand, hoping the gesture isn't too soon. 'I'm too excited to talk about that awful stuff today anyway. I'm going to buy a puppy this morning.'

'A puppy? How lovely. I adore animals. Have you any idea what you'd like.'

'A bog-standard mutt will do me.'

'Where are there puppies for sale round here?'

'I saw a sign in the pet shop when I was wandering round the town. Now where was it?'

'I'll walk you there if you like.'

They stroll along in the winter sunshine. It seems freezing to Myra, still unused to being in the open air. Her days of working in the prison garden are long gone. Sophie strides along in pale denim jeans and jacket. There's no flesh on her. You'd think *she'd* be cold.

They pass through the civic gardens with its beds of heathers and blue-leaved hebe. Across the central square is the Town Hall, a handsome Victorian confection with lots of little turrets clustered round a central clock. 'There was money here once,' says Sophie, seeing her look at it.

'I daresay there still is, judging by some of the shops,' says M drily.

To reach the pet shop they walk through a pretty shopping arcade, then cross the road and into a little ginnel. There are two cages in the shop window, one with a sleepy looking rabbit and the other with a hamster scurrying crazily round on its wheel. The sign is still there, *Batch of six month old mongrel puppies. Owners going abroad. Must be seen.* The cage is right at the back of the shop, beyond the tanks of guppies and the glass case with a malevolent looking snake sliding through it. *Corn snake,* says a little label on the tank. Sophie jumps when she sees it and instantly moves away, but Myra is drawn to its gold and brown markings, its sinuous movement. It looks powerful, exotic, and she leans down to study it more closely. The snake lifts its neck and juts forward as if to strike her, but its head meets the glass and it falls back, looking dazed, which makes her laugh. Stupid thing.

'These puppies are just gorgeous, Maria,' calls Sophie from the other side of the shop.

'Call me M. All my friends do.'

She walks over and stands close to Sophie, too close, though the little chick doesn't move away. The puppies are scrambling over each other, walking on top of each other's heads in their efforts to reach the humans. They're a liquorice allsorts of shapes and sizes, some black and white, some brown and white, some brown and black. 'Look at the littlest one,' says Sophie. 'Do you think he's a Yorkie cross?' The little fellow leaps up at her, a jumping bean of energy. 'He's so cu-ute.'

'He's adorable.'

M pokes her finger through the slats of the cage and he goes berserk, licking the tip of her finger and emitting little squealing noises. Ha. She hasn't lost her touch then.

'You've got to have him,' says Sophie.

'I think you're right.' She gets down so her face is on a level with his. He leaps at her nose, tongue working madly. 'I'd never forgive myself if I left you for someone else, would I, chuck? You want to come home with Mummy, don't you?'

That night, she stretches out on the sofa watching television, the little chap curled up on her stomach. He's so tiny, scrunched into a fuzzy ball of sleep, his funny bandy legs tucked up underneath him. Lightly she touches his shiny nose, rubs her hands through his fur. He snuffles with contentment.

He loves her already. He will always love her and she will always have him, with his rough coat and his willing eyes. She pulls softly at his ears, strokes him as he sleeps. She loves the feel of his coat, the wiry fur of his body, the downy bit on the top of his head. She loves the smell of him, the sharp honest smell of animal, not like cats with their vanilla fur, soaking up the perfume of anyone who holds them.

She will always have him. And she will have the girl too.

6 WOLFMAN AND LYNXWOMAN

From: "Hal" <wolfman@hotmail.co.uk>
To: lynx1043@hotmail.co.uk
Subject: tonight
Date: Sat, 23 November 2002 03:37:26

My darling Lynx,

I can't believe I told you. It's the first rule of operations, not to reveal anything, even to those closest to you. The thing is, you're the first person in my whole life I've wanted to be totally open with. Life in the shadows has suited me till now, till I met you.

I know you hate the woman, but please, PLEASE don't go off the deep end and talk about this.

I'd have to leave my job, and I can't afford to do that. Anyway I'm good at what I do. I like it, it's never the same two days running. I suppose I could find something else - they've made my cv look like a high-flying civil servant and people usually trust them. But I'd hate to be stuck in a desk job.

Pat, if people found out she was free they'd lynch her - you're too decent and straightforward to want that.

I wish you were here and we were curled up together with your long lynx body next to mine. I should have done my job better and kept my mouth shut but when you said you'd worked with her I wanted to know what you thought. I'm going to be dealing with her for the next year at least and I thought you'd be able to help me. What do I know about a woman like that?

My darling, I wish you were here with me instead of stuck on night shift.
Hal XXXXXXXX
From the BlackBerry of Hal Morton

From: La Barbara <lynx1043@hotmail.co.uk>

Dear Hal,

I haven't felt like this about anyone before either, not even my husband. I did love him at the beginning, though he turned out to be a bastard.

I'm not angry with you, I'm angry at THEM, whoever it is that's given this dreadful woman her freedom. Why should she be free? The mothers of those children will never be happy again. I can't imagine what it must be like to lose your child. I would die if I lost mine.

I'm sorry I stormed out. I try hard to be controlled but sometimes I get so angry I just blow. (The upside is that that loss of control seems to extend to other areas of my life as well, my wolfman!)

You know, when I think about it, maybe I can help you. I know how that bitch's mind works, that's for sure, after years of watching her on the blocks.

From: "Hal" <wolfman@hotmail.co.uk>

Look, she's not getting off scot free. If you hadn't gone off the deep end I'd have finished telling you the whole story. The woman's got cancer. She had an X-ray last year and a shadow on the lung showed up. She thinks she's being set free but really she's being sent out to die. They didn't want to have to treat her with the whole world looking on. It's a nightmare trying to get her in and out in secret. This way she can just trot quietly along to her NHS hospital and no-one knows who she is, including her doctor.

From: La Barbara <lynx1043@hotmail.co.uk>

Good, I hope she rots quickly.

From: "Hal" <wolfman@hotmail.co.uk>

My Lynx,
 I love your fierceness. I'll dream of you now, and your long lynx legs wrapped around me. I want to howl my love for you to the night sky, bare my fangs at anyone who tries to do you harm, make love to you in the open air, with the silvery light of the moon spilling over our nakedness. Hal XXXXXXXX

M hasn't got used to mornings yet. No bells to wake her, no women clattering and battering around, no guards shouting. She loves her big double bed with its plump mattress, at least three times thicker than the one she had at bloody Highpoint. She finds herself sleeping longer here, sometimes waking only when the children in the local school start their racket.

This morning she comes to early, to the sound of magpies clacking in her neighbour's back garden. It feels bizarre to be in a town, yet surrounded by all this wildlife. When she was growing up, the most you ever saw was a few grimy sparrows squabbling over crumbs. Or mice of course. Some of those old houses in Gorton were overrun by them.

She sits up in bed, reaching for her fags. The dog stirs beside her. She pats his head to soothe him but he bounces into wakefulness, jumping around the bed and licking her hands wherever his rough little tongue meets the target. 'Come on then.' She puts her dressing gown on and scoops him up, sitting him on her knee while she has a widdle.

Downstairs she lets him into the back yard and puts the kettle on. Breakfast is an adventure for her these days—she can't believe how much stuff there is in the supermarkets. Her mug of tea and chocolate chip cereal bar don't fill her up so she has a mango yoghurt as well. Last week she had a real mango, first time ever. They only had huge big ones that they'd reduced to seventy-five pence, but she bought it anyway, just to taste it. When she tried to cut into it the knife stalled on the big stone in the middle so she sliced into the rind, splashing golden juice all over her nose when she held it up to smell it. The fragrance was sensuous and perfumed, the way she imagines amber would be when they pick it up in the forests.

She gets herself a second cup of tea and sits in the living room with her National Enquirer. There's a picture of some midget actor called Mini-Me flexing his muscles at the camera and grinning like an idiot. Over the page it's Britney Spears in cut-off denim shorts and a blouse that shows her belly button. That's more like it, she looks a right slut, that Britney, hot. The dog paws at her ankles and she picks him up. 'You're my little Mini-Me, aren't you, poppet? Mini-Myra.'

It's after eleven by the time she's ready. She'll walk into the town centre, that should help her lose some weight. Her pace is brisk at first but the little dog is struggling, so she picks him up. By the time they reach the town square they're both tired and M sits down on one of the benches—after so long inside she's just not used to walking any more. Minim snuffles round the flower beds, jumping back when one of the heathers scratches his nose. Then, a silvery laugh. 'He's so cute.' The little chick has come up behind her.

'Hallo, Sophie. Were you at Mass?'

Sophie sits down beside her. She's all in black today, thin black coat, black jeans, black shirt. They give her a lot more authority than the faded blue she had on the other day. 'Yes, me and two old ladies.'

'At least you didn't have the banjo bashers, I hope?'

33

'No, they were only there the other day because of the schoolkids.'

'You look cold, love. Fancy a coffee?'

Sophie smiles. M suspects not many people call her 'love.'

'I should have worn my heavy coat, shouldn't I? I am cold,' she says. She shivers dramatically, her slim shoulders hunching up. 'A coffee sounds great.'

Myra's eyes flicker away from the sight of her nipples under the sheer fabric of her blouse.

'Minim. Come here.' The little dog carries on rooting through the heathers.

'I don't think he recognises his own name yet,' says Sophie. 'Why did you call him that?'

'Well, he's about the minimum amount of stuff you can get that adds up to a dog, isn't he?'

The cafe is chintzy and warm, its clients' faces as doughy and round as the scones they're stuffing into them. Sophie orders tea and jam roly poly with custard. Myra has tea too, making a point of pouring when the waitress brings their tray.

'How do you stay so slim?' asks Myra, genuinely puzzled. 'I've always had to watch my weight.'

Sophie shrugs. 'I suppose I must burn it off. I was always the hyper one of the family.'

'How many of you are there?'

'I've got two brothers and two sisters.'

'Handy for providing a steady supply of boyfriends, I'd have thought.'

Sophie hesitates, glancing at her from under her lashes. Go *on*, chickie. Myra's willing her on so hard she almost chokes on her tea. These damn fags.

'I've never had much success with boyfriends,' says Sophie slowly. 'Anyway my brothers are a bit older than me.'

'Never mind, love. You'll find someone one day.'

Sooner than you think. Sophie smiles at her. In spite of her posh accent she seems grateful for every kindness. That augurs well for the future. Her blonde hair flops forward while she eats. It's so shiny and pretty, M would like to stroke it. She wants to light a fag but supposes she'd better not while Sophie is eating. Course, you're not allowed to any more, anyway. Why didn't she order a cake? The fudge brownies at the next table look bloody good.

'Then there's all the nephews and nieces and aunts and cousins,' continues Sophie. 'People always think big families are marvellous, but they have their drawbacks. Do you have a big family?'

'No. I'm the only one left. I had a sister but she died.'

'I am sorry.' Her pale face has gone quite pink. 'Were you close?'

'We were, but circumstances … well, I won't go into that now. We hadn't seen each other for a while. She had a brain tumour and couldn't get

34

down to see me. And of course I couldn't ... oh well. Let's talk about something else.'

Sophie is silent for a moment. 'I'm frightfully sorry. I didn't mean to intrude.'

'You're not intruding. Of course not. Like I said the other day, I feel I could tell you anything. I'm just ... to tell you the truth, it's the anniversary of her death coming up in a few days. Usually I'm right as rain talking about it.'

'You poor dear. We won't mention it again.' She's really quite sweet. Eager to please. Good.

They talk for a while but Sophie says the hubbub of dishes clattering and people chatting is driving her mad, so Myra says she has some shopping to do anyway. She stands first and rests her arm lightly on Sophie's shoulder as she moves round to pay the waitress. The little chick looks up and smiles. So, she's not disturbed by the intimacy of the gesture. 'I'll get it next time,' she says. Myra is pleased. That means there'll be a next time.

With the little dog tucked in her handbag, M watches as Sophie strides away, her long black coat flaring out behind her. How beautiful she is. Myra catches sight of her own image in a shop window and blenches. She's got to lose weight and she's got to get some decent clothes—she looks like the sort of middle-class, middle-aged type who watches gardening programmes on the telly.

There are plenty of those women in the clothes shops she passes, sticking their fat little trotters into designer clothes. Why should these snobs have money while she has to make do with a pittance? She finds her steps turning to the large department store in the middle of the high street. The warmth of the shop, the scents from the perfume counters drench her as she enters. Minim sighs contentedly to be out of the cold.

All the makeup is on the ground floor and M wanders around for a little while, trying on the Christian Dior lipsticks and spraying the *Obsession* tester all over her neck. 'Can I help you, madam?' the smarmy assistant says. She wants a punch in the mouth, that one.

'It's so long since I've worn this I just wanted to smell it again.' The assistant doesn't bother to hide her disbelief, cheeky cow.

Upstairs in Ladies' Fashions Myra heads for the coats. Sophie's was gorgeous, too fine a fabric for the winter of course, but the movement in it, its stylishness ... what must she think of M in her stupid anorak? Methodically she works her way through the different designers, MaxMara, Windsmoor, Planet, Episode. She's beginning to recognise them now, though they're too expensive for her, of course. All the same, she tries various coats on, just to eliminate them from her enquiries. This one's too long; that one makes her look plump; a third is so short she looks as wide as the kitchen table.

At the last section on this floor she finds an unusual black coat with a French label inside. It looks a bit militaristic before she puts it on, with its deep cuffs and padded shoulders, but instead of frogging there are black embroidered buttons down the front, and when she looks at it in the mirror

35

she knows it's the coat for her. It's long and slim fitting with a slight flare at the hem like Sophie's. The fabric has cashmere in the mix and feels softer than anything she has ever owned in her life. As she stares at her own reflection it's as if she sees the possibility of a new self rising from the glass, a stylish, artistic self, a self who might paint or write or make pots like Demi Moore in *Ghost*. This is a coat to give her confidence in her free life.

The price tag says £300 and that's in the pre-Christmas sale. She's shaking, hasn't wanted a garment this badly since she was a girl. But she doesn't have £300. Slowly she slides the coat off and puts it to the back of the rail. There's only one in her size and if she can't have it she won't make it easy for anyone else to get it. 'Come on, Minim,' she snaps. This time the little dog comes trotting obediently up to her. She sticks him in the top of her handbag like the starlets in the Enquirer do with their chihuahuas. Her heart is pounding as she walks away. She'll never find a coat as good as that one, never.

In the ladies' room she takes out the fine mixed powder and cream that the girl sold her last week—the sales assistant told her that no-one's worn loose powder for years. Carefully, slowly, so that she doesn't pull the skin too much, she applies it to her face in long sweeping motions, outlining her lips in plum and filling them in with a translucent berry colour. Her eyeliner is still OK but she blends in some more of the pale brown eyeshadow that the girl said she suited so much. She needs that coat.

She heads for the store's coffee shop and sits there with an espresso in front of her. Even with a cigarette it tastes bitter. The blood is pumping too quickly round her body for her to be able to savour it. She tries to think of something else, but there's nothing in her head but herself in the coat. Her new self.

There's a public phone behind the restaurant. She takes out the phonecard she bought yesterday and dials the number of the home her mother is in. Let her bloody do something for her daughter for once. 'I'd like to speak to Mrs Nellie Moulton,' she says.

'Who shall I say is calling?' says the dimwit on the other end of the line.

M taps her nail impatiently on the metal of the box. 'It's her niece who met up with her the other day.'

'She's been a bit poorly since then. I'll just see if she'll talk to you.'

She'd bloody well better talk, you idiot. Her mother takes an age to shuffle to the phone. The damn phone card will be used up before she gets there.

'Mam, I need some money for a winter coat. It's freezing up here.'

Her mother's voice is frail and wispy. 'But I already gave you some money, love.'

'I know, but it's not enough. You've no idea what things cost these days, Mam.'

'I suppose it's the most expensive coat in t' shop, our Myra?'

'Mam, for crying out loud, don't say my name.'

'Oh, sorry love.'

'I need a decent coat, Mam. I can't go around in this ridiculous anorak all the time. I look like a cleaning lady.'

'Nothing wrong with cleaning ladies, love.' Her mother sighs. 'I suppose t' money's no use to me in here.' She goes into a prolonged bout of coughing, on and on, spluttering away as if her guts are going to come up. It's enough to drive you mad.

'Are you all right, Mam?'

'Aye,' says her mother shortly. 'Don't worry, you'll get your money.'

M raises her fist in triumph as she walks away from the phone. Yesss! She goes back to the concession and takes the coat out again. Maybe she could ask them to put it by for her till the money arrives. Carefully setting down her handbag so Minim doesn't topple over, she slides her arms into the sleeves. There's no doubt about it. This coat is hers.

'Can I help you, ma'am?' Another bloody sales assistant. But she turns to her with all the charm she can muster. 'It's beautiful, isn't it? But I don't have enough cash on me just now. Would it be possible for you to keep it for me and I'll come in at the end of the week?'

The girl has a slightly blank look about her. 'Cash?'

It seems to be a foreign concept to her. 'Have you thought about taking out one of our store cards? You'd get ten percent off the price of the coat if you bought it with the card.'

She holds her breath, doesn't want to reveal her ignorance. Of course she's heard of credit cards, but has no idea what you do to get one. 'Do you want me to check it for you, ma'am?' asks the girl.

'Well, why not?' she says, smiling encouragingly back at her. She's a nice looking girl, though maybe a bit cheeky. She'd need slapping down. Sophie is more malleable, she hopes. The girl takes her name, Maria Spencer, and her address. It's hard to remember her new date of birth but she gets it just in time. Not that the girl notices her hesitation—her head is down as she types in the address. 'I need some identification from you,' she says. Her dark hair is cut in a rough bob and her big breasts strain at her blouse.

'I've got my library card,' says Myra.

'Have you got a utilities bill, gas, electric, anything like that?'

'I've only just moved here, I'm afraid.'

The girl looks doubtful. 'A letter from someone to your new address?'

'I've got a letter telling me what I have to pay the phone company every month. Would that do? It's at home.'

'That would be fine, Miss Spencer.' She presses a button on her computer and reads a message on the screen. 'Your application has been accepted. If you nick back home and get the phone company's letter you can walk out of here today with that coat.'

She can hardly believe it. She strokes the fabric of the coat, twirls round to look at herself again. In the mirror a new self is beckoning. Is life on the outside always going to be this easy?

37

Beth is there first, as always. She sits down in the corner, where she can see everyone in the room. There are red flower candles in dishes of water on every table and poinsettias ranged along the windowsill. So pretty ...

She should have waited before coming, should have known they'd be late. It's always the same, her sitting in some restaurant looking lame while they rush about doing whatever big, important things they do on the weekends. Do they think their time is worth more than hers? She could have finished that last batch of marking instead of rushing out, leaving the bed strewn with the four different black tops she'd tried on to see which was the most flattering. She tugs at her scoop-necked jumper. She should have worn the Lycra. It pulls you in a bit more.

They always assume that they're more important than Beth is, but one works for papers full of trash and adverts and the other works in a prison. It takes a particular type of person to be comfortable with controlling another human being's life so completely. Locking someone in at night, hearing gates clang behind you every morning as you walk to your office, how do you get your head around that?

Pat strides into the restaurant twelve minutes late, youthfully slim, though Beth notes deep crows' feet at her eyes. They weren't so pronounced last time, were they? 'Why are you wearing your suit on a Saturday?'

'I'm going to have to go back into work this evening. Sorry I'm late.'

'I've ordered a bottle of white. That suit you?'

Pat frowns. 'I'm not sure I'll have a drink.'

'It's supposed to be our Christmas lunch.'

'I know, but ... I think I'll start with a mineral water.'

Oh God. She hopes Pat isn't going to have one of her austere days. The black suit is a bad sign. Even when the three of them were sharing that flat at university, all those years ago, Pat had the power to dampen any atmosphere. Often Beth dreaded going home in case she was in one of her dark moods. Those sudden irrational flashes of anger, where did they come from? There was a summer they went travelling up in the north of Scotland, all together in Jude's old Morris Traveller, a brown and white monstrosity that looked like a two tone coffin. It was baking hot, the one-track roads crowded with Germans and French. Every time they came to some little hamlet the whole stream of cars would watch as one lucky person got the last bed for the night. Pat finally exploded. 'I'm not going another step,' she said, pulling at the door handle.

'Oh God, we haven't a chance now,' moaned Jude as their friend stormed off towards a small loch just off the road. Beth, always the placatory one, got out of the car to bring Pat back. The ground was hard, the marshland all dried up. Beth could feel the grass crackle under her feet as she walked, the stalks as spiky as Pat's mood. Oh, the tyranny of temper. She wanted to sock Pat. 'Come on,' she said gently. 'This isn't helping anyone.'

'No? It's helping me.' Pat's tone was so savage Beth took a step back.

'I'm sure we'll find somewhere in the end.'

'Go away.'

Beth tramped back to the car. Jude was leaning on the side, smoking. 'Well, that was successful.'

'She'll come round.'

'Will she? I need a drink.'

Pat trailed back eventually, but still said nothing, just got in the car with her face grim. They drove more than a hundred miles in silence, till they found a little licensed hotel in the middle of nowhere. It was only halfway through the second bottle of wine that they were finally able to tease her.

'Too much turkey on this menu,' she hears Pat say now.

Beth quickly scans the menu. 'Yes, I think I'll have the brie and redcurrant tart. That sounds a bit more fun.'

'D'you know, I'm just going to have Dover sole.'

Beth can hardly say that Dover sole bores her rigid. For all her years of gentrification she has never acquired the delicacy of taste to appreciate white fish. Fish came in batter with chips and peas when she was a girl and she finds its nude flesh repellent. 'We'd better wait till Jude comes before we order, hadn't we?'

'I suppose so. She always does this.'

Beth refrains from saying that being on time is relative round here. Jude's entrance, when it finally comes, is a relief. In she sweeps, a sunburst of movement and colour with her red sweater and shiny eyes. 'Sorry, sorry, sorry, darlings. Oh goody, you've already started on the wine. Pat, get rid of that boring old mineral water. It's Christmas. Don't you look wonderfully slim? I like the suit. Very sexy governess. Sweetie, have you been losing weight too? You both look *luminous* in your black. Now let's have a starter, shall we? This wine's divine. What is it? Oh, super. I think the fish terrine to start, definitely. It always *looks* so wonderful here, beautiful strips of pale yellow and pink, far too pretty to eat. And the tart to follow. Yes, yes, I think definitely the tart. Waiter, could we have another bottle of your *delicious* wine? Thank you. How sweet of you. Oh, it's wonderful to see you both. We do this far too rarely. Now before I forget, here are your presents. But you've not to open them till Christmas Day—you must promise. Or shall we have a tiny peek? No, no, we mustn't. You're quite right.'

Pat grimaces. 'I'm sorry. I just haven't had a moment yet. The whole Hindley business, you know. It's made the women very unsettled. Lots of them knew her in our place.'

'Oh, I'm the same,' says Jude. 'All that scouring through the files, trying to find something new to say. Impossible.'

She's so … un*stop*pable, Jude. Beth relaxes now she's here. They are in safe hands. Her gifts are wrapped in shiny red and gold paper with huge red bows on top. Beth knows her own will look very dull beside them. She brings them out and places one by each plate. The bottle green paper and gold ribbon that looked so elegant in the shop now seem simply safe.

'So, how *are* you?' Jude sits back in her chair and looks at them. 'Pat, darling, you look pale.'

Beth watches as Pat too begins to relax. 'It's all been very stressful. We couldn't walk out the door without one of your lot sticking a notebook or a microphone under our noses, even though she hadn't been in Styal for years. Thank God, it's all over now.'

'Yes, the great British Christmas will suffer no obstacle in its way,' says Jude. 'What I have to do for my art. I've been looking into presents you can buy on the internet and you wouldn't believe some of the stuff that's out there. Executive ball scratchers, inflatable robots, pink plastic vibrators. Just gross.'

'Don't try and kid us your paper wants that sort of rubbish,' says Beth.

'Well no, but that's what you have to wade through to get to the cashmere cardigans and designer handbags.'

Jude always had the best, even as a student. Beth sneaks a glance at her feet. She's wearing a pair of the softest black leather boots, with a spiky heel at least four inches high and buckles across the top. 'Versace,' says Jude, laughing.

'Hmmm, thought so,' says Beth without shame. *It's where you started from that counts*, she tells herself. Jude's family were rich. She spent her weekends on yachts or going parachute jumping. She spoke like that from the start—*Darling* this and *Sweetie* that. People poked fun at her at university but Beth knew it was how she'd been brought up. She wishes she'd had that advantage. Even now, after years of opening up her vowels and censoring her own grammar, she knows that people can tell she's from Manchester.

'So did you manage to find something new to say about Hindley?' says Pat, a sly smirk flitting across her face.

'What do *you* think?' says Jude. 'You weren't exactly spilling the beans, were you?'

'More than my job's worth.'

'That's all our friendship means to you.'

'No, but I like to pay my mortgage.'

'Why did you hate her so much? I know she did terrible things but that was a long time ago.'

'She was a piece of shit, Jude. But if you'd met her she'd have fooled you into thinking she was a caring, sharing human being.'

'I remember one of our art teachers meeting her when she was at Styal,' ventures Beth. 'She was in the middle of a class when this woman strolled in. Sue had no idea who she was, but everyone in the class went quiet. She had a walking cane and she just sat down in a chair with the cane across her knee. So Sue asked her what she was doing and she said, *Just watching*. Sue said, *No-one just watches in my class. You have to paint*. Well, I don't know if Hindley was rotten at painting or what, but she didn't like that one bit and she just got up and walked out. Then everyone told Sue who she was.'

40

'Oh yes, she likes ... liked to be in control,' says Pat. 'Some of the women were very stupid about her. They treated her as if she was some kind of big crime queen—when she was just another idiot woman sucked into something because of a man.'

'Darling, I don't think that's right,' says Jude. 'These people have to find each other. You can't buy a fellow murderer off the peg.'

'I know that, but she wouldn't have harmed a child on her own. I loathed the woman, but even I don't think she'd have done that off her own bat.'

'Why did you hate her so much then? Wasn't she a bit of a victim too?'

'A victim—are you kidding? He didn't hypnotise her. She was an adult woman who chose to do this to please her man. And presumably to please herself too.'

'It wasn't just the children—you didn't like her personality either, did you, Pat?' says Beth.

'No, I hated her. She was cunning, so manipulative. And there was something creepy about her. I remember when I was working at Holloway and she was there. She was a real queen bee. This young girl came in and she'd just read something in the paper about the Moors Murderers and what they actually did. It was the tenth anniversary I think. Anyway, she attacked Hindley and Hindley just went limp. It was the weirdest thing, like a possum playing dead or something.'

'That's just biology, fight or flight, isn't it?' says Jude.

'I don't know. I've seen a lot of fights in prison but I've never seen a woman do that. There was an animal quality to it. It was a reflex, no thought there. I think she lived in her body like an animal, no matter what Lord Longford said.'

'Oh, the dotty Lord,' says Jude. 'Mad as a snake, wasn't he? Terribly sincere, of course. He really believed she'd repented, didn't he?'

'She believed it,' says Pat. 'That's the kind of liar she was.'

Jude scoops up a forkful of the fish terrine the waiter has laid in front of her. 'Told you this was divine. Isn't it darling, the way it's presented? So Beth, how is it, now that Will's fled the nest? Are you and Charles having passionate rumpy pumpy in every room?'

They all laugh at the image. 'I wish,' says Beth, though she doesn't, not really.

'I saw him on the way here. Had his nose in a shop window. I won't say which—he was probably buying your present.'

'I doubt it. I usually have to tell him what I want. He hasn't a clue.'

'He's a chap,' says Jude, as if that's an end to it.

Later, when they leave the restaurant, he is there waiting for Beth, hands shoved into the pockets of his overcoat. 'Ah, the absent-minded professor,' says Jude. He goes pink, as he usually does around her. 'You should have come in and had a drink with us, Charles,' says Pat.

41

'Oh well, driving, you know,' he says, holding up his keys and rattling them. Beth ignores Jude's cough, which she recognises as vestigial laughter. 'Yes, you've got to get me home safe,' she says, tucking her arm in his.

It takes a long time to get out of the centre of Manchester. Charles tuts impatiently at every hold-up but Beth is dozy from the wine. Only when they finally get on to the M62 does she wake up. 'I adore this road,' she says. 'It's so dramatic.'

'A little over the top, don't you think?' asks her husband.

'Absolutely. That's why I love it.'

He raises an eyebrow. Good, it does no harm to surprise him. The traffic crawls three-legged up the side of the moors, a giant scarab mounting the hill. Light from the lamps lining the central reservation skids off the hard shells of the cars ahead. As always, Beth has a strange feeling when they pass the sign for Saddleworth, the creep of recognition followed almost immediately by nausea. Those poor children, buried out here in this lonely place … How would she ever cope if something happened to Will?

It's so cold out here, so dark. How could Myra ever have left them here?

Midnight, and too alive to sleep. Fucking De Sade, getting him all wound up over an unreadable book. Stomach-turning, stomach-churning crap. 120 Days of Sodom? 120 days of boredom, more like, though you have to laugh at some of the man's tastes. Not the most aesthetic of substances, shit. Still, it was quite funny, the bit about the fat bastard dropping his greasy turd in the wee whoor's mouth.

At least De Sade achieved something, which is more than can be said of Ian Brady-Stewart-Sloan. A few grand plans. A few petty robberies. They don't amount to a hill of beans in this crazy world.

Light falling on the pavement outside the house. Cobbled streets with no-one in them. A lone dog growling at him till his foot flies out and he kicks the cur. Stupid animal. Doesn't it know he prefers animals to humans? It shouldn't have made him do that.

Down to the canal, the dank water's stink infused with the smell of piss. Along the bank, alone. No-one else awake in the world. Suburban troglodytes, caved up in the torpor of their stupid lives. No money, no power, no will, no desire. What would it take, what *would* it take for them to wake up and see what the world is doing to them?

He walks along the towpath, straining to see in the dark. A rustle in the blackness. Is it a rat? or a piece of scrunched up paper? He can't stop thinking about the girl, the girl … she's not like the rest of them in the office, silly lassies prattling about lipstick and Cliff Richard. There's something unfinished about her, a sullen tug of dissatisfaction at the corner of the mouth—maybe something to work with there.

She didn't flinch once during the film. *Trial at Nuremberg*. Nice first date, holding hands on the way home. If she was bothered by the movie she didn't show it. Not even the concentration camp footage. Well, why should she? People make too much fuss. It's pure sentimentality, getting upset at a bunch of elongated cadavers, pulled out of recognition on the Nazi racks. She didn't know any of those people. It wasn't her gran or her mum or her precious sister—why should she care? Not a comfortable way to die but if you're on your way out, what does it matter? They were weak, those people. Went along like cows to the abbatoir, shuffling and jostling maybe, but not making a serious attempt at freedom. How could you respect that?

The canal goes under a railway bridge and he has to pick his way carefully along the tunnel. Some sodding kids have knocked the light out and it would be easy to go arse over tit on the mud-slicked ground. The bridge has a long, low span, like the Vienna sewers in *The Third Man*. Smells pretty rank too. Dah rah dah rah dah, rah dah … that damn zither tune is going to go round and round in his head. He'll be talking like Orson Welles all night. *Nobody thinks in terms of human beings. Governments don't. Why should we? They talk about the people and the proletariat, I talk about the suckers and the mugs—it's the same thing. They have their five-year plans, so have I.*

43

Where will he be in five years time? Please, not in that damn office going out of his head with boredom, the only break in the routine when he gets told off for nipping out to place his bets. It's a dull job, not a job for a man. Things have to change. He has to *do* something, *be* something. Greatness requires it. You just have to have the nerve.

Will he, when the time comes—or is he just another dreamer? There can be no going back, no bleating you didn't mean it. His foot connects with a small shard of stone and sends it skittering into the water. A cat mews somewhere in the darkness, a piteous cry, evoking memories of an earlier cat, entombed in slabs of stone in a cemetery in Glasgow. Eight days he kept it there, going back every day after school to see if it was still alive. It was angry at first, hissing, lashing out at him with its claws. After a couple of days it was plaintive, pathetic, staring at him with unblinking eyes when he came to the grave he'd made for it. Its pupils were the size of gobstoppers. At the end it was too tired to be frightened of him, barely able to open its lids to look at him.

Scientific inquiry, that's all. He wasn't being cruel. He doesn't mind cats, though he prefers dogs—more loyal. He just wanted to see how long it took to die, how long it clung on to its paltry existence. Impressive in a way, its persistence, though baffling. What's in a cat's life, scurrying out of the way of humans' feet, chasing after even meaner creatures than yourself, subsisting on scraps from people's tables? A sordid little life really, though it was interesting when it actually died, the way its eyes rolled back and the head lolled to one side.

Not much of a show, though, not like the Clydesdale that died in front of him when he was a kid. That was a real death, that huge beast going down on the frosty cobbles. It slipped, too cumbersome to manoeuvre its way on the treacherous surface. They all heard the crack as its bone broke in two. He supposes it was the leg though he was too wee to tell. Here by the dark canal he can still hear its panting breaths, see the dark eyes filling up. A primeval creature, a throwback to days when greater men walked the earth. Its magnificent head fell to the side, too heavy to be supported when the pain really bit. To see suffering like that, borne so patiently by the animal, was to see something noble being snuffed out.

Not that the gawping crowds could recognise it. They herded round, staring at the horse, shuffling their feet to keep warm in the cold morning. Clods, too stolid to care that beauty was being extinguished before their eyes. They felt no shame that this pure animal was dying for the sake of them having their pint down the pub, no shame that it spent its day dragging heavy barrels of beer around for their putrid appetites. What crass exploitation of a magnificent creature.

The draymen at least knew the stature of the beast. One of them stroked its shaggy mane of black hair. The other actually had tears in his eyes. They worked with the animal. They understood its value, a value far beyond that of the meretricious human being, his miserable existence devoted to scrounging a living and screwing his fellow humans.

44

He stops to light a cigarette, cupping his hands round the flickering match. How much of all this does the girl understand? He recognises her, recognises something in her, but she is untutored, raw. Could she be like him? She seems eager to learn, eager to be with him, but how far will she go? Will she be able to rise above the puny values of this sumphole slum.

He likes the way she look, the square jaw, harsh as a man's, the athletic body with its neat breasts and wide hips. She's feminine but not midget-brained like those idiots in the office. There's something to her, something more. She doesn't smile like the other girls, all coy and placatory. She smiles as though whatever she finds funny, she can keep to herself. She smiles as though she could be cruel. Could she be like him? Could she have black light inside her, waiting to be released?

Dogs howling, cats crying. The sound of a single motor prowling the nearby streets. The rest of the world sleeps. Let them dream their venal dreams. He will be ready when the time comes ...

This place is so Jude, roof gardens and a restaurant called Babylon, how dramatic. Pat stares out the window at the trees and beyond to some kind of water feature—surely that's not a flamingo she can see? Personally she would prefer some nice little pub with ordinary food like fish and chips, but she knows Jude would dismiss that as boring. Oh well, confit fillet of sea bass with roasted baby aubergine will have to do. The Tortoise Mountain sauvignon's good anyway. Thank goodness she got here first. Twenty quid a bottle is quite enough to be spending on wine and Jude has a terrible tendency to order champagne at three times the price. A family of ducks chugs into Pat's eyeline, the little ones strung out behind the mother like beads on a string—worry beads, that's what children are.

She closes her eyes, savouring the wine. She can't get him out of her head. Oh Hal, Hal. Monday night was perfect, his lithe body, the complete conjunction of the two of them, not just their bodies but their souls, their spirits. She has never found it so easy before, so free of performance anxiety or whatever they call it—or is that just supposed to be for men? Well, she gets it too, only not with this man, not with Hal. It can't last, can it?

'Earth to Planet Pat.' Jude's voice is as light and amused as ever, though when Pat looks up she wonders if her friend is a little more tired than usual, a little less triumphantly alive. Sometimes she makes Pat feel old, she's so full of energy and enthusiasm. 'Oh good, you've ordered white.' Jude slips into the seat opposite, pouring a generous helping of wine into both glasses. Pat doesn't even bother to stem the flow. Why should she? It's a lovely day and all is right with her world.

'You look, now what is that cliché I'd use if I was still working for the Daily Mail? *Radiant*. You must be in love.'

Pat smiles but says nothing.

'It's written all over your face, sweetie. Who is he? Is he gorgeous? Young? Has he a brother?'

'He's definitely gorgeous, he's younger than me—and if you think I'm letting you anywhere near him you're off your head.'

'How cruel you are,' pronounces Jude, scanning the menu. 'Have you chosen?'

'I'm going to have the sea bass and then rum cake for pudding. Listen, rum mousse layered with sponge, nougatine, raisin and orange caramel sauce. Sounds great.'

'How on earth do you stay so slim? I take it there's lots of athletic sex to counteract the calories?'

'Never you mind about the sex. It's fine, more than fine. And private.' Private and perfect.

Jude smiles and puts her hand over Pat's. 'I'm so happy for you, darling. You deserve it after all this time. You've had a hard road, I know.'

'Arid, certainly,' says Pat. 'I know it won't last, but I'm enjoying it while it does.'

46

'You never know. Who is he?'

'No-one you'd know, just a civil servant,' a statement she knows will instantly make Jude lose interest. 'I met him on the internet.'

'Oh darling, how modern of you. So it really works? Everyone I know keeps telling me to have a go but it seems so lame somehow.'

'Lame?' says Pat, knowing her frosty tone will alarm Jude. It does.

'I didn't mean you, darling. Of course not. But you know, there are so many ways to meet men, I'd feel a bit of a failure if I had to resort to the internet.'

Pat simply looks at her.

'Oh God, sorry, sorry, sorry. Dig a hole time. Look, let's order.' She beckons the waiter over, as usual managing to catch his eye immediately, a knack neither Pat nor Beth has ever been able to master. 'You must have the truffle risotto as a starter. It's wonderful here. And we'll have another bottle of this.'

Pat watches with affection as she debates the freshness of the langoustines and the Loch Duart salmon with the waiter. 'You're such a foodie, Jude.'

'I know, I'm a dreadful pig. Left to my natural inclinations I'd be the size of a house.'

Normally Pat finds Jude's affectations grate on her, but today it is simply delicious to be in this restaurant, anticipating fine food, looking out on to the trees and water, and beyond, the city rooftops. She is happy, an unusual state of affairs for her.

'I feel so jealous of you,' says Jude. 'It's ages since I've had that blissful feeling of just having fallen in love.'

'No-one on the scene then?'

'No-one I want,' says Jude. 'Maybe I'm just tired of men. They're all so shallow in London. Do you think I should come back up north where the real men are?'

'Actually, Hal's from Kent,' says Pat. 'I don't get to see him nearly enough. Not because he's from Kent—his shifts, my shifts.'

Jude sighs. 'There's always a price to pay, isn't there?'

'Jude, you don't seem yourself. Is something wrong?'

'Nothing and everything really. Flat, stale and unprofitable, you know? Do you think it's our time of life? I thought only men had mid-life crises, but here I am, apparently in the throes of one. I'm bored with work, bored with the men I know, bored with everything. My life has become sadly predictable. Actually, I'm thinking of writing a book.'

Pat frowns, unable to imagine flibbertigibbet Jude having the concentration. 'I thought you liked journalism because you have a low boredom threshold?'

'Yes, but I had this great idea to interview all the serial killers being held in Britain. I suppose it was because of being sent to cover Myra Hindley's death. I had to do all this research and people said such different things about

47

her. It was quite strange, and rather fascinating. I can't talk to her but I can talk to Ian Brady and Peter Sutcliffe and Rosemary West.'

'Do you really think they'll send visiting orders to a journalist?'

'Maybe they won't talk in person but these people are bored rigid in prison. If you write to them they'll write back. At least that's the theory. I started with Ian Brady because Hindley's death kicked it all off—he wrote back very quickly.'

'Really?' Pat holds some risotto on her tongue, savouring its creamy texture, the earthy scent of the truffle. Why are journalists so interested in these low-lifes? Doesn't Jude know what pathetic creatures they are underneath?

'You're enjoying that, aren't you?' says Jude. 'You don't usually bother about food.'

Pat shrugs. 'What's Brady like then?'

'Angry. He's angry about politicians, the middle classes, anyone who's richer or better educated than he is. You should see his writing—it's minute. Proper serial killer writing, darling. It gave me quite a turn when I saw it.'

'Just as long as you don't believe everything he writes.'

Jude, as usual, has eaten her starter in a couple of minutes. 'Course not. I don't believe everything anyone writes or says. It's in our union's code of conduct—we're not allowed to. You know, I thought I'd enlist Charles's help.'

'Beth's Charles?'

'Yes, he's a professor of forensic psychiatry or psychology or something, isn't he? I thought he could make assessments of the letters the killers send me.'

'Well, that sounds like a plan.'

'You don't think much of it, do you?'

'I work all day with people like that—I don't want to think about them off duty as well.'

Jude finishes her second large glass of wine and reaches for the new bottle. 'All Brady wants to talk about is his childhood in the Gorbals. Bit odd to be nostalgic for a slum, don't you think?'

'I think he's nostalgic for his innocence.'

'What a sentimentalist you are. You obviously don't remember much of your childhood. Children are the cruellest, least innocent people on the planet.' Her langoustines are set down in front of her and she digs her fork in to taste almost before the dish is laid on the table. 'Divine. Darling, we're all born psychopaths. Only a few of us ever graduate to civilisation—alas, Mr Brady is not among them.'

God, this better be worth it. A fat slug of rain slithers under her collar and leaves its cold trail down her neck. She cups her fag in her palm like the old men of her childhood hoarding their precious half Woodbines. It's hard to draw properly, as if the tobacco is infected by the dampness of the atmosphere. The smoke creeps into her throat but doesn't make it as far as her lungs, and she chokes.

She peers through the gap in the shrubbery. Still not here yet. Has coughing her bloody guts up made her miss Sophie? 'Sshh, poppet,' she says to the dog, who's yelping and snuffling round her feet. She picks him up and tucks him in the top of her coat. 'You'd better not tear Mummy's good coat.' What a fucking idiot, wearing cashmere on a day like this.

She's got to come. The chick *will* come. A Sunday and the Feast of the Immaculate Conception? Yeah, course she'll make time for Our Lady. She'd better. This is the best day for launching her campaign, a *proper* holy day. After this it's obscure stuff, like St Lucy, virgin and martyr, or St John of the Cross, the weirdo mystic, all the way through to Christmas. It's got to be today.

At last. There she is, trotting down the road. Always in a rush, always too many things on her plate. She looks nice, has a sort of ethnic-looking coat on today, with shaggy fur at the collar and wrists like they used to wear at pop festivals in the sixties. Let her get in first. M nips the fag in the middle, tossing the butt on the ground as she heads for the door of the church. 'Ah, the last smoker,' says the priest, in so jovial a manner she understands he hates smokers.

She smiles at him. 'Got to break the habit, Father.'

The little chick turns, hearing her voice. 'Hallo, M,' she says. 'You do look lovely. What a beautiful coat.'

'Thank you, shouldn't have worn it today, I suppose. But it was still dry when I left the house.'

She and Sophie have a whole pew to themselves. There are no children in the church today and the place seems even more soulless and modern without them, its whitewashed walls dimmed by winter light as pale as consommé. Sophie's damp coat gives off a funky animal smell, but hovering above is the sweeter smell of her perfume, heavy and rose based today. Paris, maybe? Ha, all that hanging round the Perfume Shop, asking to look in their bible of fragrances, is beginning to pay off.

Sophie leans forward to pick up a hymn book, her slender hand brushing against M's. Oh, she does smell lovely, and that white skin of hers … They're singing one of M's least favourite hymns, 'Hail, Queen of heav'n, the ocean star, guide to the wanderer here below.' What a fucking dirge. The quavery voices of the five old ladies in the congregation scrape up to the high notes like kids learning to play the violin. 'Thrown o-on life's surge' … Sophie's body, white as the foam on the sea, thrown down on the billowy bed … rose petals drifting over her … hundreds of rose petals … that smell …

yes, but the smell is only on the top half of her body, on her breasts and neck. Down below she'll smell sharper, not fishy like they say in books but salty, like the chicken soup you used to get from the machine after the swimming baths. You'd come out, your body warm after splashing around for an hour and then putting your clothes on, but you pretended you were cold when the air from outside the pool hit you. You shivered all the while the coin went into the slot and the little plastic cup dropped down, filling up with thin, green-flecked broth. Shivering made you enjoy the soup more. It wasn't much more than a stock cube really, but comforting, a warm smell; the little chick'll smell warm. 'Pra-ay *for* the wanderer, pray for me.' Yeah, pray for me. Me, me, me.

As the Mass meanders through the Kyrie and the Gloria she struggles to concentrate. Sophie is too close, with her heat and her scents. M focuses instead on the priest and his white vestments, the shiny rectitude of the figured brocade, its sparkling cleanliness. God knows what a to-do he'll make of the immaculate conception.

Father Murphy walks up the stairs of the pulpit, gazing bleakly out over his small congregation of mostly elderly women. He knows he's talking to the wrong people. Purity is irrelevant to these old biddies. They don't have the chance to be anything but. He launches into his usual sermon about how important it is that Our Lady is a virgin. That hard-faced woman beside Sophie Ferrers has a very cynical look on her face, not the sort he'd expect Sophie to be friendly with. Lovely girl, Sophie. From a top family of course. That helps.

'Woman is God's loveliest creation,' he says. 'He made her not just to be man's helpmeet, but to be a symbol of grace and goodness in the world. What use would Mary have been to God if she was some flibbertigibbet young lady who didn't know how to keep herself to herself? Would that have sent a message of goodness to all the raw boys lusting after her? Would that have expressed God's grace?' He mops his forehead with the impeccably ironed handkerchief that Mrs Johnstone, his housekeeper, lays out for him every morning.

'It's hard for us in these sex-obsessed times to get our minds round the idea of the immaculate conception, isn't it now? But think about it, could the baby Jesus, the Son of God, really have come from the body of a female who was no better than she should be, a woman who revelled in the throes of animal passion? What kind of an insult would that have been to that baby boy?'

Sophie raises her eyebrows. 'What respect for women,' she whispers in M's ear. M shakes her head in eager disgust, enthralled by her closeness, her silky hair, her mingled aromas of wet fur and roses and freshly showered skin. Oh God, don't think of her naked. Focus is what's needed here.

As the priest resumes the Mass M bows her head in determined piety, willing herself to concentrate. She raises her eyes only at the elevation of the host. It's easy to drain herself of colour, to let her whole body relax, imagining the blood level going down, down, down. Her face must be pure white by now. A gleam of silver as the priest raises the chalice, and the church slides in front of her eyes. She grips the pew, doesn't want actually to faint, just look the part.

Finally, the commemoration of the dead. 'Remember, Lord, those who have died and have gone before us marked with the sign of faith, especially those for whom we now pray. May these, and all who sleep in Christ, find in your presence light, happiness and peace.' The church is silent, no-one shuffling or whispering. Who can she mourn? Not her bastard father, that's for sure. She can see him inside her head, his black hair, the grim jaw jutting his anger forward into the world. Is it peaceful to be dead? Will *he* ever be at peace?

Better to think of her sister. Poor Maureen, her love, her little dove, too young to have a brain haemorrhage. Seeing her lying there, on the hospital bed, white as the sheets around her ... They said she was dead already, but she wasn't. What do nurses know? The dead don't sigh like that. She waited for M, then she went. Darling Moby. She were a funny little thing as a kid—brave, always standing up for herself. Pity she ever met that no-good husband of hers. M would be free today if it wasn't for that grass, David Smith. Gutless fucking bastard.

Moby didn't have a chance. And her baby, poor little mite. If only M could have spent more time with her when the little soul died. That was Brady's fault. He never understood real people, always had his nose stuck in a book. It's not sentimental to be upset when a baby dies, just normal. Not that he saw M crying over her. She wouldn't give him the satisfaction. What was it Moby called her? Angela, was it? No, Angela Dawn, such a pretty name. That wreath M ordered was one of the nicest she's ever seen. Little white flowers with purple pansies. She meant every word on the card. *God has gathered another little flower for His garden.* Beautiful, that.

Sophie is shaking her. 'Maria. M. Are you all right? You look awful.'

'Do I?'

'You're a ghastly colour. What on earth's the matter? You look as if you're about to cry.'

That's a good idea. M takes a gulp of air. She read once about Liza Minelli not being able to produce tears for some sad scene. The director told her, *Don't try to cry, try not to cry.* Yes, it seems to work—she can't stop the tears flowing. Once she's started there's no holding it back. Her nose will be red and ugly now, but why shouldn't she cry? Who else has had a life like hers?

'I've got to get out of here, Sophie.'

'Of course. Come on. I'll look after you.' The little chick puts a hand under her arm, guides her down the aisle. All those old biddies staring at them. Yes, look. We're together. We're friends, me and this beautiful young woman. Doesn't she look like an angel? Doesn't she look like Botticelli's Primavera? Not that you lot would know what that is anyway.

It's stopped raining now, thank goodness. 'I'm going to take you to my house. It's not far from here.' This is better than she had hoped for. They walk up the hill opposite the church, away from the town. It's steep and she finds herself short of breath, but she tries not to let the little chick see it. Don't want her thinking M's old.

The house is a semi-detached stone villa right at the top of the hill. While Sophie opens the door, M turns back to look. She can see the church and beyond it the river. To the left is the main part of the town, with the square and the town hall and beyond it all the little streets and alleys where the shops and restaurants are. To the right is the park and her own terrace on the far side of it. And in the distance beyond the river is the lowering bulk of the former cotton mills, now disused and derelict, waiting to be given purpose again.

'Come in,' calls Sophie.

M turns back to the house. 'Quite a view.'

'That's why I chose it really. It was a terrible mess when I got it. Thankfully my brother Sebastian is just marvellous with renovations. He's made quite a killing doing up old houses.'

She leads the way into the living room. Its wooden floor has been sanded and polished, every little knot in the wood gleaming under its coat of varnish. The wood looks old, not that cheap laminate stuff M's got in her kitchen. There's already a chip in it where the dog tried to lift one of the corners. 'I'm going to put the kettle on and make us a nice cup of tea,' says Sophie.

M studies the room, intrigued by the fact it doesn't have a single new thing in it. Even the carpets are old, almost threadbare some of them, and the colour faded. She's leaning forward to study the hunting prints on one wall when the grandfather clock in the corner whirrs into action. Midday already. That Father Murphy must have wittered on longer than she thought.

A flock of photographs in heavy silver frames stands on a side table. M picks up a hand-tinted picture of a young woman in a tightly-waisted riding jacket, standing by her horse. 'That's my mother,' says Sophie, returning with a tray of tea things and a plate of fig rolls and shortbread. 'And Maid Marion, of course.'

'Of course,' says M.

Sophie laughs. 'I take it you don't ride?'

'I've never even been on the back of a donkey at Blackpool.' She sits down, suddenly exhausted. The effort has been a bit much.

'You poor thing. Here, put this cushion behind your back.' Sophie pours the tea. 'You looked ever so pale inside the church.'

'I'm all right. Really. It was just a bit hot.'

'Nonsense. If there's one thing it wasn't it's hot. It was bloody freezing in there. What was really the matter?'

M leans back on the needlepoint cushion with its pattern of old roses, half closes her eyes. 'It was all that talk about the baby. The baby Jesus. I had a baby once.' She can feel the tears massing under her eyelids again, ready to go into action for her. 'They took her away from me. That's what they did in those days.'

'Oh no. How awful. What was the baby's name?'

'Angela. Angela Dawn.'

'Maria, don't cry. Please don't cry.' The little chick comes over and sits on the sofa beside her, holding her hand.

'It's today. She was born on the feast of the Immaculate Conception. I shouldn't have gone to church. I might have known it would upset me. All that stuff about the throes of animal passion.'

'I know.' She can feel the heat of Sophie's body next to hers. 'These priests. I sometimes wonder what God thinks of them.'

'She'd have been forty today.'

'Gosh.'

'I was only a girl when I had her. But you know, I think of her as a baby. It's as if she never grew up. All I can see are her tiny little fingers and her little button nose.'

Sophie strokes her shoulder. She's sweet. M feels so tired she would like to lie down with her head in the little chick's lap.

Not yet.

'Maybe she'll get in touch with you one day.'

'I doubt it, not after where I've been.'

'What do you mean?'

'In the mental hospital. My mother thought I must be either mentally ill or evil so she sent me to the nuns. They ran a place in North Wales, a kind of home for young unmarried mothers. It was a registered psychiatric hospital.'

There is silence. Sophie looks shocked. 'I can't believe it. Not in this day and age.'

'It wasn't this day and age. It was forty years ago. You've no idea what it's like to be locked up for most of your adult life.' She tries to get her breath but great gusty sobs well up inside her. She's crying, and choking as she cries. Damn fags. 'I wasn't mad. I wasn't evil. I didn't deserve that.'

'Oh God, Maria. I'm so sorry. I can't begin to imagine how you're feeling.'

M turns and the little chick puts her arms round her, lets her sob, strokes her hair. The dog stares up at them both, alarmed. 'Just let it out. You cry.' M lays her head on Sophie's breast, drawing in the scent of her, the heat of her. Finally she straightens up. 'I'm sorry. I don't usually behave like this. It's because it's Our Lady's feast day, Angela Dawn's birthday. I feel kind of alone at this time of year.'

'You poor thing. It must be hard to make a new life after being locked away from the world for so long.'

'Yes, it's not easy to make friends at my age. It's like being a teenager all over again, only you're not as appealing when you're a woman approaching sixty.'

'Don't worry. You're such a sympathetic person I'm sure you'll meet lots of people.'

'I sort of don't know where to start, you know?'

Sophie pats her hand. 'Here, drink your tea. She holds out the china plate with the biscuits. 'Have a shortbread. That'll make you feel better. It's nice and sugary.'

M takes the biscuit. The pattern on the plate is old-fashioned, with full-blown red and gold roses. Pretty.

'I shouldn't really. Now I'm out I want to lose some weight. You get used to institutional food. In fact it's about the only thing to look forward to in those places.'

There is the sound of something thudding on the mat and Sophie gets up. 'Excuse me.' She comes back into the room a moment later, brandishing an envelope. 'First Christmas card of the season,' she says, sticking the card on the wooden mantelpiece. It shows a garish Christmas tree liberally sprinkled with glitter and with an enormous teddy bear standing beside it. 'That's my neighbour. She's always terribly organised. Oh Lord, I suppose I'd better buy some cards tomorrow. I can't believe how much there is to do for Christmas, and I haven't even started yet.'

'I suppose you have loads of presents to buy, when there's so many of you.'

'We try to stick to little things, really. Except for the children, of course.'

M finds herself wondering what the chick's family would class as little. Posh stuff for sure.

'What do you do at Christmas?'

'Oh, it's usually chaos. There are so many of us and once you add in partners and offspring and old aunties and friends the house is bursting at the seams. I don't know how Mummy copes.'

M drinks her tea. She lets silence develop.

'What do you do at Christmas?' asks Sophie.

'I don't know. I'll buy a bit of turkey for me and Minim, I suppose. Watch the Queen's speech.'

Sophie looks at her. Good. The little chick's brain is whirring in there. Let her work it out. Poor M, just out of the loonie bin after all these years. Alone ...

'All on your own?'

'Oh yes. But don't you worry about that. I'm just happy to be out and able to celebrate Christmas any way I want. I'll be fine.'

The little chick pours another cup of tea for her. 'I'll go and fill the pot up.' She goes through to the kitchen and there is the hiss of steam as the water boils again, then the sound of footsteps in the hall. Her voice is soft, but M can still hear. She makes sure she does. 'Mummy, will it be all right if I bring a friend for Christmas? She's had the most awful bad luck in her life ...'

'No, she's not like that at all. I don't know exactly how old she is, around sixty.'

'Course she's not here. I wouldn't put you on the spot like that.'

'Mummy, you are a darling. She's a most interesting person. You'll like her.'

'Bye, Mummy. See you soon.'

Sophie comes back into the living room, eyes bright. 'That's settled. You're coming to us for Christmas.'

'I couldn't possibly.'

'Don't worry. There's oodles of space. We always have house guests over Christmas.'

Myra shakes her head. 'I can't believe you'd ... you're a very kind person.'

Sophie's head ducks as she pours the next round of tea, but M can see she's pleased. So, the little chick collects lame ducks. Well, not this time, chickie. Not this one.

From: "Hal Wolf" <wolfman@hotmail.co.uk>
To: lynx1043@hotmail.co.uk
Subject: shifts
Date: Fri, 13 December 2002 01:54:33

Dearest Lynx,
            I'm really fed up I won't see you tonight. Damn them and their
shifts. I'm wandering around here with a bottle of red and the hots for you,
with some scraggy fox barking outside the window. Gives me the creeps, that
sound. It's so unearthly. You'd think it's in agony but it's probably just hungry.
            Aren't we all?
            I'm hungry for your skin and the salt taste of you, hungry for those
long, lean legs of yours, hungry for the space on your neck just above your
breastbone - that's my space, my land, my territory. Mine, mine, mine.
            Are you out there? speak to me, my lynx.
From the Blackberry of Hal Morton

From: La Barbara <lynx1043@hotmail.co.uk>

Darling Hal, it's so good to hear from you. I wish I was with you, curled up
against my warm wolf man.
But you should be asleep, my love. It's late.
From the BlackBerry of Pat Shields

From: "Hal Wolf" <wolfman@hotmail.co.uk>

I suppose so. Guess I'm just fretting about work. Our favourite person has
discovered the joys of shopping, which doesn't bode well for the future. She's
like a kid in Aladdin's cave. I suppose there wasn't so much stuff around in
her day.
She has expensive tastes - she bought a 300 quid coat the other day. The
salesgirl offered her a credit card, would you believe? It's criminal the way they
just offer these cards to anyone. She'll get herself - and us! -in trouble if she
doesn't watch out.

From: La Barbara <lynx1043@hotmail.co.uk>

Just herself, darling. Nobody knows who she is.

From: "Hal Wolf" <wolfman@hotmail.co.uk>

I hope you're right, but there's a lot of pressure on our team. We're supposed
to head trouble off at the pass. Can you imagine if she starts wanting lots of
expensive stuff that she can't afford? What if she started shoplifting or got

56

involved with criminals? You couldn't put it past her - when she was with Psycho they were hell bent on armed robbery. That was what all his plotting and planning and grooming the third man was leading up to.

From: La Barbara <lynx1043@hotmail.co.uk>

The third man?

From: "Hal Wolf" <wolfman@hotmail.co.uk>

You know, the brother-in-law, the one who shopped them to the police. They tried to blame him.

From: La Barbara <lynx1043@hotmail.co.uk>

Yes, I remember now. But surely she wouldn't be stupid enough to get involved in anything criminal again?

From: "Hal Wolf" <wolfman@hotmail.co.uk>

You're the one who knows her. You tell me.

From: La Barbara <lynx1043@hotmail.co.uk>

She certainly wanted the best of everything inside, expensive clothes and good quality curtains in her cell, that sort of thing. There was a limit to how much they would put up with, of course, so she couldn't indulge herself totally, but she's a hedonist, without a doubt, so it wouldn't surprise me if she went a bit wild at first.

From: "Hal Wolf" <wolfman@hotmail.co.uk>

She's already fallen for some woman - the girl's very pretty, blonde and quite posh apparently. It's all a bit puzzling as the girl has no history of batting for the other side. Or should that be the same side?
I think she's bewitched.

From: La Barbara <lynx1043@hotmail.co.uk>

Course she is. M can get people to do things. She even bewitched the prison governor once, persuaded her to take her to the park.

From: "Hal Wolf" <wolfman@hotmail.co.uk>

Oh yes, I think I remember seeing something about that in the News of the World.

From: La Barbara <lynx1043@hotmail.co.uk>

That's right. She was a lovely woman, good-hearted. Crims find it easier to manipulate good people. Don't you remember our friend had a love affair with a warder who was an ex-nun? She'd been in a convent for years so wasn't exactly worldly-wise - an innocent waiting to be plucked. You can rely on M to spot a mark. The poor little nun ended up in prison herself - escape plan that went wrong.

From: "Hal Wolf" <wolfman@hotmail.co.uk>

Wasn't M supposed to be madly in love with the psycho?

From: La Barbara <lynx1043@hotmail.co.uk>

She was, but of course she realised she'd never get out if she was still linked to him, so she just ditched him.
She always had lovers - always the prettiest, freshest girls.

From: "Hal Wolf" <wolfman@hotmail.co.uk>

How on earth does she do it? She's not exactly the best looking woman in the world, is she?

From: La Barbara <lynx1043@hotmail.co.uk>

She's not the worst either. She broke her nose and had to have an op and everyone was sure she'd persuaded them to lop a bit off for her. And she has real magnetism, a perverse kind of glamour that doesn't depend on what she looks like.
Of course her real trump card in prison was who she was. It's like a mirror image of society in there. They admire the people we despise.
She'll cause havoc out there - she can scent prey from a mile off. Anyone vulnerable or soft, anyone with no allies.

From: "Hal Wolf" <wolfman@hotmail.co.uk>

Really? I've always thought she was blinded by love and dragged into it by him.

From: La Barbara <lynx1043@hotmail.co.uk>

You're sweet, my love. Most people think she's just an evil bitch.

From: "Hal Wolf" <wolfman@hotmail.co.uk>

I suppose I can't really believe a woman would do things like that of her own free will.

From: La Barbara <lynx1043@hotmail.co.uk>

What a romantic you are! If you'd met some of the women I worked with you wouldn't be under any illusions. Women can be just as violent and cruel as men. Why do you think I hate her so much?
If she'd felt the slightest remorse I'd have given her the benefit of the doubt, but she revelled in being queen bee in there. She loved swaggering round with her little acolytes following her.

From: "Hal Wolf" <wolfman@hotmail.co.uk>

So, why did people like Lord Longford campaign so hard for her then?

From: La Barbara <lynx1043@hotmail.co.uk>

She could talk the talk. Hal, if you met her I swear she'd have you wrapped round her little finger. She looked remorseful, said she was remorseful, but I don't believe she lost a minute's sleep over those children. As far as I'm concerned she's the biggest hypocrite I've ever met. She never faced her guilt, ever. He did. He even tried to make some kind of reparation by doing Braille books for the blind.

From: "Hal Wolf" <wolfman@hotmail.co.uk>

I've always thought she couldn't have lived with herself if she didn't repent.

From: La Barbara <lynx1043@hotmail.co.uk>

It's the other way round, surely? You couldn't live with yourself if you did repent.

13 THE HUNT

What the fuck do you wear at a posh country house? M studies her wardrobe in dismay. The lilac suit she loved so much inside looks starchy and dated now, even if she was thin enough to get into it, which she's not. Not really. The navy pleated skirt makes her look like a Wren or a prison warder and her pink blouse with the pussy bow is just silly. It's wrong, all of it. Wrong, wrong, wrong. People don't wear these stiff clothes any more.

But what do they wear? How on earth is she going to find out? She could ask Sophie, but that might make her look *too* vulnerable. Weak, even. And what do you *do* in country houses? She's going to look wrong and sound wrong too, for sure. No matter how much she tries to disguise the backstreet accent, she's never certain she's succeeded. Telltale signs of her boiled cabbage upbringing always slip out.

Her jaw sets hard. She has never panicked at anything in her life before, why is she like this now? It's *clothes*, other people, nothing to get yourself aereated over, yet here she is falling apart. Her face in the mirror looks grim. Better try and think some nice thoughts or she'll look like a sodding gargoyle.

There must be a way out here. The money from her Mam hasn't come yet but she's always got that credit card. She's going to need it for the Christmas presents anyway. Better get the list. M goes into the little room she's made her office. Everything is filed in different coloured document wallets—purple for Christmas, red for bills, blue for personal correspondence. Huh, that one just has a letter from her Mam, nothing interesting. The pink one is for her own writing. There's nothing in there yet, but she hasn't had much time, with all the new things she's having to learn about the outside world.

There's too many of these Ferrers. Mummy and Papa, Alexander, Bunty, Serena, Sebastian, Cassandra and of course, her Sophie. She closes her eyes for a moment, thinking of elegantly choppy hair and clear grey eyes. How can she woo such a little goddess? Maybe a love letter? She's had some success with those in the past. *My dearest one, I burn till I see you once again, my heart consumed in the flames of desire.* No, that's probably a bit too full on for the little chick. Something gentler, more romantic. *My dearest one, I ache with longing to see your sweet face again. You are the light that illumines the path ahead of me, my will-of-the-wisp, my lodestar.* What the hell is a lodestar anyway?

She'd better get moving. There's a lot to sort out this afternoon. 'Mini-me, where are you?' she calls. He comes scampering up the stairs, his little chest heaving with the effort. 'There's Mummy's little darling. Who's a good boy, then?' She sticks him in the top of her handbag and goes through to the bedroom to get her coat. 'Let's go and spend someone else's money.'

It's a bit puzzling, this credit card business. There was none of that in the old days. Mam had that kitty thing in the local drapery store where you all put money by every week and then when it was your turn you had the whole lot in tea towels or net curtains. Da had tick down the pub sometimes. They were just starting to bring in hire purchase agreements when she got sent away, so she never had one. Now she's got this card and it feels as if she can buy anything she wants in the whole world.

As she leaves the house she sees the bus coming and runs to catch it. That's good luck. She hasn't time to walk, too many jobs to get through today. What on earth *do* you wear in the country? As the bus pulls away the words are repeating themselves over and over in her head, all the way into town. What do you wear in the country? You'd think she'd never been there, the way she's going on.

In the little streets off the town square she drifts from shop to shop, looking in the windows. One shop has green waxed jackets and tweed fishing hats, but the jackets cost hundreds of pounds. Not even the credit card is going to run to that *and* the presents. Loud music is thumping relentlessly from one of the shops, giving her a headache. She's about to hurry past when she sees a skirt exactly the same as one she once wore all those years ago, on the moors. It was white with dark blue squares that undulated in the folds of material. When she moved the squares went all spiky and jagged, as if they were breaking up. It was pretty, feminine. Brady liked it, especially when she crouched down, looking up at him, in their secret garden …

Why would a skirt like hers be in a shop today? The blood inside her starts rushing, pounding, making a noise in her ears. 'Don't you bother, just block the whole doorway,' says a young woman, coming out of the shop and roughly pushing past her. M stumbles aside, her balance shaken. A middle-aged lady walking past offers her a hand to steady herself.

'Get your breath back, love.'

'Honestly, young people today,' says M.

The skirt is not exactly like hers after all, though these full skirts are obviously back in fashion again. She can't imagine herself in it now, but she did wear that sort of thing when she went to Saddleworth with Brady— fashionable clothes and sling-back shoes, sometimes a warm jacket. They went in the car of course, and she never really walked that far. He did, thought it was a spiritual experience to become immersed in the landscape. Said he drew his power from it. She musn't think about that now. No, no more country.

Briskly she heads for the department store. She'll get the presents first. Sophie's bathroom is full of Penhaligon soaps and fragrance, so that seems a safe bet. M's breathing gradually returns to normal as she walks, but she is disappointed at the store. 'We don't stock it, I'm afraid,' the assistant tells her. 'You'll have to go to Bilbo Bags in the arcade.'

Oh God, only the most expensive gift shop in this whole poxy town. There were no shops like that in the old days, leastways not in Gorton. The town centre had big department stores though they didn't go in very often. Her Mam took her to Kendal Milne's on Deansgate once. Da had won at the races and gave her mother money to buy a new dress. 'Treat yourself, love,' he said, the only time she can remember him saying such a thing. He said it as if he loved her mother, though he was always slapping her about. Maybe that was what they both liked.

What M liked was the tunnel under the main road that took you from one side of the street to the other. You felt you were going on a secret mission when you went down into the dark passageway. It smelled dank and mysterious and really she'd have liked to play in there, but she was a big girl, out to help her mother buy clothes, not to behave like a tomboy. That day she looked back as they left the tunnel and it was as if her childhood was slipping away from her.

Her Mam bought a suit with a nipped in waist just like the young Queen was always wearing. She had a set of pearls too but you could tell they weren't real. They looked like Poppets, those plastic beads that snapped apart when you pulled them. How on earth did Mam bring herself to wear them? Fit only for kids, they were. M would die rather than put on rubbish like that.

Bilbo Bags is a small, discreet boutique, much more elegant than you'd expect from the stupid name. It's tucked away in a corner of the arcade and is stuffed with fancy Italian bags and shoes, their leather imbued with the sweetness that comes from paying a fortune for them. The Penhaligon's display is along the back wall. By Appointment to Her Majesty the Queen, say the labels. M loves the names: Artemisia, Elisabethan Rose, Malabah, 'the Indies in a bottle. Exotic, cool and confident, for the born traveller.' It contains spices, lush flowers, precious woods. She turns the bottle over to look at the price. For God's sake, it costs fifteen quid just for a few soaps. It's going to be well over a hundred pounds if she gets this stuff for all of them.

She needs to think this through, not to panic. She takes out her list and unfolds it. Lily of the Valley for Mummy, or should she get Bluebell, which 'echoes the beguiling coolness of an English wood?' Oh God, is Bunty a boy or a girl? Something gender free. Maybe English Fern, a classic Fougere? Whatever that means—it sounds stuffy and old-fashioned, the sort of thing old Lord Longford would have approved of. That'll do.

The girl offers to gift wrap them, putting them in some posh paper, then scoring gold ribbon with a knife to create a waterfall of curls. Her hands are quick and deft and M is impressed. Is it a new kind of ribbon? She's never seen any like that before.

What on earth is she going to get for Sophie? Can't be the same as these bastards she's never met. There are ranks and ranks of handbags but despite their obvious quality and expense they look solid, conventional, with none of the classy quirkiness of her little chick. Christmas was never this difficult in the nick. You got your girlfriend sweets or fags, one or the other. Occasionally she'd needlepoint them a cushion though they weren't always appreciative of that, seemed to think she'd just run it up on a machine.

If only she'd thought of that in time she could have made Sophie a tapestry waistcoat—she'd have worn that, just different enough to be funky, as she puts it. Before, M would have said that meant it smelled, but she knows differently now. Things are either funky or cool. There doesn't seem to be any other term of approval. Neither seems a very desirable quality to her. Brady always thought he was cool, but when it came down to it he had passions far hotter than those of an ordinary man.

She leaves Bilbo Bags, clutching her Penhaligon's shopper. It's nice stuff, the best, so it's OK to have spent so much on it. They won't be able to look down on her. She sets off down the arcade, looking for something for the little chick, but it all seems impossible. The clothes in the shops are irrationally expensive, the jewellery solid gold and too fussy for Sophie anyway. There's a gift shop, Bear Necessities, which looks promising but the teddies are overpriced, no doubt made in some sweatshop in China. Or Doncaster.

She wanders in and out of streets and arcades for hours, coming back to where she started. Should she just settle for Penhaligon's for Sophie too? The shops are open late, but there's only half an hour left, she'll have to make a decision soon. And what about the clothes? She is weary now, sits down on a bench for a while. After just a couple of minutes some woman sags heavily down beside her, patting the dog's head as it pokes out of her handbag. Bugger, people always start talking when she's out with him. 'Oh, you're a lovely little chap, aren't you? How old is he, love?'

'He's just a pup.'

'It's hard work, this Christmas shopping, i'n't it?'

'Bloody hard.'

That's it, she'd better move. She picks up her bags and sets off again. They feel awfully heavy. It's not until she's halfway down the next street that she realises she's lifted one of that old bat's bags. Well, buggered if she's going back now. She stops and looks inside. There's a little wooden duck with a name tag round its neck. *My name is Hayley.* That makes her laugh. Like that daft transsexual in Corrie. She's not even like a butch girl, much less a trannie.

The duck, though, is sweet and beautifully carved. She strokes the wood, so smooth. It's the perfect gift for Sophie. 'You're a little wizard, you are,' she says, ruffling the dog's head. She's exhausted, can't take any more of this shopping lark. Her clothes will just have to do. They can sodding well take her or leave her.

By the time she gets home, wraps Sophie's present and packs her case, all she wants to do is sleep—she's just not used to walking so much. Minim goes into the back yard to do his business and then they head for bed. What a relief to lie down. If only you could turn your brain off. What will it be like in the posh house? Will her bedroom be next to Sophie's? Will they play that game, what d'you call it?—Sardines?—and all squash into cupboards together? To lie next to Sophie, in the dark, to feel that taut bum ...

M's eyes drift shut. She's being pulled down a long tunnel, into the dark ... Sophie is at the end of it, naked, lying face down across the bed ... there are stripes across her buttocks. Flash, bang, wallop. Wallop. Who knew it could be like that? The zebra thrusts powerful haunches at the camera and backs right through the closed door of her grandmother's house, the house in Wardle Brook Avenue, where the police found them. He tip-toes up the stairs, the zebra, laughing ... he doesn't laugh much, just smiles sometimes, his teeth pulled back over big horsey lips. 'The old lady'll think I'm giving you what you deserve. She knows I'm your lord and master.' Yes master, please master, how's your lord and master today?

The radio goes on next door. Gran's playing Dean Martin again. *When the moon hits your eye like a big pizza pie, that's amore.* The zebra has a cane in his hand ... M bends over the bed, but she doesn't want to go down the gloomy tunnel ... she runs up the steps, towards the bright lights of the department store, but it's just a cupboard. Sophie looks over her shoulder, slides her jeans down, but M is suffocating. The stripes are biting into her flesh ... she needs to get the cane off the zebra ... she needs out, out of the tunnel, out of the dark.

'Good Lord. What on earth are you doing here?' Charles hurriedly takes his glasses off and lays them on his desk. Standing looking down at him, Jude sees the clear lineaments of a little monk's tonsure on the top of his head. Poor dear, he's going bald. How ghastly to be a man and have to go through all that.

'Darling, you haven't been answering my e-mails, have you?'

'Sorry,' he mumbles, his face slightly pink. 'So much to finish before the end of term, you know?'

'No I don't know. I think you're beastly,' she says, looking round the spacious office with its view on to the cropped grass of the campus. Everything in the room is so tidy. He's even working through what appears to be his in tray. How very methodical of him. 'Look, I won't take no for an answer—you and I are going out for dinner, my treat, while I tell you my wonderful idea. I'm rather hoping you'll help me with it. Now you just pick up that phone and tell Beth she's to bin the shepherd's pie or whatever she's made for you—I'm taking you both out.'

He coughs, uncomfortable. 'No need. She's going to a play tonight. Some children's thing.'

'Oh no, am dram, how awful. She is a love. I suppose some friend of hers is in it. Well, all the better, I shall have you all to myself. I warn you, Prof, I'm going to pick your brains all night.'

Charles shuffles his papers together and stands awkwardly, banging his knee off the side of the desk. Frowning, he bumbles over to take his coat from the hook. 'I'm not sure ...'

'Don't you worry about a thing, sweetie. I know a divine little restaurant where we can be totally quiet.'

'I doubt even you can manage that at this time of year,' says Charles, the glimmer of a smile at last flitting across his face.

'Wait and see,' she says, striding ahead of him into the corridor, then turning to watch as he fiddles with the key. He is a clumsy man, or perhaps he just gets anxious around her. Jude regards him with some amusement. Best not frighten the horses tonight.

In the car park she walks over to her Alfa Romeo, holding the door open for him. 'We're going to a little place I know in the country,' she announces. 'I'm staying there and it's not too far away from you. That way you can easily get a taxi home and we can both have a drink.'

'Why don't I drive behind you, then I can pick up my car on the way to work tomorrow?'

'OK, whatever suits. Do you think your wheels can keep up with mine?' she teases.

'We'll just have to see, won't we?' Good, he looks a bit more relaxed now they're out of his office. Perhaps he was afraid she'd pounce on him with nobody else around. Must curb the flirting.

She keeps his Ford in her sights as she negotiates the early evening traffic. God, it's so slow. Why on earth is it called it rush hour when they're crawling along like motorised tortoises? Even when they hit the M62 there are too many cars and they're forced to dawdle along in convoy. Not until the road reaches the moors does the traffic finally begin to thin out as people peel off to their little villages. Jude signals she's turning and Charles follows her off the motorway, hugging her back wheels as she leads him across black, bleak land barely visible in the dusk.

The pub is tucked away down a lane in a remote hamlet. Low-beamed and traditional, it has fairy lights strung across mullioned windows in honour of the season. Charles should find it charming.

'Mmmm, nice.' He nods approvingly at the dark wood tables, the flames of the open fire.

'It's always quiet in here,' says Jude. 'At this time anyway. It does get pretty busy later on, I have to admit. Here, have a look at the menu.'

'Ha. That sounds interesting,' he says, with the satisfaction of a dedicated foodie. 'Cumbrian spring lamb with leek and redcurrant sauce.'

'Don't you want a starter?'

'What do you think?'

'Why not,' says Jude. 'We might as well make a night of it.'

A slight flush creeps across his face and he turns to the wine list, poring over it for minutes and obviously enjoying the ritual of choosing. 'The Rioja should do very nicely.'

'Let's have the Gevrey Chambertin. I feel like splashing out.'

'Not at all,' says Charles. 'You mustn't think of paying.'

'I insist,' says Jude, waving her credit card at the barman. 'Stick it all on that, will you, sweetie? And we'll have a bottle of champagne to start.'

They settle themselves at a table in the corner. He seems uneasy, almost shy, a syndrome Jude has noted before with men who're attracted to her. If only she could tell him to relax, he's not her type. 'I'll get straight to the point,' she says. 'I'm writing a book on serial killers and I'm hoping you might help me.'

'Really? I didn't think you were the book writing type.'

'Too stupid, you mean?'

'Not at all. On the contrary, I'd say you were the brightest of my wife's friends. I just thought you preferred the sprint of writing articles.'

'I thought I'd start with Ian Brady and Myra Hindley,' says Jude. 'I did a bit of research into her when she died, though I'll obviously need to do more. I've been writing to him.'

'And he writes back?'

'Yes, but he just seems to want to talk about his childhood in Scotland. He's very nostalgic.'

Charles takes the first bite of his black pudding and scallop starter. Jude knows he won't say anything till he's thoroughly savoured and assessed it. 'Very good,' he nods. 'The scallops aren't overdone, which is always the big danger with a dish like this.' He sniffs his wine, closing his eyes to drink. 'Nostalgic, hmmm? Well, I suppose we all look back to our childhood as an age of innocence.'

66

'That would be the obvious conclusion to draw except that Brady wasn't innocent then. He tortured a cat when he was only eight.'

Charles looks at her sharply. 'You're right. And of course he'd been abandoned by his father before he was even born, so there should be little comfort in the past for him.'

'Abandoned by his mother too. She came to visit him at his foster parents' house but she didn't take care of him, and in the end she moved to England. During the trial she was very supportive but no doubt the damage had been done by then.' Jude sighs. She's surprised by how much Brady's story has taken her over, how sad it makes her feel.

'We see a lot of criminals in forensic psychiatry who've been abandoned in childhood in one way or another,' says Charles slowly. It interests her to watch him turning it all over in his mind. She's known him for years, knows how he behaves, but this is the first time she's been alone with him, the first time she's heard what he really thinks. 'It can have complex effects. On the one hand they have low self-esteem because they blame themselves for the abandonment—if only they'd been better children the parent wouldn't have left. But on the other, they're thrown on to their own resources, so survivors can end up feeling all-powerful. Like Brady. He was a special person so he had the right to commit the ultimate crime.'

Jude regretfully eats the last mouthful of her lime-scented crabmeat. 'That was delicious,' she says. 'He insists his childhood isn't to blame. He seems not to approve of blaming the past. I suppose that's why he's nostalgic about it. It isn't the real past that he thinks about because that would hurt him too much—his is a made-up one.'

'That's why you get that curious mixture of cruelty and sentimentality in psychopaths ...'

'You mean they can't think too deeply about their own pain, so they don't think at all about the pain of others,' interrupts Jude.

He smiles at her eagerness. 'Yes, that's a good way to put it. Or else they relish the pain of others because so much has been inflicted on them.'

The waitress clearing their dishes raises her eyebrows. This is clearly not the normal run of conversation at the Black Swan. 'He sends me letters with stickers from the Royal Humane Society, pictures of little dogs with chocolate drop eyes.'

'Is that an animal charity?'

'Yes. He seems to prefer animals to humans.'

Charles laughs. 'He's not alone in that.'

'Have you worked with him?'

'Brady? No, but of course we do all swap stories. One of my colleagues works part-time at Ashworth, so she knows him.'

'Why is he on hunger strike?'

'They moved him out of the ward he was on.'

'Yes, but it's gone on for three years now. Is that what it's really about?'

'Really? It's about control. The usual.'

67

Jude tries to sip her champagne slowly. She's drinking too quickly and it's going to her head. 'What does he think he's controlling?'

'The only thing any prisoner can—what goes into his body or what goes out.'

'Like the dirty protests in Northern Ireland, you mean?'

'Yes, only Brady is too fastidious to smear faeces round his room so he has to starve himself.'

'Does he really want to die?'

'Maybe. But if he does, he wants it to be an embarrassment to the authorities, to symbolise the fact that they're not looking after him properly.'

'I'd want to die. I couldn't bear to be locked up like that. I think I'd try to kill myself too.'

He studies her for a moment. 'I don't think you would, you know. You're not the type. You're a survivor, a clinger on to life no matter what.'

Jude looks up, meeting his gaze in a moment of both recognition and curiosity. 'D'you think so, Prof? What about you? Are you a clinger on to life no matter what?'

He concentrates on the plate of lamb the waitress is placing before him. 'I'm not sure that I am,' he says. 'I don't think I have your super life force. You like challenges, don't you? Adventure? I'm all for the quiet life.'

Challenges? Yes, she does. But she mustn't, not this time.

The case is in the kitchen, all packed, with Minim snoozing beside it. When the car horn goes M is in front of the mirror, trying to close the zip on her lilac trousers. How could she have let herself get so fat? Flesh seethes at her waistband, like a chemistry experiment about to explode. Not that she was ever any good at science at school. The only bit she enjoyed was when they boiled up geranium leaves in iodine and she'd compete with her pal to see who could stick her face longest in the beaker. Goodness knows what the point of the experiment was. The leaves went all purple and pretty though smelled unbearable, sort of sulphurous, which made you gasp for air and want to retch. She always used to win though she's not sure whether it was because she had a strong stomach or a strong will.

Now she tips Minim into her handbag and lugs the suitcase out to the car. The little dog scampers off as she locks the front door, but Sophie calls to him and he pauses in his flight to go bouncing up to her. She opens the door and Minim jumps on to her lap. 'Who's a little love, then? Yes, yes, yes, yes.'

It's freezing outside but M is suffocatingly hot with her new coat on as well as the damn suit. Minim is absorbed in licking Sophie's hands with a complete disregard for M. She feels enraged. Doesn't he know who his owner is?

My dog. My fucking dog.

'Sophie, can I put this in the boot?'

She must have spoken too harshly. The little chick looks startled.

'Sorry. Of course.' She deposits the dog on the passenger seat and scuttles to the back of the car. 'Why don't you take your coat off or you won't feel the good of it when you get out.'

'Yes, I won't need it with my own personal hand warmer here.' M scoops Minim off Sophie's seat and settles herself in the front. 'That's my poppet.'

Sophie runs back, nearly slipping on the frost. 'My God, it's freezing. I hope we're going to be all right. The weather forecast was a bit grim.'

M's waistband is digging into her, the fabric tight across her thighs. She yanks at it, suddenly angry at how constrained it makes her feel. Why didn't she just wear a tracksuit? Who cares what these fucking snobs think? She wants to feel comfortable. The car engine roars. She wants to feel free.

Sophie heads out of town, the car chugging up the sides of the valley. Even in the bleached light of the car headlights, M can see that the grass and bushes at the side of the road are coated with frost. She feels uneasy, unsure of where they're going. She wants them to go further east into Yorkshire, not back to Lancashire. She can't go over Saddleworth with the little chick. 'It's called Melham Hall,' Sophie had said, as if she ought to know it, though M hasn't a clue where it is. Now Sophie concentrates on steering the car through the frozen darkness, her lips pursed as she negotiates patches of black ice.

They climb up the steep-sided hills surrounding the town, then back along the twisting roads that first brought M to this place. Minim curls up on her lap and goes to sleep, his little snuffling breaths punctuating the purring of the car through the winter night.

At last they approach the big roundabout on to the M62. Turn left, turn left, turn left. Please go the other way. Don't go over the moor. Please don't go over the moor.

Sophie almost stalls as they reach the roundabout. The grinding gears grate on M's ears as the car jerks forward in a series of hops. *Move it. Move it— bitch.* She feels like screaming, needs to know which direction they're taking. The indicator clicks on and Sophie pulls on to the roundabout. Oh no, they're going right. She leans her head against the window, the cold glass setting her teeth on edge. Not Saddleworth.

'I'm sorry,' Sophie says. 'We're setting out awfully late, aren't we? You sit back and have a rest.' She switches on the CD player. The music is soft and slow and unbearable. M knows she's heard it before. She doesn't want to think about it but it infiltrates her mind, the long, stately melody sneaking its way into reluctant memory cells, forcing her to remember. Neddy and Hessie, glasses of sweet German wine by their sides, his pallid face suffused somehow with light. Her reading her magazine till he wrenched it out of her hand and whacked her on the head with it. 'Have you no soul, Hessie? Forget the bleeding Woman's Own. This is the greatest artist mankind has ever known and you've got your nose stuck in knitting patterns.'

Sometimes Brady conducted, eyes closed, drawing the music up out of his chest, his bony hands graceful as they twisted and turned to the long lines of melody. He was, she now realises, the first creative person she had ever met. He *felt* the music, embodied it.

As the slow movement ends, she glances at the little chick. Sophie's face is all contorted. The grimace makes her look ugly, not herself, her face a troll's face, screwed up and comical. She scrubs her cheek with her hand as if to rub out tears. Then she realises M is looking at her and starts to laugh. 'It's so beautiful, Tristan and Isolde, don't you think?'

'Yes, terribly sad,' she says, though she never was a fan of the idea of dying with your lover. Would he have asked that of her eventually? Would she have agreed?

Sophie ejects the disc. 'Let's put on something else. We don't want to go careering off the road because I'm going all Wagnerian and dewy-eyed.'

With the music off they can hear the wind above the sound of the car. Outside, the fields lie thick with snow. The music Sophie chooses this time is soft and slow too. M doesn't know it. She relaxes back in her seat and closes her eyes but she can still see herself, sitting on the moor with her Neddy, blue skies beyond them, the crisp air. They were happy then, in their secret garden, the hidden flowers of their love lying beneath them. Nobody could ever understand how it was between them.

But how come he was a jolly Goon and she ended up Hitler's deputy Führer? It didn't start like that. He called her Hessie after Myra Hess and her

70

beautiful piano playing, not after a Nazi. It was the bastard press that turned it into someone else.

'Do you like the Goons?' she asks Sophie.

'God, no. They're about as funny as a dentist's drill.'

'I suppose they were a bit before your time.'

'Well, yes, but Papa was a great devotee. He and my uncle used to do all the voices. My brother loved it but it drove the rest of us mad. What on earth made you think of the Goons?'

'I don't know. A friend just popped into my head. He used to do all the voices too.'

'I take it he was a computer geek? Or a train spotter?' Sophie's voice is teasing. She seems to find the idea hilarious.

'Something like that.' M laughs, but underneath is shocked at the casual dismissal of Brady. How dare she? Silly little ninny. That's her lover Sophie's talking about, her only, well, not her only lover but her real lover anyway. Is that all he was, a geek? He certainly liked making lists. Stupid idiot. If the police hadn't found that one in the left luggage they'd never have been able to pin the other murders on them. She'd have been out in a few years. She'd have had a life.

Is that how other people saw him? They didn't use that term in those days, didn't call people anoraks or nerds or any of those other words they use nowadays. Maybe these people who're always banging on about falling standards have got it wrong. Maybe people have a bigger vocabulary to choose from now than there was before.

God, she can't imagine Brady's response if you called him something like that. Not a man to insult. He could be really scary sometimes. She strokes Minim's fur, feeling suddenly empty.

The weather worsens as they reach the summit and start the descent to the other side. Mist begins to creep round the lamps that divide the motorway, refracting light back, like golden gossamer spun by giant spiders. The road surface is slick with ice. As they edge slowly forward, the fog swirls and rolls around the car, enclosing it in its own mobile world, separate from the other cars moving along the road. The vapour is so dense that they can hardly see a foot ahead of them. 'I think this is what they used to call a peasouper,' says Sophie.

'Mmm.'

'God knows where we are.' Sophie peers at the petrol tank as if it will reveal their location. 'I think we must be round about Saddleworth. Gives you the creeps, doesn't it?'

'I don't like to think of it.' She tries not to answer curtly. She mustn't arouse suspicion. But she wants to howl, with shame, with fright, with sheer unadulterated fury that she can never escape who she is, what she did. At least what Brady did anyway.

The car is slowing almost to a crawl now. The mist is so thick they can barely see the lights of the car in front. 'I wish we could stop,' says Sophie.

71

'I can't see where the road begins and ends. We could end up on the moor at any minute. Or in the ditch.'

'You'd better stop and put the hazard lights on. We'll be up the backside of the car in front if we carry on.'

Sophie sighs. 'Yes, I can't even see it. I think you're right. We can't go on like this. I just hope the people behind are doing the same thing.'

M peers through the back window. 'I think they've stopped already.'

Sophie brings the car to a halt. 'I suppose I'd better call Mummy and tell her we'll be late. Of all nights for this to happen. I can't bear it if we miss midnight mass.'

The phone call is brief. 'I hate this place,' she says, leaning back in her seat. 'It wasn't just Brady and Hindley, you know—there were all sorts of horrible murders here. An innkeeper got battered to death in Victorian times. They found two and a half pounds of coagulated blood splattered over the doorway.'

M can hear the hiss of the heater, the clicking of the hazard lights, her own heart thumping. She must get control of herself. 'How did they weigh it?' she asks.

Sophie laughs. 'Ughh, what a thought. They must have let it dry and then scraped it all off into a bag or something. It doesn't bear thinking about, does it? You know, you're right—other people are doing the same as us and parking up. I wonder how long it'll take to clear.'

'I used to love it up here when I was a girl. I came all the time with this friend of mine. We used to go for long walks across the moors.'

She didn't, of course, never had the right shoes for that walking lark. Her white winklepicker slingbacks were bang in fashion, which was what counted. He loved it up here, loved the bleakness of it, the unending expanses of rough grass.

'We have nice moors by us. You'll be able to get some walking done there if you want,' says Sophie.

Oh shit. 'Think I'll pass if the weather's like this.'

The little chick laughs. 'Not exactly conducive to jolly hikes, is it?'

The fog tumbles and swirls in the car headlights, completely opaque. M feels they are caught, submerged in a strange, immaterial underworld cut off from normal existence, swimming in tides of mist. 'There were other ghostly children round here, you know,' says Sophie. 'Not just the ones Brady and Hindley murdered.'

Oh God. She's not going to give up, is she?

'There used to be a village called Forty Row, full of these tiny houses that they built for the mill workers in the nineteenth century. Pauper children came from all over to work there, poor darlings. Years later they found all their little bones squished together in a common grave.' She leans across M, reaching for another CD in the glove compartment. Oh, her perfume ...

Some sort of choral stuff drifts from the speaker. The voices have an otherworldly quality to them, as if emerging from a luminous planet out in the infinite darkness of the sky, or perhaps seeping out from a pearly cave gleaming underwater. Separate lines of melody thread their way through the misty night, entangling M and Sophie in a web of sound, one intricate strand overlaying and replacing the next. They are caught, trapped by the purity of the music, like birds held in a hunter's net. The music is so *good*. This must be what angels sound like, disembodied voices untouched by anger or desire.

Outside, through the fog, M is sure her eye catches a flash of white. Her chest drums out a blizzard of heartbeats. The night around her seems filled with spirits, spirits inhabiting the mist, always beyond her in an eternity of movement. Are they angels? Are they the restless dead, the ones who cannot sleep, unburied in sacred ground? the ones who died violent deaths? Perhaps they're the souls of the dead children flitting through the dark, evanescent little beings shimmering accusingly for a second, and then gone? She feels a terrible fear, that their tiny fingers will reach into the car and haul her off to perdition. To judgement. They will tweak her and tease her and drag her to the land they live in, to gloat over her powerlessness. They will pull her and pound her and crush *her* head into a mass of coagulated blood. She can hear them howling in the night, faces daubed red with her blood.

Is she never to be free of this torment? She made one mistake in her life, listening to Brady, following him into debauchery and death as if he were a god and she his helpless follower. For God's sake, she was so young.

Through the ethereal waves of music that threaten to overwhelm her, she begins to hear the sounds of individual mill children, their clogs clattering on the cobblestones, and their laughter, horrible laughter. Have they become ghosts, vengeful ghosts? Will all of them, all the dead, all the people she and Brady killed, come back to haunt her? The voices surge, expanding into the night-time sky, resonating in her ear-drums. The music of death. Not everyone gets to hear it. They were privileged, her and Brady, to hear the choking in the throat, the death rattle, the gurgling. Like that last one, Edward wasn't it? Edward Evans. How much blood was there? How much would it have weighed if they hadn't cleaned up so meticulously? Would there have been two and a half pounds on the walls that night if she hadn't got the mop out?

The sound fades as the next strand of music takes over, and over the angelic voices she begins to hear the awful sound of Lesley Ann Downey. The child's voice. 'Can I just tell you summat? I must tell you summat. Please take your hands off me a minute, please. Please— mummy—please … I can't tell you. I can't tell you. I can't breathe.' The words are running round and round, hamster-like, in her brain. She can't get off the wheel. Her ears are going to burst with the pain.

'Maria. Maria. Are you all right?' Sophie is shaking her. 'You look ever so pale.'

She shudders. 'Just need a fag, probably. Would you mind?'

'Are you sure that's the best thing for you?' She looks alarmed.

M concentrates on drawing the cigarette out of the packet. Christ, that was close. She must be losing it, going soft in her old age. That bloody music. The smoke rolls down her throat, soothing her with its familiar warmth. The sodding fog. Why won't it lift?

She rolls the window down. The smoke curls out into the mist, the noxious fumes disappearing into the wider vapour. With the sudden breath of moisture-laden air it's as if she feels the moors beyond them, though she can still see nothing. Some freedom this, to be out of jail at last and yet plagued by stupid thoughts about the past. She must make sure she gets out and meets lots of people. She mustn't be too much on her own. 'All that talk of dead children,' she says to Sophie. 'You really had me going there.'

The little chick leans over and squeezes her hand. Her skin is soft and warm. 'I'm sorry, M. I just open my mouth and spout rubbish sometimes.' God, she's so ready to make it her fault. Good. M leans back in the seat, exhausted. If only they could go. She can't bear this waiting. Too much time to think.

It seems a long time later when the tooting of horns all around signals they can move, though when M looks at her watch only twenty minutes has gone by. 'Oh jolly good,' says Sophie. 'We might make midnight mass after all.'

The car edges slowly forward, following the red brake lights of the one in front. All around them horns are going off, in jubilant cacophony that finally, this Christmas Eve, they can all get off Saddleworth Moor and reach their homes. As they move away from the moor, M leans back in the seat, relieved. She never wanted to come back here, thought she had moved beyond it, but now she wonders if she will have to come back, alone next time.

They start the long descent back into civilisation. The mist is gradually fading, like a scent just gone. Somewhere beyond Rochdale they turn left off the motorway and follow long country roads. Even in the darkness M can see they are hemmed in by high hedges on either side. It feels claustrophobic and strange, a journey through the night to a fairytale castle.

Finally a crossroads and a sign for Melham Hall. Sophie stops the car and hauls back two massive iron gates. 'I'd have done that,' says M.

'It's all right. They're a bit tricky. We were supposed to be getting them electrified but Papa's hopeless at organising that sort of thing. Ask him to catalogue rare books and he's in his element. Just don't expect him to do anything practical. He couldn't open a tin if he was left on his own.'

The little chick seems cheerful and energetic now that they've arrived at her home, though she must be tired after that drive. M is. The car plunges erratically along the overgrown track, then they turn a corner and the house is there, at the top of the hill, all lit up. M is disappointed at first—she thought it would have been
bigger—but as they approach, she realises that the front facade is the least of it, that it sprawls back in a series of wings of different styles, a conjuror's box of hidden compartments and sliding doors. She wishes she could remember some of the architecture stuff that Oxford graduate taught them in Holloway. What was she called? Helen? Ellen? Nice arse anyway. It would be useful to be

able to discuss some of it now, just so they don't think she's a complete moron.

'Ten minutes to spare,' says Sophie, relieved. Minim shakes himself on M's lap, looking confused as the night air hits him. Oh no, M feels a warm dribble down her good lilac trousers. 'Minim, you naughty boy.' She holds the little dog away from her in disgust, watching the yellow liquid stream from her. Sophie leans against the car laughing. A male voice drawls from the porch, 'Well, that's some entrance.'

Sophie rushes over and throws her arms round him. 'This idiot is my brother Bunty,' she says. 'Don't stand there laughing, you oik. Help Maria with her luggage.'

The brother, M decides, has more edge than the sister, for all that they share a certain wayward eccentricity. He's good looking in a solid English way, with high cheekbones and high colour and springy, unmanageable hair. 'Stop laughing yourself, sis. Oh Lord, she's got the giggles,' he says, picking up both cases.

They follow him up the stairs into the house. M glances up as they reach the lighted porch. A dozen vicious hooks hang down from the ceiling like miniature gibbets. Sophie catches her look. 'Don't be scared. They're just for hanging up game.'

'What, pheasants and things?'

'Yes, we always have people here for the grouse. And of course the pheasant season goes on for months.'

The wet patch on M's trousers feels cold, even inside the house. Bunty, instead of taking their cases upstairs, stows them beside the hall table. 'Best hurry, sis-let. Mummy's been shitting bricks that you wouldn't arrive in time for old Macalinden.'

'Mummy,' says Sophie, 'wouldn't do anything so inelegant.'

M turns to Sophie. She must change before she meets the parents. But Bunty puts his arm firmly round her shoulders. 'I don't want to frighten you, Miss Spencer, but Mummy, when aroused, is a fearful beast. Let's not let a little bit of chihuahua tiddle come between friends, shall we?'

'He's not …'

He steers her along a long narrow corridor. Sophie follows, still laughing. The furniture is dark oak and cumbersome, too much of it crammed into too small a space. M bumps into it constantly. God, she must be covered in bruises.

They reach a heavy studded door. 'Family chapel,' whispers the little chick. 'I think you might like it rather better than St Stephen's.'

M's first impression of the interior is of brilliant light. The altar has been decorated for Christmas with hundreds of candles, their flames floating free against the dark walls of the church as if suspended in space. It's like bloody Geraldine Hargitay's birthday cake, the only birthday cake with candles she ever saw as a child. Mam didn't have the money for things like that. Sometimes she even made their gifts, a rag doll for Mo one year and a golliwog for Myra. They got their one present and that was it, though Gran

75

always slipped Myra some extra sweeties or a few comics. There wasn't much left over for luxuries once their Dad got sick and was off work. If he was sick, the pig. That Geraldine got half a crown a day for sweets. Every single day. Probably a total porker by now, she was a right barrel then.

The church is very hot and as M takes her place between Sophie and the brother she realises that the smell of Minim's wee is floating up to her nostrils. 'Phew,' says Bunty, glancing at the little dog. Sophie leans over M to smack his hand. 'Shush, you. It's not Maria's fault.' Minim licks M's hand, excited by this new playground. M knows her cheeks are bright red.

She feels uncomfortably hot, trussed up like the sodding Christmas turkey in these tight clothes. The church, though, is beautiful, all dark wood and antique gold, gleaming softly where the candlelight catches it. Sophie sees M looking at the stations of the cross, icons painted in dark blues and reds. 'Unusual, aren't they? You don't often see icons used for the Stations of the Cross. Mummy and Papa brought them back from Russia after the war. They found this marvellous artist from the Ukraine and asked him to paint them for the family chapel. He leapt at the chance, of course, would never have been able to do religious painting at home. He'd probably have ended up in a Siberian gulag or something. Mummy says he was thrilled to be asked. Papa always thought it was because he was madly in love with Mummy, though she says he wasn't. I expect he was, though. She was awfully beautiful when she was young.'

'Stop chattering, Sophie,' says Bunty. 'You're supposed to be in the house of God.' Sophie sniggers and puts her head down.

M gazes at the images. She likes their stiff moon-faces, their straight, correct carriage. They're probably the least dramatic stations of the cross that she's ever seen, except for the dark, ravaged eyes of Jesus. The scourging at the pillar merges wholly into the dusty, gold-stippled pattern till you can't see where the whips end and the scars on Christ's body begin. Were it not for the candles and the gleam of gold, the whole place would be imbued with that profound gloom and darkness which brought her to the Catholic faith in the first place. Poor Maureen, her sister, God rest her soul, could never understand why M signed up for it. They weren't brought up to think much about religion—Moby didn't even care whether there was a God or not. The only thing that bothered her was whether she had enough money for the dancing on a Saturday night or for that beige Miners lipstick she liked. Teddy Bear, that's what it was called. David thought she was dead sexy in it.

Fucking David Smith. If that pathetic, potato-faced wimp hadn't lost his nerve she wouldn't have had to spend the last thirty-four years in jail. What an apology for a man, afraid of a bit of blood. And he had the nerve to say he was afraid of *them*. After all the books Brady gave him, the bottles of wine, the gun practice—he'd never have learned to shoot if they hadn't taught him. Must come in handy now he's a blinking country squire or whatever he is these days.

She would like Smith to suffer the way she has. Let him know what it feels like to have his head smashed in like Evans. But not to die like that stupid little poof, she wants him still alive to feel the pain. Let him lie, brains spilling out, gasping, gurgling his last at her feet. If only she could make him pay for what he did to her and Brady, for all the dead years, the years and years of prison.

Finally the priest makes his entrance, resplendent in the white and red robes of Christmas. She must calm down, concentrate on the Mass, otherwise she'll be in a right state when it's time to meet Sophie's family. The parents are a couple of rows in front. The father looks distinguished, though vague, with the air of one who has spent his life in libraries. The mother is beside him, rangy and practical-looking, with great bone structure. She has the air of one who has spent her life with horses.

M sits and stands when she should but takes little in. Minim is squirming on her lap, disturbed, as she is herself, by all the new people. The aromatic, heavy smell of incense surges over the chapel in a tsunami of scent. She undoes the top buttons of her blouse. She can hardly breathe.

The priest has a wrinkled face like a chimpanzee. His wavery voice has to be amplified by a microphone even in this little church. Imagine having a private chapel all to yourself. Maybe old Longford had one too.

By the time they reach the sermon M is exhausted, discombobulated, not even bothering to pursue the erotic possibilities of the little chick's thigh pressing against her own in the narrow pew. God, please don't let old monkey-face rabbit on too long. 'Coming to Melham Hall is probably the most pleasurable event of my calendar year,' begins the old toady. 'You may have noticed that the chapel smells particularly sweet this year. That is because I was recently given a very special gift by my niece. Like the Three Wise Kings who followed their star to Bethlehem, she brought gold, frankincense and myrrh, in the form of a gold bag containing small lumps of these precious materials.

'They look like scruffy little bits of wood but their scent, as you can no doubt smell tonight, is extremely powerful, like the Word of Our Lord Jesus Christ. We cannot see him but he is all-pervasive. His influence reaches into every aspect of our lives.

'I want to talk to you especially about myrrh. Myrrh, as well as being pungent, is also the most poignant of the gifts the kings brought, symbolising, as it does, the bitterness of the future that lay ahead of Jesus Christ. It is a heady, heavy perfume, as you can perceive yourselves, but it was also used for the anointing of the dead. It falls from the tree in the form of a teardrop and represents for us the bitter tears that Our Lady shed when her Son died on the cross.'

'Oh God,' whispers Bunty. 'Hellfire and damnation coming up.'

'You'd think he'd find something cheery to say at Christmas, wouldn't you?' says Sophie.

'Myrrh, this aromatic resin,' continues the canon, 'is gathered by making cuts in the bark of a small tree that grows in the desert. The liquid oozes out just as the blood of Our Lord oozed from the gashes cut in His skin by Roman soldiers' whips, when they scourged Him at the pillar.'

Bunty shakes his head and turns to M. 'The canon is the most grim, puritanical, old-fashioned priest you will ever meet.'

'And one of the most egotistical,' says Sophie. 'He's forever getting his picture in the papers with the bishop.'

'For me, this year, it has a special resonance. I apologise for introducing such a grisly topic to our Christmas celebrations, but even in the rejoicing surrounding the birth of Jesus, his suffering and death were prefigured.

'Some of you may know that I was privileged to be pastor to one of the families whose child was cruelly taken from them by the Moors Murderers, Ian Brady and Myra Hindley.'

'The whole world knows it,' whispers Sophie. 'He's forever talking to journalists about it.'

A ripple of surprise moves round the church. Even Lady Melham glances sideways at her husband. As if the priest senses his audience's discomfort, his voice becomes louder, its frail croak amplified by righteous anger. 'Can you imagine what Christmas is like for those families? Every year, that missing place at the table. Every year the memories. But this year, for the first time in a long, long time, there's a ray of hope for them. That evil woman Myra Hindley has died, just a month ago. The very name *Myra* comes from myrrh, this bitter, bitter substance that represents suffering, death, cruelty.

'Originally I thought the name *Myra* was a corruption of the name of Our Lady, a corruption of the name *Mary*. It seemed apt, for this woman was a perversion of the very idea of womanhood. She was not fit to bear the name of Our Blessed Lady. What woman could carry such hardness in her heart as to betray and torture innocent children?

'In fact the name *Myra* was created in the seventeenth century by a famous poet. He linked it to myrrh and therefore to suffering and death. Now that Myra Hindley, the most evil woman of the twentiethth century, is at last dead, I have lit this myrrh to thank God for taking her from our midst. I believe that she burns, as this bittersweet perfume burns, but in the fires of Hell.'

M is in shock. Here, of all places … how dare he desecrate the Mass with such rubbish? She stares straight ahead at the altar, even though her eyes ache from the flare of the candles. The most evil woman of the twentieth century? What about Irme Grese, the Beast of Belsen, that concentration camp guard that Brady gave her a picture of? She carried it in her handbag for ages because he wanted her to. What about …? She can't bloody think, he's got her so upset. Chimp-faced git. What kind of Christian is that? Has she not paid for what she did, year after sodding year?

He's wittering on now about the phoenix and how it built its funeral pyre from myrrh and frankincense. What the fuck has *that* to do with Christmas?

'Year after year we rejoice anew in the birth of Our Lord. Like the phoenix He too rises, but from the ashes of our sin, not His own.'

He can go fuck himself, the stupid prat. *She* is the phoenix. She will rise, from the very ashes of the Hell they're always consigning her to. She will shake her burnt feathers and fluff out her newly healed wings to soar on air currents far above them. They think they have killed her, but she will not die.

Look out, you bastards. I am not myrrh. I'm Myra.

The dormitory is empty, the long line of beds as bleak as a row of coffins. At home, Will knows, his dad will be putting the finishing touches to the Christmas decorations, pouring himself a glass of port or sherry in deference to the season. He doesn't normally drink such things so why should he at this time of year? Just another of the mysterious ways of his father. If there's a boring old fart thing to do he'll do it. Why won't he support the Army, seeing he's so keen on tradition? Prat. He's too much of the bloody liberal to stand up for his country.

Will takes the medal from its velvet box and agonises for perhaps the fifth time this evening. Does it say what he wants it to say? She must know he likes her. Hers was the most difficult present to buy. She won't get him anything at all so it couldn't be anything too lavish or romantic, but then again he doesn't want her to think he's cheap either. She's a girl, she'll be bound to notice it's pure gold, won't she?

She'd better. It cost him a fortune, so the earrings he sent his mother this year had to be just sterling silver. Still, Kezza's going to war—she might never come back—which is why he thought the St Christopher medal would be the perfect thing to give her. Now she'll know someone cares about her. He can get Mum a good present any time. The worst thing she has to worry about is whether her new stuffing recipe from Good Housekeeping will turn out all right.

He can just imagine the way she'll have the house, all the tinsel and the angels and the baubles. They've had most of them since he was a kid. His favourites were the red toy soldiers with their little rifles and the gold trim on their jackets. He gets a twinge thinking of them but dismisses it. The barracks look just fine. Who needs more than a few sprigs of holly? And wouldn't it be cool to kiss Kezza under the mistletoe?

He'd better wrap the thing up now before one of the others comes in and finds him. Yeah, the shiny red paper looks nice. He slips the box into the jacket he's going to wear tomorrow. Thank goodness they've both got KP together. He'll be able to slip it to her when no-one else is around, maybe when they're peeling the potatoes, halfway up spud mountain when she's getting really fed up.

She's not like any of the girls he knows at home. Nice girls, good girls, girls who drool over Brad Pitt and other people's babies. Boring really, not girls you can do anything with—except fuck them till their brains pop, of course. Not that he ever got much of that action—he was shyer at home. God knows what his mother would make of Kezza. Mum's so refined, so ladylike, middle class really. She's always led a sheltered life, wouldn't have the bottle to get up to the stuff Kezza does. Dad would hate her, call her common. But then nothing new about that. Will's never been able to please him.

Oh Kezza, Kezza, Kezza … he can feel his face getting red as he remembers her dancing on the bar the night the regiment was posted. She had on some flimsy little mini-skirt and kept flicking it in people's faces when they tried to stuff money up her knickers or pat her bum. She was *hot*.

He groans. Time to go, the lads will all be down the pub by now. Just as he gets to the outside door he is suddenly knocked off his feet. Kezza! Flying into him! What's she doing back here? 'Wotchit, tosser,' she says, but her eyes are bright, as if she's about to cry.

'What's wrong, Kez?'

'Nuthin',' she says, her mouth setting hard. She walks away from him, her shoulders rigid the way his mum's sometimes are. Maybe he could massage her shoulders. That usually does it with Mum. He pulls her back by the arm. 'Has somebody hurt you?'

'What if they did? Like *you* care.'

'I do care, Kezza,' he says, staring into her sharp-eyed little face.

She looks at him for a long time, then gives a slight shrug, as if conceding that maybe he does. 'Come in here,' he says. 'I've got something for you.'

Reluctantly she follows him into the dormitory. 'No funny business. Right? I've had enough tonight.'

He reaches into his locker and brings out the little parcel. 'Christmas present for you.'

She stares at him, suspicious. 'Wot you givin' me a presie for?'

'Duh ... because I like you, dummy.'

'I ain't got nuthin' for you.'

'I know. Open it.'

Slowly she tears the sellotape. He's wrapped it too tightly and the paper rips.

'It's gold.'

'Yeah?'

She opens the little box and takes out the medal.

'That's St Christopher. It's to keep you safe in the war.'

She laughs. 'A protective shield, yeah?'

He laughs too. 'That's me.' He pulls her down on to the bunk and sits beside her. 'What happened to you tonight, Kezza?'

'That fuckin' Yardley. He's got no right. Just cos I like to have a laugh.'

Will feels an inexplicable rage take him over. He knows he has no right to feel angry but he wants to thump Yardley, mangle his stupid face for daring to touch Kezza. His throat is dry as he asks, 'What did he do?'

'You know how the toilets are out back down the Dog? Well, he was waitin' for me there and he had me up against the wall, with his hands up me skirt. I thought he were going to rip me knickers off. He really hurted me. Inside, you know?'

'Bastard.' Will finds himself on his feet, in a fury. 'Let's go,' he says.

Kezza looks up at him from the bed. 'What you goin' to do?'

'I'm going to knock his teeth down his throat.'

'But Yardley's about nine feet tall and built like a brick shithouse.'

'I don't give a flying fuck.'

She smiles.

'Kezza, I really like you.'

'Put me necklace on, then.' She stands up, holding her hair away from her bare neck. A little blonde tendril trails over her soft skin. He stands behind her, finding it hard to breathe, fumbling with the catch. Why do they make them so damn fiddly?

She turns, bumping against him. 'Why are you so excited, posh boy? You haven't even seen it on yet.'

'Sorry.'

'That's all right.' She presses herself even harder against him.

'Oh God, don't.'

'Why not? Don't you want a Christmas present from me?'

As Will watches in fascinated silence, she walks across to the door of the room and wedges the nearest locker under the handle. He catches a glimpse of red lace at the neck of her shirt, breathes in the heavy scent of her perfume. Then he's lost ...

It's cold on the moor and bleak. Why isn't it sunny as it used to be? Where is he? where's Ian? She is all alone here, wandering in her white dress. The winds are howling round her and she's shivering. 'Heathcliff, it's me, your Cathy, I've come home now. Let me in at your window.' Round and round ... she's trapped, trapped in a Kate Bush song. She sits up in bed. She is Cathy, battering away at the windows of a life she can never get back to.

God, she needs a fag. She reaches out for the bedside light. The room has a kippered look to it, probably hasn't been painted in years. A mahogany four poster, though without curtains, thank God—she's had enough of being shut in. The carpet is dark red and blue, but faded and threadbare, like the carpets in Sophie's house, only worse. She prefers her own bedroom at home, much prettier.

Where is little Mini-Me? Good boy, you tuck in close to Mummy. You gave her such a showing up though, you naughty boy. The look on that Cassandra's face when she realised what the smell was. Snotty cow. Lady Whatsit was a lot more down to earth. 'Good God, Cassie, the whole place smells of dog. Don't be so rude to our guest.'

Sophie was sweet to her. 'Are you all right, Maria? You look a bit ... cross?'

'I suppose I didn't really think that sermon had anything to do with the Christmas spirit,' she'd said. 'A little depressing.'

'Oh, I know.' Sophie's agreement was almost too eager. 'It's inverted snobbery with Father Macalinden. He works with some of the victims' families so he's obsessed with her.'

'It didn't seem a very Christian message to me. Not much forgiveness there.'

'I suppose you're right,' though the little chick's look of doubt undermined her agreement. 'It's hard to find anything good to say about Myra Hindley, though, don't you think?'

'They should have hanged her years ago if you ask me,' said Bunty.

'Oh God no. Hanging's too good for her,' said the wispy one, Serena. 'It's just a pity we weren't allowed to torture her the way she tortured those poor little children.'

'You're so sentimental, Serena,' said Cassandra briskly.

'Sentimental? What's sentimental about that?'

'If it hadn't been children ...'

'And a woman,' added Sophie.

'She was totally under Brady's spell,' M said firmly. 'It was quite obvious at the time. They just demonised her because she didn't break down and rat on him like most girls those days would have.'

They were all silent then, outflanked by someone who had been old enough when it happened to have an opinion. Later, in the drawing room as they called it, Sophie made the proper introductions—Mummy, Papa, Seb. Did none of them have normal names? Hot little rolls of bacon wrapped

83

round chipolatas and prunes were brought in by a housekeeper. 'Oh goody, devils on horseback,' said Bunty. 'Angels on horseback, you mean,' said Cassandra. They all stood around and drank sherry. M tried not to eat too much but she was starving after such a trying evening.

Now she leans back on her bed, relieved that she can have a ciggie. You could never do that in bed in the nick. She supposes you shouldn't really do it in someone else's house but what the hell? Just have to make sure she doesn't fall asleep with the fag in her hand. Setting the stately home alight might not go down too well with the parents.

It's important that they like her, though why, when she may never see them again? She never used to worry whether people liked her, always thought it better for them to respect her, or maybe even be a little bit afraid, the way the other girls at Milwards were when she and Brady worked there. 'Overbearing,' one of the bastards there called her. 'Surly and aggressive.' She read it in a book by that scummy News of the World journalist. People always ham it up for journalists. Morons.

It would be nice to get back some of the fighting spirit she once had. No way she should be intimidated by a bunch of nobs. Focus on the little chick, that's the way to get through this.

She stubs out the cigarette and snuggles down to think about Sophie. Would a love letter frighten her off? Or would it be just the hook to reel her in, the way it was with Trish. Oh Trish, that was her finest hour. None of the girls could believe it, that she'd persuaded a warder to have an affair with her, especially an ex-Carmelite nun. She was a darling, Trish, so innocent. That first letter to her was one of the best she's ever written. *You are my whole world, the very breath in my body. Only you can bring me light in this place of darkness ... I long for the day when you and I will be one, twin souls forged as one in the flames of a pure love.*

Trish wasn't as soft as she looked. It took bottle to have an affair with the most notorious woman in Britain. Huh, not that they should be calling her that any more—anything she and Brady did was chickenfeed compared to that ghastly Rosemary West. What kind of person kills their own daughter? Animals, that's all she and Fred West were. They didn't have an idea in their heads. Brady's might have been half-baked, but at least he had some. He believed in something. Being a superman, better than anyone else, trying to reach a higher state of being. It was a philosophy. Ordinary people wouldn't understand it, transcendence through shedding blood. Human sacrifice, that's all, as old as time. Just like the Church, where you eat the Body and drink the Blood of Christ.

For fuck's sake, what's she doing, thinking about Brady? It's Christmas Day. Far better to think about Sophie, darling little Sophie with her lovely long legs and that bum, or buns, as they say now, much better. Round, sweet, good enough to eat. She can just imagine kissing them, rolling her tongue round the taut softness of the little chick's flesh. Or stroking her, one hand resting on each bun. Or what if she was naked, and dancing? It'd be like those peaches jiggling around in the car ad. Juicy, pink, shaking that ass, shaking that ass, shaking that ass.

She leans over to get some Vaseline from her sponge bag. It's a bugger, the menopause.

Peaches, buns, sweet … what would they look like with a stroke of the cane across them?

What happened to those S & M photos of her and Brady? They ought to have given them back to her after they were used in evidence. They were her bloody property after all.

Would Sophie like it? The humiliation? Would she pretend not to, all the while secretly longing to be *made* to bend over, the way he made her do it. That first time, 'I am your Master,' he said, in this quiet voice. It still sends shivers up her when she hears a Scottish accent.

If only she had the photos …

'I am your Mistress.' God, could she say that? She'd laugh. Not if she was in a leather basque—that would be good, laced tightly up the front so she couldn't breathe, pushing her breasts up. Not her breasts now, course not. Too saggy now. But then, when they were firm and strong.

'You will do as I say. You are my slave.'

Would that be a bit much for the little chick? She's clever, educated, why would she go for that?

Oh Myra, you stupid bitch, she's probably not going to go for any of it. But there's something there, a whiff of, what? Submission? Anxiety? Does little Sophie want someone else to make the decision for her?

Concentrate. She can feel herself engorged with blood, the heat spreading outwards through her body. Gently, not too hard, don't wreck it. Sophie, Sophie. Images of the little chick, her blonde hair next to the leather basque, her pale honey skin pressed against black lacing. *You will do as I say. I am Myra.* God, if only Sophie could call her by her name. It's so unfair. Wonder what underwear she wears. It'll be white cotton probably, boyish. Bet her voice goes lower when she's aroused. Say it. *Oh Myra, Myra, Myra, Myra.*

Course Myra won't come. What a fool to send her that cash. She's got what she wants now.

She wouldn't have come anyway. She'll say she can't, that the police won't let her, but she could if she'd a mind to. She could always do anything she had a mind to, could Myra.

Nellie can't stand the thought of another Christmas in this place. What do she want wi' wearing a paper hat at her age? And if that lass calls her 'honey' one more time she'll swing for her. *Just one more step, honey. Eat another spoonful for me, honey.* Kids get tret wi' more dignity than old folk nowadays.

Where did she go wrong?

She even lost her first grandchild. Course she did. Why would God let her have little Angela Dawn when her Myra done what she done? And Mo's boys, course she never sees them. Why would God let her have anything to do with them after her daughter destroyed the lives of those children, of those parents? Thank goodness she at least has Mo's Sharon. Lovely girl she is.

But He could have left her Maureen. Why did He have to take her away too? *She* done the right thing, went to the police straight away, even though it were her only sister.

How can it be Nellie's fault? Her one daughter knew what were right and what were wrong. Why couldn't the other?

Poor little Maureen. She were happy in the end, once she got rid of that scumbag, David Smith. Nice looking lad, but no good. Whatsisname were better for her, even if he were a bit older.

Oh God, they're going to start a singsong now, all them croaky old voices singing *Roll Out the Barrel.* Weren't the dried up turkey and cheap sherry enough for them? She's never liked sherry. Why are you suddenly supposed to take a fancy for it just because you're old? Give her a nice vodka and Coke any day.

Her own Mam were lucky. She never had to live in a place like this wi' no-one to come and visit her. Mind, maybe you couldn't call it lucky to have to live wi' them two through all of that. They were no use to her, she said. Myra never had time to talk to her any more. As for him, he were a nasty bastard, couldn't be bothered wi' an old lady like her.

Folk couldn't believe she never heard a thing, not even Myra shouting—she had quite a set of lungs on her. But that Brady used to drug her and anyway, he made sure and got her out of the way when they did the Downey girl, poor little mite. He were cunning.

She wishes they'd take old Mrs Harper off and get that pad of hers changed. They think none of them have any sense of smell left, but you'd have to have your nose cut off not to smell that. *Lovey, could you come over here, please?* Don't think she's heard. No wonder with that godawful racket going on. Why can't they sing some decent songs? Moon River, that's a lovely song. Or Catch a Falling Star. Some hopes, around here. He were gorgeous, Perry Como.

Johnny Mathis were a bit of a darkie, but Perry Como were ever so handsome. Sitting in that hay stack on the telly, wi' all them girls in gingham frocks around him. Lovely, it were.

She supposes she deserves this, but Myra never understood how little money there was, that she couldn't afford to go to the prison every week. Durham, Holloway, on her wages? Not that she wanted to, if the truth be told. What would she have said? How could she have looked at her own daughter? Knowing what she done. She got there sometimes. That should have been enough.

Yes, love, Mrs Harper. Maggie indeed. Since when did young lasses like that call old folk by their first names? There's no respect … oh well, maybe there were too much respect in their day. Maybe Myra felt stifled or summat. Her Da didn't help, did he? He wouldn't make a lass feel confident. Always too quick to raise his hand. Myra didn't get the brunt of it, though. He saved the worst for his beloved wife.

Poor Nancy Higginbottom … why on earth have they given her ice cream that's already melted? She's got it all over herself, all over the carpet. Anybody would. It makes you mad. They know she can't control herself. It's not her fault. *It's not her fault, love. You shouldn't have given her it like that.* Poor old soul, she's crying now because she's made a mess. It's no way to treat a human being. She used to be such a well-groomed woman. It must be torture for her, sitting there wi' a big stain on her jumper.

Christmas used to be such a lovely time of year, even though they didn't have much. It weren't about presents, it were the fun of it, the two of them staying up half the night putting tangerines and walnuts at the end of those net stockings from Woolworth's for the children. Little chocolate coins. Nothing big, just things like bubbles and scraps and chewing gum with film star cards. One toy in the morning, two at most. Course they never ate the fresh stuff, just the sweets. You'd find wizened tangerines months later, rolled underneath the beds.

She could at least have sent a card.

She looked so different. Wouldn't have known her. Terrible, that, wouldn't have recognised her own daughter. Her voice were right rough from all the fags, though her accent were right posh. That were always Myra, though. Didn't need Lord Longford to give her airs and graces. She were lovely when she spoke nice. She were just trying to pull herself up in the world. Why shouldn't she? Nothing wrong with the likes of us.

There were summat wrong with her though. Maybe she were born like that. Maybe it weren't her fault, just summat in the genes, summat she couldn't help. Summat from her Da's side of the family. Maybe it were Brady, like she said. But she always had a mind of her own, did Myra. She weren't some shrinking violet.

Oh God, why don't they turn the heat down? Why don't they stop that ruddy singing? Why don't they stop pretending everyone's feeling happy because it's Christmas?

87

Maybe it's better not to see her. The letters are lovely. She writes a lovely letter, does Myra ...

Thud ... thud ... what the ...? It sounds like fucking kids playing football. The light in the room is a queer half-white colour, as if it's snowing outside. M reaches for her fags. Is it morning already?

'Cris-pin, you blithering idiot.' The tones are as clear and as cutting as an icicle.

'It's all right. I haven't broken it.'

'Shh, you'll wake Mummy.'

The little tykes. It *is* kids.

'I *want* her to get up now. I want my presents.'

"Mummy's not likely to give you any presents if you keep that racket up.' The voice is deep and masculine.

'Papa!'

'All right, darling. Let's tiptoe downstairs as quietly as we can. Maybe if we make Mummy a cup of tea she'll get up quicker. Come on, Piers.'

The little boy goes running after the others, then the ball clatters down the stairs. God, that'll bloody wake everybody up. She stubs the cigarette out. Better get in that bathroom before the rush starts. She pulls on her dressing gown, wishing it shut better. Where's her sponge bag? The floor feels cold when she walks to the door. No wonder, with this sodding threadbare carpet.

She sticks her head out the door, then makes a run for the bathroom across the way. There's no warmth here either. She puts on the wall heater. Aren't these people supposed to be toffs? You'd have thought they'd have central heating. And oh God, the shower's just a little rubber shampoo spray jammed on to the taps. She runs the cold first, then adds the hot. The water starts clanking in some tank which sounds as if it's buried in the bowels of the earth and operated by bloody spastic dwarves. The water stays stubbornly cold in spite of the spastics' efforts, so she tries running the hot first. It's still fucking freezing.

There's no way out of it. She won't be able to wash her hair while she's here, that's all. The soap looks as if it's cut from big cakes of the stuff. These people are probably like the Queen, going round turning all the lights off and saving bits of soap. M's skin recoils from the water's icy onslaught. No wonder the upper classes stay on top of the heap. They have to be tough as nails to survive their own bathrooms.

It's only when she steps out of the shower that she realises the curtain hasn't been tucked in properly and there's water all over the floor. Oh God. Is there a cloth? She's just bending over to look in the cupboard under the sink when she hears the door opening and shutting quietly behind her. Fuck, didn't she lock it behind her? In fact, fuck, fuck, fuck, fuck, fuck, where's her sodding towel? She's only gone and left it in the bedroom.

Bugger this. She pulls the skimpy cotton dressing gown on—with great difficulty because it drags on her wet skin. There's muffled laughter from the corridor and someone's whispering something about Crinkly Bottom. She knows he doesn't mean the stupid television show. Does he think she's deaf? Take a deep breath. She must compose herself, though the only way to do that is to make her face stony, which makes people hate her.

When she steps into the corridor, Bunty is still there, dressed in a dark patterned silk dressing gown and striped pyjamas. He's leaning round the door of the bedroom next to hers, talking to whoever's inside, but turns when she comes out. 'Awfully sorry to barge in like that, Maria. I was half asleep, I'm afraid.'

'Sorry. My fault. I didn't realise I'd left the door unlocked.' She knows she sounds curt, but it's awfully hard to relax when she knows he's been sniggering about her.

'Merry Christmas, Miss Spencer.'

Patronising bastard. She tries to smile and scuttles into her bedroom. 'Oops,' she hears before she shuts the door. Some Christmas this is going to be. First that ranting priest, now total humiliation. Why is she here? What *did* she think she was doing? At least the towel is soft and fluffy and she snuggles into it, letting its warmth soothe her. She's deciding what to wear when there's a knock on the door. Sophie's there in blue and white striped pyjamas, looking very cute.

'Cup of tea for you, M. Breakfast's being served in half an hour and then it's presie time.'

'Oh, thank you. What a lifesaver.'

Sophie looks pink and deliciously sleepy. 'You've had your shower already?'

'Rather sprayed the bathroom, I'm afraid.'

'Don't worry about that.' Sophie darts a glance at her bare shoulders above the towel, then flits back out of the room. M hears her hammering on the bathroom door. 'Out this minute, Bunty. Better people than you are waiting here.'

'Get back to your own side of the house, Snuffy.'

The tea is lukewarm after its transit from the kitchen below up through draughty corridors and stairs to the bedroom. Sweet of Sophie, though. M dresses as quickly as she can. She has difficulty squeezing into her bottle green dress until she remembers her elastic knickers. It'll be uncomfortable wearing them all day but there's nothing else for it. The red patent belt is a little tight too, but looks nice with her shiny red bangles and earrings, quite Christmassy really. She spends a long time getting her makeup right—not too much eye pencil, she doesn't want to look hard. Finally she fastens her gold and pearl brooch in the pussy bow at the neck of her dress. Just little Minim and she's ready.

Downstairs there seem to be hordes of people milling about. And children, loads of the noisy little beggars. This is going to be a long day. Sophie's down already, looking elegant in black trousers and a creamy blouse. Dainty spiky-heeled sandals. Hmm, they're nice. A little girl of about seven comes running over to M. 'Look, Charlotte. It's the most gorgeous little dog.' Minim licks her hands, happy to be the centre of attention, as the two children

90

cluster round the dog. 'Be careful,' says M, more sharply than she meant to. 'You'll frighten him if you crowd him too much.'

The first child looks up at her, anxious. Best keep on the right side of these kids. M smiles at her. 'Here, sweetheart. Just pat him, very gently like I'm doing.'

Sophie turns and watches with interest as M leans forward and whispers to the child. 'You know what he did last night? Tiddled all over me as soon as he got here.'

The little girl giggles. 'He's lovely,' she says shyly. 'Are you staying here for Christmas?'

'Yes, I'm Sophie's friend Maria. You can call me M if you like.'

'I'm Em too, short for Emily.'

Sophie comes over, smiling in approval. 'You're really good with children, aren't you?' she says in M's ear. 'They trust you.'

'I love kids,' says M.

'We'd best get breakfast, I think. Have you two had yours?'

'Yes, Aunt Sophie. I had scramblers on toast. Yummy,' says Emily.

'Maybe that's what I'll have too then, Em. Sounds scrumptious.' She guides M away from the children and into a large dining room, its polished mahogany table gleaming. 'Coffee, I think, before we face the scrum,' says Sophie. M gazes in astonishment at the large chafing dishes filled with scrambled eggs, kidneys, bacon, sausages, fried eggs and tomatoes. Surely these things exist only in BBC costume dramas, like *Brideshead* or *Pride and Prejudice*? She takes a tomato and a small helping of scrambled eggs. She'll be sick if she tries to eat too much.

Sophie heaps her plate high, to M's astonishment. 'I've got one of those metabolisms,' she says, laughing.

'You're a greedy little pig, Snuffy,' says the voice of Bunty. 'Got your coffee, ladies? I hope you've left some for me.'

The meal is punctuated by endless children whining. Why didn't Sophie tell her there were going to be so many of them? She hasn't got a thing for them, nor for the various husbands and partners who come in and out. Were there that many last night in the church? This is going to be really embarrassing.

She's just wondering if it would be all right to smoke when Lady Melham comes in. 'Oh good, you're here. Christmas tree time. There's going to be a riot if we don't give these children their presents soon.'

'I think I'll riot all on my own if you don't give me mine,' drawls Bunty. Sophie stands up. 'Will you help me, M? I've got some rather large toys up there.'

'I'll just get my gifts from the room too,' says M.

'You shouldn't have brought anything,' says Lady Melham. 'There's far too many of us.'

'I didn't know quite how many. I'm afraid I don't have something for everyone.'

'I should think not,' says Lady Melham briskly.

91

Upstairs Sophie waits while M collects her bag of presents, then they go along to her bedroom, on the other side of the main central staircase. Would you call that the other wing? It has the same threadbare carpets but the bedding here is prettier, white cotton with little lilac flowers. Sophie must look so adorable here, in her little boy's pyjamas.

They struggle downstairs into the drawing room, Sophie with black plastic bin bags full of brightly wrapped parcels. It all seems different from last night, shabbier somehow, the gold sprigged wallpaper worn through at the bottom where dogs have scratched it, the disgusting old carpets again. She almost trips over a rip in one of them. 'Ooh, I say,' says Lord Melham, putting out a hand to steady her. 'We really ought to get someone in to see to that rug, you know, Esther.'

M is astonished at the very idea. Surely they'd be better to chuck it out and get some nice wall to wall carpeting? They must be tight as ticks. Lady Melham shakes her head regretfully. 'The only person who could do it round here is old Andy Braithwaite, and he's poorly at the moment.'

'What about that place in Birmingham?'

'Yes, I suppose so. They did a good job on Esme Charteris's Aubusson rug.'

'Grandma, do stop talking about smelly old carpets,' says little Emily.

'Emily! Those are very valuable antique rugs,' says Cassandra. She must be the mother.

'You're quite right, my darling,' says Lady Melham to the child. 'Come along now. Let's see what's under the tree for you.'

'Charlotte. Char. Presies,' shouts the little girl, provoking a clatter of footsteps from all corners of the house. How many of the little terrors are there, for God's sake?

'My God,' says Bunty. 'Overrun by the Mongol hordes. Should we have a little snifter to cope?'

'It's a bit early for that, isn't it, darling?' says Lady Melham.

'Nonsense, Esther,' says Lord Melham. 'It's Christmas. I should think a little glass of something wouldn't go amiss. What about some of that marsala we got from Avery's?'

'Or a nice glass of fizz,' says Sophie hopefully.

'The very thing. You see to it, Bunty, would you? There's a good chap.'

M retreats to a chair by the window as Lady Melham delves under the Christmas tree for the children's gifts. It's a huge tree—off the estate, someone said last night—festooned with red tinsel and countless little shiny ornaments, some of them rather battered looking. Valuable antique tree baubles, no doubt. Bunty comes back with several bottles and a tray of glasses. The adults cluster round as the children rip the paper off one present after another. Greedy little sods. It's unbelievable how many things they're getting, expensive stuff too.

92

Sophie brings a glass of champagne over to M. 'We exchange ours after the kids have finished,' she says. 'Mrs Hargreaves takes them for a walk so we can have a bit of peace.'

M takes a sip. She's never tasted real champagne before, just Asti Spumante or Babycham. It's fizzy and chalky and a little sour.

'Jolly nice, isn't it?' says Sophie. 'Papa always gets decent stuff. I can only ever afford Moët. Or Tesco's cava if I'm really broke.'

'You don't,' says Cassandra in disbelief.

'We haven't all got husbands in high finance, you know.'

'But Snuffy, we have *standards*,' says Bunty.

'Snobby lot, aren't they?' says Sebastian, one of the other brothers. He seems quite nice, blond like Sophie where the others are mousy or dark. M just smiles in return. She can't think of anything to say back to him.

'Who bought so many presents for these ghastly little wretches?' says Bunty, snatching up a blonde-haired child from the sofa. She squirms in his grip.

'Uncle Bunty, you're horrid.'

'Me horrid? Who gave you those delicious pink high heels crammed on your grubby little feet right now?'

She clasps her arms tightly round his neck and lays her head against his cheek. 'I love you, uncle Bunty.'

'I love you too, precious,' he says. M is perplexed. Is this the way men are these days? She's never seen a man behave in such a soft way to a child before. They'd have called him a big poof round Gorton if he'd gone on like that there. Gosh, she'd better try and phone Mam some time today, wish her a happy Christmas. See if she got the lavender talc and the Milk Tray.

At last the children come to the end of their present opening. A tide of Christmas paper, shiny ribbon, boxes and cards has washed over the room. Minim bounces contentedly round in it, pouncing on the occasional ribbon as if on prey. There are bikes, rocking horses, computers, dolls, mobile phones, coloured hair clasps, footballs, torches, teddy bears, clothes, CDs all piled high on the sofas. The place looks like Santa's grotto.

The lady who brought in the supper last night comes in to round up the children. Cassandra bustles about picking up discarded wrapping paper while Sebastian pours out more champagne for everyone. Already M feels a little tipsy—she should have eaten more of the breakfast. It's much quieter when the children leave. She sits down on the sofa, relieved that the noise has stopped. Now just the presents. If only they'd get it over with. This is going to be embarrassing—all these rich people. They'll think she's a right cheapskate, just giving them soaps and things. For all she knows Penhaligon's is the cheapest stuff they ever use. Mind you, that soap in the bathroom looked a bit like the carbolic they used for scrubbing clothes and things down at the public wash-house. Probably made by appointment to the Queen or something.

Sophie flops down beside her, limbs totally relaxed. Seems like the champagne's gone to the little chick's head as well. The smell of the Christmas

93

tree surges through the room, earthy and fragrant, the smell of the open air, of walking wherever you want on God's earth, of being free.

Lady Melham starts to draw shiny things from a giant plastic crate beside her. She squints at the name tags as though she needs glasses. 'Sebastian. I think this is Serena. Check the names, you two. You wouldn't want to get each other's present. Bunty. Cassie. I can't read this one. Oh, I think it may be for you, Miss Spencer. Sophie, would you check?'

M brings out her beautifully wrapped gifts. She's spent a lot of time and effort making fancy decorations for each one, some from nuts and pine cones, some from dried flowers, others from that ribbon that you make into little curls and frills. She hands one with red berries and glitter to Cassandra, who barely glances at the decoration, ripping the paper off as if she were seven years old. 'Gosh, Penhaligon's, how super. Thanks ever so much, Miss Spencer.' She glances at her mother, who hands M a second gift from the crate. This one doesn't appear to have a name tag on it. The mother has obviously stocked up well in case of emergencies.

Bunty starts to laugh, a loud hooting noise like an owl. 'I say, I like *this.*' He's fiddling about with a newly opened present. Next thing M feels something hard pinging off her breast. 'Bullseye!' shouts Sebastian. Bunty is laughing so much he can hardly speak. 'Sorry, Miss Spencer. That wasn't intended, I promise you.'

'What on earth is it?' says Sophie, glancing in alarm at M's immobile face.

'It's my new pig catapult,' howls Bunty.

M looks in disbelief at the tiny pink plastic pig nestling on the sofa beside her. She wants to smile but can't seem to manage the practicalities of it. It doesn't matter, the next moment there's another hooting laugh, this time from Alexander, the oldest of the family. He's something in the stock market, plump and middle aged, with thick silvery hair like Richard Gere in *Pretty Woman.* 'Yes!' he shouts, punching the air with one hand while fondling luridly pink rubber breasts with the other. 'What on earth is *that?*' says Serena in disgust.

'It's for when I have my sex change,' he says, mincing across the floor with the fake breasts clamped to his chest.

Bunty snatches them off him and drapes them over his own head. 'Just the job for the man about town.'

'Who gave him those?' says Sophie reprovingly.

'That's a very useful present,' says Sebastian. 'It's a dispenser for shampoo and shower gel.'

'Well, that's all right then,' says Sophie, rolling her eyes.

M opens the first of the gifts she's been given. A rubber Charlie Chaplin doll filled with bubble bath. The next is a blue plastic Martini glass that lights up. She can hardly believe it. Nearly two hundred quid she spent in the end and all they give her is this junk. Sophie drops a little box into her lap. 'You mustn't pay any attention to these idiots. They'll never grow up.'

94

'No fun in that,' says Alexander, his mousy wife watching him dispassionately.

The box contains a pair of earrings, pearls set into a little daisy cluster. They're really tasteful. M feels quite shy, they're so pretty. 'Thank you so much,' she says, uncomfortably aware that she's mimicking the way they all speak. 'They'll go perfectly with my brooch.' She takes out her red earrings and slides the pearl ones into her ears. Sophie is opening her duck. 'I *love* this,' she says. 'Oh look, *My name is Hayley*. What an unusual gift, Maria. Where on earth did you find her?'

God knows where that woman got the duck. 'Somewhere in the arcade, I think it was,' she says. 'I don't know the names of the shops too well yet.'

The adults' present opening leaves the floor strewn with socks, fur handcuffs, coasters in the form of gel hearts, hankies, scented candles, keyrings with copulating pigs dressed in England rugby shirts, and chocolate spread for licking off someone else's body. Never has M seen so much tat gathered in one place before.

'I'm going to do some stuff in the kitchen,' says Sophie. 'Then do you fancy a walk?'

M scrambles to her feet. She's not going to be left on her own with this lot. 'I'll give you a hand.'

The kitchen is huge, with a dark green Aga on one wall and a conventional cooker on another. The air is saturated with the smell of hot fat and crispy animal skin. 'Goose,' says Sophie. 'And turkey in the oven for the kids. The goose is too rich for them. Now, I promised Mrs H I'd do some of the veg.' She pulls two sharp-looking knives from a drawer. 'You mustn't worry about my brothers. They're clowns.'   'They're charming.'

Sophie laughs out loud. 'They're a pain in the butt. I think boarding school does that to them.'

M smiles at her. It's a relief to be alone with Sophie. 'What do you want me to do?' she asks.

'Well, first we'll have another glass of fizz. Cooks' perks.' Sophie brings a full bottle of Avery Brothers' premier cru champagne out of the fridge. The cork shoots out like a firework. 'How about you start the broad beans? They're just here,' says Sophie, bringing out a tray filled with long green pods. 'Mummy's favourite, imported at vast expense from goodness knows where.'

M has only ever seen broad beans in a tin and once some frozen ones in Holloway kitchen. She takes the knife Sophie offers her and cuts the top off a bean, sliding it open with her finger. Inside is the softest, whitest, furriest little bed with four beans tucked up inside, like children in a cradle. It seems a shame to take them out of there.

'Let's get in the mood,' says Sophie. She flits out of the kitchen, still waving her champagne glass around, then returns with a CD. 'We Wish You a Merry Christmas,' she reads, pressing the disc into the music player on the work counter and singing along while peeling a huge mound of carrots,

95

though her control of the knife and the tune becomes progressively more unsure the more champagne she sips.

Oh little town of Bethlehem, how still we see you lie ... M joins in, enjoying the feeling of being with Sophie, working only a couple of feet away from her, close enough to smell her scent. Not close enough to smell *her*, though.

Away in a manger.

The piles of carrots and broad beans mount up, bright orange and pale green, as the level in their glasses goes down.

Silver bells, silver bells. Sophie's voice is clear and silvery, M's rough and low. They complement each other, that's all. She is happy, for the first time since coming here. Carefully she prises the beans from their fluffy nests, marvelling at the comfort of each miniature womb as it yields up its treasure.

Then it starts, the rat-a-tat of the drum rolling out a warning. *Come they told me, pa rum pum pum pum.* She can't believe it, *The Little Drummer Boy*. Her hand shakes as she cuts the top off the next bean. She feels too hot again. The wine must be going to her head. She can hear the scream of the little girl inside her head. If only Brady hadn't taped it, it wouldn't have stayed with her like this. She couldn't believe it when they played it to her in the police station that first time. She read later that she'd said she was ashamed but she couldn't remember saying anything at all. The sounds on the tape were too awful, much worse hearing them there than it had been at the time or later, in the court. Everyone hated the two of them so much by then that it was easy not to care, easy to shut your ears to it.

But here, in this hot, fragrant kitchen, with Sophie singing sweetly by her side, the song seems obscene. M tries to control the knife but her hands feel slippery and her eyes struggle to focus. Goddamn it, she's sliced right through her finger. Blood starts to ooze out, thick blood.

'Oh no, what have you done to yourself?' says Sophie.

'I feel sick. I hate seeing my own blood.' She's lifted her hand away from the beans and the dark liquid is dripping on to the counter. Her heart is racing. She's going to die, she's going to bleed to death. Sophie rifles through drawers looking for a bandage. 'Hold it under the cold tap,' she says. The pain is excruciating, and the fear. On and on, the stupid song with its piddling little drum rolls just goes on and on.

Sophie puts some white cream on M's finger, then binds it with several elastoplasts. 'You look white as a sheet. Why don't you go and lie down for a while. I'll finish off here.'

M stumbles gratefully from the kitchen. She never wants to hear that poxy song again. She climbs the stairs to get away from it but the words follow her. *I played my drum for him, pa rum pum pum pum. I played my best for him, pa rum pum pum pum, rum pum pum pum, rum pum pum pum.*

Why did he have to make the tape? Why did everything have to be recorded, detail after detail, condemning them both to this living death? He was like a clerk, filing away his sordid little catalogue of murder mementoes. All that talk of liberation and immortality and all the time he was just a bloody stamp collector.

96

She feels her blood pumping away through her hand, tick-tocking its way through her body as a relentless reminder that she too will one day die. She needs to vomit. She needs to lie down. Minim barks at her, unnerved by her strange mood, as the bandage on her hand effloresces into strange and repellent blossoms of blood.

The eerie barking of the fox wakes her. He's running up and down the garden, calling for the vixen in that raucous, breathless wheeze that is at once threatening and yet seems as if he might be breathing his last. Beth raises her head from the pillow. Good God, it's ten o'clock. How did she manage to sleep so late, and on Christmas Day too? She lies back. Her heart goes out to the poor creature, missing his mate.

She closes her eyes for a moment. It's Christmas morning, she should be happy, yet her heart drums out a beat of foreboding behind her ribs. Of course. Will isn't here. It's just her and Charles this year. Yesterday she saw her mother at the home, though whether her mother knew her is debatable. Charles's parents are going to his sister in Norfolk, so they'll be all alone, just the two of them. The room is cold and it's with reluctance that she swings her legs out of bed, not wanting to leave its warm cocoon.

'Morning, darling. Happy Christmas.' Charles kisses her cheek when she appears in the living room. The tree lights are already on and he's trying to get a wood fire burning.

'How lovely,' she says. 'What a treat. I just adore the smell of woodsmoke.'

'I've made fresh coffee,' he says.

'You're an angel. Happy Christmas, love.'

He squeezes her hand. 'We *will* have a happy Christmas without him, don't worry.'

She tries to smile. 'I know. It's just taking a bit of getting used to.'

'Damn.' The fledgling fire gutters into extinction. 'I'm useless at this.'

'Just let me get a cup of coffee and I'll do it. I know the knack.' She walks into the kitchen. At least there won't be as much work as usual, without Will here. A pan of potatoes she peeled last night sits ready to roast, the special chestnut stuffing that Charles is so fond of is in a bowl in the fridge, and the roasted Mediterranean vegetables are all cut up in a plastic bag in the freezer. Other than that she just has to stick the duck in the oven. 'No point in a big turkey without Will, is there?' he'd said and she was relieved. It would have been too sad, doing the things they normally did. Gosh, he's only in the barracks. Anyone would think there'd been a death in the family.

The coffee galvanises her and she nudges Charles out of the way. 'You need an extra firelighter in that lot,' she says.

'Ah, I'll leave it to the expert, then.' He pushes his glasses back up his nose and goes to choose a CD, studying the covers as intently as he studies wine labels. Handel's Messiah for Christmas, she thinks.

'A bit of Messiah, seeing it's Christmas,' he says. 'Should we have a little port to help the coffee down, do you think?'

'Why not?' she says, though she doesn't like port much and doesn't feel like drinking this early in the day. Flames start to lick around the logs and she stands up. 'You pour it out and I'll just go and get my shower.'

In the bathroom she relaxes. She can cry in the shower and he won't be able to tell. She has the water really hot, wishing her grief could drain away down the plughole too. Her face is all pink when she comes out, as if she's been taking part in a cross-country race.

She puts on the pale blue dress that was Charles's present to her last Christmas. She knows she looks pretty in it, pretty and feminine, if a little insipid—it's the dress of a wife, not a woman. Perhaps a little discreet makeup to disguise her tears? Finally, Will's gold star earrings from last Christmas. 'Because my Mum's a star and always forgets it,' the card said.

When she comes through, Charles is lying back with his eyes closed, conducting the music. The room looks as it always does on Christmas morning, the tree swathed in red tinsel garlands and the baubles they've collected since Will was a little boy—shiny purple balls, gold angels blowing trumpets, wooden toy soldiers with red uniforms and blank faces. A pile of presents sits on each armchair. The fire is blazing, its acrid sweetness permeating the room like incense in a church. Squeaky is curled up on the sofa, snoozing. All looks as it always does—except that Will is not here.

She drinks a little of the port. The ritual requires that she bring in mince pies while they open their presents, but she can hardly be bothered. Not until she sees the pull of unspoken disappointment at Charles's mouth does she relent. 'Oh, I forgot to put the mince pies in,' she says, and is rewarded with a child's smile of pleasure.

As she puts the tray in the oven it occurs to her she's left the remains of the chicken they ate last night. Charles doesn't like her feeding the foxes but it's Christmas after all, everyone deserves a present, don't they? She tears the meat off the carcass and puts it on some old plates she uses for the cat. Squeaky's safe in the living room, so she can put this out now.

Quietly she opens the kitchen door and walks halfway down the garden, not too close to the house. They mustn't get too familiar. 'Should we phone Will now?' she calls to Charles.

'Good idea. He said we should get him early.'

She heads for the hall and dials her son's mobile. 'Oh no, it's on answer.'

'Never mind, he's probably on some duty or other. We'll get him later.'

She goes back into the kitchen, the feeling of loss back in her chest again. Looking out the window she sees the fox is already there, nose down in the chicken. Just beyond him, the vixen lurks, more timid than he. She's so dainty, with her delicately pointed ears, her sensitive nose, quivering now as if to scent out danger. Silently Beth urges her forward. *Go on, love. You'd better hurry or you won't get any.*

The dog fox looks up from the plate and sees Beth watching. Coolly he stares at her, then lifts a large piece of breast meat from the plate with his teeth. He trots back to the vixen and lays it in front of her, then stands guard, staring at Beth as if telling her to keep her distance. She feels oddly cheered as

99

she turns back to take the mince pies out of the oven and bring them to her husband.

The mist has lifted now. In the night it lay over the land like a pall. M was too hot after all the rich food, felt as if all the calories she'd eaten were roiling and boiling around inside her, a witches' brew of meat, hot fat, brandy butter and chocolate liqueurs rushing through her arteries like poison. She couldn't sleep and stood at the window. There should be lots of animals to see here at night, deer maybe? rabbits, badgers ... well, whatever. But there was nothing to be seen through the fog, only the blurred lights from a few insomniacs' bedrooms. Maybe Sophie's was one of them.

Dinner was a nightmare. One of the children was sick, another lay wailing and kicking her heels on the sofa. Bunty got progressively more exuberant and kept making jokes about breasts; Serena got progressively more distraught and ended up sobbing about all her failed love affairs. Lord and Lady Melham discreetly retired to some private drawing room with the poisonous priest when their offspring became too personal. It was enough to make you nostalgic for Christmas inside, with its quiet Mass in the morning, the tasteless turkey dinner with its thin gravy and waterlogged sprouts. At least it didn't give you indigestion.

This morning there has been clattering and calling outside the window for hours. There are all sorts of people milling about, most of them wearing green waxed jackets and wellingtons. M pulls on her anorak over the lilac trouser suit and goes downstairs. Lord and Lady Melham are standing on the steps at the front of the house. Beside them is the housekeeper, presiding over a table with glasses and a bowl of mulled wine. 'Master's coming any minute,' says Serena, her nose and eyes still slightly red from her liquid excesses of the day before.

M has no idea who Master is and doesn't care. Where's Sophie? She's nowhere to be seen in the crowd. The little boy Crispin is asking after her too. 'Where's Aunt Snuffy?' Serena barely looks at him. 'Oh, she'll be off hiding somewhere. She thinks if she doesn't see it, the hunt doesn't happen.'

It's all rather exciting. Of course M doesn't approve of cruelty to animals but this is a British tradition. The closest she's been to it is once a year on the television news when they count up all the protestors. 'Don't you ride?' she asks Serena.

'Well, I do, but I've got a sprained wrist,' she says. Hmm, didn't prevent her raising her glass to her lips hundreds of times last night.

There is the sound of metal-shod hooves striking the ground and a collective roar from the watching crowd as the hunt gathers in front of the house, the Master leading them. What a handsome man, with his dark hair and fresh complexion whipped into ruddiness by the cold. He sits astride his horse like a king entering his capital city, his thighs splayed across the creature's back with supreme disregard for onlookers—or perhaps in invitation. At his back is a cavalcade of riders, many of the men in bright red jackets that splash the morning with warmth, though the women are disappointingly drab in black or grey. Last of all come the hounds, eyes bright, tails up, led by a wizened little man who looks like a monkey in his scarlet coat.

The housekeeper pours hot wine into little glass cups, the liquid splashing down like steaming blood. Oh, fuck it. She always has blood on the brain on Boxing Day. She must keep her mind off bloody Lesley Ann Downey. It's the worst day of her year. Regular as clockwork, somebody in prison would start taunting her. 'Wish you were on the moors now, Myyy-ra?' one woman drawled, dragging M's name out as if the very name were a curse. 'Want to be drinking wine with your fancy man, torturing a little lass? I'n't that how you like to spend your Boxing Day? Shoving cock in a little lass's mouth? Awwww, it weren't cock, it were a scarf or a sock or summat? Well, that's all right then. That's fucking all right then.' Mental bitch, the other women had to drag her away.

Steam is rising off the horses' flanks, but the hounds are silent, waiting for the signal to be off. Where is Sophie? Bunty is riding, just to the right of the Master. He looks good, sitting erect on his black hunter, virile, healthy. You'd never dream he was so drunk last night that he could talk only of female parts. Tosser. And how sexy horses are, for some reason. She studies the beasts milling about in front of them. The dogs are like children, for all their feral instincts, their predatory drive. They're eager to please. But the horses, the horses are like gods with their gleaming haunches, their eyes like bruises smudging their skin, their manes streaming.

A couple of rows in front of her Cassandra is talking to Sebastian's wife, M can't remember her name. 'Goodness but she's a ghastly woman. I can't imagine why Snuffy invited her to stay.'

'Do you think Sophie might have *unusual* tendencies?' The voice of the sister-in-law is wispy, sly.

From her vantage point above, M can see Cassandra jerking like a marionette whose strings have just been pulled. 'What on earth do you mean, unusual?'

'Well, M's a bit hard, wouldn't you say? A bit *dominant* looking?'

'Oh my God, you cannot be serious!'

'It's nothing to be ashamed of these days.'

Cassandra's voice is so low M can hardly hear her. 'Mummy would die.'

'Mummy would just ignore it, the way she ignores everything else that's happening to her children. Let's face it, she doesn't want to know. It's too uncomfortable for her.'

'You are a bitch, darling,' says Cassandra. 'You have to make the worst of everything, don't you?'

The sister-in-law's voice is mild. 'I just call it as I see it, Cassie. Didn't you notice her last night at table, staring at Sophie? She's a games player, that's all I'll say.'

Cassandra stares off into the distance as though she no longer sees the assembled horses and riders and hounds. Someone gives the signal on a strangulated horn and they're off. M tries to concentrate on the beauty of it, but she's too angry. Enough of this. Who do these people think they are? She turns to watch the hunt leave and sees, as she turns, that Serena has overheard and is trying not to snigger. Stupid, stupid bitch. 'How droll,' says M, and walks away.

Who cares if she looks hard? She knows she can. Let the rest of them contort their faces into silly simpering—if that's being sociable you can keep it, she'll have none of it. She fumbles for a cigarette but can't find one. This is it; she's got to find the little chick. You don't invite someone for a weekend and then abandon them to the idiot siblings. She strides away from them all, back into the house. 'Sophie?' she calls. 'Where are you?'

There is silence, save for the muffled sound of the dishwasher in the kitchen. M marches upstairs and knocks briskly on Sophie's door. 'Sophie? Are you in there?'

The door swings open and Sophie stands there looking surprised. 'What's wrong?'

M looks past her into the pretty sprigged bedroom. 'I'm sorry. I can't do this on my own. They all hate me.'

Sophie looks stricken. 'Of course they don't. Whatever makes you say a thing like that? Come on in.'

She stands back to let M enter the bedroom. M sits heavily on the bed. 'I shouldn't have come. I don't fit in.'

Sophie is about to say of course she does, till she sees the warning look on M's face. No massaging the truth then. 'You know what families are like—they all have their own way of doing things.'

M stares out the window. In the distance the horses move across the frosty fields with the instinctive synchronicity of a flock of birds. 'Don't you like hunting, then?'

'Not really. I used to hunt but I hate the thought of what happens when the fox gets caught. Now I just kind of avoid the whole business. What about you?'

'Never seen it.' M knows she's being curt but feels too angry to stop.

'You must watch it, M,' says Sophie timidly. 'They'll ban it soon enough. It's part of English history.'

'We didn't do much of it in Manchester where I grew up. It was more greyhound racing and pigeon lofts.'

Sophie laughs and then checks herself, not sure how to read M's expression.

'You know what your family are saying about us, don't you?'

The little chick looks alarmed. 'No. What?'

'That we're lesbians.'

Sophie colours. 'Why would they say such a thing?'

'You tell me.' M's tone is blunt, her expression unyielding.

'You surely don't think I ...'

'For God's sake, how would I know, Sophie?'

'You're far more likely to have had a relationship with a woman than I am.'

'Am I?' M studies her, knowing she has made Sophie feel afraid. When Sophie finally dares to look at M, she sees something measuring in her look, a calculation in it that she cannot compute. Then M's whole body relaxes, its plump curves becoming shapeless, spongelike—for all Sophie knows, a deadly pulsating sponge that will absorb her into its clutches. M's voice is slow and somehow taunting. 'How do you make that out then?'

'Well, you're older than me.' Sophie finds herself stuttering.

'Oh, yes. Much. But so what? Your mother's older than me. Do you think she's slept with a woman?'

Sophie can't look at her. Bet she was bullied at school. 'Course not,' she mutters.

'Then why do you think I would? Eh? You think I'm a lezzo, is that it?'

'No. No.'

Softly now, don't take it out on the little chick. This moment holds the key to what will happen later. It must be managed. She must steer things to a suitable conclusion. She wills her voice to go quiet, calm. 'Sophie, love. I'm middle aged and I know I must look ancient to a young woman like you. Even if I were that way inclined why would someone like you look at me?'

Sophie looks at her in surprise. Good. Hold the eye contact. 'But you're a handsome woman. Anyway, I'm not that young.'

M holds the silence for a long moment. God, she's getting excited. This is a high stakes game. Is Sophie looking a little pink? Is she getting to her? The sun has come out and she can see dust motes swirling in the light, like little ethereal beings tumbled around, willy-nilly, by the air currents. Not her. She is going to be in control, she is going to win here. She touches the little chick's hand, ever so softly, feeling the leap of electricity through her skin. 'You're a very sweet person, Sophie.'

'Am I?' The younger woman's voice comes out in a croak.

'I won't have them talking about you like that.' She's hooked, M can see it, those big grey eyes limpid with gratitude, begging to be looked after, to be loved. To be told what to do. 'Come on, dear. Let's go and watch the rest of the hunt.' Yes, let's make a public declaration, join the rest of them, clearly having spent private time together. Let's see what the fuckers make of that.

She puts out her hand so that Sophie can help her up from the soft bed. Sophie, respectful, proffers two, pulling M towards her. M looks into her eyes for a long time before saying, 'Thank you, Sophie.' But it is she who breaks off first. Leave the little chick on the back foot, not knowing what will happen next.

As they drive along country lanes she allows herself to contemplate what that might be. Should she make her move tonight, soften the little chick up with tales from the nuthouse and stories of dead babies, or should she wait till they get back home, where there's no brothers and sisters around to poke their noses in? Morons, the dribbling siblings. She tries not to think about Sophie's berry nipples, her creamy skin. In the fields, their rich green bleached by frost, are a few cows looking disgruntled at the cold. 'They shouldn't be out in this weather. What's Mr Fanshawe thinking of?' says Sophie, but all M can think of is licking the sweet berries, lapping the cream.

They hear the hunt before they see it, a cacophony of horns and hounds and then the low shiver of hooves along the ground. 'We'll go up to Wenford Edge,' says Sophie. 'Then we can see them from above.' They drive up a steep lane, towards a wide road running through moorland. Alongside it runs a dark ridge of pleated rock. About a mile further on, Sophie pulls into a passing place and stops the car. Down below is a flat stretch of open land scattered with grey stones.

The fox appears first, running along, belly low to the ground. It heads straight across the space, ears back, looking neither to left nor right, a concentrated streak of survival. Halfway across, it encounters a small stream, which it flits across, hardly seeming to jump at all. It's a full five minutes before the hunt comes into view. The hounds arrive first, making a strange baying, a pure, ghostly sound like banshees crying of death to come. When they reach the stream they hurl themselves across it, but they seem puzzled on the other side, as if the water has washed away the fox's scent. They start to mill around, noses to the ground, utterly silent. 'Oh, look, there's one feathering,' says Sophie. The dog is trembling all over, its tail waving. As the others realise it has found the scent, they gather round, yelping excitedly, before all moving off together.

The riders appear shortly after, a blizzard of red and black moving across the moor. It's as if they're a world within the world, contained in their own private universe of flight. They're too far away for M and Sophie to make out individual features or the lines of individual bodies, but even from this distance the riders project a sense of massed power, like redcoated armies laying claim to a land not their own. A surge of energy goes through M as she watches. What must it be like to sit on top of such a magnificent animal, gripping it into submission with your thighs? To storm across the landscape, taking it for yourself, your pleasure?

As the last rider disappears, Sophie touches her arm lightly. 'We'll go down to Holby Woods. That may be where the fox is heading.'

'Are you sure? You don't want to see the kill.'

'We'll probably miss it anyway. You hardly ever see it. The hounds are usually too quick.'

'At least it's over quickly for the fox, then.'

They get back into the car, shivering now. 'Let's get a nice fug going,' says Sophie, putting the heater on. They head back along the edge of the pleated rocks, then round the corner before descending into a wooded valley. Sophie frowns. 'I wonder where all the followers are. Maybe we're ahead of them.'

She plunges along a forest path, the car bumping over ruts in the ground. 'Not good for the suspension, this,' says M. In the gloom of the pine trees it seems an eerie place, all hemmed in and hidden. Every time they catch a glimpse of sunlight through the trunks M thinks she sees a ghost. It's a trick of the light, she knows, but it's Boxing Day and she knows whose spirit walks

105

abroad today. Damn that child. Damn her, wandering round the fairground on her own. Did she think that was what the world was like, full of shiny lights and fluorescent colours? Did she think all those people smiling and laughing were her friends? Silly little sod. She was too easy, trotted into the car like a lamb.

Sophie draws to a halt near a clearing in the middle of the woods. M has a cigarette while they wait. After about five minutes the ground starts to shiver again and the thud of running hounds reverberates along the path. The sound of their crying rolls around the trees, hangs suspended in the branches. 'Where's the fox?' asks M, but they can't see either it or the dogs yet. At last the animal runs into the clearing, panting, its tongue lolling out of its mouth and its eyes frantic—a scarecrow fox, pathetic, nothing like the proud male she sees in her back garden. 'It's exhausted, poor beast,' whispers Sophie.

The hounds are on it before the words are out of her mouth. M stays very still as they swarm on top of the animal, ripping its red fur with their sharp pointed teeth, their jaws slavering with blood. Amidst the yelps of the dogs, the fox's last cry is almost lost, but M catches it, notes the moment when the breath leaves its body and it becomes a thing, no longer living. The dogs are magnificent, ripping and clawing and tearing, exulting in the taste of blood.

Sophie stands beside her, tears streaming down her face. The red-jacketed Master clatters into the clearing, followed by the rest of the riders. The hounds are circling and calling, excited by the kill. One of the huntsmen walks over to the fox's carcass. He bends down, holding a circlet of wire, and swiftly clips the animal's brush, handing it to the Master, who asks, 'Who shall we blood today?' Bunty looks down at M from the heights of his horse. 'What about Miss Spencer?' he says. 'She's a guest of the hunt.'

She looks up at him, eyes black with loathing, not taking her gaze off him as she walks forward. Around her she can hear a little murmur of surprise, but she ignores it. No doubt it breaks all their silly rules, but let them say what they want. 'It would be a privilege,' she says. She knows he wants her to crumple, to cry, but she won't do it. For a boy like him? For a little spot of blood? *You don't know what you're dealing with, sonny.*

Sophie looks on in horror as the warm blood is smeared across M's face, but M doesn't want her sympathy. She wears her blood like woad. She is a warrior woman. Let none of them forget it.

From: "Hal" <wolfman@hotmail.co.uk>
To: lynx1043@hotmail.co.uk
Subject: boxing day
Date: Fri, 27 December 2002 11:05:17

God, would you believe it - M at a fox hunt? I couldn't believe my eyes. I was acting the hunt sab this time. Good fun actually. I can see why the toffs like this sport, really exciting and it looked quite dangerous. Certainly is for the poor old fox.

I think she's really getting it on with the posh girl. Can't tell for sure yet as even Her Majesty's government doesn't listen in to every minute of her day, but the two of them seem very close.

The rest of the toffs smell a rat - they're rather looking down their noses at her - but that just makes the young girl stick closer to her. Obviously one of those who always stands up for the underdog.

Sorry to go on before I've even asked you about your Boxing Day. It just seemed so surreal I had to tell you.

From the BlackBerry of Hal Morton

From: La Barbara <lynx1043@hotmail.co.uk>

Thank God to hear from you, my darling. Boxing Day was a desert. I longed for you to be there.

Eddie came over with the latest wife (third since me!) to give Alex his present, so I had to pretend to be civilised all afternoon. I find that quite a stretch when my ex is around.

Alex spent the time a) sulking because the extremely expensive hi-tech present was not the one he wanted and b) ogling the new wife, whose blonde hair was not of a tint which denotes intelligence.

Mother is going deaf so I went hoarse from shouting at her all day. Not in anger, you understand, just asking her would she like another cup of tea or a sherry. She finally had one at four o'clock, by which time I'd been in the kitchen for three vodka tonics! You know I'm not a big drinker so you can see how enjoyable it all was. There is an upside to not ever knowing your family!

From the BlackBerry of Pat Shields

From: "Hal" <wolfman@hotmail.co.uk>

Yes, I guess this way you never have to know that your parents are bores or drunkards. I remember my mother a little bit but haven't got the foggiest about my father. And you know what Nietzsche said - a man without a father is like a wolf.

From: La Barbara <lynx1043@hotmail.co.uk>

Is that why you chose the wolf thing for your e-address? I just thought you were being romantic in a macho Hemingway/Jack London sort of way.

From: "Hal" <wolfman@hotmail.co.uk>

So you admit it's romantic?

From: La Barbara <lynx1043@hotmail.co.uk>

Of course. As soon as I saw it I knew you were for me. I chose the lynx because she's beautiful and fierce and people are always telling me I get angry too quickly. I thought you'd chosen the wolf for similar reasons, though when I think about it you never do get angry. You're a saint compared to me.
I've never actually heard that Nietzsche thing before and am not sure I understand it.

From: "Hal" <wolfman@hotmail.co.uk>

You can't settle. You have no-one to tell you how to be a man, so you become a rabid animal, roaming the forests and mountains, searching - for food, for sustenance, for you don't know what.

From: La Barbara <lynx1043@hotmail.co.uk>

That sounds lonely.

From: "Hal" <wolfman@hotmail.co.uk>

It is. When you don't know your own father you don't know who you are, what you've come from, where you belong. In the end you become your own creation.
I chose the wolfman a long time ago, when I was quite young. I don't think of myself that way now - except in bed, of course!

From: La Barbara <lynx1043@hotmail.co.uk>

There you're right! In bed you're ferocious, insatiable, a BEAST!!!!!
XXXXXXXXXXX

Mist and drizzle in Manchester. Small expectations. What's the point? They don't know how to do New Year here. The clock ticking, ticking, ticking. The gas fire hissing. Tick tick tick. Hiss, hiss, hiss.

Time to go.

Luggage? Minimal. A bottle of rum, a bottle of whisky. Cigarettes. The 38 of course, carefully laid in the inside pocket of the black leather briefcase. The black suit, black shirt, black overcoat. He scribbles a brief explanation. Leave them a note at least.

Runs for the bus. Just catches the 34 as it pulls away from the stop. Impatient as it winds it way through the sulphurous streets of Gorton, past the railway yards with their rolling stock lying there, waiting to be brought back to life. Rolling, rolling, rolling. Fire flares out of the foundry, sending sparks—and hopes—flying into the grey sky.

Cobbled streets, redbrick back to backs. How strange they were at first after the grandeur of the tenements. They do it better where he comes from. Stone, solid stone and an artist's eye shaping it.

City centre. Come on, no time to waste. Get the bloody bus through these crowds. Out of the way. Idiots. Stuck in offices all day, do this, do that. No guts, no hearts, no brains. Don't know they're alive.

The station at last. Victoria, with its grand facade like a posh hotel, all windows and turrets. Rush on to the platform. The train is still there, lowering and quivering like a bull about to charge. Smoke pours from its chimney and he tastes soot crawling into his throat. It's not unpleasant. A quick slug of the whisky in his briefcase would take it away.

Hazy air in the railway carriage. It's a corridor train, all the compartments crammed with Scots like him, going home for New Year. Soldiers in a huddle, their kitbags piled up around them. The sound of laughter and liquor from the compartments, glasses clinking, people singing. The smell of soot and wet wool. Foreigners must think the British stink when they meet them on a rainy day.

A grumbling below and the wheels clank and jerk forward before beginning to roll. The guard's whistle and then the high-pitched scream of steam as the train streams into motion, picking up speed across the railway bridge. Below, the pallid streets of Manchester lie slug-slick with rain and rottenness.

He elbows his way through the packed corridor. People move aside for him, smiling little half-smiles as they look down at the wet city, thinking of where they are going, hugging the thought of the journey and its end.

A long queue at the bar but eventually he gets to the front. The girl is wiping sloshed tea off the counter. 'A bottle of beer and a pie,' he says, ignoring her attempts to make eye contact with him. Not that she's bad looking, with her blonde beehive and her tight jumper, but what's the point? She doesn't have half the possibilities of the girl. The girl, the girl, the girl. She's tough. But will she join in the existential exercise? ... he chooses not to think about her. No place for that soft stuff in a crowded train. The pie is steak and kidney, not as good as a nice peppery lamb pie from home, but warm and the gravy is brown and rich.

Manoeuvres his way to the window to eat, keeping his briefcase between him and the next person so that no-one can come close enough to knock over his beer. Grey light as the train ploughs through Lancashire, but once they get into Westmoreland the sky brightens. He turns his face to the afternoon sun, eyes scanning the scenery. Rocks, hills, the occasional rushing burn. God, it's beautiful.

He opens the window to stick his head out and soot flies back into his eyes and up his nose. Ma Sloan told him he'd get his head cut off if he did that but he always does, always imagines the head dripping blood and bouncing back along the track, grinning at him. Hah, never happened yet.

'Hey Jimmy, it's no' that warm yit.'

'OK, pal.' He shuts the window again, savouring the roughness of the Glaswegian's speech. Whisky and fags voice, sound of the tenements. They pass black crags, plunging valleys thick with trees and bushes. It reminds him of the tangled growth mantling the Southern Necropolis when he was a kid during the war. They played Tarzan there, bending the trees back and lashing them into native noose traps. In the comics the traps always catapulted their victims into the air, but whenever one of them set theirs off, accidentally on purpose, all he did was dangle there. They shrieked their heads off, of course. That was part of the game.

It's early evening by the time the train huffs and puffs into Carlisle. Lit-up cathedral, small and solid, the little frilly bits at the front black against the twilight sky. Peaceful in there probably. Larcenous peace, of course, extorted by the clerics at the cost of the rebel soul. This was the cathedral they hung the Jacobites in, wasn't it? A right rabble, them, swaggering into all those English towns in their kilts, affronting the local females by publicly pissing in their gutters.

Satisfying.

He gets a seat after Carlisle, thank God. Long way to stand. Half-empty compartment with two old ducks snoring in the window seats. They should just die right now. What's the point of being old, dribbling and drooling down their frocks? He falls asleep to the steady swish of the train along the rails. Wakes only when the engine clanks to a halt. Dark, with the swooshing sound of the steam, the train pawing to be off.

Motherwell.

Time for a walk. He heads down the corridor, free hand steadying himself as the train lurches along. Everyone else is semi-comatose. Bang, bang. He laughs. Deserted corridor as he positions himself at the window, ready for the familiar approach into Glasgow. Eglinton Toll and the Plaza ballroom, with its mirrored ball and the fountain with coloured lights gushing over it. Elsie McEvoy from the next close used to go there on Friday nights, running down the stairs in her sticky out balldress, dark hair still in kirby grips that she took off on the bus. Her Dad could have taken her in his motor if he wanted. Rich by Camden Street standards with his butcher's shop, but always out himself on a Friday night, usually at the dog track, or so they said.

The train is crawling now, waiting for another one to clear the platform. The Bedford cinema all lit up, gold stars in a blue sky over its frontage. The doorman there always smelled of drink. You saw him sometimes when the film was on, taking a sly nip from the quarter bottle of El D tucked in his uniform pocket. Strong stuff, these fortified wines. He'd have been seeing two of everyone on the screen. Guy must have got the sack by now.

Now the Coliseum, big and brash, with its Cinerama screen. He queued there with his pals to see Ben Hur one Saturday matinee. Cracking chariot race. Shame about the asinine mush that passed for an ending. Why the hell would Ben Hur go through all that shit from the Romans and fall for the *turn the other cheek* stuff at the end? Poisonous, moronic pap.

Crossing the river now, Carlton Place and its bastard lawyers' offices. The moral relativism of the ruling class enshrined in stone. Corpulent cretins bursting with self-satisfaction as they rape the honest criminal classes, the trick of self-deception acquired with a university degree. The train inches across the railway bridge and he pulls the window down. Lights and dark water and the smell of the river, both pleasurable and dank.

The platform is spattered with frost. He pulls the overcoat up to his neck, wishing he'd brought gloves. Only ten thirty, plenty of time before the bells. Down the back stairs to the Hielanman's Umbrella, its iron fretwork overlaid with soot. The cafe across the road is still open, windows steamed up in the frost. Pie and chips, a proper pie. And a cup of tea. The waitress is a big raw Glasgow lassie with hands like ham hough. 'Park yer bum there, son. It winna be lang.'

'Is this your fancy man, Winnie?' Some wee wifie sitting in the corner.

'Looks like the man fae the Pru, wi' yon briefcase,' says a middle-aged man nursing a cup of tea and a fag.

'Naw, he's got a million pounds fae the pools in there. He's gonnae take me away fae here. Flying down to Rio, we are.' She plonks the food down in front of him with a wink. It's all he can do not to shudder. Hard to imagine anyone less like Ginger Rogers. But the pie is piping hot and the chips fresh. Not bad at all.

Eleven o'clock and he'll need to shift if he wants to get to Pollok in time. Too big a queue for taxis at the station, so he hits the street, manages to flag one down. Back across the river, along Paisley Road West. Elegant stone tenements and then along the side of the park. Who knows what's going on in that darkness?

The taxi follows the 49 bus route, up Corkerhill Road past the cemetery, then across the river Cart, where he made his escape after a robbery once. Gardens, football field, trees, all are crystal white. He gets the driver to set him down at the Braidcraft roundabout. He'll walk the rest of the way. Imperative that the visit be clandestine.

111

The hall light is out in the close at the end of the road. Perfect. He stands, upturned collar, waiting. Inside the houses he can hear the sounds of the White Heather Club, with Andy Stewart singing that daft song, *There was a soldier, a Scottish soldier*. Sentimental claptrap. What the fuck's a Scottish soldier supposed to be doing in the Tyrol anyway?

Just over the border from Switzerland, the Tyrol. He's dying to sing Harry Lime's theme tune. *In Italy for thirty years under the Borgias they had warfare, terror, murder, bloodshed, but produced Michelangelo, DaVinci, and the Renaissance. In Switzerland they had brotherly love and five hundred years of democracy and peace. And what did that produce? The cuckoo clock.* He lights a cigarette. Must be nearly twelve now.

Windows open so that people can hear midnight strike. If the wind is right and there are enough ships on the river, it might be possible to hear their foghorns blowing all the way up here in Pollok. A few men come on to the street, all dark-haired, of course. Cheating, though. Impossible to hoodwink fate like that. The first foot has to be someone from outside the family—you can't choose.

Whisky. He slides the bottle from the briefcase, undoes the seal with his teeth. In the darkness of the close he can hear the countdown to midnight on all the tellies. Five, four, three, two, one. Muffled cheering. Doors slam above him and people go across the landing to shake hands with their neighbours. He takes a long, slow pull on his whisky, silently toasting all.

Laughter outside. People coming into the close. *Happy New Year, pal.* If they are surprised to see him alone, in the dark, they do not say so. Hands are shaken, bottles offered. *Have a drink, Jimmy.*

Have one yourself, mate. Whisky is exchanged for rum. Honours even, they head upstairs, leaving him to his solitary post. He pulls his coat collar up, stands in the shadows staring out at the frosty street. Further up the road he can see Mrs Semple, the lady next door, knocking at his house. A voice, *Come away in.* Was that Ma Sloan? Or maybe her sister? Black bun handed over and a bottle of Bertola Cream sherry, by the looks of it.

Constant to-ing and fro-ing. People carrying bottles of whisky, Babycham for the ladies; the ladies in silver Lurex and high heels, tripping across the snow with plates of hot sausage rolls. The inevitable drunken Sinatra impersonator. *One for my Baby (and One More for the Road).*

A new year, new life? Maybe the girl … across the road a young woman comes out of a house with a dark young man. They're holding hands and stopping to kiss every ten yards. She'll be knocked up within six months and he'll have to be dragged screaming to the altar, but Brady feels too mellow to despise them. *Slainthe.*

Most of the bottle gone now. Shadows dance behind every set of curtains, to all sorts of different records. The Shirelles, Ricky Nelson, Roy Orbison. Here in the darkness it's like having your own jukebox.

At two o'clock he moves. Safe now. Up towards the house. Lights still on behind closed curtains. He stops at the gate and lights a cigarette. He can hear the murmur of voices, the clink of glasses. He wonders how many of

112

the family are there tonight. Maybe all of them, with their wives and husbands of course. There's certainly a lot of noise going on in there.

The bloke from three doors down comes up the street with his girlfriend. They nod at Brady, but fail to recognise him. Don't expect to see him there.

He turns up his collar and walks past his childhood home, back towards the city.

PART II

UNASSAILABLE

Weary, M feels weary. She's eaten too much, drunk too much—felt too much. She slides on to the wooden bench, its slats immediately slicing into her thighs. Oh Lord, she's got to get the weight off. What chance will she have with Sophie if she stays this big? Slim Sophie with her slender legs, slipping in and out of M's life like a mermaid. Will she, *could* she ever stay?

She can't work out whether Christmas was a success or not. The family hated her, but that seemed to make Sophie more protective. It was wise to wait, though, no point in frightening the little chick off by making her move too early. Pulling the last of her clothes off, M studies her naked body in the dressing room mirror. If she stands up straight and holds her stomach in she looks about a stone lighter. Not bad at all, especially with the fluffy towel wrapped round her. She just has to keep herself together when she walks in. No-one will look twice at her if she's confident enough.

Sometimes it all seems too much, harder than being inside. At least you knew where you were pretty quickly in there. No long courtships or trying to read people's minds. They told you straight out in the nick. Why didn't she keep her mouth shut, like Brady? What did she think was so great about being outside, that she had to keep pushing and pushing to be let out?

A gust of heat makes her look up, as the door opens and a woman comes through from the baths area. Her face is pink and a thin caul of moisture covers her skin. She has a dreamy look on her face, as though not quite awake. 'No-one in there, love. You'll have total peace,' she says. M smiles and heads for the door. After all, this is not an experience you could have in prison.

Inside the steam room the heat is colossal and she instantly feels her skin prickle. The room is square, its walls covered entirely in green and blue tiles which fan out in a series of peacock tails. A marble bench runs around the walls and she lies down on it, legs stretched out. After only a few minutes she is overwhelmed by the sensation of being bathed in heat. Is this what it's like abroad, in hot countries?

Every inch of her skin seems to pulsate with the heat, the cells underneath in a gentle dance of transformation, like molten chocolate bubbling up to the surface. She lies along the bench, torpid as a cat in sunlight, luxuriating in what must surely be tropical temperatures? Vivid pink and turquoise parrots throng in the rainforests of her dreams, their crazy screeches ripping the molten air. She is in the jungle, with the sound of a roaring river pounding in her ears. Must be the Amazon, it's so huge. The current powers through her head, then there's roaring as if a waterfall is
nearby—danger. The river turns into a snake, the most enormous thing she's ever seen in her life, an anaconda, writhing its way through the water like some primeval monster driving her from paradise. She has to make it change, has to. Just as she's about to wake up it transforms itself into Sophie, the mermaid, thank God, slipping through the waves with consummate elegance, her hair long and golden in the dream.

'Hallo. I didn't expect to see you here, M.'

M's eyes open. She can't believe it. Sophie is standing there in a skimpy towel, hair scrunched up on top of her head, revealing her slender neck. It's as if M has conjured her up. She struggles to sit up, feeling herself turn even pinker with heat and embarrassment.

'Good grief. What are you doing here?'

Sophie slides on to the bench beside her. 'Trying to detox after Christmas, just like you, I suppose?'

'I do feel a bit wodgy.'

Sophie laughs out loud. 'Is that a word you made up?'

M shrugs. 'Don't suppose you'd know what that feels like anyway.'

Sophie stretches, with an animal confidence that M envies. She was like that once, for a few years when she was with Brady, when she had a man to love her. The first time they had sex she felt as if her brain had been cracked right open. All those years of hiding herself away when she had her bath on a Saturday night. *No-one's to come in*, she'd tell them. Sometimes she'd put a chair against the door just in case. How great it was to get rid of that old tin bath when they moved to Wardle Road. It was all scratched, horrible to touch, sort of matt, setting her teeth on edge. The water was always too hot at the bottom when you first got in, but had a thin layer of cold at the top, before it all settled into tepid mediocrity around you. You came out two-toned, like those desserts with clear red jelly at the bottom and milky pink blancmange on top.

She hated her body then. Moby was much more petite, small-boned like Mam. Why was *she* stuck with big hips? and broad shoulders like a man? Brady made her feel sexy, though, especially when they got into the heavier stuff later on and he'd order her to do things. Her insides disintegrated then as if an electrical charge had gone through her. *You will take that skirt off.*

'Why?'

Because I'm telling you to.

Now the knickers.

'Why?'

Because I want to see your cunt.

She felt like a proper woman then, standing half naked in front of him. Obeying him. How seductive that was, as if she wasn't the toughest girl in Gorton but soft and feminine like all the others. It wasn't till later, once all the dungaree feminists came into Holloway, that she realised how stupid it was. 'You fetishise obedience,' one of them said. 'No wonder you ended up in here. Learn to think for yourself.'

You've dared to question me. You'll have to be punished.

I know. Then the delicious waiting …

'M, did you enjoy the break—or did you just loathe my family?' Sophie's crystalline voice cuts through the heat.

'No, no. I enjoyed it very much, but I think they loathed me.'

'Of course they didn't.'

'I'm not daft, Sophie.'

116

Beads of sweat glisten along Sophie's arm. 'They're snobs,' she says flatly. 'Don't worry about them.'

'I'm not. I don't suppose I'll ever see them again anyway.'

'Course you will.' Sophie shifts on the bench, the already short towel riding further up her thighs. M is mesmerised by the colour of them, a light golden colour at odds with her pale face. 'How are you so brown?'

'I go to that tanning place at the back of Debenhams. You stand between the sunbeds so you get an all over tan, but I always cover my face completely. I don't want to get skin cancer.'

M is intrigued. She could change her skin colour entirely if she wanted, transform her appearance even more. She could probably go really brown if she tried. Maybe that would make her look sexier.

'Shall we go through to the other room?' asks Sophie.

'I didn't realise there was another one.'

'Oh yes, there's one more hot room and then the plunge pool.'

M, enervated already, drags herself up and follows Sophie. The heat in the next room is like a barrier as they enter. A high-domed ceiling of stained glass causes pools of red and blue light to form on the tiled floor and ripple in little rivulets round the dolphin mosaic. M has to sit down, she's so hot, but Sophie seems perfectly comfortable, as if this submarine world is her natural home. She stretches her arms upwards and the towel she's wearing slips a little. 'Oops,' she says, but makes only a perfunctory move to secure it. M can clearly see her nipple and the cup of her breast. She ties her own towel tightly at the front and lies down on one of the day beds set around the room. The heat feels dry, nibbling away at her as if a mouse were scampering over her skin.

Sophie is fiddling with her hair, removing her scrunchie and starting all over again. She's not yet ready, it seems, to lie down. Her movements are languid, elegant, as if she is aware of her own grace. What a beautiful body she has, with her long legs, her narrow hips, the thin sheen of sweat making her seem polished, shiny, a glass mermaid to keep for ever.

As the heat rises, Myra's skin starts to prickle. Why doesn't the little chick lie down instead of flaunting herself in front of her. Doesn't she know what it's doing to her?

'It's beautiful, this room, don't you think?' says Sophie suddenly. M nods in reply. 'The Victorians really knew how to do things well. There's not many of these baths left. We're very lucky to have this one.'

'The ceiling's beautiful,' says M.

'Yes, but the technology's very interesting too, you know. The air currents are being heated all the time. They go round the furnace and through all the rooms. It's the dryness of the heat that makes it special.'

'Is that so?' says M, trying not to let her tone become dry too. Why is Sophie telling her this—and how the hell does she know about it anyway? Has she been reading a guide book or something? She seems to know about the strangest things. 'The Victorians thought dry heat was terribly healthy,' she continues. 'Along with taking regular exercise, and making oodles of money, of course.'

'Of course.'

Sophie yawns and stretches her whole body upwards. Lord, if she doesn't watch out, that towel's going to go. M catches a glimpse of golden skin, and is that a flash of hair? Her heart is pounding, her mouth very dry. Sophie closes the towel and walks to the daybed. A slight smile flashes across her face, so fast that M isn't sure she's seen it. Oh my God, she's flirting, the little chick is flirting.

Sophie's eyes close over as she sprawls on the bed, legs splayed. M tries not to look but the towel is little more than a hand towel. She must have been given a bath towel by the attendant, so why choose the smaller one? She can't have known M was here. Did she intend to flirt with whoever was in today? And if so, has the little chick been leading her up the garden path? Naughty girl, maybe she's not so innocent as she seems. Can't let her get away with that.

M relaxes on her own bed. The luminous blue and red lights lap across her face, casting strange shadows in the room. She can see the curve of Sophie's leg, dappled like the scales of the slippery little mermaid she is. A nymph, a goddess. The heat builds and builds, in layers of light and warmth, a cathedral of heat where she is a worshipper.

Her hair is flat against her head and she is damp and sticky, but she feels a certain satisfaction. She knows now that things will move forward. How lucky there was no-one else here today. She closes her eyes. It's so hot. The dryness of the heat is like desert wind, harrying the moisture from her body till it leaches into her towel. She drifts into sleep, with waves of sand breaking over the desert and the mermaid gliding effortlessly through the golden sea.

'We'd better not stay too long here,' says Sophie's voice. M starts awake. As Sophie stands up her towel drifts open a little. Dreamily she pulls it shut. 'This is when the Victorians would have been shampooed all over and given a massage.'

'Sod the Victorians,' says M, standing up and letting her own towel fall.

Sophie gasps. A small smile shimmers across her face as she walks to the door. She turns and looks over her shoulder, feminine and flirtatious, as M walks towards her. M knows that her own face is intense, her eyes staring. The room they walk into is tiled in cool white, with a deep green plunge pool lying ahead of them. Sophie walks to the steps and drops her towel, but turns to wait for M. Together they walk into the water ...

M runs her hands through the new hairdo, mussing it up—she likes it. Maybe it's a bit too like Sophie's, but the rough, choppy effect makes her look younger, more modern. The colour's pretty too—champagne the hairdresser called it, which makes her sound like an old English sheepdog or something— but it's soft and not too ageing. She flicks it to and fro like the girls in hair adverts. *Because you're worth it,* she tells her mirror.

She can't seem to settle to anything today, can't stop thinking about Sophie and the baths, the empty dressing room afterwards, their bodies becoming pure liquid, as wet inside as out.

Really there's washing to do and Minim needs a walk, but she can't dredge up the energy somehow. 'Come here,' she says and scoops him up into her arms, but once he's licked her face he just wants to squirm out of her grasp and go snuffling round his food tray again.

When will she see Sophie again? She mustn't sit by the phone, must take the initiative. Sophie hasn't been with a woman before and won't know what the next step is, much less take it. M will have to take charge. Take charge of herself too, get fit and under control, get rid of her clothes and find a new look, streamline her life, bend it to her will. The stuff she's seen other women wearing is nothing like her A-line skirts and secretary's tops. And when did pussy bows go out of fashion? She hasn't seen a single other person wearing them.

Sophie was so pretty yesterday, slipping weightlessly through the water, her skin so firm, she so elusive and yet so willing, in the end, to be caught …

Upstairs M flips through the wardrobe. The neat dresses and suits ranged there look like the clothes of someone else, an older, more staid type of person than she is herself. She will walk away from them, leave them discarded on the beach of her life like that MP who faked his death in Australia. She needs to look younger—she's a woman with a toygirl lover after all, can't afford to appear middle-aged. First for the binbag is her navy suit. Its pleated skirt seems old-fashioned, its jacket matronly. That sort of thing was all right in prison, where you needed to look as powerful as you could, but out here it just looks dowdy. She flings it on the bed, with a faint whisper of regret for its fine wool and immaculate tailoring. It was the most expensive thing in that catalogue.

The dark green dress she wore at Christmas is definitely going. She'll never feel the same about it again, will always associate it in her head with humiliation, with the braying of upper class yobs. Where is it? She rakes through the cupboard till she finds it, tosses it down with relish. Talk about being trussed up like a turkey ready for basting. Sod that. She's going to wear bohemian clothes like Sophie, artistic clothes that make her feel free and light and adventurous.

She's an adventurer out here. That's the odd thing. Out here they think lesbianism is exotic, shocking. Inside it was just taken for granted. Not

119

that she's a lesbian herself, she just sleeps with women sometimes. She flops down on the bed, wondering how it will be if Sophie comes here. Will she admire the funny curtain, as M does? It's called a festoon blind, according to the lady next door, though she didn't seem impressed by it. 'I'd have thought she'd have got rid of that by now,' she sniffed. 'It looks ever so dated.' Maybe she should think about changing it—she doesn't want to seem old-fashioned.

Jeans, maybe she'll wear jeans, dark ones, not the light-coloured ones that Sophie wears. Maybe V-neck black sweaters with chunky jewellery at the neck? And bright red nail polish. You can get brilliant false nails in the pound shop.

Oh, get a move on. She gets up and starts going through her chest of drawers. Bras with black lace, red shiny ones, little camisoles with ribbon trim. Her underwear is *pretty*, thanks to good old Lord Astor. Pity she has to be dead, she could do with the money he and his family paid her. Two hundred and fifty quid a month is not to be sneezed at.

She should probably get rid of that lilac trouser suit, but she can't bear to, lets it stay for the moment. How great she always felt in it, sort of professional somehow, yet still feminine. She could have been a manager or something, for sure. If only she'd got her degree on the outside, there's no knowing where she'd have ended up. She might have gone into business for herself or become a teacher. She should have written books, though not that turgid psychological stuff Brady wrote. *Gates of Janus* indeed. Anus more like, pretending he knew why murderers murdered people. What explanation could he give for what *he* did?

No, she'd prefer to be a romantic novelist, like Charlotte Vale Allen or that Yorkshire one that thinks she's gritty—Barbara Bradford, is it? Maybe, with all the women she's had, she should write raunchy stuff like Jackie Collins, only for dykes. She'd look good in black leather, talking about herself on the telly.

The tweed skirt's going and all those crew-necked jumpers. She pulls them down from the shelf, sending them tumbling across the bedspread. Powder blue, lilac, pale green—what on earth possessed her to choose such naff colours all the time? She needs to look bold, dramatic, like the strong woman she is. The slacks are going too, all of them. The very word is out of date. She'll get herself a couple of pairs of jeans and some nicely cut trousers for going out. No more mousy clothes. She wants to look chic now. Not elegant chic but chic in the arty way Sophie and her friends are.

There's quite a pile on the bed now. They look sad, clothes from a past life, a life that needs to be scrubbed out, obliterated, as if it had never been. She is the phoenix, rising again, her plumage shiny and new, shaking out her feathers in readiness for a new form of existence. Sophie's friends will respect her for who she is now. She'll look cool, trendy, an older woman who doesn't deny her age but isn't defined by it either, with a new style, new makeup. That magazine she was reading the other day said nothing gives away a woman's age so much as clinging to the same look for years and years while your skin gradually sags and stretches.

120

Settling herself in front of the dressing table mirror, she smooths on some makeup remover, wipes off everything with a tissue. Her eyebrows need plucking but she can't find any tweezers. Oh, nail scissors will do. Amazing how thick they've become. Oops. The scissors slip and she shears a large chunk off her left eyebrow. Bugger, what's she going to do now? She looks so odd, as if one eye is in shock. Better match them at least. She can get her eye pencil out later and fill in the shape she wants, just as she used to do in the old days, etching quizzical Joan Crawford eyebrows above the natural line of her own, pencilling a vamp's mouth over her own thin lips. It was her personal look. She was an artist in her way, creating that face. People read the wrong things into that mugshot.

Could she ever look like that again? Slowly she unzips her makeup bag, smears foundation all over her cheekbones and chin. It's not quite as pale as the stuff she used to wear but if she doesn't bother with blusher she might be able to achieve that pallid, unwell look. She'd been up half the night when the photo was taken. No wonder she looked like hell had opened before her.

Dark, plummy red lipstick next, giving her mouth luscious Clara Bow curves. She holds her face rigid, feeling the pull of the muscles in her neck, till her lower lip juts out, full and sulky looking.

Now deep grey shadow on the lower part of her lids. She was wearing none that day but the harsh light of the police photographer cast dark shadows into her eye sockets. She puts lilac shadow underneath the eyes. How strange that all these years on she has no bags there, fewer wrinkles, softer skin than she had then, at twenty-three. Did the murkiness of their joint project seep into her very skin cells, transforming them into the tough hide everyone thought she had?

How soft Sophie's skin was yesterday, their underwater embraces like swimming with silk.

Was she really as hard as they all said? What did they expect, that she would fall apart and blurt everything out, condemning her and Brady to a life apart? He was everything then. She clung to the idea of the two of them as long as she could, the denials and prevarications like a hedge of thorns to keep the world at bay. Anyone who loved would have done the same.

She turns back to the eyebrows again. To hell with it. They both have to come off. She takes her ladies' razor out of the drawer, briskly draws it across her brows. There, gone. A moment's hesitation, remembering. The line came to a steep peak above the eye, then faded away in a fine line like the makeup in Japanese theatre. It looked fierce, dramatic, nothing like the soft line of her natural eyebrows. She didn't want to look soft then, she wanted to look strong. For him.

Will she be able to draw her eyebrows as she used to? There's a black kohl pencil in here somewhere. She rifles through the bag, discarding the brown eyeliner. Not dark enough. The navy one is no good for eyebrows. She finds the black at last, producing it from the bag with the triumph of a diver bringing up a pearl.

121

She draws the steep, upward line, but somehow it's not right, makes her look like a man. That won't do. Too many people accused her of that at the time, as if she couldn't be a real woman because she hurt those children. Idiots. It's women you see cuffing heads in supermarkets, women who do the day to day clattering their kids. They call women the weaker sex as if that means they're powerless, but tell that to the kids and old people they knock about.

She frowns. This is proving harder than she thought. Closing her eyes, she tries to conjure up the exact image. How often has she seen that mugshot staring at her from some crap tabloid paper? inviting people to think that that was her, the whole of her. It never was all that she was, but because it was there in black and white they thought it was the truth.

Lord, she ought to know what the bloody thing looked like after forty years of living with it. Yes, this is the right angle ... slowly now. She needs a steady hand for the long horizontal line. No, that doesn't look right either. Damn. Slowly, painstakingly, she builds her face into the way she used to look, in those few short years after she met Brady, when she stopped being Myra and became The Girl, kiddo, M.

The eyebrows done, she smudges more grey shadow on to the lids, then adds some below the eye. The lilac doesn't work, too pale. However the light fell on her face that night it left black tracks beneath her lashes. Maybe it was Brady's black light, shedding darkness, not illumination.

Finally she stops. That should be it now.

But the reflection staring back at her looks strange, a wax devil mask somehow devoid of the demonic. The peaked eyebrows, the sullen mouth are hard, as the girl's were, but her nose is shorter now than it was before the nose job, narrower across the bridge. It doesn't have that bump in it. Without it her face looks ordinary, not particularly pretty but not malevolent either, not the face of a serial killer. But then people are so stupid, the way they think murderers should be ugly. That Ted Bundy was good looking, really pleasant. How else did he get the girls to trust him, that and playing the cripple? If she'd looked like she did in the mugshot, none of the kids would ever have got into the car. They'd have run off in fright.

Why doesn't she look as she did then? Is it just the hair? It's the wrong colour, no longer that platinum blonde that looked like it had been sloshed on by some backstreet hairdresser. Which it had, sort of. She and Moby used to dye it themselves, rinsing off the colour for each other with that silly rubber hose that was always coming off the taps.

No. It's not the same. She is not the same. She looks into the mirror for a long time but the face she seeks has gone, evaporated. She has vanquished the malign twin. But if the woman in the mugshot is no longer there, who is there in her place?

Her hand shakes a little as she reaches for the makeup remover. She smears it liberally over her face, watching the dissolution of her features. The wax is melting. She can never be that person again. There should be liberation

122

of a sort in this, relief, but somehow she is not at all sure she feels either free or happy.

Sophie sits on her bed and wonders what she's done, what *was* she thinking of? She can hardly believe she's had sex with a woman. She can see her face in the wardrobe mirror opposite, her cheeks pillarbox red. How pathetic she is, blushing when there's no-one around to see her.

Oh, but it was so good, M nuzzling her breasts, pinioning her arms against the side of the plunge pool, holding her there till she wanted to scream out with the cold. Then the heat of the steam room again, their skins popping like firecrackers with excitement. Was it just a fling, a wild aberration because of the surroundings, or will M want to sleep with her properly?

God, she can't think of this now. She's got to get to work. Swiftly she stands and heads for the shower. The hot water soothes her, unravels the knots in her neck. She's not bad looking, is she? Why wouldn't M ring? Sophie dries herself, eyes riveted to the mirror. Normally she just scrubs herself with the towel and throws her clothes on but she needs to take an inventory today. Long legs, slim waist. Her breasts aren't big but they are pretty. She touches her nipple, feeling it harden quickly against her fingers. She's still excited.

M will ring. She has to.

'You look all rosy cheeked this morning,' says Sue when she arrives at the school. 'Have you been out doing something disgustingly healthy or summat?'

'Or summat,' says Sophie, turning away to hang her coat up.

'Lucky you,' says Sue. 'Anyone I know?'

'Oh no, I didn't mean that.'

'Liar. You can't keep the grin off your face, love.'

'Nonsense,' says Sophie.

She follows Sue into the empty art room. The stacked pots of paint, sheaves of paper, pine desks, the paintings pinned round the walls are as they always are, but somehow it's as if she's seeing them more intensely. How blue the walls are, how caked with paint Sue's white coat is, like Utrillo's Paris walls, splodged with pink and yellow and grey. Les Buttes de Montmartre, Le Lapin Agile ... bunnies bouncing all over the place, their floppy ears signalling their readiness for the act of love, or at least the act of coitus.

'What's funny?' asks Sue but Sophie merely shakes her head in reply. Sue is busying herself with a cafetière. 'Real coffee,' she sighs. 'My special morning treat. I've brought in a little pannetone for us as well. It's no wonder I'm this shape, is it?'

'You're fine,' says Sophie, though she would hate to be so large. That short hairstyle of hers makes Sue look quite butch. The pupils' work is laid out on a table, a lot of chalk drawings of ancient looking people, probably the kids' parents, undoubtedly younger than Sophie herself. A bald eagle stares up at her from a pile of acrylic paintings. 'Have you got an American pupil?' she asks.

'No, that's our Eddie. He's a bit lazy, didn't think he'd manage forty shades of brown for the golden eagle.'

'He has a point.'

The harsh coffee catches in Sophie's throat but somehow soothes her nerves. Normally it makes her hyper so she must be wired already. What a night. She feels the way she used to after hockey at school, all that running in the fresh air, the exhilaration of scoring goals, her nerves alive and tingling as if they were about to pop through the surface of her skin. She must calm down.

An awful clanging sound like a prison bell marks the beginning of the next lesson. The children sidle in, all scuffing feet and shuffling bags. Sophie tries to do a mental rollcall of the names, but many of them she doesn't recognise. Last one in is Jason. For some reason she remembers him, though his hair is different this time, slicked into ridges with hair gel like the young offenders she sometimes works with. He looked quite cute last time, a woodland sprite with little knots of hair sticking up all over his head like burrs. Now he moves into the room with malevolent assurance, his self-contained bearing signifying his separation from the others.

'I'm looking forward to seeing what you've been doing since I last came,' she says. Sniggers rumble along the middle row, all large lads sprawling arrogantly, their feet sticking out below the desks. 'That weren't very long ago, were it, Miss?' says the largest, and, Sophie conjectures, the stupidest.

'For heaven's sake, lads,' says Sue. 'Give Miss Ferrers a break. Can she at least get in the door before you start with the sex jokes? Get your work out on the desk and let's have no more nonsense.'

More shuffling and a lot of sighing as their jotters are brought out. Sue rolls her eyes at Sophie. 'I don't envy you your job. You'll get nothing meaningful out of this lot.'

'Oh there's always one or two bright sparks in any group.'

'This lot want locking up, not art therapy.'

'There are rather a lot of them. I wasn't expecting so many.'

There's a loud bang as Jason thumps a wooden box down on his desk. Sue jumps, her soft shoulders wobbling as she turns on the boy. 'For crying out loud, Jason. What's the matter with you?'

'He's a nut job, Miss,' calls out one of the large lads.

'Sorry, Miss,' says Jason, his voice low and controlled. His face is expressionless, though Sophie wonders if she's caught a flicker of amusement—or perhaps triumph?—in the grey eyes. Instinctively she starts at the other end of the room from him. The pupils are working on art which represents their family relations and she's not sure she's up to the job of examining the inner workings of Jason's psyche yet. Many of them, though, are staring into space, lost.

'Come on,' says Sophie, stopping by one of the large lads. 'You've done nothing.'

'I don't know what to do, Miss.'

'Why not? You're a clever chap, I'm sure.'

There are sniggers from some of the other pupils. 'He's an idiot, Miss.'

125

'Nonsense. I'll be coming to inspect yours in a minute so don't get too cheeky.'

'You can inspect mine any time,' says one of them.

'What's your name?' asks Sophie.

'Darren, Miss. Darren Sowerby.'

She walks towards him, knowing she falls some way short of menace. 'Well, Darren Sowerby, that's quite enough from you.'

There is silence in the room, except for the hissing of a large overhead heater. Sophie moves between the desks, focused on the work in front of her. This is her life. Romance, love, sex, whatever it is with M is only peripheral, isn't it? She has reached Jason's desk and stops with a feeling of dread. The wooden box is lying closed in front of him. He watches her through observant eyes.

'May I?'

Inside are two dolls with round staring eyes outlined in black, red gashes for mouths. A shroud of clear white wax like congealed fat surrounds them, as if they're enveloped in the contents of their own bodies. Sophie's stomach turns. The dolls' bodies are scored with slashmarks which have also been outlined in black. Stuffing spills from the cuts, the dry grey material in its blankness and lack of life somehow more horrific than fake blood would have been.

Sophie tries not to shudder. 'Who are they?'

'My parents.' The face is closed, all expression locked up behind those cool eyes.

'But which parents? Your real ones or your adoptive ones?'

He shrugs. 'Take your pick.'

'I can see you might be angry at the parents who abandoned you, but why would you blame your adoptive parents?'

'They didn't tell me.'

'To them you were their son.'

'No.' He says the word flatly but she is sure there is anger behind them.

'They've always treated you well, haven't they? They gave you a home. They were kind to you. Many of the people in this room have real parents who didn't do as much for them.'

He raises an eyebrow. 'What would you know?'

She looks at the dolls. 'Why? Why make something so negative?'

'Is it?' He is openly smiling now.

She senses he is angry but is not sure how she can tell—his expression is unreadable, his eyes apparently mild. All she knows is that in his rage he is terrible and that she will not get an honest answer from him.

The dolls stare blankly up at her, their damaged bodies and gaping mouths declaring maleficent intent on his part. 'We must try and work out how you can turn your anger into something more positive,' she says.

Later, in the staffroom, she is puzzled by his inner fury. 'They treated him all right, didn't they, his foster parents?' she asks.

126

Sue nods. 'As far as we know.'

'I don't understand it. Why should he be so angry at finding out he's adopted.'

'He's not who he thought he was, I suppose.'

'He's fourteen. How the hell would he know *who* he was?' Yet as soon as she says the words Sophie wonders about them. After all, her own family has lived in the same house for hundreds of years. She comes from a historical line going back to William the Conqueror, has always been told stories about her ancestors. What must it feel like if you don't know who your own mother and father were?

Sue looks at her curiously. 'You seem really rattled by him.'

'I was scared of him. There's something very unnerving about the way he looks at you.'

'I heard a rather strange story about him from his primary school teacher. She said he'd tortured this puppy when he was a kid. He trapped it in a bag and then kept poking it to watch it jump. He thought it was hilarious.'

'Goodness. Did the puppy survive?'

'Yes, I think so. But Jason was damn lucky somebody caught him before he went too far.'

Sophie sips her peppermint tea, feeling rather shaken. Maybe the boy is a psychopath. She's rattled and yet she can't put her finger on why. He didn't say anything very revealing and certainly didn't display anything. Those dolls were really gruesome, though.

'There's some of them you just know are going to turn out wrong uns, don't you?' says Sue.

'I suppose so.' Yet Sophie is doubtful. That would mean character was pre-ordained, that there was no such thing as free will.

'You mark my words,' says one of the other teachers. 'That boy'll end up in prison for murder. He's violent underneath, he is, a proper little Peter Sutcliffe.'

That afternoon as Sophie drives home she keeps returning to the image of the slaughtered dolls. Would the boy be capable of doing such a thing in reality, of slashing his parents to ribbons, or are the dolls a substitute for action, a safety valve?

What a curious day it's been. Her first love affair with a woman and now a potential pyschopath in her class. Surely things don't have to turn out the way they say? Jason is gifted, perhaps a real artist. However cruel the impulse behind his work, he made it with a power far beyond that of his classmates. She must help him, must help him achieve his potential. After all, surely no-one is beyond redemption?

27 THE THINGS LOVERS ARE SUPPOSED TO DO

From: "Hal" <wolfman@hotmail.co.uk>
To: lynx1043@hotmail.co.uk
Subject: valentine's day
Date: 10th February 2003 12:05:17

Why does work always get in our way? I wanted to take you away somewhere romantic for Valentine's Day, shower you with rose petals, drink champagne in the morning, all the things that lovers are supposed to do.
From the BlackBerry of Hal Morton

From: La Barbara <lynx1043@hotmail.co.uk>

Ha, I had something funkier in mind. I wanted to drag you into my lynx's lair. The boy's with his dad this weekend and we'd have had the house to ourselves. You come into my home so rarely that that would have meant more to me than going to a fancy hotel - though I'm not ruling that out in the future, of course!
I wanted to do simple things, like cook you bacon and eggs, and maybe even eat them myself. (None of that yoghurt and fruit when I'm with you - I just cast care to the winds.)
From the BlackBerry of Pat Shields

From: "Hal" <wolfman@hotmail.co.uk>

God, Pat, you know I'd like nothing better. It's a joke, giving her the car on Valentine's Day.

From: La Barbara <lynx1043@hotmail.co.uk>

Some joke. Off a few kids and we'll give you a nice Ford Focus. Brilliant.

From: "Hal" <wolfman@hotmail.co.uk>

Be careful. Too much information. You are deleting everything immediately, aren't you?

From: La Barbara <lynx1043@hotmail.co.uk>

Sorry, love, course I am. I'm just shocked they're giving her a car, spending taxpayers' money on someone like her.

From: "Hal" <wolfman@hotmail.co.uk>

The taxpayers aren't shelling out that much. It's just one of the pool cars. Anyway, they're worried she'll get drawn into criminal stuff if she doesn't have the things her girlfriend has.

From: La Barbara <lynx1043@hotmail.co.uk>

Best thing for her. They could lock her up and throw away the key this time.

From: "Hal" <wolfman@hotmail.co.uk>

Darling, they just want her to keep her head down, stay out of trouble. That's why I have to work the day after as well, just to make sure she doesn't get involved in any accidents after all this time. She won't be used to the volume of modern traffic.

From: La Barbara <lynx1043@hotmail.co.uk>

Don't you worry about her. She's too keen on her own self-preservation to take any chances in the car.
She was always very capable whatever she turned her hand to in prison – she won a songwriting competition and she was known as green-fingered when she worked in the garden.
She got a bloody degree, for heaven's sake – though I'm not sure she'd have managed it if she hadn't had help from some Oxford graduate who came in as a tutor.

From: "Hal" <wolfman@hotmail.co.uk>

I hope you're right that she's capable. I wouldn't want to be picking her body parts up from the motorway.

From: La Barbara <lynx1043@hotmail.co.uk>

I would!

From: "Hal" <wolfman@hotmail.co.uk>

You don't mean that, my love.

From: La Barbara <lynx1043@hotmail.co.uk>

You're such a romantic about women, my Hal. You don't know the half of what we can do!

The smell of blood and sawdust filters into the hot street ... God, it takes him back. It must be at least ten years ago now, that butcher's shop on the Paisley Road West. Why does blood always smell stale, even when it's fresh?

He peeks into the shop. She's about ninth in the queue. He's going to be here all day. And there won't be a decent bit of meat to be had at the end of it. No nice steak pies with flaky pastry, no square slice sausages. These English butchers don't know a cow's arse from its elbow. It's all scrag end of mutton and bloody oxtail with them, not fit for a man to eat.

She looks nice in there, the girl, beside all the old biddies with headscarves over their rollers. Hair dazzling blonde, just like Marilyn Monroe. Pictures of *her* all over the paper today. Just because she died a year ago. Typical of the great British public—stop going to the lassie's films but then, as soon as she's dead, go swarming all over her memory like maggots. As if death made her more important. Not a bad actress, but och, a weak woman. They like that, of course. Not man enough to accept that women are strong.

Like Myra. Who'd have thought she'd take to the existential exercise so well? He didn't know what to expect the first time he brought it up. Some girls would have laughed, thinking he was kidding, some would have been frightened. Not M. They were up on the moors late at night, in a little hollow just off the road. He put his hand on her naked stomach, ran it down her flank. 'Do you have black light inside you, Myra? Would you follow its dark flame into death, into murder?'

Her eyes stared into his. 'I would do anything for you,' she said.

In the end she plunged into the black light even further than he did. The pupil became more depraved than the master—she grabbed the Reade girl's necklace and taunted her, *You won't need that where you're going.* She actually knew the girl, lived round the corner from her for years, but didn't let cheap sentimentality get in the way. Some kid, the way she asks after Pauline every time they meet Mrs Reade. Takes nerve to do that. She's like a cadaver herself, that woman, skin and bone, the flesh dropping off her. They'll be burying her too if she carries on the way she's going.

She's taken well to everything, Myra. Everything. The way she lies back in bed afterwards, her lids all hooded. She doesn't care what she looks like then, no fussing about whether her stomach's flat or her lipstick smudged. She is only body in those moments, beautiful.

They're slow in there today. He wants to put a bomb under them, hurry them up. A fly oozes its sticky way up a flank of beef hanging from a hook in the window. He knows the feel of that dead animal, the heft of it. That first day at Wallace's, Big Jim asked him to bring the meat in from the store. It was freezing in there and he started shivering under his butcher's coat. He only had on thin school flannels and the white shirt his stepma made him wear. Not what you'd call sharp attire. His breath plumed out in the grey air. He could hear the delivery boy's transistor outside the window. The Happy

Wanderer ... *Val-deri, val-dera Ha, ha, ha, ha, ha, ha Ha.* Ha fucking ha. Bloody silly song. A travesty of what it is to be in the mountains.

He swung the first carcass along the rail, its little legs stumpy and pathetic without their hooves. Arms round its cold torso, he lifted the hook off, staggering under the weight of the beast as he struggled into the shop and dropped it down in front of Big Jim. 'That'll do for now,' Jim said. He switched on his electric saw and gouged into the dead flesh, hacking it into different sections. The harsh sound whined inside his ears. The meat was a cheery colour, not that dark red you see when it's been sitting around for a while. One part was the animal's ribs, regular as piano keys. Jim cut into them with a knife, dividing them into neat joints ready for roasting. Expensive. The sort of thing you didn't get very often in the Sloans' house.

Big Jim's face was red with effort. When he got to the loin he took out a smaller knife, sharpening it before he started. Nice blade. Wouldn't have minded one of those. You'd be ready for anyone with a knife like that. The flesh fell away from the metal like melting ice cream. Jim cut it into small steaks, laying them out on a white enamel tray with a woman's care, his raw, chunky fingers incongruous against the dainty slices of meat.

It took a long time for the dead animal to be reduced to steaks and roasts, cut into chunks for stew, minced to oblivion. Big Jim's white coat was smeared with blood at the end of it. There was surprisingly little on the floor, though Jim made him sweep up the sawdust and scatter fresh. The meat started to ooze, though, once it was in the warm. After the effort of it, the whole long process, it was, almost disappointingly, only meat. Was this all there was of the huge beast that once lived and breathed in the fields? whose blood once pulsed and curdled through its veins, pumping it into life? What of its blood and bone and sinew? What of its spirit?

It shouldn't be like that. He's proved that now. He leans against the shop window, the glass warmed by the sun. Even the pavement under his feet feels warm. Shoppers are idling past, made weary by the heat. None of them know. The girl is in there, flirting with the butcher so he'll give her a good piece of meat, chatting with the women in the queue about the price of everything. None of them know.

A short word, *Death.* Not easily comprehended. Certainly not by these vermin scurrying about their business in the streets of Gorton. Let them have their little wakes, their Co-operative funerals. Let them tend graves with worm-ridden bodies beneath them, stick their plastic flowers in the rotten ground. That is not Death. Pauline Reade may have wanted to hang on to her paltry little life, but she should have been grateful for the death they gave her. Up on the moors with a curlew calling out and the pure wind battering against her bones.

She disappointed him when she screamed and cried. People are such cowards. Crawling, maggoty little cowards. Lucky for him that Myra was there. She told the girl to shut up or they'd kill her. That was funny. They laughed about it afterwards. All that fuss over a simple physical activity. It was pretty sexy when Myra had a go with her. The Reade girl was a virgin, of course,

131

hanging on to her precious maidenhead like a Warsaw Jew hanging on to his shekels. Why on earth should her poxy pudenda be of value, when silly tarts are opening their legs and dropping sprogs all the time?

At least she lost it in style, in open country, the dark moors turning darker as the light faded. Make a wish, girl. It'll be your last. She was dry inside and he really had to force himself into her. She was crying, her nose running. Ugly, though she was a pretty girl. Not interesting, not the sort to try to talk for her life, though she fought so hard in the end he thought he'd have to get Myra to help subdue her. But what an idiot in the first place, grubbing about on the ground looking for Myra's so-called glove. He despised her really.

He'd meant to strangle her but she was too strong and he had to use the knife. Sharper than he thought. Whoosh—right across her neck. Blood gushing out from those big arteries like liquid fireworks. Her head nearly came off with it.

The wine they drank afterwards buzzed in the blood. To sit on the black rocks, surrounded by eternity, and know that you've crossed over to the other side, that you have been bold enough and strong enough to seize the mystery of life, that you are not like ordinary men ...

And she, Myra, her face alive with power, in that moment he knew they would love each other for ever, would be bound together for ever. She would keep faith with him no matter what happened, she would always be his woman. The blood of the girl was their bond. He was panting from his efforts and she touched his hand, steadied him as she poured the wine. 'It's like the mystery of the Consecration in the Mass, only better,' she said. He didn't get mad at the reference to religion. Somehow it felt right. In amongst the blood and the muck, they had made something sacred.

The real mystery was that she had survived it, embraced it even. Not many women would lure another woman for their lover, watch as he fucked her. Not many would just laugh and run back when the big spray of blood went up like a breaker at the shore. Not many would help him bury her, then clean out the car afterwards. No, she is not like ordinary women.

'Bugger. His prices are getting ridiculous.' She's fumbling about in her purse, checking her change. He can see a thin moustache of sweat along her top lip. It's bloody hot. Maybe they'll go up to the moors after tea, cool off up there.

'What did you get?'

'Lamb chops. I hope Mam's home tonight. It's too hot for me to be cooking.'

'She ought to be. We pay her enough.'

He hopes it will rain tonight, cool, clean rain purging her flesh. Washing down the topsoil below which she lies. Cooling him down. It's too soon to do another, but oh, he wants to ...

132

Will feels sick when he thinks about last night—sick with pleasure, sick with joy, sick with desire. He wants her in his bed every night, all night ...

Shit! He's nicked himself shaving. He needs to stop mooning over her but she's all he can think of—naked, in bed with him, her muscled brown arm thrown lightly over his chest. Her sitting astride him, brushing his stomach with the moistness inside her. He dabs at his cheek with a piece of toilet paper. Last night was incredible. She'd blown hot and cold for so long he could hardly believe she was there, stroking his skin with her workmanlike little hands, nuzzling into him, her honey coloured hair falling over him as her tongue sought him out.

'She's a fucking little pricktease cunt,' Jem, his mate, had said in the pub. 'Can't you see she's stringing you along?'

'No, she's not,' he said, his stomach contorting at the thought that Jem might be right.

Now he dresses with scrupulous care. Adidas polo shirt, the Levi straight-legs that cost him his last month's bonus. He douses himself with the aftershave his Mum gave him for Christmas. Davidoff's Cool Water—it smells really good, not one of those cheap ones. He's sure she didn't pick it. It was probably that pal of hers, Jude. She's pretty clued up, even if she is always making eyes at Dad. Mum wouldn't have a clue about aftershaves herself.

When he arrives at the pub the decibel levels are of brain damage proportions. He can almost see the sound vibrations being given off. Inside, the atmosphere is smoky and he can't make out Kezza at all at first, then he realises she's over at the jukebox, holding a half of lager in her hand and leaning in confidentially to talk to someone. Isn't that Yardley, the guy who's always chatting her up? the one who made a pass at her at Christmas? What's she playing at? She's whispering something in his ear, standing on tiptoe because he's so tall. Her mini-skirt is riding up at the back, revealing a very skimpy thong.

He doesn't want other people to see her body. It's just for him.

Trying to look casual he strolls over to her and slips his arm round her waist. 'All right, Kez?'

She stiffens, then turns her back to him and examines the jukebox playlist. 'How about *All the Things She Said*?' she says to Yardley. The prick stands there looking down at her like a big dozy elephant. 'Yeah,' he nods, lumbering to put the money in the machine as she gazes meaningfully up at him. How can she bear to flirt with him like this? His tongue is practically hanging out of his big red face. Her glance flicks over Will as if she's dismissing him. What's she playing at? Did last night mean nothing to her? He thought it was finally the beginning of something, but now he has to face the fact that Jem might be right.

The music comes thumping on.

All the things she said, All the things she said
Running through my head, Running through my head,

133

Running through my head.

She's dancing now, pulling her T-shirt down at the front so that that big fucker can see right down her bra. He's a bloody country bumpkin. Why is she bothering with him? Calling him Jim and making those soppy eyes at him. She's spinning round now, holding the mini-skirt out like a little girl at a party. Singing right at the bastard,

> *Wanna fly to a place where it's just you and me*
> *Nobody else so we can be free.*

Will's guts are scrunched up like a used elastic band. He wants to kill Yardley. Jem hands him his pint and he takes a long drink. The money he spent on taking her out to dinner, the fancy hotel, he's going to be broke for weeks now. Was that all she was after? He tries to ignore her but the insistent beat of the song worms its way into his head. When he sees Yardley put his big hams of hands on Kezza's bum, that's it. He can't contain himself any longer.

'You fucker. Get your hands off her.'

He shoves Yardley but the other man barely rocks on his heels. Kezza nips smartly out of the way, tucking herself in behind the jukebox. Will just has time to register her amused eyes when he feels an explosion in his stomach. Yardley's punch has bloody well displaced his intestines.

Jem puts his pint down and jumps joyfully on to Yardley's back, but his thumps make little impact. Soon half the squaddies in the pub are pitching in. Glasses crash to the ground; a table collapses underneath Yardley, leaving a huge splinter of wood in his backside. Will slips on spilled beer and skids along the floor.

He lands right at the foot of the jukebox, looking up at Kezza. She smiles at him. 'Let's get out of here, Will,' she says. He looks at her in astonishment. 'What the hell are you playing at, Kezza?'

She shrugs. 'Just wanted to see if you'd be jealous.'

He tries to keep his face grim but he feels inordinately pleased. 'Well, now you know.'

She pouts at him. 'Don't sulk, Will.' She slides out from behind the machine, her skirt riding even higher up her thighs. 'Get me out of here.'

She puts her hand out to him and heads for the door.

'Hey man,' says Jem. 'Where the fuck are you going? I'm here defending you.'

'Give him a good kicking for me,' says Will, sidestepping as one of Yardley's friends lunges at him.

He and Kezza pick their way through the mayhem and run out the door. Kezza's body is rippling with laughter. Will shakes his head. 'You're a little bitch.'

'Course I am. That's why you love me, innit it, Will? You wouldn't like it if I was one of your nice posh birds, would ya?'

He doesn't know what to make of her. No girl he's ever met would admit to being a bitch. It makes her *more* attractive. She's so petite, so dainty the way she's made, but there's a core of steel inside her. He senses he's out of

134

his depth, but it's not a bad feeling. It's a feeling of freedom. Who needs a boring, safe girl like the ones he grew up with? He doesn't want to marry his mum. Kezza's fiery, feisty, foxy. He looks at her and instantly feels himself getting hard. She's gorgeous. She's his. Who knows where this will take him?

'Who *designs* these cards?' says Jude, holding up a cyanotic blue teddy with the words *I Wuv You* spelled out in flowers above its head.

'I know. Depressing, isn't it? I always look for the most old-fashioned one I can find,' says Beth, flipping through the serried ranks of roses and hearts.

'Yes, but if you go for those you have to put up with the god-awful verses,' says Jude, holding a card at arm's length as she declaims:

I saw you and I knew you
Though we had never met.
The joy of our encounter
Lingers with me yet.

'Pathetic, isn't it?'

'I've read worse,' says Beth. Could Jude need glasses? The ever-youthful Jude of the personal trainer, with her toned body and trendy haircuts and designer clothes? Beth sighs. They're none of them getting any younger. 'Isn't being fifty hell?' she says.

'What brought that on?' asks Jude, with her characteristic blend of curiosity and amusement. No wonder the crows' feet at the corner of her eyes have got so entrenched—she's always laughing at something.

'Oh, I don't know,' says Beth. 'Charles is getting a bit deaf and I've started to get varicose veins. Not exactly love's young dream, are we?'

'Darling, I think it's splendid the way you two have stayed together. I've never managed it.'

'Well, why would you want to? You lead far too exciting a life to settle for cosy, married bliss.'

'Bethykins, do I detect the faintest whisper of disillusion?'

'No, of course not. I think I'll have this one.' She brandishes two rather pretty bluebirds bearing a heart in their beaks.

'But what does the verse say, Bethykins? What does the verse say?'

'It's private.'

'Stop smirking. You're just chicken.'

'Some things are between a man and a woman,' says Beth.

Jude snorts. 'I know very well what's between a man and a woman,' she says. 'Darling, you're the only woman our age I know who still blushes. I know what we'll do. We'll go and buy a Valentine's Day present for Charles. Debenham's have the most divine lingerie sale.'

Beth smiles. 'Oh no, I've been in lingerie departments with you before. You know what will happen, don't you? You'll get something seductive and gorgeous and all I'll see is white cotton.'

'White cotton is the new sexy. Don't you read your Marie Claire, darling? Now pay for that piece of sentimental tosh and let's get going.'

She leads the way out of the shop in a haze of Chloe perfume and jangling gold bracelets. Beth follows in her slipstream, grateful for Jude's perennial ability to make crowds part, keeping her head down as people

136

inevitably turn, wondering which celebrity they have just let through. In Debenham's Jude heads straight for the lingerie department. If Beth were on her own she'd have to check the store guide to see where it is.

'Now what would Charles like? Is he a black lace man?' asks Jude, holding up the scantiest thong. 'Or perhaps he's more red satin?' She yanks out a red satin camisole trimmed with black lace. 'Maybe he's the pervy type who likes navy gym knickers?' She pretends to search through the mound of lace and frills and frippery. 'Sorry. All out of gym knickers. He'll have to do without his fix of schoolgirl chic.'

'I'll tell him that's what you think of him.'

Jude winks. 'Don't do that, sweetie. Can't have the professor standing me in the corner tonight.' The fine gold bracelets shimmer down her wrist as she drops the camisole. 'Too many people here today. Do they think it's the weekend or something? I've just had the most marvellous idea. We'll go and get away from it all in that new bar on the other side of the town hall. They do the best mojitos.'

Instinctively Beth looks at her watch. 'Don't fret, my love,' says Jude. 'The sun is most indubitably over the yardarm.'

'It's only four o'clock.'

Jude tosses aside the cream silk camiknickers she was examining. 'This stuff's all way too large or way too small. Why don't they ever have anything for the middle-sized people?'

'Yes, we should protest, form the Middle-Sized People's Revolutionary Army.'

'Speaking of armies, how is that divine boy of yours? If I weren't one of his godparents I swear I'd gobble him up for my next toyboy.'

'Haven't you got someone on the go just now?' asks Beth.

'Well, yes, but no harm in lining up the next contender.'

They walk across the town square, picking their way through pockets of puddle. 'How do people up here get their skins that awful porridgey colour? Do you think there's a special Northern makeup?'

Beth huddles into her good winter coat. 'You've got soft, girl. Stayed down south too long. That's the way skin's *supposed* to look in winter, not like you and your sunbed tan.'

'Nonsense. I got this in Mauritius.'

Beth laughs. She feels herself today, as only old friends make you feel. 'You poser.'

'Absolutely,' says Jude. 'God bless the Mauritius Beauty Spa in Hampstead,' though they both know she really did get her tan abroad. 'Here it is. They've spent a fortune on it inside.'

The bar has a tropical theme, with fake palm trees and a fountain in the middle of the room, its jets of water suffused with pink and green and turquoise light. A green parrot with a red beak squawks by the side of the bar. 'Mojitos coming up,' says Jude. 'You grab us a table.'

She brings over a jug with crushed mint leaves floating on top of the tea coloured liquid. 'Kitsch heaven, don't you think?' The music, which Beth

137

recognises as one of Charles's records by a band of old Cuban men, is a little too loud for her taste, the lights too lurid, but she tries to follow Jude's lead and feel amused by it. The drink, its aromatic sweetness cut by the sour kick of lime, is delicious, though surely they're not intending to drink a whole jug of it?

'Don't worry,' says Jude. 'We won't go back sozzled to Charles. It's actually only two drinks each.'

'I expect he'll have opened something nice himself by now,' says Beth. 'He always does when he's cooking.'

'You mean it's not just barbecue? That's what most of the men I know mean by cooking.'

'Oh no, Charles's a proper cook. None of that Jamie Oliver bish bosh stuff for him. He does quite serious recipes from French cookbooks.'

'Oh goodie. I wish I could be less greedy. I'd have to spend far less time in the bloody gym.'

'I suppose I should go but I've never had the time till now.'

'The curse of the wife and mother, darling. I'm an expert on it.'

'How can you be? You've never had kids.'

'So what? I've written at least three articles a year on it for the last decade. Making time for yourself. Work life balance. The guilt of being a mother. Believe me, I know all about it.'

Maybe it's just the cocktail, but Beth feels more relaxed than she has for a long time. She always has fun with Jude. Like this ridiculous place they're in—she'd never have come on her own. Jude doesn't even live here but she's somehow managed to find out about it. Probably because she's a journalist. As the alcohol begins to penetrate her bloodstream, Beth finds herself even beginning to approve of the parrot, a species she usually abhors since a neighbour of hers died from psittacosis.

'This place reminds me of a place I was in in Buenos Aires once,' says Jude. 'It had all these amazing fairy lights and tinsel decorations, as if it was Christmas, but this was in July and there was no-one there but me. I knew it would be a clipjoint but I just had to eat there. Do you know, they charged me twenty dollars for a plate of pasta.'

'I hope it was good pasta,' says Beth.

'Of course it wasn't. It was foul. Oh, the trials of the international reporter.'

'Wouldn't you like to work abroad again?' asks Beth, sloshing sticky liquid on the table as she pours their second mojito.

'I'm thinking of something much more exciting than just travel journalism, actually. I'd have to get leave of absence from the paper. A TV producer I know read some stuff I did years ago on drug dealers—remember I got shortlisted for that award? He wants me to go to Iraq if this war comes down.'

'War? Surely it won't? It wouldn't be legal.'

'Oh my Bethling. You know that. I know that. But this government doesn't give a toss.'

138

'I think I've drunk this too quickly. They're awfully strong, aren't they?'

'No, darling. They're quite mild. You've lost your capacity for strong drink since university days. All that suburban, *Shall we open a half bottle?* It isn't good for you.'

'We never open half bottles,' says Beth.

'Ah, but do you drink the whole bottle in a night?'

'We do now.' Beth laughs. 'We did sometimes put a stopper in when Will was little. It seemed sort of irresponsible somehow to drink more than a glass.'

'Was that to go with your cold fish fingers?' teases Jude. 'That's the defining skill of motherhood, the thing that marks out the girls from the women—motherhood means you can eat congealed beans as you clear your child's plate.' She twirls her cocktail stirrer, a grinning little monkey climbing a plastic palm tree. 'Are you worried about Will?'

The little monkey is cute, adorable. Beth feels as if he has a personality, cheeky, irrepressible. If he were real he'd scamper away as soon as you came near him. 'Worried? Should I be?'

Jude stares into her glass, swirls the mint leaves round with the stick. 'Oh, probably not.'

'That sounds ominous.'

'Does it? Not meant to be.' But Jude still hasn't looked at her, seems intent on making the little monkey dizzy by continually stirring her drink.

'Surely they wouldn't send someone as young as him? As inexperienced, for God's sake.'

'Oh Beth, they're going to need all the able-bodied young idiots they can get. It isn't terribly fashionable these days to be a soldier, you know.'

'It's not idiotic to want to fight for your country, you know.'

Jude closes one tanned hand over Beth's white one, her cluster of gold rings making Beth's plain wedding band and engagement ring look cheap. They were. Charles didn't have a permanent positon then and it seemed silly to pay a lot of money for a big ring when they needed it for carpets and wallpaper.

'Of course Will's not an idiot. You know I love him to bits. But they'll need cannon fodder. Do you really think it's all going to be sorted out if they get rid of Saddam? You know what they say about marrying your mistress, that it immediately creates a job vacancy? Well, it's the same with tyrants. Once you knock one down every local bully boy in the country will be trying to take his place. This war hasn't even kicked off yet and it's obvious it's going to be the next Belfast.'

Beth pulls her hand away. 'How would you know? All you write about is the next new restaurant or where to go for Ayurvedic sodding massage. I can't imagine why anyone would want to send you to Iraq.'

'Because they remember what I'm capable of, even if my best friends don't,' says Jude. 'I don't always have to do the same old stuff, you know.'

139

The record of the four old men comes to an end, leaving silence. Beth wants to cry. Jude looks at her for a long minute. 'Let's go and see what that gorgeous husband of yours has made us to eat,' she says. She stands up. 'It'll be all right,' she says, though they both know it won't.

M never cries. Never. Not even when Moby's baby died, Angela Dawn. She had a tear in her eye maybe, but that was all. She didn't cry when they charged her or when they sent her down or even when they took her lover away. That day, when she saw him for the last time, she thought her heart would break, but she didn't flinch, didn't shed a tear. Her eyes were dry as she watched him led away by the guards. He was elegant in the grey suit that was made for him, not bought off the peg. Not an ugly uniform like they were wearing. His hair was combed back into a quiff, his fingers slender. He looked like a finer species altogether than the blunt, brute guards.

So why is she blubbering now? She can't believe it, that they've given her a car. Why would they? They told her she was to have a quiet life, not to draw attention to herself. Like a nun except not in a convent, she thought. Why did they change their minds? Why give her this, this thing of exquisite beauty. It's more than a car. It's her freedom, a sign that she is no longer a prisoner, that she is in the world again.

They know she's not the person she was. She's done her time, washed the sin away. They must trust her. It's one in the eye for the bloody parents, those greedy bastards, feeding off other people's pity. Why can't they let it go? It's not healthy to be as obsessed as they are. That Joan, Pauline's Mum, she wasn't right in the head anyway. Ended up in the loony bin later. They used to laugh, walking past her, knowing what they'd done, knowing Pauline was never coming back. 'Morning, Mrs Reade,' M would say. 'Any news yet?' Ian thought it was a scream. 'You're cool as a cucumber, kiddo, aren't you?' She felt good, as though ... well, maybe he admired her.

She never expected the car. The governor told her she had no chance of any luxuries like that. Yet here it is, gleaming in front of her in a halo of polish and petrol. It's dark blue, a solid, handsome colour, not too ostentatious but still vibrant. It has the Ford logo on the front and the wheels have sporty struts splayed out like that Da Vinci man with all the legs and arms. Get the wheels going, whirl him round, faster and faster as the car picks up speed.

The garage man watches her curiously. He couldn't know who she is, surely? 'It's only a car, lass,' he says. He holds the car keys out to her. 'You'd best see if you like her. Just hold on and I'll get your brother. He's having a coffee in the office.'

The man who comes towards her a minute or two later is tall and slim, unsmiling. He's wearing a dark suit and a white shirt, open at the neck. Although the clothing is formal, there's a casualness about the cut that makes him look informal. Is it the trousers? are they baggier than the trousers men used to wear? the jacket more flowing? Neddy often wore his shirts open too, felt constricted in a tie. She had a picture of him in her cell for years, taken after one of their court appearances. He was in the grey suit, cigarette smoke curling round his face, ever so handsome. They don't know what cool is nowadays. Nothing fazed him. Not even when they came to arrest him. He stood up, naked from the waist down, didn't give a damn.

'Well, Maria. Do you like it?' says the man. He holds the car door open for her. As she stoops to get in she feels a light touch on her back. It's the strangest sensation, as though moth's wings had brushed against her, yet it leaves her skin hot. The man gets into the passenger seat. His aftershave smells like woodland paths, seems to fill the car. In this small space he feels awfully close to her and she wonders is her face all red.

'Can you remember how to do this?' he asks.

'Yes, of course,' she says, but the noise of the car starting up frightens her.

'Clutch in, into first gear.'

'Right.' But she takes her foot off the clutch too quickly and the car stalls. A worm of sweat slithers down her neck.

'Take it easy. We have plenty of time.'

This time she gets it right, except that the car jerks forward. Time to pull herself together. Getting all hot and bothered because a man's sitting next to you, it's ridiculous. That's what comes of living among women for most of your life. No sooner cooped up in a car with a man than you stop breathing and start palpitating.

Now she concentrates on the driving, easing the car through the gears till she feels confident again. She was always good at this. As the car picks up speed, she relaxes, enjoying the feeling of being in command of the road. This is liberation. They bowl through the town centre, M negotiating the lunchtime traffic. No problem there.

'Do you know the industrial estate on the way up to the Manchester road? I'd like you to pull in there, please.'

She drives in silence, refusing to give the man beside her any recognition, though she has been up to the estate before, with the driving instructor, along with half the learner drivers of the town. It's a quiet place for them to practise three point turns and emergency stops. She pulls in just past the paper products factory at the end, toilet paper probably. Why don't they just say so?

'You're a good driver,' he says, unclicking his seatbelt.

'Thanks.'

'You understand, this car is a privilege. They'll take it away if there's any funny business whatever.'

'What do you mean, funny business? I've done my time. I wouldn't do anything to hurt anyone now. They know that.'

He gives a slight smile. 'I'm talking about speeding, drink driving, stuff like that.'

'Oh.'

'The car documents are in the glove compartment.'

'What made them give me the car?'

'I don't know. They must trust you.' He really has a very attractive face, weathered, sure of himself. He's not a cissy like some of the younger men you see, with their hair gelled and their man-handbags. She's got to stop looking at him. 'Is your car somewhere near here?' she asks.

'Just at the paper factory.'

'Oh, in among the bog rolls.'

'Very posh headed paper, actually.' He has a lovely smile, definitely got a sense of humour.

'I'll drive you back in,' she says.

'Don't worry, it's just a step.' He gets out of the car, then walks round to her side. The car has one of those electronic windows. Brilliant. He leans in and again she catches that scent of woods, moss, fern. It makes him seem earthy, sexy. 'Enjoy the car,' he says, looking straight at her as if he knows what she's thinking. Bastard.

She turns the car and toots the horn as she passes him walking back. Then she puts her foot down. That'll show him. She looks back in the mirror and sees he's looking amused. God, she'd like to meet him again. She frowns. Where on earth did that come from? Sophie's lovely. Why would she need someone else?

It's too nice a day to go home and park this car. She heads out of the town and up towards the M62, up through the winding lanes towards the big roundabout. She'll just go up there and come straight back round, far too soon to be thinking of motorway driving in a new car. But as she waits at the junction, a massive articulated lorry undulates its way round to the exit. It's irresistible—no-one will dare mess with that. She follows it on to the roundabout and eases on to the motorway in its wake. It's scary at first—she can hardly believe she's driving along at such speed, in so many lanes of traffic. At first she hugs the side of the road, staying in the slow lane, but after a while she becomes impatient and signals to move out. She's a little nervous but the car behind moves in and she has a free run into the fast lane.

The sky is blue and she's surrounded on either side by moorland. It stretches way off in the distance on both sides of the road. The car moves like a dream, a dream in which there is only her in the world, only her gliding along with the ease of a spirit, no body, no barriers, no obstacles. She is happy.

It seems no time at all before she reaches the turn-off for Saddleworth. Easing into the slow lane again she turns to the left. This is not the way she used to approach it—she always came here from the opposite direction, from Manchester. That was before they built the motorway. At the top of a rise she stops the car and gets out. Sheep are calling all around though she can't see them. Down below, the clustered houses of a little town are spread out in the valley, Oldham maybe? Her sense of geography is uncertain after all these years. The wind whips at the back of her neck and she hurries back inside. She's never been one to freeze.

It's bleak up here, even though it's a sunny day. The little villages have funny names, like Delph and Diggle. Eventually she sees a signpost for Ashton-under-Lyne and takes that road. Once she gets to the market she'll know which way to go. The road passes through prosperous-looking villages

143

where the houses gleam with the weekend efforts of suburban couples; mean villages where the people are living hugger-mugger on top of each other, with dustbins and bits of rusting bicycles in the gardens. Women in saris meander slowly across the streets, their hips swaying with a lazy sensuality that looks decidedly foreign in Lancashire.

In Ashton she parks in the municipal car park and walks through to the market, past the Hippodrome Theatre and the Stage Bar with its dark green tiles and Victorian lamps. There's a modern shopping precinct on the way so she dawdles, looking at the shops, though there's nothing very interesting here—it's not as nice as the arcade at home.

She reaches the market at last but it looks awfully small now, contained in a little square. The stalls sell cheap knitwear, CDs, jewellery, household goods. Ignoring the stallholders' banter, she just wanders round. There seem to be a lot of Asians here. There never used to be any. They were all white stallholders that day, the day they took the little boy, John Kilbride. He was a cheeky looking kid, hanging about waiting to earn a few pennies by running errands. They offered him a lift, told him there was a whole sixpence for him if he came with them because they had some fertiliser bags to move. 'All right, missus,' he said. 'But I need to get home for me tea.'

'Don't worry about that,' she said. 'We'll see you right.'

The road down the side of the market is one way. They'd have to go in a different direction if they picked him up now. She's cold, should buy a pair of gloves. Other than that there's nothing for her here, so she heads back to the car park. That'll warm her up. He was a funny little lad, chatting away to them as they drove from the market. 'That hair your own colour, missus? cos I bet you dye it, don't you? Don't you want to perm it 'n' all? I can get Toni stuff for half price. I'm good mates wi' Bert, y'know? him that's got the stall next to the stockings?'

He was the first *child* they ... Pauline didn't count, she was sixteen, just about grown up.

Those diamond mesh stockings were great. Ashton was the only place you could get them for that price. The lad got scared, in the end, once they drove away from the town. She walks briskly to keep the cold out. It's not so sunny over here and she doesn't feel like hanging around. She needs to get up to the moors now.

Once she leaves Ashton she knows she's on the right road. There's a bit more traffic about but little has changed. Back through Oldham and its red-brick back to backs, so like her granny's house in Bannock Street. The kids playing in the street here have those funny little topknots and white baggy trousers, not like the skint knees and holey jumpers of her day. She'll always have a soft spot for those houses. They may not have looked like much but there was a warmth to be had from living on top of one another. In one of those houses she first made love to Brady.

She's driving almost on automatic pilot now, even though she just picked up the car today. How quickly you get used to things. Her favourite village was always Greenfield, with its stone cottages and the cricket club and

144

the big houses with the moors shooting up behind them. She nearly stops for a drink in the Railway Hotel there, but remembers what that bloke said about drink driving. So many petty rules these days. Besides, the sky is grey and it looks like rain, so she presses on.

The road begins to climb outside the village. The light is really murky now and she puts the headlights on, though it's not that late. As she emerges into open country the rain comes on in earnest, drizzling great sheets of moisture that darken the sky and make the ground slippery. A trail of abandoned Christmas trees rots by the side of the road. Her hands feel clammy on the wheel. Why is she here? Has she no will power? Could she not stay away? She wanted to remember the good parts, the picnics out in the open, where the air smelt fresh and good. Damn this sodding rain.

A few miles out of the village the road curves and the moors open up around her. Down in the valley below she can see Dove Stone Reservoir, with a proper car park now, though there don't seem to be any cars there today. The hillside next to it is littered with scree, as if a giant hand has ripped the earth open and left only scrubby grass growing over the wounds.

On she presses, hoping to find somewhere to park by the side of the road. There's a patch of open ground about a mile on and she leaves the car there, its shiny blue exterior already grimy and pockmarked with mud. Luckily she has a scarf, which she ties under her chin. Bugger, she must look like the bloody Queen Mum.

Nothing for it. She starts back towards the flat black rocks where they used to stand and look down on the reservoir. There's no-one else around but the moors are noisy with birds calling and the crying of sheep. It's bleak, bleak. She's soaking already, but she must get to the rocks. Some sheep loom up through the drizzle, scaring her. They're grubby, almost black with muck. Peat bogs break out on the earth like pustules on skin.

Her shoes are not suitable for this weather. Already she can feel water seeping in. A lapwing takes flight ahead of her, whirling and diving in a spectacular display of aeronautics. It zigzags across the road, then hovers, quivering, as if to show off its athletic skills. Idiotic bird. It's far too misty for any female to see him. The females will all be tucked up somewhere nice and warm in this weather.

The rocks jut up above the road, but there's fencing all along and no way for her to climb up there, so she stands across the other side and looks up at them, quailing at their blunt timelessness.

She shivers in the rain. This place has death embedded in it. A decapitated crow lies on the road, still bleeding, its mangled little head a few feet away. Stagnant pools of water ooze from the bog like drops of blood from Christ's crown of thorns. A dead rabbit is sunk perfectly into the ground as if it has always been there. As she has, always. She turns to go, but she knows she will never be free of this place, never.

145

A nicotine miasma hangs over the hall. The noise is deafening, as if an underground train is constantly rumbling away underneath the building. As they make their way to their seats the first fighters are already in their corners. He's bought tickets not too far from the front. Expensive, but it'll be worth it to impress David.

'These are welterweights, I think,' he says, handing David a bottle of beer.

'Aye. They always have the heavyweights on last.'

'Typical. You get far more skill and speed at the lower weights but we worship these great big lumbering clodhoppers.'

'Eh oop, you couldn't call Cassius Clay a clodhopper.'

'I don't think we'll see anyone of quite his calibre at a Gorton blood tub.'

David sniggers at the dryness of his tone. 'You're right there, mate.'

The bell clangs for the start of the fight and a temporary silence settles over the crowd, a mark of respect that will be over before the first punch is thrown. The fighters dance on their toes, shuffle, throw phantom punches as a storm of support swells and breaks over them.

They are quite contrasting figures. The one in red satin shorts is stocky and powerfully built, with doughy shoulders and sturdy peasant's legs, firmly planted on the ground. Brady is more interested in the one in black. He's taller and slender, with wide shoulders and a narrow waist. Under the clamour of the lights his skin looks pale as phosphoresence in dark water; he darts and turns with mercurial grace. It is he who lands the first punch, a swift jab that leaves a dull red mark on his opponent's cheekbone.

'He's fast. D'you know him?'

David nods. 'That's Eddie Atwood, from over by Froxmer Street, I think. He's not lived here long. Happen he's fast but I don't think he'll last the course. The other guy's Ted Worple. He's bloody strong. He humps stuff at the locomotive factory.'

'He's a donkey.'

As the round wears on, a film of perspiration seeps over Atwood's translucent shoulders. His dark hair flops forward over his eyes and he flicks it back impatiently, eager to crowd the other fighter. The muscles on his back shiver when he moves, as if his skin is wrought too finely to contain them. He is another order of creature altogether from his plodding opponent—ethereal, mysterious, fashioned from some superior and beautiful material that can only be appreciated by those who are themselves of a higher order.

Atwood slumps in his corner at the end of the round. His second sloshes water all over him, leaving glassy droplets glistening all over his chest. God, he is beautiful, such slender lines, such dark eyes. If he were fighting naked, naked under the lights … Brady wants to compare him to a Greek sculpture. He could talk about how the Greeks valued love between men above all other kinds, but David might take it wrongly. It's imperative to take

146

things carefully with him. He'd look good up there. His legs are a bit shorter than the Atwood lad's but he's slim-hipped and broad shouldered and he has the same pale skin, the same dark eyes. He can fight a bit too, or so they say. What he'd be like if it came to the crunch is still to be revealed. He's not exactly a Marquess of Queensbury fighter, always got a blade somewhere about his person. That suggests one of two things, that he's determined to win and doesn't care how he does it. Or that he's a coward. Neither of these is a bad thing in a disciple.

The heavier lad lunges out for the second round with a determined look on his face, as if sheer willpower can enable him to trap his will o' the wisp opponent. Atwood weaves in and out and around him, luring him forward and then dancing away from him, wrong-footing him and then tormenting him with flickering jabs. It must be like being in Hell, with the lights full on your humiliation and the baying crowd in the darkness beyond. Taunting you. Making you feel stupid.

'I wish I'd put a bet on this boy,' Brady says to David.

'Nah. He won't last the pace. You'll see.'

Will David last the pace? Or will that rough little wife of his snooker things? She's determined to domesticate him, tame him. Huh, the pram in the hall is the enemy of creation. Damn it, who was it said that? Was it George Bernard Shaw? Not that Maureen Hindley would know or care. Ignorant wee tart. She'll be the slave of her own biology, that one. Let her drop as many sprogs as she wants. Other people have more important things to do.

Thank God M isn't like that. She never comes whining around saying she wants children. It's a myth that all women have maternal instincts. Of course, the run of the mill ones do. If you have no other aims in life what else is there? But not women like M. She's a warrior, a Boadicea. She could be up there in that ring taking on all comers.

It's the end of the second round now and Atwood is looking exhausted. Maybe Davieboy is right. Maybe he won't last the pace. In the third round he comes out on his toes but you can see he's tiring now. There can't be much in it. He still looks fast beside the carthorse Worple but there's less of a contrast now. Now the peasant boy's punches start connecting. That's the difference a fraction of a second can make. Precision, precision is the thing.

As the round wears on Atwood's skin starts to take on a blue, bruised look. He staggers a little under the weight of the other man's punches. He's weaving still but the way a drunk man weaves over the road, not the slick way he was before. Suddenly Worple lands a colossal punch and a fine mist of blood sprays up over them, like the spray when you stand at the front of a Clyde steamer. 'Oh my God,' says David, scrambling back out of the road. Brady stays where he is. He can taste the other man's blood and sweat on his mouth.

Atwood's milky skin is flecked with red, his face daubed with purple bruising. There's something very beautiful about the defilement of such a pristine surface, the way a plum looks beautiful with the verdigris of mould creeping over it. He sways on his feet, looking confused, then crashes to the

147

floor, a dead weight in spite of his delicate build. It's excruciating to see such a fine performer succumb to the brutality of mere power. For a moment Brady's heart sinks as if he himself has been defeated.

Worple's arm is lifted aloft and the two fighters exit. A sigh comes from the crowd, whether of relief or sadness it's impossible to tell. 'You know the girls' dad used to fight in the blood tubs?' says David.

'No, I didnae. When was this?'

'I dunno. After the war, I think. He were a hard man, Bob Hindley. I bet he made a bob or two.'

'He'll have drunk it straight away, mind.'

'Oh aye. Maureen's mam had a right hard time wi' 'im.'

Brady shrugs. 'I don't suppose he made more than beer money in a wee local hall like this.' He looks around the crowd, many of them men he recognises from the bookie's or the pub or the factory gates at closing time. 'This is just chicken feed, David. You need to keep your eye on the big pickings. There is *money* to be made if you're brave enough. What do you reckon? Are you brave enough?'

David nods. 'Oh aye, I'm up for anything, me.'

Brady's eyes rest on him, measuring.

'I need a piss,' says David.

'Aye, me too.'

They make their way out the back of the hall. Men are standing around smoking, sharing nips from flasks. The red brick wall is already dribbled with other men's urine. They stand together and watch the twin yellow arcs hit the bricks. It feels like a moment of communion.

148

She never comes when she says she will. Always got some excuse, she has. Nellie leans back in the chair and closes her eyes. She hasn't the energy to get mad today. Probably for the best anyway. It's dangerous, of course it is. A niece that suddenly pops up out of nowhere? Someone'd be bound to smell a rat.

The room is warm and she's just about to drift off when a sickening stench forces its way through the usual cocktail of urine-soaked pads, lily of the valley talcum powder and watery soup. She opens her eyes to see Mrs Harper fishing about in her knickers. Oh God, she's bringing out a bit of shit, looking at it like she's never seen a turd before. She puts it down on one of the blue velvet armchairs and starts rolling it like a bit of pastry. Nellie wants to vomit. 'Nurse,' she calls. 'Nurse,' but she knows they're in the other lounge watching that Irish singer on the widescreen telly. Daniel O'Donnell, that's it. Lovely feller. Good to his mam, you can tell. Has all his fans round for tea once a year. They queue right across the hill outside his house, they do. Nancy Higginbottom went over there once, daft mare. She said it were just for a laugh, but you can get laughs a lot cheaper than that. She were old enough to be his grandma by then, any road.

Maggie Harper's studying her find. 'Ah needle needle needle needle noddle,' she says, in that singsong way she has. Says the same nonsense over and over. Nellie's going to be sick if someone doesn't come quick and take that away. 'Maggie,' she says sharply. Too sharply probably, because Maggie looks up, scared. She wonders were Myra and little Mo scared of her when they were girls. She were known as nobody's fool in them days but she doesn't think she were too harsh. A quick smack on the bot when they were naughty, none of that rough stuff their Da went in for. Everyone did the same. How else would you keep up with them?

'Needle noddle, needle noddle, beedle boddle,' says Maggie. What a wreck of an old woman she's become. Nellie can't walk any more and her lungs have just about had it from the fags, but at least she's still got her marbles. Whatever they are. Honestly, some of the phrases people use are plain daft.

Maybe it'd be easier if she *had* lost it. Then she wouldn't know what a hellhole she was in, wouldn't see the depths that human beings can sink to. Maggie Harper were funny once. She were never a great beauty but she had that kind of dry sense of humour that makes you laugh in spite of yourself. Needle noddle indeed. Now look at her. For crying out loud, she's going to tuck that turd under the seat and the next person that sits there'll squash it flat. 'Maggie,' she says. 'Put that in the bin, love.'

Maggie glares at her. 'Noddle boddle, noddle boddle, noddle boddle,' she says in an agitated voice. If you knew what were waiting for you when you got old, no-one'd ever live past forty. There's no dignity, no privacy, no peace. Maybe she should ask Myra to bring her in a nice lethal cocktail. She shouldn't mind—she's killed folk afore.

149

As soon as she's thought it, Nellie wants to take it back, but you can't stop thoughts, can you? Now she can't help herself wondering, why didn't Myra kill some old ducks, put them out of their misery, instead of robbing fresh young lads and lasses of lives they hadn't had? Maybe that were why Maureen died—it were the universe balancing things out. Gaia they call it. She read about it in the Daily Express when Emma Thompson had her baby.

So long ago now, but she still thinks of her Mo every day. She were no soft touch either but she were a good girl. She knew right from wrong. She wouldn't leave her poor Mam rotting in a home, brain going to mush. Stomach going to mush with the stuff that's going on around here.

She were brave, little Mo. You couldn't ever be sure you'd do what she did, shop your own family. She didn't hesitate. Took her three hours to get that piece of shit David Smith to do the right thing but he did it in the end. Oh God, Maggie Harper's putting a hankie over her turd and tucking it up like it's a little baby. It'd be funny if it wasn't so disgusting.

Must have been the longest three hours of her life, in the middle of the night too. Three o'clock in the morning he came home, white as a sheet, she said. Imagine finding out that your own sister was mixed up in all that blood, that she was sitting quite calmly with her feet up, having a cup of tea, after that psycho boyfriend of hers splattered someone's blood and brains all over the wall. It doesn't seem human, but then Myra always were a bit hard. Had to be, maybe?

Maureen were in her shadow as a lass but when it comes down to it, who's got more bottle? The little un that speaks out about summat wrong, or the big flamboyant one that follows a murderer round like a gormless sheep? She can dress it up how she likes, Myra, but she were the weak one, letting a man dictate to her.

Well, that's how she dressed it up any road. Maybe she egged him on? Maybe she got turned on by him being the big hard man. That bloody long drink of water, she must have been joking. Not even a man, from what they say. He were a queer, picking up that Edward Evans in a poofters' place. What on earth did Myra make of that? You think you know your own daughter, but who knows what goes on inside another person's head? Sometimes it feels like there were two Myras—the one that got herself dragged in the mire and the one that writes the lovely letters saying what she's going to do for you. Never does it, though, does she?

They've stopped singing. Thank goodness, the Daniel O'Donnell thing must be over. Yes, she can hear all the zimmers crashing into the chairs as they leave the room. Or is it their false teeth clattering? 'Nurse. Nurse,' she calls.

One of the teenage Nazis comes in the room, almost gags at the smell. 'Now Maggie,' she says. 'We don't play with that, now do we?' She turns away as if she's going to get a cloth but Hettie knows that one won't be back till it's all safely cleaned up and disinfected.

Funny how they all do the same job, they all look after you, but you can't help having your favourites, can you?

150

Oh no, the usual table arrayed with plastic nametags. Jude loathes them. Well, damned if she's going to pin one to her new cashmere sweater. She hooks it on the handle of her handbag. Let them search for it if they want to know who she is.

Coffee first. It's too early for her to be functioning without some drug or other. Probably it'll be that wishy-washy stuff in a vacuum flask, but it must have some trace element of caffeine, surely? She wanders into the conference hall, to be pleasantly surprised by the smell of real coffee. Bliss. Now she can really look at the programme.

First though, as always, she checks out the other people in the room. Too many rumpled men and harassed women, but then that's academics for you. Not her usual beat, but this will help the book and she'll probably get lots of contacts to follow up. She's concentrating on working out the really useful speakers when she hears a familiar voice behind her. 'Jude, I saw your name on the delegate list and looked for the most vibrant colour in the place.'

'Charles, what a lovely surprise. Oh goodie, you can tell me who they all are and if they're talking sense.'

'That, my dear, you're perfectly capable of working out yourself. You've been hiding your light under a bushel.'

Jude feels absurdly pleased. 'You liked the chapter I sent you, then?'

'Yes, indeed. Very insightful, I thought. I'm sorry there was some delay in getting back to you but all the computers were down. I'm afraid I always treat that as a holiday and ignore my laptop, so I only read all my e-mails yesterday.'

'I know you're busy. I just don't want to make a fool of myself.'

'You certainly won't do that,' says Charles.

He sits down beside her but before they can talk a stream of people come up to speak to him—a corduroy man, an earnest young woman, a brisk older one, two scruffy postgraduate students. Professor Hunter this, Professor Hunter that.

'Gosh, Professor Hunter, I can see I'm with a very eminent man in his field,' says Jude.

Charles, smiles, not displeased. He seems more confident in this setting, has a very attractive smile when he relaxes. 'I'm lucky,' he says. 'A few of my books are set texts now, so people know me.'

'They're classics, Charles,' says Jude firmly. 'Absolute classics.'

'You've read them? I am flattered. I'd have thought they'd be a bit dry and dusty for you.'

'Why does everyone in your family think I'm a lightweight?'

'Do they? Beth's never said such a thing to me.'

Jude laughs. 'She just says it to my face. At least I don't have to worry what she thinks of me—I know already.'

'She thinks the world of you.'

They sit companionably as the conference begins. Jude has circled the speakers she wants to talk to afterwards and slips quickly from her seat at the end of their speeches to exchange cards.

'You're quite an operator,' says Charles after her third sortie.

'That's just the job,' she says, though she's pleased at the remark. Nice when a clever man compliments you.

Lunch is a buffet at the back of the room, so they help themselves and bring the food over to their seats.

'Any more letters from Brady?' asks Charles, struggling with an over-filled egg mayonnaise sandwich.

'Yes, I had one recently where he referred to the murders as 'the existential exercise.'

'These chaps' heads are always filled with pseudo-intellectual rubbish. Always the same things—Dostoyevsky, De Sade, Nietzsche. It's a shame for someone like Brady. If only he'd had a proper education, encountered some rigorous thinking, then he might have done very well for himself.'

Jude frowns. 'That's what he thinks, but I wonder. Would a job and a bit of money compensate for the bizarreness of his desires?'

'Someone I read recently said the only thing to do with revolutionaries is to give them a responsible job. They finally have a bit of approval and something they can put all their energy into. I suspect it might be the same with psychopaths.'

'Is there such a thing?' asks Jude. 'After all, plenty of people commit acts that seem psychopathic in wartime. Isn't calling people psychopaths just a convenient way of saying they're different, not the same as us.'

'Is it your profession that makes you question everything?' asks Charles.

Jude laughs, flattered. 'That's the job description.'

He considers her, his interest clearly piqued. 'You're right, of course. The word *is* a sort of shorthand. People talk about it as an absolute but psychopathy is a spectrum like everything else. As you say, people can be temporarily psychopathic when they're under pressure, as in wartime. Or rather, temporarily behave in psychopathic ways. I do believe there's a difference.'

How precise he is. It must be his academic training. Jude wonders if she'll ever reach his level of clarity. 'Maybe some people are just caught up with the excitement of being with psychopaths, being allowed to indulge in behaviour they'd find abhorrent if they had time to think. Do you think that's the way it was with Myra Hindley?'

'My colleague says hers is a histrionic disorder. She would mimic the behaviour of whoever she was with.'

'Just a shame she happened to be with Brady and not the Dalai Lama,' says Jude.

'These people will always find each other. They're like bats. They have some kind of built-in radar so they can pick each other out in the

152

darkness.' He pokes at his skewers of chicken satay. 'I'm not sure these are really edible.'

Jude hands him one of her fish goujons. 'Dip it in the mayonnaise,' she says. 'They're really quite good. You know, Hindley did actually have time to think. She was having an affair at one point with a nice policeman but he was married and she was with Brady—breaking the rules seems to have turned her on in some way. But as soon as Brady said he wanted to commit another murder she ditched the policeman.'

'My word, she could have stopped it there and then, just by telling her lover.'

'Brady was her lover,' says Jude. 'The policeman was just her toy.'

'Of course. Married lovers usually are.' He leans forward, stacks her plate with his. 'I believe they're about to start again. I'll just get rid of the rubbish, shall I?'

As the afternoon wears on, she finds herself watching him. He falls asleep during one of the sessions and she is able to stare. Why has she never noticed the fineness of his hands before, his sensitive lips? She's sorry when the last speaker finishes and the conference is wound up.

'I've enjoyed today so much, so stimulating,' she says. 'And it's wonderful to be able to talk to someone about all this stuff, especially someone as clever as you.'

'You flatter me,' he says. 'But I've enjoyed it too. Enormously.'

Jude gathers her things, stuffs her papers into her handbag. All around them is the clatter of opinion, people discussing this idea or that, this speaker or that. She can't bear it if she and Charles get caught up in some mass descent on the pub. She wants him for herself, wants to talk more. That's all it is.

'I'm staying at the Black Swan again tonight.' She tries to say it casually but waits anxiously for his response. 'Fancy continuing the discussion over some more of that lamb?'

He hesitates, pulls nervously at his tie, then seems to make a decision. 'Yes. Yes,' he says. 'I'll let Beth know I'll be late.'

It's hot. Brady leans back against the car, sucking the juice from the end of a blade of grass. One ruined church looks much the same as another to him. M is walking in bare feet along the wall, skirt tucked up. Her legs are strong and a light golden colour you don't expect from an English girl. Maybe she has some coloured blood in her. Not nigger blood—he wouldn't stay with her if he thought that—but something exotic like Burmese or Malayan.

Her father's got really swarthy skin. Maybe she's just a bloody tinker. He remembers seeing them in Arran once. He was on holiday with the Sloans in a wee cottage near Blackwaterfoot. In the daytime the family would walk past the farmer's field and see the tinks all crouched over, howking tatties. At night they played the fiddle round a campfire at the corner of the same field they worked in. It sounded romantic, but in the morning you could see they were just dirty men and women in filthy clothes. They lived in little green curved tents they called 'benders', with no sense of irony.

He lights a cigarette, letting it dangle between long, elegant fingers. A funny thing, heredity, that he and M should be so different, yet so much the same—she with her sturdy, farm gir's build and he like a concert pianist, she tanned and he potato white. Yet when it comes down to it they are the same, both shunted out of their own parents' homes, both willing to explore things that most people would be too chicken to contemplate.

At least she knows her father, though maybe that isn't such a good thing when he's so violent. No wonder she hit him with his walking stick the other day. Cracked him right across the back with his own stick, no mercy. Now that he's so frail the bugger can't hit back. Serves him right. If Brady ever saw his own father he'd give him a kicking too, spit in his bloody face. Deserting his wife and kid like that. That's not a man. A man accepts responsibility. His father was just a ponce, some middle class twat coddled by his family.

Not that he blames him really. Who wants a woman and a squawking kid hanging around? Being a journalist would be a much more interesting life. It would be good to know where his father ended up. Did he see the world? Or did he not get further than Glasgow? Did he work for a quality paper or just one of those scummy tabloids?

Brady could have been a journalist himself if he'd had the chance to stay on at school. He was clever enough, but they didn't do that in the Sloan family. Once you got to fifteen you had to earn your keep. Everyone was the same down the Gorbals. Fair enough. They looked after him and he wasn't even their flesh and blood. Ma Sloan always used to say it didn't matter, that she loved him as much as her own children, but he knew it wasn't true. She was a good woman, Ma, but he never fooled himself that she cared for him the way she did for her own.

It's not bad, this place—you can see right across to Arran from here. Monks built it, but it's overgrown now. M has walked right round the wall and come full circle. She jumps down and stands in front of him, with that slightly challenging way she has, like she's going to say something that'll fetch her a smack. She wants to watch out. She might get one.

'The guide book said summat about a dreamin' tree, but I can't see one.'

'What the fuck kind of tree is that supposed to be?'

'An ash, right at the end of the chapel. Lovers'd come and eat its leaves together to see if they'd get married or not.'

'We don't need a sodding tree to tell us whether we'll get married— we're not. Who needs that kind of bourgeois rubbish? We've got something better than that.'

He leans back, watching her through his dark glasses. He knows she'll come to him. She does, presses herself up against him. 'Do we? What's that, then?'

He doesn't answer, lets her make the running. She unbuttons her shirt and pulls her bra down so that he can see her bare flesh. 'You're not scared someone will come along and see us?'

'Makes it more exciting, doesn't it?' she says.

'I don't know. I like it when we do things in the dark.' Behind the glasses he closes his eyes. It's as warm now as it was the day of the last one, in June … the boy in the ravine. In his mind he can hear the wheezing sound the child made as the string squeezed the breath from his body, the way his skin was warm to the touch. Brady holds himself very still, remembering the fucking glory of that moment, riding him like a bucking bronco, him thrusting, the boy face downward, and her, standing above, watching.

Control. He must stay in control. He moves away from her. 'Stop it. I don't want to be caught here with you looking like some cheap tart. Button yourself up.'

She jerks away. 'Who do you think is going to come to this godforsaken place?'

'Hardly godforsaken. It's a monastery.'

'Oh, very funny.'

He walks over to the wall she was walking round. It's a circle of massive stone blocks, overrun with nettles at the centre. 'What is this anyway?'

She's sullen. 'It was a kind of stronghold they could hide in if someone attacked them. And then later they used it to punish the monks if they sinned.'

'Punish them? Hmmm …'

'Don't you be getting any ideas.'

'Like what?' He makes his voice as seductive as he can. He's enjoying this game.

She flounces away from him. 'It's called the Devil's Cauldron, so you should be at home in it.'

He stands on top of the wall and looks down at her. 'Oh, I am.' He unzips his trousers.

'This is supposed to be a holy place,' she says.

155

'Good. Here's what I think of that.' He releases a long arc of piss into the centre, watching with satisfaction as the golden liquid spills over the nettles.

She starts to snigger, but nervously, hand over her mouth.

'What's the matter? Afraid your God is going to smite me down?'

'You know I don't believe in God,' she says, but he doesn't know anything of the kind. He suspects she indulges in that histrionic Catholic stuff when his back's turned. What is it about women, that they can't stick to things? They've got no self-discipline, no staying power when it comes to abstractions. They can't stand the idea of a universe with no-one in it to look after them. They'll always go scurrying back to their beloved holy water and candles. But what God worth his salt (if He existed, of course) would pay any attention to a puny little flame flickering in some suburban vestry when He has the stars and the sun at His command? when the strongest power in the world is the black light hidden inside the human heart?

Brady jumps down suddenly. 'Come on. I'm bored with this old wreck.'

'I think it's got a lovely atmosphere,' she says. 'Sort of spiritual.'

He raises one eyebrow, which she can see above his sunglasses. 'Sort of spiritual? Oh aye, it's almost as spiritual as Eva Petulengro telling fortunes in the Woman's Own or whatever it is.'

'Didn't realise you read my magazines,' she says, smirking as she trots past him.

'Oh, I never miss Eva,' he says.

He puts the radio on in the car as they drive back to Rothesay. It's a country music special on Jim Reeves and they sing the words to each other as they drive along:

I love you because you understand, dear,
Every single thing I try to do.
You're always there to lend a helping hand, dear.
I love you most of all because you're you.

He's choking with laughter. 'That line kills me. *You're always there to lend a helping hand, dear.* Yes, dear, you're wonderful at scraping blood off the walls.'

No matter what the world may say about me,
I know your love will always see me through.

She snorts with laughter too. It's infectious. '*No matter what the world may say about me.* Like, "You murdering bastard, you." If people only knew.'

'If people knew, they'd string us up,' he says, which shuts her up.

They park the car next to the bed and breakfast they're staying at and walk down to the cafe on the corner for something to eat. At this time of year the town is quiet, despite the good weather.

'I used to come here as a kid and it was always mobbed,' he says. 'People would put their towels down on the beach about six inches away from the next family. You'd get sand in your sandwiches, sand up your bum, but we all thought that was really living, going doon the watter.'

'Is that the way you say it?'

156

He nods. 'You'd go down into the steamer engine room and see the big pistons working. And you'd get a hot pie on the boat if Pa Sloan was flush, though the best pies in the world were the ones you got in Rothesay itself. Oozing jelly.'

She looks disgusted.

'Try one. You might like it.'

The cafe is called *The Pirates' Cove* and smells of fried food and fags. It has mock fishing nets and floats strung across the walls. Every blue Formica table has an empty Chianti bottle with a candle in it and orange wax encrusting the neck of the bottle. M picks idly at it as the waitress comes to take their order. The girl is short and plump, with her blonde hair teased so it stands up round her face like that teenage singer off the telly. Her breasts brush Brady's shoulder as she leans over to light their candle. 'Padded,' whispers M as the waitress walks away.

'Nice anyway,' shrugs Brady, amused when she looks cross. He walks over to put some money in the jukebox. 'Anything you fancy?'

She shakes her head. 'You choose. You will anyway.'

The waitress pulls at a long piece of pink gum as she tells them the food will be a few minutes. 'Ma da's just put another load of chips in.' Brady leans back in his chair, inscrutable behind his dark glasses. The girl looks at him nervously. 'You famous, mister?'

'I will be,' he says.

She walks to the jukebox and starts dancing, her tartan kilt flicking up underneath her pink jumper. Her tightly held breasts cling to her chest like a small animal as she bounces about. 'Stop that,' says M when she realises Brady is watching.

The record changes to something slower and the girl strikes a languid pose, leaning her head back as if in sexual surrender, eyes looking dreamily at Brady. M is getting really annoyed. The girl's father sees her expression and calls to his daughter. 'That's enough now, you. Leave the customers alone.'

'I'm not doing anything,' says the girl. She brushes past their table with a sulky look on her face. M is triumphant. Brady lights another cigarette, impassive. What would it be like to force that silly tart's chunky wee thighs apart? Would her skin be soft, or would it feel dry to the touch? She's standing at the counter now, still watching him. The jukebox starts to play M's current favourite. Brady looks at his woman and favours her with a brief smile. *I sit and watch as tears go by.*

'How many is that now?' Sophie looks sternly over the top of her wine glass. No matter how many times she does it M always finds it delightful. She's such a soft creature that her assumed severity becomes deliciously sexy.

'Are you my keeper now?'

'You smoke far too much. You know you do.'

'Don't you worry, love. I'm strong as an ox, me.'

Sophie shakes her head. 'It's frightfully bad for you, you know.'

'Course I know. I'm sick of hearing about it. I'll tell you something, the National Health Service would go bankrupt without all us smokers dying young.'

'Debatable. Here, have a nibble instead.'

As M leans forward to take a jalapeno-stuffed olive, their hostess comes back into the room. Behind her are two more guests, a man and woman of indeterminate age, appearance and character. Twin geeks, she can see why they're married. 'Can I introduce you to Beth and Charles,' says Sue. 'You know Sophie of course. This is her friend Maria.'

M rises to shake their hands, wondering if she's met the woman before. She looks familiar, though how on earth could she have met someone like that inside? Unless a prison visitor of some kind? She has that subdued, half-alive look that comes from living too comfortably. Last week M was stood behind one of these women in the supermarket queue while the man in front fidgeted and fumbled, trying first to pack his shopping and then to get his money out. When the transaction was finally over, the checkout assistant closed the till and said she was going for her tea, leaving them all standing there like lemons. 'Oh? Thank you,' said the idiot woman in front. *Thank you,* after being shoved around like cattle? M wasn't about to act like a ninny, and gave the assistant a piece of her mind, but maybe that's the sort this Beth is. She has a bland, deferential look, as if apologising for taking up room on the planet.

The man is a mild, civilised type. A do gooder probably. 'Charles, how lovely to see you,' Sophie is saying. 'Last time it was just Beth on her own—remember we met at Sue's Christmas pantomime? Well, not pantomime, *The Snow Queen*, with a wonderfully baroque wicked queen.'

'He wouldn't come with me,' says the woman Beth. 'Refused to support Sue's beautiful designs.'

'I'm sure it wasn't that at all,' says the man, neck flushing above his glass of red wine.

'Work, I suppose,' says Sue. 'Don't worry, Charles, I demand that my colleagues attend but I don't expect their husbands to trot along too.' She's a kind woman really. M wouldn't have let him off the hook like that. As she holds out her glass for a refill, the lights of a car roll over the living room. It's so deserted, this place. M would find it spooky living here. She settles back with her wine, watching her young lover talk to the beige people. He's a professor and she's a teacher, it seems.

Sue returns with the owner of the car. Now, *she's* a bit different. Class, she is. Long legs, blonde hair that she's paid a fortune to have tousled. That professor's getting even hotter under the collar now she's come in.

'Jude!' says the teacher woman, though M wouldn't be so delighted to see her if the prof was her husband. 'I didn't know you knew Sue.'

'Jude knows absolutely everyone,' says Sue. 'She came to my show at that gallery in Helmsley.'

'I bought one of Sue's marvellous abstracts,' says the Jude woman. 'Such glorious colours.'

'What are you doing here midweek anyway, Jude?' asks Beth.

'Oh, the PM's having a secret meeting about Iraq. Very hush hush.'

'So hush hush that your paper has front row seats?' says the professor.

'Well, it is the hotel we use for some of our management shindigs. We put a lot of business their way. Let's just say we have a good relationship with some of the lower grade employees.'

'Of course. None of the real management would give that away,' says Beth.

'How have you managed to get away tonight?' asks Sophie.

'Oh, I'm not filing. I've just been doing background stuff on the hotel. What the bedrooms are like, what freebies you get in the suites, that sort of thing. Easy really—I get all my lovers to take me there.'

'*À table,*' says Sue, in what even M can tell is a duff French accent. She leads the way through to the big farmhouse kitchen, where the lights have been dimmed and the table is covered with shoes sprayed gold and filled with anemones and daisies. There seem to be dozens of little candles dotted all round the room. 'That looks divine,' says Jude.

'Typical Sue flair,' says Beth. What a prat. M is sure she saw exactly the same table decorations in *Cosmopolitan's* December issue. Sue motions her to sit beside the Beth woman, which is fine by her—she can stare across the table at Sophie. God, she's delicious, that posh voice, those edible nipples. She can tell M is looking at her and is trying not to smile.

'And where are you from?' asks Beth.

'Manchester, same as you, judging from your accent. What part are you from?'

'Gorton, though it's all pulled down now. I go back there and I don't recognise anything. What part are you from?'

'Hulme actually, though I've not been back in many years.'

Sue places a large orange casserole dish on the table. 'I always get excited when I see a Le Creuset steaming away in front of me,' says the Jude woman. 'I understand perfectly why Jeanette Winterson offered sex in exchange for one.'

'I'm sure she didn't really,' says the professor. 'Just another of her little publicity stunts.'

'Oh Charles, course she did. It's far too good a story not to be true.'

'There speaks the journalist, I fear,' he says with a smile. 'Never let the truth get in the way.'

'Absolutely not,' says Jude. 'Anyway, who wouldn't give someone sex for a gorgeous dish like that. They're so useful and they do make a statement. Gosh, I'd have sex *in* one of them if they made them big enough.'

'Oh, Jude,' says Beth, half-appalled, half-amused. M wonders who Jeanette Winterson is. The lid of the dish is removed to reveal pieces of chicken in a tomato sauce. Sue dips a large ladle into the mixture and puts a piece of chicken smothered in sauce on a plate. Then she scatters croutons over it, slides a fried egg down beside it and piles a heap of what look like prawns on the other side. What a godawful mess. The first plate is handed to Sophie, who instantly nibbles at one of the little prawn things. 'Crayfish, how delicious,' she says. 'What a super idea to put them with chicken.'

'Not mine, I'm afraid,' says Sue, serving up the next portion. 'Napoleon's cook.'

'Really? An unusual combination,' says Beth.

'What's it called, then?' asks Charles.

'Chicken Marengo. I saw that gorgeous French chef making it on television and thought it looked fun.'

'He's divine, isn't he?' says Jude. 'Keep fingers and toes crossed for me. I'm supposed to be interviewing him soon.'

'Why did Napoleon's cook have the idea of putting the crayfish together with the chicken?' asks Charles.

'You see? Now that's why Charles is a prof and the rest of us are running around in our paltry little jobs,' says Jude. 'He focuses on the question in hand.'

'Well, the cook must have been expecting Boney to lose, because he didn't have any food around the place,' says Sue. 'But reinforcements came and Napoleon started to win so the cook sends out a foraging party. They come back with four tomatoes, three eggs, a handful of crayfish and this very scrawny chicken. So the cook cut the chicken into pieces with his sabre ...'

'As you do,' says Jude.

'And fried it up in garlic and a bit of olive oil, with some cognac nicked from Napoleon's own canteen. Next time he had a battle on, Napoleon wanted the same again. The cook thought the crayfish didn't go with the chicken and used mushrooms instead, but Boney was superstitious and told him to put it back in.'

'So this is the historically accurate version,' says Charles.

'Apart from the sabre,' says Sophie.

'Oh, you never know what Sue's got hidden away among all her theatrical props,' says Jude.

'Rather appropriate, given that it looks as if we'll be going to war ourselves soon,' says the prof guy.

'Do you think so?' asks Sophie. She looks anxious, which is very becoming. It makes her seem sweet, and vulnerable.

160

'Almost certainly,' he says authoritatively. 'Wouldn't you say so, Jude?'

'Oh yes. Blair's absolutely determined, according to our political guys. He doesn't care whether there's a single weapon of mass destruction in Iraq—he just wants his Churchill moment.'

'What is it about all these politicians? Why can't they just get on with making the National Health Service work?' says Sue.

'We'll have to do something,' says Sophie. Her pupils are all dilated from the wine and M would like to just take her away and make love to her right now. Somewhere out there in the darkness, with a high moon throwing its light on to her silvery hair and a soft wind caressing their bare skin. The way it used to be out on the moors ... Course, it's bloody cold out there tonight.

'I'm going to ring my church,' says Beth. 'They had a demonstration before the last Gulf war.'

'That worked, then,' says Jude.

'Well, it's better than doing nothing,' says Beth. Good for her. About time the little worm turned.

'Mmm, you can taste the cognac in this,' says the professor. 'Delicious, Sue.'

'Thanks, Charles.'

'I'm sure there'll be a big demo,' says Sophie. 'We'll go on that, won't we, M?'

'Course,' she says, though the idea sounds outlandish. Go on a demo? with all those daft hippies and beatniks? Get trampled under a police horse's hooves? No thanks. The big range in the kitchen is pumping its heat towards her and making her feel drowsy. It really is very pretty this, the candles, the flowers. How different from the way she was brought up. The only entertaining they ever did was when Maureen came round for her tea with that creep husband of hers. They'd have the check tablecloth out on top of the formica table and she'd get Mam to make them a nice pork chop or something. It would be five thirty or six o'clock, none of this eating in the middle of the night, at eight or nine o'clock.

But she does love this. This is how it could have been if she and Brady hadn't been brought up in bloody slums. He was naturally elegant, the only person she knew who drank wine—nobody else did in those days, unless you count the jakies and their gutrot South African fortified stuff. Everyone drank either beer or else gin and whisky, sherry at Christmas. She looks round the room, its surfaces gleaming with the patina of money, of the middle classes. This is the way it *should* have been for them. They were clever enough. None of these people have anything they didn't.

After the cheese and the charlotte russe, as they wander back into the front room for coffee, she feels Sophie's hand slipping into hers. 'You looked sad in there.'

'Did I? I didn't mean to. It was lovely. I just wish I'd had more of this in my life.'

161

'Poor M.' The little chick squeezes her hand. They sit together on the squishy sofa, in a haze of animal warmth. Sue goes over to pull the curtains.

'Oh my God,' she shouts. 'What the hell's that?'

They all rush to the window, feeling the coldness of the glass after the fug of the kitchen. Outside, lights are bobbing in the darkness, suspended seemingly in nothingness like Japanese lanterns. M thinks of will o' the wisps, seductive, drawing them out into the vast blackness of the night, only to lead them into danger and death. It's scary out in the dark country. She'd never live there.

Sue moves briskly towards the door. 'It's bloody lampers,' she says.

'What's that?' asks M.

'You're a real townie, aren't you?' teases Sophie.

They all troop to the door, Sue flipping the house security lights full on. Across the lane, men with lamps are starting to rise up from the hedge opposite the house. Sue runs right across to them and stands in front of one.

'How dare you?' she says.

'We're entitled,' his voice sullen. 'Thae foxes are nowt but vermin. They'll have my lambs just for t'sport o' it.'

'This is my land,' says Sue, plump and dogged, though M can see a tiny tremor at one corner of her mouth.

'We've been lamping here for years.'

Out of the corner of her eye, M notices the professor and his wife melting back into the house.

'I don't care. You have no right,' shouts Sue.

'Ah suppose you'd sing a different tune if they came after your pet poodle,' jeers the man.

'You patronising idiot. If you don't get off my land right now, John Heppenstall, I'm going to call the police.'

The men behind him are shuffling their feet, uneasy in the glare of the floodlight, and doubly so now that one of their number has been identified.

'Bunch of lesbian twats,' says Heppenstall as he turns away.

Jude puts her arm round Sue. 'Come back in, darling,' she says. 'You mustn't let them upset you.'

M and Sophie watch her lead Sue back towards the house. 'It's a gorgeous night, isn't it?' whispers the little chick. M pulls her towards the barn.

'We can't,' says Sophie.

'Just one kiss. They're not going to send the search parties out yet.'

They stand against the wooden half-door, the smell of hay drifting around them. The kiss is soft and long and M doesn't want it to stop. It's Sophie who tugs at her. 'Come on. They'll all know what we're doing.'

M laughs. 'Who cares?' she says, but she turns to follow.

She can see the men's lamps bobbing along the hillside as they walk up the valley towards the main road. Their grumbling rolls back towards the farmhouse but the words dissolve in the wind, the words of malignant, unseen spirits.

162

'It's eerie here,' she says.

They are moving towards the house when M's eye is caught by a sudden gleam across the lane. What is it, the eyes of an animal or a trick of the light? She crosses to see, Sophie trotting after her. Stretched out along the top of the fence is the body of a fox, its blood dripping down the wood, its eyes dulled.

M can't believe what she's seeing. 'Murderers,' she screams. 'Murderers ...'

Sophie catches her arm and pulls her in. 'Don't, Maria. Please don't upset yourself. It's a country thing. They do it to crows sometimes too, to scare the rest.'

The others come crowding to the door of the farmhouse again, wondering what's happening. M looks in horror at the lolling head, the animal's tongue hanging out. Such a beautiful creature, dead, its paws nailed to the fence. What did the poor fox do to deserve this? Who would treat an innocent creature in this way, draping its head in this humiliating fashion, splaying its limbs to make it look ridiculous? There's no respect for life here, no care, no soul. M hugs her arms to her chest. 'Whoever did this is one sick bastard,' she says.

It's the voice that gets to Beth, that nasal squawk as if parrots came from Essex. But the girl is pretty enough in her way. These young people call sexy girls foxes and that's what she reminds Beth of, with her bright eyes and sharp features.

'Thank you dear, that's kind of you.' She takes the profferred plant but the girl has already moved on to Charles.

'Will's told me all about you,' she says. 'He thinks 'is old man is the business.'

Charles looks surprised, but is immediately flattered, his face relaxing into its most expansive expression. 'Now what would you like to drink?' he says. 'Should we have a little champagne to welcome Kezza to our home?' Much to Beth's surprise, he says the name with no hint of distaste. She'd have thought he'd find it common. And champagne? He didn't tell her that was on the menu.

Will slips his arm round his mother's waist. He's such an affectionate boy. 'I've put you two in the blue bedroom at the top,' she says. He gives her a grateful grin and turns to take their cases upstairs. Charles holds the living room door open for Kezza. Gosh, he's being courtly today, though his eyes are drifting rather too frequently to the girl's low cut top. Is he having a mid-life crisis or something?

The champagne puts Beth in a more mellow mood. She mustn't be the clinging mother. Will's obviously head over heels in love with the girl. Her Will, her little boy. It seems no time at all since he was running round in short trousers, exuberantly playing football with the kids next door, telling them he was going to marry his mum when he grew up. They poured scorn on him. 'You can't marry your mum, you knobhead,' she heard one of them say, but Will was adamant. 'Well, I'm going to.'

The meal is simple, prosciutto and melon to start, followed by roast beef. It's only when Charles carves the joint and she sees the look of distaste on Kezza's face that she remembers how long it took her to get used to pink meat. 'Charles, give Kezza some from the end. I don't think she likes it rare.' The girl nods her thanks, but turns almost immediately back to Charles.

'So you're a professor, then? You must be dead clever.'

'Only moderately so, my dear. I can't lay claim to any more than that.'

'Will's clever too. He always solves problems quicker than anybody else. I fink he's gonna be a general one day.'

Beth and Will exchange smiles. She's so proud of him, her beautiful boy.

'Will, tell them about the survival exercise.'

'They're not interested in that sort of thing, Kez.'

'Of course we are, son,' says Charles.

Will blushes, touched by his father's interest. 'It was pretty awful at first. We were left out on the Brecon Beacons and had to get by on our wits for three days. Trapping rabbits to eat and that sort of thing. We slept in the open the first night but it was bitterly cold and we decided we weren't doing that again. Then I realised from our bearings that we must be near your friend Jude's holiday house, Mum.'

'Told you he was clever, di'n't I?' says Kezza.

'So we made our way over there and checked it out. We managed to get in a window at the back. Well, Kezza did. It was the pantry and she was the only one small enough to squeeze through. Don't worry, we left some money for the food we took.'

'Very enterprising,' says Charles. 'But what did your commanding officer think about it.'

'He didn't seem to mind. Said we'd used our wits at least. Hey, Mum, this beef is delicious.'

'Glad you're enjoying it, son. I'll get the pudding in a minute.'

She's decorating the sherry trifle when Will brings the dishes in. A bit surprising. You'd have thought Kerry or Kezza or whatever the heck her name really is would have wanted to get in with her boyfriend's mother, but clearly she reckons it's better to get in with his father. It's a little obvious as a tactic. Beth's sick of watching the girl flash her bra at Charles. What an idiot he is, falling for it.

'Thanks for putting us in the room together, Mum,' says Will, stacking plates next to the dishwasher. 'I'd have felt a right plonker if you'd made us sleep in separate beds. Totally uncool.'

'You young people and your cool this, cool that. Don't you ever get hot about anything?'

'Not in public,' he says, in a dry tone reminiscent of his father's.

She looks indulgently at him. He seems healthier than he was before he went away. His skin's fresher, less pasty. All that yomping probably. She wonders do the girl soldiers yomp as well, whatever that is.

'Do you like her, Mum?'

His tone is shy and Beth is taken by surprise. She wasn't expecting it to matter whether she liked the girl or not. 'Your father seems to like her very much,' she says.

'Yes, but do you, Mum?'

'Darling, if she makes you happy I'll like her.'

'That means you don't, then.' He seems disappointed.

'What that means, my darling, is that no girl is good enough for my son, that's all. I'm sure she's a very nice girl. We just didn't wear our underwear in public in my day.'

'That's the fashion, Mum. Anyway you didn't even wear underwear at all if what I hear about bra burning is right.'

She laughs. 'There wasn't much of that going on in Manchester, love. Not down our street, anyway.'

He picks at the end of the roast beef. 'What don't you like about her, Mum?'

'Nothing, love. I hardly know her.' She shoots the leftover broccoli into the waste disposal, which clunks and grinds and reduces the conversation to mulch. Why does she instinctively dislike the girl? Is it that she's what Charles would call common? Let's be honest, her own mother would call that girl common. There's something feral about her, something musky, despite her heavy perfume and gaudy makeup. She gives off the whiff of a cornered animal.

Back in the living room Charles is fussing around, plumping up the cushions. 'Have you seen my keys?' he asks. 'I thought we'd take Kezza down to the country club.'

Beth frowns. 'Kezza? She'll hardly like it there, Charles.'

'Oh, she and Will can have a drink with us and then pole off wherever young people pole off to,' he says.

She shrugs. 'If you like.'

'You might make a bit more effort,' he says. 'Will's serious about this girl.'

'Will's infatuated with her. If she told him to assassinate the Queen he'd be on the road to Buckingham Palace within the hour. Where are they anyway?'

'Kezza's gone to freshen up, she said.'

'Heaven help us,' says Beth. 'I've already seen more of that girl's underwear than I want to.'

'What are you talking about?' asks Charles.

'Didn't you realise that's her bra you've been ogling for the past two hours? Making yourself ridiculous.'

'The frill round her top?'

'Yes, dear. You didn't know?'

'Oh really, Beth. It's hardly a capital offence. You're not yourself tonight. Should you be taking an extra dose of evening primrose or something?'

'I'm going to start the car,' she says. 'I expect you'll want me to drive so you can drink.'

She marches out to the garage, slamming every door on the way. The others, when they join her in the car, seem subdued. Will slips into the front seat before his father can. 'It's ages since we've been down the country club, Mum,' he says, patting her hand. She turns to smile at him. Such a sweet boy, her Will. 'It's nice to be all together again, love,' she says. 'I wish you weren't going away.'

'That's the choice you make, Mum.'

'I know, son.'

She feels herself calming down as she drives. The roads are wet and she takes her time, enjoying being in control of the moving car, of her little world. The noise of the heater blots out the sound of Charles and Kezza chatting in the back. Who'd have thought he would unbend with that little piece? Normally he hates those sharp-faced blondes.

166

At the country club, Will waits with her as she locks up the car. Charles and Kezza go ahead to sign in.

'It's a real club then? And you're a member?' asks Kezza.

Mauvaise foi, thinks Beth suddenly. Bad faith. Not a concept she's thought of much since university, but watching the girl contort herself into what she thinks is acceptable middle class behaviour sickens her.

Kezza turns from the register as Will steps forward to sign. Beth is shocked. There, in the girl's ears, are her own earrings, heavy gold-faceted hoops with a sapphire at the centre, expensive earrings that Charles gave her on their twenty-fifth wedding anniversary. She couldn't have afforded them herself. So this is how Kezza freshened up? She just can't believe it, knows she's gawping. Kezza stares at her, mocking, as if daring her to say something. Neither Charles nor Will seems to have noticed.

It's Kezza who takes the initiative, much to Beth's chagrin. 'Like them?' she asks, touching her right ear. 'My gran gave me them.' 'I have a pair exactly the same,' says Beth, trying to keep her voice level.

'Yeah? Small world, innit?'

'Now dear, what would you like to drink?' Beth goes to answer Charles, but Kezza gets in first. 'I'll have a vodka tonic,' she says. 'No, we're in a country club. Make that a gin and tonic please, Charles.'

'Right you are. Now how about you, dear?'

'I'll just have the tonic, thank you.'

'Oh my God, you was. talking to Beth, wasn't you?' says Kezza. 'Sorry, Beth. I'm always butting in ahead of people. No patience.'

Will leads them over to a table by the window while Charles gets the drinks. Beth always loves coming here. The elegance of the high-ceilinged room, the rich chenille sofas in muted earth tones speak of a world of safety and peace, a world far away from the world she grew up in. She should be more compassionate towards Kezza. Maybe her grandmother really did give her the earrings, though Beth can't wait to get home to search her jewellery drawer. She's only trying to blend in, as Beth did when she went to university.

Or is she? There's something faintly derisory about her chumminess with Charles. Beth looks at the crystal chandelier, the heavy Jacquard curtains, then at Kezza's short skirt and tanned legs. Kezza doesn't really want to be part of all this. She'll probably tease Will about the country club once they're away from here.

Charles arrives with the drinks and a bowl of peanuts. Kezza dips her hand in the bowl. 'Shouldn't eat these,' she says. 'You know what they say about pub nuts. Always got little bits of people's pee in them. They're really pee-nuts.'

Ah, at last, Charles flinches, distaste written all over his face. 'That is certainly not the case here,' he says. 'These nuts came straight from the packet. It's hardly a pub, you know.'

'No, it's lovely here,' says Kezza with a sweet smile, though Beth's sure she's highly amused at the mollified look on Charles's face. Will's looking tenderly at her too. Are men blind? Don't they see she's teasing them? Will's

167

like a puppy dog, so eager to please his father, so happy that his father and the girl seem to be getting on. Charles has often been too hard on him in the past. It would be nice if they could have a better relationship now that Will's grown up.

Will's suddenly scrambling to his feet. It's Sophie Ferrers, and that older woman they met her with, at Sue's dinner party. She seems a strange person for Sophie to be with all the time, a lovely young woman like that. The older woman makes Beth feel uneasy. She has a hard look about her, cynical. Didn't she have some terrible thing in her background, like illness? Or was it a mental problem? There's something …

'Do join us,' Charles is saying. He and Will disappear to the bar, followed by Sophie, who's clearly uneasy at Charles having to pay for their drinks. Such a sweet girl. She's rich herself but seems to be very aware that other people might not have what she has. Beth's noticed that about her before—must be because she works with disadvantaged people. The older woman, Maria, sits next to Kezza. 'You've got an amazing voice,' Kezza is telling her. 'I bet you drank a lot of whisky to get like that.'

'Wish I had. Smoked a lot of fags, I'm afraid,' she says.

'I'd die without my fags,' says Kezza. She seems very chatty with the woman. Beth can't imagine why she'd take to someone like that, but perhaps she's trying to behave well socially for Will. God, she'd better treat him properly. Forget the earrings, if she hurts Will … if only she could go home right now and look. She knows exactly where she left them—in a blue velvet box that Will gave to her as a young child. If she's taken that box as well …

The others return with the drinks. Will trails his hand down Kezza's arm as he sits beside her, while Sophie touches Maria's hand. It hits Beth with the force of an epiphany—when did Charles stop touching her? While Will and Sophie create a ceremony around the pouring of the drinks, he places her tonic in front of her as if he were a stranger.

Maria smiles at Sophie, but Kezza turns almost immediately to the older woman, leaving Will looking tense. There seems to be some sort of mutual fascination between the two of them. The older woman stares right into Kezza's eyes, leaving the girl flushed. Beth can't understand it. She's clearly straight, so what's all the excitement?

'Yeah, we're going to Iraq,' she's saying now. 'That's why we're up here seeing Will's parents.'

'You're what?' says Beth.

Kezza looks at her. 'Has Will not told you?'

The room suddenly seems unbearably hot. Beth struggles to her feet, rushes to the door. Kezza runs after her. 'He should have told you,' she says. She seems almost kind. 'I'm sorry. I thought you knew.'

She puts a hand out to touch Beth. 'You'll get'm back,' she says, but Beth doesn't know whether she's talking about her earrings or her son.

Brady looks at the boy on the bed but can't say what he really thinks, which is, *Why would you want to do what millions of people do every day—spawn children?* One less or more makes not a jot of difference in the world. But Angela Dawn has only been dead a week or two. No doubt if it's your own child that's died, you can't be logical about it.

David is lying there dumb, not talking to any of them. He went mental when he heard the news, tore the hospital room apart. Even ripped the lamp out of the ceiling. Then when he got home he took all the wee matinee jackets and nappies and stuff that they'd been buying for weeks, and stuffed it into a suitcase. He went out the back and chucked it over the railway embankment. Never went back to the house again. Still, that was good. He got a transfer from the council and now he and Mo live just a quarter of a mile away.

'Leave him to me,' Brady tells Maureen. He goes into the bedroom, takes in the frilly yellow bedspread and the purple wallpaper that they haven't had time to change yet. David's lying on his back, staring at the ceiling, not even smoking. The lassies couldn't get through to him at all. No wonder, hovering about gushing at him, talking in whispers as if he's old or deaf or something.

Brady doesn't talk about the baby, he talks about the dog. The council wouldn't let them keep their retriever in the new flat. What does his old man do but go and have her put down? Brady breaks out a packet of fags. 'Here, heard about Peggy. That father of yours is a right bastard. He's the bleeder who should have got the needle, not the dog.'

The boy cheers up instantly. It's intermittent warfare between him and his dad. People are always feeling sorry for Brady because he never knew his father but they needn't bother—Brady senior could have been a right old prick, like David's dad. 'Let's go out on the moors,' he says. 'Shoot all our troubles away.'

They load up the van with wine and beer. M drives, Mo up front beside her while the men sit in the back, drinking wine straight from the bottle. It's one of those golden afternoons where the light seems almost amber. Through the little villages they rattle, past that nice wee pub down the bottom. As the road begins to climb Brady feels his spirits rising too. The boy is his now. The boy is in. He can feel it.

Up past the reservoir they drive, up to their favourite spot. M parks the car and they climb back off the road to the rocks. High above them a hawk rides the air currents before swooping suddenly and snatching a rabbit from the ground. It's so close they can hear the squeal of the creature as the bird's talons dig into its flesh.

'Ohhhhh,' say the girls in unison.

'Don't be such hypocrites,' says David. 'You eat rabbit pie for your tea same as the rest of us.'

169

'Unfeeling creep,' mutters M, but David just laughs. He's coming out of himself. Good. They walk side by side, David bouncing along on springy feet. He bumps shoulders with Brady, almost like a girl sidling up to him. 'Lay off,' says Brady, but beneath the embarrassment he's not displeased.

Maureen runs ahead and sets up empty beer cans on the rocks. She's not interested in the guns, not like the girl. Brady takes out the Smith and Wesson, savouring the heft of it, the sheer weight. He knows it'll annoy M but he hands it to the boy. 'Here, you take this one,' he says. She glares at him but he just winks at her. That'll quieten the daft bird down. Sure enough, she preens, smiles at him.

Doesn't stop her competing like hell, though. The boy knocks two of the four cans down. 'That the best you can do?' she says, swaggering forward with her Luger. Got to hand it to her. Four in a row. Bang, bang, bang, bang. Most folk would seize up after boasting like that, but not her. She seems to get even cooler under pressure. If she was an athlete she'd be an Olympic champion.

He leans back against the rock, takes a long pull on the bottle of Riesling. Here, on this moor, is where he feels most alive. He wants to laugh at the pure beauty of it. God, it's so peaceful, though not quiet, what with the sheep calling to each other, the constant twittering of birds. Down below, Dove Reservoir glitters like a long streak of mica set in tar. The hill opposite is covered with scree as if a giant hand has tossed sweeties up in the air and let them fall where they may, like a wedding scramble at home with all the kiddies elbowing each other out of the way for halfpennies and farthings. He closes his eyes and smiles as he breathes in the clean air.

'You'll have to do better than that if you want to get involved,' he hears M say. The boy almost trips over a rock in his eagerness to show her. Brady opens an eye. 'Careful,' he says. 'That gun's loaded if I'm not mistaken.'

'You don't want to blow your balls off, love,' says Maureen. She and M snigger like a pair of wee schoolgirls. Brady flinches a little. That's not the sort of word he likes to hear a woman say in public. Mo looks challengingly at him, sensing his disapproval. 'Got to go for a pee,' she says gleefully. She gets to her feet and starts picking her way behind the rocks. Stupid bitch, wearing those silly shoes.

'Tell you what, David,' says Brady. 'I'll show you how to make a dum dum bullet.'

He slides the knife from his jacket pocket and painstakingly carves a deep cross in one of the bullets, which he then places carefully into the chamber of the Smith and Wesson. 'This'll splatter anything.' Over by the rocks a sheep looks up from chewing the springy grass and gazes blankly in their direction. A shame to destroy an innocent beast but this is clearly one of the stupider quadrupeds on the planet. He aims the gun and pulls the trigger. The blast reverberates in his ears as the animal explodes in front of their eyes. Its innards spurt from its body, leaving a great crater in its bloody side.

'Man,' says David. 'That is really something.'

170

M looks indignant, but Brady shrugs. 'If we're really going to go for it we have to be prepared to do anything.'

He could swear these two are going to go for each other any minute. That's OK. As long as they're loyal to him it doesn't matter how they are with each other. Divide and rule, isn't that what they say?

'Well, David. Are you prepared to do anything?' says M, her eyes looking not at him but at the blood-soaked sheep.

'You know I am.'

'Do we?' says Brady. 'What if it was the driver of a security van we had to shoot, could you do that? Or the night watchman at a bank, could you do that?'

Maureen comes tripping back over the heather and stands beside David, looking curious. The boy gazes at him through alcohol clouded eyes. 'I can do anything, me.'

'We'll see,' says Brady softly. 'We'll see.'

From: La Barbara <lynx1043@hotmail.co.uk>
To: wolfman@hotmail.co.uk
Subject: where?
Date: Tuesday, 29th April 2003 09:24:26

Hal, where have you been? I've been dying to talk. Was even tempted to use work email - don't worry though, I didn't.
From the BlackBerry of Pat Shields

From: "Hal" <wolfman@hotmail.co.uk>

Darling Lynx, they told me to do an extra surveillance that I wasn't expecting. I tried to call you but couldn't get a signal - we were on our way to some farm in the
country. Afterwards we had to turn our phones off. There was nothing I could do.
From the BlackBerry of Hal Morton

From: La Barbara <lynx1043@hotmail.co.uk>

I missed you, wolfman. I wanted you in my house, my bed for a change. I want you to know me, to know the very depths of me. I want you to know what brand of soup I buy, what colour sheets I have, where the dust lurks in my house. I want you to see me. I love you so much it scares me.

From: "Hal" <wolfman@hotmail.co.uk>

Believe me, I wanted to be there with you. We had to scope out this Sunday supplement type farmhouse she was visiting with the posh girl, Sophie. You'll never guess who was one of the guests - that friend of yours who grew up in Manchester.

From: La Barbara <lynx1043@hotmail.co.uk>

Beth? What if she'd known her? That sort of thing just shouldn't happen - she shouldn't be placed anywhere near her home county.

From: "Hal" <wolfman@hotmail.co.uk>

Ah, but nobody would expect her to be right here under their noses. Anyway she knows criminals all over the place - except in Yorkshire!

From: La Barbara <lynx1043@hotmail.co.uk>

Beth would be really spooked if she knew who it was - she's quite soft. Was it a dinner party or something?

From: "Hal" <wolfman@hotmail.co.uk>

I guess so. We didn't bug it or anything. I think mixing with these middle class people is giving her ideas above her station. Her house is perfectly fine but she went shopping with the credit card the next day and bought wallpaper and some lace curtains that cost an arm and a leg.

From: La Barbara <lynx1043@hotmail.co.uk>

She was always changing things around when she was inside. One of her famous supporters gave her an allowance every month and she ordered really nice stuff in from catalogues. It didn't go down very well with the others sometimes. She'd always want what other people had - only she had to go one better. Say someone got a satin bedspread sent from home, hers would be satin with flounces or satin with fancy embroidery. She always had to be top dog. Let's be gender specific - top bitch!
I bet someone she knows has a set of lace curtains.

From: "Hal" <wolfman@hotmail.co.uk>

Sophie does apparently. I wouldn't know but my partner reckoned they were old lace, much finer than anything you get in the shops nowadays. She studied them minutely through the binoculars.

From: La Barbara <lynx1043@hotmail.co.uk>

The prison psych said our friend has a hysterical disorder, that she takes on the characteristics of the people she's with.

From: "Hal" <wolfman@hotmail.co.uk>

So I was right - not a psychopath after all?

From: La Barbara <lynx1043@hotmail.co.uk>

She didn't have that excuse.

Oh blast, another pair of Marigolds gone. She can feel the hot water nipping the raw skin on her hands. It's a pain, washing dishes. She never used to have to do crap stuff like that inside, was rarely given kitchen detail. Now she's supposed to be free yet she spends half her time on housework. Wouldn't it be nice to have a dishwasher, like that Sue whose house they went to the other night?

That was a good night, except for the fox. How could anyone do that to a defenceless animal? It was more than just clearing vermin. Whoever did that was evil, interfering with the poor creature's body like that. She shudders as she thinks of it, the way the legs were pulled in different directions, the tongue spilling out from the lips like that grotesque Rolling Stones logo, with its gaping mouth and gross tongue. A beautiful creature like a fox doesn't look like that. Whoever killed it had a very macabre sense of humour.

She wonders where *her* fox is. She hasn't seen him or the vixen round the back for ages. There's a bit of cold chicken in the fridge. Maybe she'll put that out tonight when she gets back from Manchester, see if they come.

Christ, she'd better get a move on. It's almost ten o'clock and she's still to iron her blouse. Maybe she should start wearing T-shirts all the time, like Sophie. They only cost a couple of quid from the supermarket and she looks all right in them now that she's started to lose weight. Mam—oops, need to remember she's Aunt Nellie now—will notice quite a difference in her style over the last few months, since she's been with Sophie. Much more modern now, not nearly so stiff and starched. Mam'll get a right shock when she walks in in her new gear. So what if they told her she wasn't to go again? It's inhuman not to let you see your own mother.

Poor love, what she's had to put up with in her life. Not just the moors business but losing Moby like that. It's not right for a child to die before a parent, goes against the natural order of things. And from a brain tumour too. It doesn't bear thinking about, those creepy cancer cells worming their way through Maureen's skull. Mo was a good sister really, even if she did shop them to the police. It takes a long time to get over that sort of betrayal, but thank goodness they were talking again before the end.

Actually a lot of big sisters wouldn't have bothered with Moby at all, not after getting chipped out of the house to make room for her. *She* didn't have to stay at Granny Maybury's, did she? Oh no no, she was the one that got to stay at home. She had it easy. Mam always favoured her. You shouldn't do that with your children, you should treat them equally.

Still, no mother should have to bury her child.

She's not had it easy, Mam. Worked hard all her life and for what? If only things had been different, they could have been going abroad now, maybe to one of those quiet little French villages you see on the relocation programmes on the telly. Little cobbled streets, local baker's shop. Or a Greek island, with blue skies and the sea. She wouldn't consider Spain—too many

174

Brits there. Too common. But maybe a villa in Florida, one with its own pool. It might be easier there, because of the language, and the sun would be good for old bones. They could make juice in the morning with oranges from their own trees, have a dip in the pool. She'd lower her mother gently into the blue water, watch it ripple over her withered skin. She wouldn't mind a bit. Tenderly, she'd support her skinny body, making her feel safe. They could get to know each other all over again.

Too bad Mam's not up to it any more. She's in the best place really, in the home.

'Right, poppet, let's get going.' She pops Minim into her bag and heads for the car. It's still a thrill to know it's hers. She wipes a speck of mud from the wing. What a gorgeous colour of blue it is, exactly what she'd have chosen herself. She puts it into gear and hurtles off at speed. Damn, better remember the new traffic cameras this time. She nearly got done last week. Luckily the thing flashed as the guy in front went through, so she was able to slow down.

It's a bright day and she opens the car window, turns the radio up. Oh no, it's that bloody Mozart clarinet concerto again. Why do the English love that reedy sound so much? She has to get a CD player put in so she can listen to what she likes. There must be something better than this. Loud rock? no. She runs through the stations till she finds something more to her taste. It's slow and sad, always the best. When she wrote songs herself she always made them like that—that's how you get to people. It was one of the best days of her life, winning that competition in prison. What a buzz, beating Janie Jones, a professional. Just shows what kind of a life M could have had if she hadn't met Brady. A fool for love, she really was.

Janie was gorgeous, lovely curvaceous little figure, those green eyes. Just a bottle blonde, probably, but hot stuff. Pity she never managed to get her into bed—she wouldn't have bleated on afterwards about M being a liar if they'd had a thing together. Absurd really, what was she supposed to do? Declare to the world that she'd killed two more children? That would have done her chances of parole a lot of good. Brady was right, people are sloppy and sentimental in their thinking when young people are involved.

M was born out of her time. She should have lived during a war. That's when you need tough thinking, people who've got the stomach to do hard things. Life's too soft nowadays. People have too much. They're drowning in *things*—I-pods, Pot Noodles, duvets and drinks cabinets, tellies in every room, toilets in every room, it's never-ending. It's like that telly game show where they brought a whole load of stuff out on a conveyor belt and you walked away with everything you could remember. Nowadays people wouldn't thank you for it, they've got it all already.

Oh God, it's 12 o'clock. Lunchtime at the home in quarter of an hour. Not much point in going now—she'll never make it in time. And the old dear'll be asleep afterwards anyway. Might as well go down to Ashton Market.

She takes the turn-off at Saddleworth and follows the road across scrubby moorland. This is the scrag-end of the moor, not the bit she and

175

Neddy liked. She stops the car and gets out to look down over the town of Oldham, all scrunched up in the valley below. The grass by the roadside is rough and dry-looking, as though the terraced houses below have sucked out all the moisture from it. That's what poverty does, drains the juice from a person, leaves you with no defences. She was ripe for the plucking in those days, bloody ripe.

She follows the long, familiar road down, through the endless back to backs. The market, when she eventually gets there, is heaving with people. It seems much more interesting than it did the other day, when there was no-one around. The stall-holders are all bloody Pakis. She's not saying there's anything wrong with Pakis, but there's just too many of them. How come they're the ones with all the money nowadays?

'Here love, you look like you need cheering up. Why don't you treat yourself?' says one of them. Cheeky sod, though he's quite good looking. She likes that dark hair and the brown skin. What's he selling anyway? She peers at his stall—lots of hair ornaments, a few wigs. '100 percent human hair,' he says. 'An' all for thirty quid.'

'Get away,' she says. 'How could you offer a wig made of human hair for that money?'

'It's them bloody Chinese,' he says. 'They're giving it up cheap, taking food out of the mouths of good Muslim women.'

'Oh yeah, they don't need their hair, do they? They can just hide the lot under those stupid veils.'

'Watch it, love, a bit of respect here, please. Look, this one'd suit you, pet. Nice and feminine, wi' them waves. You'd look like a film star in that, you would.'

The wig he's holding out has long rippling curls and blonde streaks. She hesitates. It does look awfully glamorous. She deserves a bit of fun, doesn't she? All those years inside. 'You'll have to try it on wi' a wig cap,' he says. She crams what looks like the top of a pair of tights on top of her hair. Oh lovely, it makes her look like she's going to rob a bank. Ha, she almost did once.

But the wig is stunning. She gazes at herself in the little mirror he holds out, seeing a different person in there, someone much younger and softer. She pulls at the wispy fringe. The stallholder hovers, predatory, sensing he's about to make a sale. 'That looks right good wi' them jeans,' he says. 'You look twenty years younger, love.'

'Twenty?' she says, raising her eyebrows.

'Naw, not twenty, love. But a good few years, you know?'

'Mmm ... how much did you say it was?'

'Thirty quid, darling. An' I'll throw the wig cap in for free.'

'Just in case I don't know how to cut the top off my tights?' she asks.

'Tell you what, I'll throw in a nice styling brush 'n' all.'

'All right, done. I think I'll keep it on.'

'D'you want the box, love?'

'No, I'll not bother,' she says.

She jams the combs at the front of the wig into her own hair. 'We don't want it moving, do we?'

'That's right, love. You experiment wi' it, get it right for you. You look a right cracker in that.'

She walks away from the stall, knowing that even her walk is different; she's moving in a sexier, freer way. A man on the corner turns his head as she goes by. *Yes-s-s, you look, boyo, but you can't touch. This is me ... Myra ... I'm way beyond you.* She feels incandescent with light, as if some secret source of energy has suddenly been ignited inside her. This is how Marilyn Monroe must have felt when she decided to turn it on and become Marilyn. M strides forward, shedding the cares of everyday life and gliding through a world filled with possibility.

But after all, it's only Ashton and the poxy little market. There must be somewhere more interesting. She walks back to the car, aware of glances from several men. Manchester itself is just a stone's throw away, there's bound to be action there. Why not? It takes her a long time to make her way through the centre of the city, but she eventually finds a car park. Now for a pub. It's so long since she's been here, everything seems different. The bars are no longer the traditional brown male enclaves, tucked into little back streets. They're bright and open and they gleam with chrome and fluorescent lights. Through their plate glass windows she can see young women in mini-skirts balancing cocktails and cigarettes. Will she be too old for these places or will her sexy new self carry her through?

She chooses one near the theatre. It won't all be young people there, surely? Inside, a number of couples linger over late lunches. She watches them for a moment. Wouldn't it be nice to be part of a normal couple? The barman approaches her and she orders red wine. She's too pumped up to eat, though she really ought to because of the car. These drink driving laws nowadays are ridiculous. She never had a problem in the old days. They'd always have Liebfraumilch or something once they got up to the moors—and no accidents afterwards. A crack of loud laughter comes from a large table in the corner. That must be the actors. She noticed from Janie Jones's crowd that performers always make more noise than anyone else.

That's not for her. She needs quiet, intimacy. She takes her drink to the opposite corner of the place but immediately realises her mistake. No-one will approach a woman on her own if she's stuck in a corner. She lifts the glass and goes back to the bar. 'Forgot to order my fags,' she says. 'Twenty Benson and Hedges, please.' She perches on a stool and lights up. The wig makes her feel sophisticated, striking, unassailable.

The crowd in the corner are shrieking with laughter. 'Bloody students,' says the barman with contempt. There's one man who's a bit older than the rest. He must be the one in charge, the lecturer or whatever. He's dressed in a black suit and a white shirt and she bets he smells lovely, like that man who handed over the car to her. Suddenly he gets up from the group and heads towards the bar. 'You have a very frank way of staring,' he says, in a soft accent that she thinks might be Irish.

177

'Was I? I'm so sorry. I didn't mean to.'

He leans over and whispers in her ear, 'Oh, I think you did.' She can feel his skin brush her neck. 'I'm Aidan O'Connor. Can I join you for a drink? One needs breathing space from the young, doesn't one? Do you think we were ever so silly at that age?'

'I expect I was anyway.'

'What'll you have?'

'I'll just have a mineral water, thanks. I'm driving.'

'But not yet.' His tone is seductive but she feels that an order has just been given. She will have her red wine and then she will see how unassailable she really is.

The place Brady's heading for is in a side street at the back of Deansgate. It's piled high with dusty cardboard boxes containing batteries, fusewire, light bulbs, tapes and reminds him of the old hardware shop in the Gorbals except that all the shopkeepers there were Jewish and the guy here is an old Paki. At least his stuff is cheap and there's no-one around to watch you going in and out. Half of Manchester would see you if you went to Kendal Milne on a Saturday afternoon.

It would be great just to walk into a big department store and order the best, but he hasn't got the money and he won't steal on such a petty level. It would be too humiliating to be huckled out by some sub-moronic store detective. No, his crimes will be on a grander scale than that. He will choose his moment, and when he does, even the big boys will have to sit up and take notice. He's got contacts. After Borstal he made sure he had—getaway drivers, safe-breakers, sons of important criminals. He'll show those guys he can organise, at the most meticulous and complex level. The training, the endless lists in preparation for robberies to come, the grooming of his accomplices, they'll all pay off.

Myra's more than an accomplice of course. She's his lover, his soulmate, she makes him not complete but replete. He always functioned perfectly well without her but with her he is finally—not happy, that would be a silly word for someone of his quality and temperament—but content. She is not like other women. Most of them are silly little ninnies, scared of their own shadows, but she, she's as bold as he is. Who would have dreamt he'd find a woman like her? A man, maybe. They have tougher minds, aren't afraid to take what they want. Women are always waiting to be given permission. Well, he gives M permission and she him.

Smith is another matter. Brady frowns, is so busy thinking about the boy that he nearly walks in front of a car and sets off furious horn-honking. 'Pay attention to what you're doing,' he shouts, much to his own amusement, though not perhaps the driver's. It's difficult to mould a scally like Smith. On the one hand he's uneducated, green, ripe for introduction to important ideas and philosophers like De Sade and Nietzsche. He drinks that up, though of course you can only feed him summaries—he's not got the concentration for the real thing—but then you don't need it, there's always the lurid little under the counter books that provide the same thing, *Kiss of the Whip*, *The Passionfruit of Corruption*. On the other hand Smith's prone to mood swings and violence. He doesn't understand that these matters have to be controlled, that the pleasure to be gained from inflicting pain is enhanced when it's deferred, planned for, anticipated.

Still, he's coming along. The question is, is he ready? Does he really understand their project? He doesn't like work, is more than willing to make money by holding up a bank or burgling some rich fucker's country house, but will he go all the way? Has he got the stomach for it?

There's only one way to find out and it's risky. It's one thing having a flutter on the horses but lose at this and it's the rest of your life down the chute. That reminds him, he hasn't put his bet on for today. There's a William Hill's in the next street, he'll head there before the electrical shop.

He loves the atmosphere of betting shops, the seediness of floors strewn with discarded slips, of fluorescent tube lighting, of places thronging with men, the only woman some hard-faced blonde behind the counter. They know him in here, despite the fact that he doesn't waste time bantering with them, simply nods in greeting.

A race is on and he waits respectfully till it's over before crossing the room to fill in his slip. *Secret Enterprise* catches his eye. It's done not badly on its last three outings, might be worth a couple of shillings. He's won a pound or two with *The Girl* in the past, checks to see whether the going's rough or not—the mare can't handle heavy going, unlike his own girl. One more—the name *Ultimate Test* leaps out at him. He's already proved he's got what it takes, hasn't he? You can't go much further than he's gone. The wee girl was the best so far. He's broken the taboo, smashed convention. It takes a clear, unsentimental mind to do what he's done.

What's so special about wee girls anyway? They're not angels. They're not fucking fairies spun from some ethereal substance. They're not even uncommon. There are millions of them in the world. Nobody bothers the same way about wee boys. Are they any less vulnerable? Was he supposed to be tough and macho as a child, when his mother dumped him at the Sloans', when she turned up every once in a while, arms laden with cheap toys that were supposed to take his mind off the fact that she'd abandoned him, when she shut him up every time he asked about his daddy? He can see the slim-waisted coat she wore, smell her scent still, light and flowery, the essence of what a mother should be. Ma Sloan didn't wear any.

Och, it didn't do him any harm. Who needs to know where they came from? It's where you're going that counts. And it wasn't as if she could help it. The proletariat have limited options. A single mother, scrabbling to make a living, how could she find a new life with a bastard child to look after? It's different if you've got money. There's always someone else to palm the sprog off on, someone else to pay the bills. He wasn't unhappy. The Sloans were good to him, looked after him as well as they could. Still, he had to learn how to be in their family, knew he wasn't one of them. It wasn't their fault that he was different.

Money changes the course of people's lives. Actually, if Lesley Ann had had more money, he and Myra would never have been able to snatch her. She only had sixpence to spend at the fair and that was gone pretty quickly. Lack of money that separated her from her friends and left her wandering about alone. She was a pretty thing, little Miss Downey. Those big black eyes, the round child's face. He wishes now he'd had a cine camera. It's all very well recording on audio tape but you can't beat pictures, especially moving ones. A collector would pay a lot for film of that wee girl naked except for her socks and shoes. A nice touch, that.

180

He starts to walk more slowly, struggling to maintain his composure. Not that he'd sell a film recording his greatest masterpiece. He mustn't get turned on, but it's hard not to, thinking about the child and the way she begged them not to hurt her, not to take her clothes off, the way she cried silently, eyes huge above the gag. That was the best Christmas ever, starting off on the moors on Christmas Eve with little Pat Hodge. It amused him to have her there, innocent of what could happen to her. He wouldn't touch her, of course. Far too dangerous to kill a next door neighbour, or even mess with her. She'd probably do anything they asked, though. She loved the beer and wine they gave her, seemed to take to it naturally.

It was beautiful on the moors, counting down the minutes to Christmas Day, drinking wine out of the bottle. The snow on the ground looked almost blue in the darkness. Who needs all that sapsy Jesus stuff? The smell of the earth, the sound of water in the distance, the calling of some daft bird that doesn't realise it's night, and beyond that the roaring of the universe; if humans need to feel in awe of something, what more do they need than an infinity of stars and planets and galaxies streaming into the darkest reaches of space?

The bell clangs behind him as he enters the hardware shop. He looks round the grimy shelves with distaste, wishing he was in some posh shop examining state of the art cine cameras. 'I need a spool of carpet tape,' he says.

The very act of lifting the jar of cold cream from the bathroom cupboard excites her. It adds a sense of possibility to the sameness of her morning rituals, the careful smoothing of body lotion into her legs, the dusting of freesia talcum powder over her breasts and stomach. Younger ones don't use talc any more, but they're fools—it makes your skin so soft to the touch.

Carefully, so that she doesn't take too much, she dips her fingers into the jar and eases herself back on to the bed. The cream feels cold but instantly excites her. She tried Vaseline for this before but it was too thick, a kind of liquid condom, deadening sensation. In the old days she never needed anything, she was always ready, responded instantly to a touch.

She strokes herself gently as her breath quickens and her skin suffuses with heat. Maybe Sophie will pull her down on the bed as soon as she arrives, enfold her in caresses, elegant limbs entwined around hers. She closes her eyes, feasting on the image of Sophie's slim shoulders shimmering with golden light, her flat stomach. She must stop. She'll be late. But it seems she can't and the heat builds up and up inside her. God, she should never have started this. Slow, smooth … strokes … she is gasping, but it is not Sophie she thinks of any longer. It is Aidan's face she sees, his skin she dreams of touching.

Should she feel guilty? Maybe she has an infidelity gene and can't help wanting more than one person at a time. Even when she was with Brady she had her policeman, Norman. He was a good looking man, better built than Brady was. And gentler. Making love with him was so sweet, so normal. If only she'd stayed with him she could have had a nice ordinary life, a home, a family. Once she'd got rid of his wife, of course.

The first day he came round to buy the van, he sat there stroking the dog. That was the sign of a good man. When they made love it was like gliding through rose scented pleasure gardens, like plunging into a pile of newly mown grass. They were innocent, like children. There was no violence in it, no pain. Hmm, but maybe no heat? You couldn't imagine him getting into a rage like Brady. Neddy was fine about Norman at first. It made him laugh that she'd sold the van to a copper. They were having a picnic when she told him and his beer frothed right up out of the bottle, he was shaking so hard with laughter. The sound took her by surprise. It started as a low, hooting noise and built to manic, uncontrollable glee. Here they'd committed the perfect murder using that van and she'd only gone and sold it to a cop.

He wasn't quite as cheerful when he realised she was still sleeping with Norman weeks afterwards, swore he'd kill him. Norman thought he was a lunatic. Ha, little did he know. She and Brady had a bloody fantastic night that night. He was really passionate, bit her on the shoulder just to show her who was boss.

He was the boss. That's the way it's supposed to be. Sophie's lovely but she does run around after M like a little panting dog. He brooked no disobedience. She did as he said. There was a kind of voluptuousness in yielding to him, in knowing that he would make the decisions. That was why she dumped Norman in the end—he was a man to have fun with, not a man to follow. 'We've had our fling. Now it's over,' she told him.

'A fling? Is that all it was?' he said, and she didn't know, not for sure. It had been fun to have him there, just for her, a part of her life that was nothing to do with Brady. He had his trips out on the bike after all, didn't he? Looking for experiences, he called it, though God knows what they were—going with queers, they said in court. He certainly didn't share any of it with her.

But she knew that nothing—not what she had with Norman, not what he got up to by himself—none of it compared to what they had together. Ian let her enjoy herself with Norman, even enjoyed it a little that she was knocking off a policeman, but when he clicked his fingers he expected her to come to heel.

They were watching Sunday Night at the London Palladium when he said he wanted to do another one. She could hardly believe it at first. They'd committed the perfect murder when they did that daft Pauline Reade. There was no reason to do another one, nothing more to prove.

Maybe the person he wanted to prove something to was her.

That night she dreamt that she was in a cave. She inched forward in the dark but the ground started giving way beneath her feet and she was plunged into a deep pit. Thick black water, viscous as tar, rose around her and drenched her dress, but suddenly Brady was there, reaching out to her. She grasped the warm flesh of his hand and the next minute they were floating above the tar, up, up, riding in the night sky like the bride she'd seen in a picture, wearing a blood red dress, while a musician with a goat's head sawed away on the cello.

The next day she took Norman back to hers after night class. They made love in the front room. Granny Maybury went to the bingo on a Monday night so the house was empty. She savoured every kiss, every caress and then she told him it was the end, that she couldn't see him any more. She had to give everything she had to Brady. He couldn't understand it, didn't know what she saw in Brady.

Sighing, she rolls over. It will never be like that again. How could the little chick or Aidan ever be like Brady to her? They're nice people, but unremarkable. He was an artist, to the core. He changed the world for her. He made a world for her.

If only she'd never met him …

When she reaches Sophie's house she's a good half hour late. 'You look odd,' says Sophie bluntly. 'Are you OK? Has something happened to upset you?'

She shakes her head and gives a smile she knows to fall under the definition of wan. 'Just thinking about the past. Strange, the way you think you've put it behind you and suddenly it comes back to haunt you.'

Sophie squeezes her hand. 'Oh M, I know …'

183

'Come on,' says M. 'We'd better get a move on if we're going to save the planet.'

Sophie slings her overnight bag in the back of M's car. It's a relief to be driving. Too much time to think if you're a passenger. They head out of the village and on to the M62. M can't work out whether she loves or hates this road. She loves its grandeur, loves the moors stretching either side of it, but to be on it, with someone else, is to be stepping through a nest of vipers.

They pass the Saddleworth turn-off without comment and she begins to relax and enjoy the theatre of the road, the long, slow inclines, the slow-moving columns of cars inching forward like snakes through grass. The moor is blank, almost grey, at this time of year, with the light leached from the sky and the car headlights on even though it's early. It holds within it the possibility of infinity. She is almost disappointed when they reach the turn-off for the M6 motorway north.

With Sophie dozing beside her, the drive seems featureless until they cross the border into Scotland. Brady's country, the hills curving in on one another like molluscs reluctant to reveal themselves. This, he told her, was bandit country, a country of robbers and reivers who went marauding, stealing their enemies' cattle, raping their women and torching their houses.

They'd pulled in for a picnic on one of their weekend trips up to Glasgow. His voice got rough and excited, even more Scottish than usual, when he told her about the families who ruled the Borders—the Bruces, the Stuarts, the Douglases. 'The Douglases had a very famous girl,' he said, making two syllables of the word 'girl' in the way that always seemed a caress to her. 'Catherine Douglas, Kate Barlass, the Queen's lady-in-waiting. She was alone in the chapterhouse at Perth one day when some of the Graemes and Stuarts stormed in, brandishing knives. Determined to get to the King's chamber. Catherine Douglas tried to stop them getting in. She held fast, wedged her arm in the door till it broke.'

He looked her straight in the eye then, sent a shiver down her spine. 'You'll need to be my Kate Barlass.'

'You're a king, are you?' she said, looking straight back at him.

'Actually, I could have royal blood in me. My father's name was Stewart.'

Well, she was his Kate Barlass. She bloody was. Held fast till her arm broke and her life broke. And what good did it do her? She didn't protect him any more than Catherine Douglas protected her king. 'Did they get the King?' she asked Brady.

'Aye, they did,' he said. 'But her descendants still have a broken arm on their family crest.'

It seemed scant reward to her for losing the use of an arm, but then posterity always mattered more to Neddy than it did to her. She didn't care what they said about her afterwards so long as she was having a good time in the present.

'M, you're looking sad again.'

Sophie has woken up, her eyes heavy-lidded still with sleep.

184

'You're missing the best scenery here,' says M, unclenching her jaw.

'The Borders are beautiful, aren't they?' agrees Sophie. 'I remember we used to come up here quite often for house parties. My cousin has a castle over by Roxburgh.'

'A castle? My God.'

Sophie shrugs. 'The grown-ups did the huntin', shootin', fishin' bit but us kids had a wonderful time just roaming round the estate, looking for brambles and things. There was this ruined tower that we were forbidden to go in but we did, of course.'

'Of course.'

'There was all this rubble inside and we were always grazing our hands and knees when it slipped, but we'd just say we'd fallen in the drive or something.'

'I can't imagine you doing something you were told not to. Weren't you a good little girl then?'

Sophie laughs. She really is sweet. 'I was, but all kids want to do the forbidden, don't they?'

'Not just kids.'

The road crosses a fast-flowing river, then plunges back into the secret folds of another glen. 'I love these hills,' says Sophie. 'When we were younger Nanny used to tell us that the little people lived in them. If it was very dark and we were very quiet we'd hear the sound of goblin shoemakers hammering away. She used to let us put out saucers of milk for them. They were always licked clean in the morning.'

'Plenty of cats around, no doubt.'

'Cats? Of course not. It was definitely the little people,' says Sophie.

The road begins to flatten out and they start to see proper towns. They speed through the last miles to Glasgow. M is astonished at the shortness of the journey. When she and Neddy used to come up here it took twice as long—the motorway petered out somewhere around Preston. It's so built up now, and the amount of traffic on the road, well, it's scary.

Once they get into the city centre it's easier as the traffic slows right down. Sophie has booked them into a hotel and directs M to the car park nearby. M tries not to get excited, but she's never stayed in a real hotel before, just the odd bed and breakfast with Brady, lumpy beds and the bathroom so far down the corridor you had to put your coat on to go to the toilet in the night. Life nowadays seems to involve leaving your own house far more than it ever did when she was young. The only place she went was the pub or the occasional dance. Now you have meals in restaurants; you stay in hotels or other people's houses; even children go abroad. They know what croissants are when they're five years old.

The hotel lobby is full of people in smart suits drinking cappucinos. Sophie said this place was cheap but it seems pretty posh to M. The room is decorated in lime green and hot pink.

'Cool.' Sophie nods in approval though M prefers something more traditional. 'This is really funky, isn't it?'

185

'Mmm. Very ... unusual,' says M.

'Don't you like it?' asks Sophie.

'Oh yes, I love it. It's fun.'

'The jets on this shower are amazing,' says Sophie from the bathroom.

'Are you going to jump on the beds next?'

'Sorry, just like to test these things, you know?' She's giggling like a kid, but composes herself. 'Let's go and get dinner now. The food here's supposed to be very good.'

The restaurant has an open brazier which sends flames leaping upwards dramatically against the dark red walls. M looks with bemusement at the leather-bound menu. Pac choi? Pancetta? Wasabi? And that's just the starters. She shuts it over. 'You choose. I haven't a clue what half of this is.'

'Oh? I'll order for both of us, shall I?' Sophie smiles at the waiter. 'Sushi to start with, then the grilled prawns with ali-oli and spicy fries. And a bottle of the house white, please.'

'You're so *competent*,' teases M.

The starter arrives on an oblong black dish with pink slivers of ginger and a murky green paste. M's seen sushi in Tesco's but the rice is usually filled with tuna mayonnaise or little bits of cucumber. This appears to have bits of raw white fish sticking out of it. 'Try it. It's delicious,' says Sophie. 'Much better than the stuff you get in the supermarket.'

She smears a slick of green paste on hers and adds a slice of the ginger. 'Mmmm ...' For someone so slender she has an inordinate enjoyment of food. M follows suit. She finds that if she closes her mind to the fact that the fish is raw it doesn't taste too bad. The ginger's nice. The main course, though, is totally daunting. Huge prawn things still in their shells. She dips one of the spicy fries into what looks like mayonnaise. *They're* all right at least. Sophie sees her looking dubiously at the langoustines. 'Here, I'll show you.' She lifts one of the beasts from the plate. It has eyes, for godssake. And big pincers that reach blindly outwards as if to strike.

Sophie looks into her eyes. 'First you have to pull off the head.' Her dainty fingers close round the creature's neck, then she rips the top part away. The big claws clatter next on to the plate. M finds she is breathing hard. Next Sophie pulls off the tail, yanking the sides of the thing apart till the rib cage cracks open. She holds the little carcass out for M to see, like a child offering a gift, then prises the white meat out with the blade of her knife. Delicately, her eyes always on M's, she draws the knife right down the beast's back and removes a kind of black vein. Blood? shit? The insides of living organisms are messy.

'Here,' she says. 'Taste it.' She dips it into the mayonnaise stuff and slowly glides it into M's mouth. M closes her eyes. 'That's divine,' she says. There are two vivid circles of colour on Sophie's cheek. Her hair shimmers in the light cast by the brazier's flames. The food is delicious but they do not linger over their meal.

186

The next morning M wakes with the feeling of being sated. She can hear Sophie in the bathroom, the sound of the water changing timbre as she moves around under the shower's powerful jets, first pattering like rain, then drumming down like hail. It was never like this when she came to Glasgow with Neddy, never this luxury. This peace. They were always sitting outside his foster parents' house in the slums and not going in, or drinking in dark little bars where the people grunted like a bunch of warthogs.

Sophie orders a taxi to take them to the demonstration. As soon as it pulls up at the big gates, M recognises it. This is Glasgow Green. It used to have sets of rings where men did athletics exercises. She can see Brady hauling himself up there, trying to impress her with how strong he was. It would have been comical, really, if it wasn't such a turn-on. He was tough, even though he was wiry.

There are more people than she thought possible gathered in one place. She thinks it's futile, this protesting against a war that's going to happen anyway, but the atmosphere is almost festive. Face paint, anoraks, piercings, balloons. Brightly coloured banners bob amongst the crowd and there is the sound of drumming. People are chattering, though not always about war. 'What an amazing collection of people,' whispers Sophie. 'You can't believe it, can you?'

M looks around. There are Goths, nuns, pensioners, students, a whole band of women drummers, housewives even. 'Oh my God,' she says. 'There's that friend of yours.'

'What, here? I thought everyone from Manchester would go to the London demo.' Her eyes scan the crowd. 'Wouldn't you know, it's Beth.'

She waves and Beth comes over, looking matronly in her flat shoes. Nurses' shoes, thinks M.

'Sophie, what on earth are you doing here?' she says in that silly voice of hers. She barely glances at M.

'Oh, we thought we'd make a little trip out of it. Why are you not in London?'

'This is where Blair is,' says Beth, her face solemn. 'This is the man who may send my son into war.'

'Of course,' says Sophie, chastened.

'Why aren't we starting?' asks M.

'We have,' says Beth, looking at her as if she's an idiot. 'The people at the front have been moving off for the last quarter of an hour.'

'Oh.'

There is a tinkling sound which M recognises as a popular piece of ragtime. Beth fishes in her pocket and brings out a mobile phone, a rather large and unfashionable one, M notes with some satisfaction.

'Oh bugger.' Beth looks furious. 'They're moving Blair's speech forward. He'll be gone before we ever get there.'

'What a coward,' says Sophie, though M wonders what else a politician would do. He's in Glasgow to avoid a baying London mob. Why would he set himself up for a bunch of howling Glaswegians?

187

Beth is texting furiously on her mobile. 'Was that Jude?' asks Sophie.

Beth nods. 'She's up near the front. She has to hear all the speeches.'

M turns to watch the crowd. A man in clownface is juggling, sending Indian clubs spiralling into the cold air. A child tugs at his father's hand. 'Let's go, Daddy. What are we waiting for?' All around is that voice, the Glaswegian voice, rough, guttural—beloved. It stirs her as nothing else could.

'Ah was in the Second World War and ah've never been on a demonstration in ma life. That fucker Blair doesn't know what he's letting our boys in fur.'

'He's a twat. It's no' his son that's goin."

'Jamie, will ye leave yer sister alone.'

The voices weave in and out, whispering to her of what she once had. What she lost. In the midst of this immense crowd she feels desperately alone.

There is suddenly an air of purpose in the people immediately in front of her. Marshals with yellow stripes on their jackets usher the crowd forward. Someone in front sets up a chant: *Who let the dogs out?*

Bush, Bush and Blair, comes the antiphon.

People move forward slowly, the crowd stretched out like a giant reptile dragging its length behind it. Policemen stand watching with benign mouths but folded arms. Pigs. M starts to walk, caught up in the chanting and the sense of excitement. The women drummers have sprung into action and are pounding out a primitive, driving rhythm. It looks punishingly hard to do. M stares at their arms, the muscles defined even in the older women. Sophie dances up beside her. 'How d'you fancy that, M? Looks fun, doesn't it?'

'Looks bloody hard work if you ask me.'

'Jude says there are fifty thousand here today, and two million in London.'

'And none of it'll do any good.'

'It's a big chunk of your electorate to ignore,' says Sophie.

'I know, love, but he wants to be a hero. No amount of protest is going to get in the way of that.'

'I want one of those banners,' says Sophie, darting over to the side, where a young man is handing out placards emblazoned with the name of a tabloid paper. As the young man starts to chat Sophie up, M suddenly realises she has been joined by Beth. 'You gave me heart failure there. I thought you were somewhere behind.'

Beth is staring at her. 'You're her. I'd know your walk anywhere, the way you saunter along like you own the place. You're Myra. You're Myra. '

'Who? Who's Myra? My name's Maria Spencer.'

'It may be Maria Spencer now but you were Myra Hindley back then.'

M gives her a long hard look. 'My God, what an awful thing to say. How could you think I was that terrible woman? You'd best watch what you're saying. Anyway, you must know Myra Hindley died last year.'

'I know you. You can get a new nose and a new hair colour but you still walk the same. Don't you remember me? Betty from round the corner?'

Of course. She knew there was something familiar about her from the start. That gangly lass who used to hang about after school and offer to run errands. *'Hey Myra. D'yer want me to get yer fags, Myra?'* She can feel her heart pounding in her chest. *One, two, three, four, We don't want your fucking war,* chant the crowds. She's hot and cold by turns and her head is going to explode with those sodding drummers. Oh God, what's she going to do? She can see Sophie coming back with her placard. She turns to Beth, her face cool, expressionless. 'I suggest you keep your ridiculous ideas to yourself. I don't want Sophie upset by this nonsense.'

She turns away from Beth and smiles as Sophie comes back clutching a placard that says, *No War.* No war? That'll be right. This is war. 'All right, love?' she says to Sophie. 'Let's get on with changing the world.'

PART III

DEAD MEAT

Bloody hell, Aidan wasn't joking. He really is an alpha male. Earlier this afternoon, at the hotel, he was teasing her. 'A woman who loves being on top. You only go for alpha males, do you?'

'Why, are you one?' she'd asked.

'And how, baby,' he said in that soft Irish voice of his.

Now he walks slowly on to the altar, surrounded by young men. God, he looks gorgeous, one dark lock of hair falling over his forehead. A priest, a fucking priest, she can hardly contain her excitement. Aidan sees her looking at him and the merest smile catches his lips. He has very sexy lips.

The sex is so much better with a man. She'd forgotten, forgotten the hardness of the man's body, the stronger smell of his sweat, the way he can make her do things as no woman could. She can hardly concentrate on the Mass for looking at Aidan. When he comes into the pulpit to give his sermon she tries to look at the flowers on the altar, at the woolly hat of the woman in front of her, but her eyes keep drifting back to him. She feels as if he's making her look at him. His deep brown, intense eyes can't possibly be looking just at her, but it seems as if they are always focused on her, as if he wants to see inside her head, take control of her, as if he's speaking only to her.

'Can we not buy a car or spend time surfing on our computers without having to contemplate the naked female form?' he is saying. 'Must all our purchases be accompanied by pornography? The good Lord gave us beautiful bodies to love each other with, not to display in public for the purposes of lust or vanity.'

She can hardly believe what she is hearing. Already? *To love each other with?* The breath is trapped in her throat, her body tense. Her head is filled with the thought of him, this afternoon, in that little hotel room, the muscles standing out on his neck as he pinioned her to the bed with his strong arms. A woman couldn't do that, not unless she was some Russian shot putter.

'We're obsessed with sex,' he continues. 'In our society we act as if there's no better or finer human activity than to exchange bodily fluids with one another. Yet in the Church's eyes, sex outside the sacrament of marriage is a mortal sin. That has been Her position for hundreds of years and it is *still*, despite what the more liberal of us might think. What does this mean for the way we behave?'

M feels a thrill inching up her spine. He thinks sex is a mortal sin and yet he dares to sleep with her, to touch her naked body, to enter her. She closes her eyes in euphoria, blocking out the sound of his voice. She feels boneless, all sensation, as if her flesh has been converted into pure energy. Around her she can smell the earthy scent of people's wet wool coats, but she herself is all light and heat, incandescent with life. She looks up and the stained glass window above the altar flares with ethereal light, burning, as she is inside. Is it wicked, to like sex so much? Will she burn in the fires of hell for it? Do they really exist?

191

'We live in a world where the temptations of sex, if we are at all human, set us alight day after day,' says Aidan. 'Jesus would understand our confusion, our yearnings. He was, after all, a man. What he will not understand or forgive is if, in the midst of our confusion and yearning, we treat other people as objects for our lust, if we use them and toss them away without caring for them, if we steal their bodies and throw away their souls. Love is the finest gift that God gives us. We must cherish it and nurture it and if we are weak enough to share our bodies without the benefit of holy matrimony, then we must make sure it is with someone we love.'

Oh God. He's telling her he loves her. She watches in a dream as he walks back to the altar and the flock of altar boys cluster around him again. They're teenagers, skinny and pimply. Beside them, moving around in his green robes, he looks like a god. She knows what lies underneath them, feels her heart seized by a blizzard of palpitations. Here she is in church, a handsome church with stained glass saints dancing floodlit around her and the crucified Christ looking down on her in his agony, and yet all she can think about is the priest's penis, warm and slippery to the touch. A surge of satisfaction shoots through her body. Aidan is hers. She is his. They are bound together in a dark covenant more powerful than the Church and all its rules. They are beyond rules, beyond ordinary reality. She feels sick and afraid and ecstatic.

She has felt like this before.

He's broader and maybe stronger physically than Brady, full of the confidence of being a powerful man. Ian, she realises, with a strange feeling of tenderness, had no power at all, though he was a far superior being to anyone else at work. He was bold, grasped power for himself. Aidan has power because of his office.

Maybe it will be different this time. Please God it will be different. It must be. The other was too dark a path, cost her too much. She was a lamb to the slaughter with Brady. He must have known how it would end but he didn't care. He was too much in love with nihilism, too obsessed with blood and power. That night when they watched the London Palladium and he said he wanted to do another murder, he'd turned to her when Bruce Forsyth did his silly catchphrase, *I'm in charge.* 'You know that's what it's all about?' he said. Heaven knows what Brucie would think if he heard that, a child murderer adopting his catch phrase. She has to check her laughter. This is a church, after all.

When the Mass ends she hesitates, wondering whether to stay and see if she can speak to Aidan. The congregation files out slowly. There's always a lot of people at a Saturday night vigil Mass, all the lazy buggers that don't want to get up for church in the morning. It doesn't seem right to her somehow, all this slackening of the Church's rules. Is it so much to ask that people get out of their beds to go and worship God? You don't have to eat fish on Friday either any more, so long as you mortify your flesh some other way, but how many of them bother? How many even remember now?

192

Rules are important. If there are no rules, then you can't break them. Nothing matters. At least she and Neddy never thought like that. It all mattered. They knew they were crossing a line. That was what made it so exciting, so very deep a ... not *pleasure*, that's too mild a word. It was more than pleasure, more than life itself.

She walks past the collection plate in a trance. Outside the church people are standing chatting. There's a little flurry of excitement in the crowd as Aidan comes out, no longer wearing his liturgical robes but dressed all in black. Several well-preserved ladies surge towards him, twittering about his sermon. They'd give anything to have him rip their knickers off. She doesn't look at him, though she senses he's looking at her. Let him wait, the bastard. That'll serve him right for not wearing a dogcollar. She keeps her face stony. That always makes people nervous.

For fuckssake, he's twinkling at her. Irish git. 'Miss Spencer! How good of you to come.'

'I enjoyed your sermon very much, Father.' She can't prevent herself smiling, but at least she's not flaunting herself at him like those other old bags.

'It's important to tell it like it is, I think,' he says.

It's too much. She bursts out laughing.

'Hush,' he says. 'Our secret.'

'So what is it you're really doing tonight?'

'Working with young people, like I said. Youth club disco tonight.'

'Oh. Well, I hope it all goes well, Father.'

'I enjoyed our meeting this afternoon, Maria. I'll ring you about that matter.'

'Thank you, Father. I'll look forward to your call.'

'You drive carefully now.'

'Goodnight, Father.'

She walks away from him, trusting he's watching her legs. She's exhilarated, can't wait to see him again. What a damn shame he's working tonight. When he said it was with young people she thought they were students. The barman in the place where she first met him had said the kids with Aidan were students so she just assumed he was a lecturer. She never dreamt he was a priest. Now that she knows, it only adds to her pleasure.

She backs her little blue Ford out of the church car park. Her head is buzzing and she doesn't want to go home, but she heads back on to the main road. Now to find the M62. It seems she's not concentrating tonight. She gets confused by the direction signs and takes the wrong turning. Drat, this is the road to Warrington. Something tugs at her brain. Warrington and then St Helen's and then the M58 ... that's it, she remembers looking it up on the map. She's fucking going to Ashworth. Brady is there, just off that M58.

Why is she doing this? Did she always intend to come here? It's strange. When she was in prison it was as though her brain was cooped up too—she didn't think about the past. But now that she's out and supposedly free it seems she can't stop thinking about it, can't keep away from the places that remind her of it.

She puts on the CD as she drives, ignoring the darkening countryside on either side of the road. Ian's favourite, the Gotterdämmerung. I-an. She rolls the name round her lips. For years she thought of him just as Brady, the man who got her locked up for life, but being out has changed things. Slowly she is beginnning to re-make him in her head, remember him as he really was. It's disconcerting to feel the passion he aroused in her, as if she is twenty again—she thought she'd gone beyond that. Has she been Brunnhilde, sleeping inside a ring not of fire but of steel, sleeping through her life for the last forty years? learning nothing? Is Aidan her Siegfried, the hero who will re-awaken her? Not from sleep, but from the terrible dreams of the past?

The twilight of the gods. As the sonorous music rolls its way through the car she realises that that's what they thought they were, gods. They defied the norms, lived life at a more heightened pitch than ordinary people did. In that grotty little slum, at least their ambitions were not small. What could they have been if they'd had a proper education, proper chances in life?

She grips the wheel angrily. Whoops, better watch her speed. That's the last thing she wants, a bloody fine. For the last ten miles or so she drives with decorum, calming herself down in the process. She loves to drive, loves the feeling of being in control. No-one can get at her here, in her portable world.

The turn-off is for Maghull, she thinks. She must concentrate. As the car enters the outskirts of Liverpool, the road is lined with mean little houses, mean little shops. It's only a mile or two once you're on Maghull Lane, if she could only find it. It's no use, she'll have to stop and ask the way. She winds the window down and stops an elderly man out walking his dog. 'Yer nearly there, love. You turn right into Park Lane, right into Parkbourn Drive and then right again on to Parkbourn itself. They're all tight turns. But you'll not gerrin at this time of night.'

'I might be applying for a job there,' she says. 'I thought I'd have a look anyway as I'm passing.'

'Too right, love. See what yer letting yerself in for.'

'Thanks,' she says and smiles at him. He winks back. Probably fancies her. Not a chance, mate.

His directions lead her to the long grey Victorian building she recognises from the internet. It looks grim, its high mesh fence blocking out the lower half of the building. What a place to live in. She sits in the car staring at it. How Brady must regret asking to be transferred here. He really snookered himself, asking to serve his time in hospital instead of prison so that he'd get a softer ride. Now he can't get out because they say he's too insane to decide for himself. It's like bloody Colditz.

Now she's here she feels depressed at the thought that this is what he has been reduced to. It starts to drizzle, sending motes of rain dancing in the perimeter floodlights. Just yards away from her he is sitting in some yellow painted room, rotting. He must be weak after so many years of hunger strike and being force fed. Nearly four years now, isn't it? What can that be like, to be manhandled by poxy guards, have them shove tubes down your throat,

194

making you gag, all so they can give you some tasteless gruel? She couldn't do it, but then he's always been strong, burning with conviction that what he thought was right. She can imagine him spitting the stuff out at them. Or maybe they just inject his arm.

She shudders. The pictures of him in the paper make him look like a wizened old man, much older than his age. If she met him now she'd never be attracted to him. He'd snap in her hands if they were in bed together.

Nothing would make her want to die.

The rain goes off and she gets out of the car, stares at the lighted windows. Which one is his? Maybe he's in one of the modern blocks inside the complex, no view of the outside world at all. Is he still clutching a hot water bottle to his stomach like they said in the News of the World years ago? That's probably the only comfort he has.

Poor sod. It's not right what they're doing to him. He was better than that. Better than them. She turns to go. They never understood. He was always more than the sum of his crimes. She can't bear that that fierce life is being crushed out of him. Is that really it? Are we just the sum of what we do?

44 DEAD MEAT

From: "Hal" <wolfman@hotmail.co.uk>
To: lynx1043@hotmail.co.uk
Subject: same
Date: Thu 24th April 2003 23:06:15

I've worked so many hours I'm exhausted but I still lie awake at night thinking of you, Pat. I really am the wolf who roams the night. Without you, without my mate, I'm nothing.
From the BlackBerry of Hal Morton

From: La Barbara <lynx1043@hotmail.co.uk>

Love, why do they need you to spend so much time watching that bitch anyway?
From the BlackBerry of Pat Shields

From: "Hal" <wolfman@hotmail.co.uk>

They're worried. She's doing so many things they didn't expect. She went on a jaunt to Glasgow with the girlfriend for that big anti-war demo, stayed in a nice hotel. A bit ironic really, to demonstrate against the government that freed her. (The boss was rather miffed by that.)

From: La Barbara <lynx1043@hotmail.co.uk>

That woman has a greater sense of entitlement than the bloody Queen Mother! She no doubt thinks it was her due to be let out.
My friend Beth went to that one too. Manchester was nearer but Tony Blair was supposed to be speaking in Glasgow and her son's a soldier so she wanted to throw stones at him or something.

From: "Hal" <wolfman@hotmail.co.uk>

Blair's not daft. He moved up the time of his speech so that the demonstrators would miss him. He's a slick operator.

From: La Barbara <lynx1043@hotmail.co.uk>

Yes, well so is our mutual friend. It makes me sick that she's out there enjoying herself at the taxpayer's expense. A nice house to live in, a car, a credit card - where's it going to end?

From: "Hal" <wolfman@hotmail.co.uk>

It's only an old terraced house, not a palace. But she is moving in higher circles just now. She was at a country club recently, the same night your friend Beth was there, actually. You will be very careful what you say around her, won't you?

From: La Barbara <lynx1043@hotmail.co.uk>

Of course I will. I don't want it all to blow up any more than you do. I want you right here beside me, not back down south somewhere.

From: "Hal" <wolfman@hotmail.co.uk>

Guess what, as well as shagging the posh girlfriend, she's also picked up a guy in a bar in Manchester. We checked him out and he turns out to be a priest. God knows what he'd think if he knew who she was. Another brilliant own goal for the Catholic church!

From: La Barbara <lynx1043@hotmail.co.uk>

She's bloody unbelievable. You'd think she'd try and live a quiet life, wouldn't you? Because if anyone ever discovered who she was she'd be dead meat in days.

From: "Hal" <wolfman@hotmail.co.uk>

Don't scare me, Lynxwoman!!!

From: La Barbara <lynx1043@hotmail.co.uk>

It's true, love. People would come after her. It would be acid in the face time. Or vigilantes in the night.

From: "Hal" <wolfman@hotmail.co.uk>

Which would make those people no better than her.

From: La Barbara <lynx1043@hotmail.co.uk>

You think so? I think they'd have a point. And when she takes my wolfman away from me I want to hunt her down, let her feel my hot breath at her back.

'Look, don't be ridiculous, Beth,' says Charles, as if she's a particularly obtuse student. 'There is no way that woman is alive.'

'I saw her,' says Beth, wondering if she's just being stubborn.

'You saw someone who looked like her, darling.'

'It was her,' says Beth. 'I'd know her walk anywhere.'

Charles sighs, lays down *The Daily Telegraph*. 'You can't seriously think the government would allow her out?'

'Why not? If they thought they'd get away with it—less embarrassment for them if she's suddenly off the scene and not able to take them to the European Court any more.'

'For crying out loud, woman. I think all the lefties you're meeting at these idiotic political rallies have turned your brain to mush.'

'Political? It's not political. He's your son too and you haven't raised a finger.'

'Will chose his own profession without consulting me. He now has to live with the consequences.'

'Or die with them.'

'Beth, what has got into you? You come home from Glasgow babbling about a woman who's been dead for months. You talk as if the government were some third world dictatorship. Be serious.' He closes his eyes and sips at his wine as if at salvation.

Beth feels a red wave of anger washing over her, in a way she hasn't felt since she was a girl and her mother slapped her across the head for hanging about on the street. 'Your precious government killed Princess Diana. They're capable of anything.'

He bangs the glass down on the table, spilling red wine over its polished surface. 'Now look what you've made me do. After it's just come back from the French polisher's.'

'Oh, for heaven's sake. Who cares?' says Beth. 'I never liked that table anyway. Just because your precious mother had it by her bedside.'

'My dear Beth, you are hardly equipped to judge fine furniture, now are you?'

'I may not have *had* any before I met you but I'm just as good a judge of it now, thank you very much.'

He gives her a long, cold look as he heaves himself up out of the armchair to find a cloth. Good, why should she do everything round here? She stomps into the hall and snatches her coat from its hook. 'Where are you going?' asks Charles, but she ignores him. Snob. Who does he think he is?

She bangs the door behind her as she leaves. What on earth's wrong with her? She feels so shaky. She *knows* that woman is Myra Hindley, just as she knows Will's going to be sent to Iraq. Everything seems so bleak, hopeless. She's felt like death since she came back from Scotland.

The air is crisp and cold and she starts walking down the street towards the main road. It's too dark to go into the park, she decides, then walks in anyway. All she wants is to smell the trees, the grass. There won't be anyone around at this time of night and anyway, why would they bother her? She's just another middle-aged woman of no interest to anyone. Even to her own husband? She huddles into her coat. He's so dismissive of her these days, never wants to hear her opinion.

She draws the scent of greenery down into her chest, feeling oddly comforted by its medicinal dankness. Ahead of her she sees a man she recognises from down the street, out walking his dogs. Funny, she thought he only had the one but there are two in front of him. She breathes more easily now. The park is so calm, so soothing somehow, as if the trees are giving off some narcotic that quiets all anxiety. If it is Myra—and it is—how on earth will it be possible to act normally when she sees her next? What should she say? Should she say something to Sophie? She feels a shiver of fear rustling through her. What if Myra turns on her? Even if she's supposed to have reformed completely she's still proved herself capable of great violence.

More than violence. It's impossible to imagine how she could bring herself to do what she did. Beth couldn't even bring herself to smack Will when he was naughty; she can't conceive of what it takes to batter a small child, to murder one. Their skin is so soft, you want to stroke it, smother it with kisses; a child's skin is one of the wonders of the universe. To hurt it, you'd have to be practically inhuman. You couldn't be like other people.

Once, she heard some of the tapes Myra and Brady made when they were torturing Lesley Ann Downey—a policewoman she knew from Gorton played it to her. She didn't want to listen, but Myra had been so much a part of her life she had to. On and on it went, not just the one they played in court but others. Worse. Unbearable. How could any woman slap a frightened little girl like that, tell her to shut up? It's unbelievable what one human being can do to another, but to a *child?* What was inside Myra Hindley that she could care so little about a small, defenceless creature? Or what was missing, what vital part of the human heart did she not have? God, she cared more about her dog than about the children she'd killed.

What if it had been Will? What if he'd been younger and she'd met Myra when she was with him? To think of a woman who'd murdered children, casually bumping into kids at the supermarket. Her stomach is churning, she feels sick. Myra was always so good with the little ones—everyone wanted her to babysit. Would she have put her hand out to touch Will's? coaxed a smile from him?

Beth's got herself so agitated that she almost walks into the back of the man from down the street. His dogs are trotting ahead of him, one after the other. He turns and smiles at her, puts a finger to his lips. 'Look, it's a fox,' he whispers.

Beth peers into the gloom. 'My goodness,' she says. Sure enough, the man's dog has a little fox padding behind it. It's the vixen she sees in her garden, not the dog fox, and obviously thinks the mutt in front of it is the leader of a pack or something. Such a dainty creature, with her sharp little teeth and her sensitive nose. Does she think she's a dog too? Can she really believe she's the same species?

Maybe she is. She's just wilder, more vicious than a domestic dog. Could she adapt? learn to do as she's told? become tame? Would it be a good thing?

'Whatever next?' she says to her neighbour. 'You never know what foxes will do, do you?'

'Aye, the more they live in towns the bolder they get. They made a right mess of my daughter's cat last week. You want to watch yours.'

'Oh, I don't think she roams too far. Cats aren't natural prey for foxes anyway, are they?'

'That doesn't stop them. I think some of them like the taste of blood. One of these days they'll go for a child, you mark my words.'

Beth walks along in silence. How bleak the world is becoming, how strange. 'You shouldn't be walking on your own at this time of night, love,' says the man.

'I know,' says Beth, with a placatory smile. 'But sometimes you just get fed up staying in, don't you? Maybe the bad people should stay at home for a change.'

'You're right there, love. It's got that decent people can't walk down t'road in safety.' They've reached the end of the park and he turns to go back. His dog follows him but the vixen seems surprised to be changing direction and suddenly takes off, scurrying out the gate and off through the lanes. 'She were a right pretty creature, weren't she?'

Beth nods, eyes straining to see the last of her. 'I'm off that way too,' she says. 'Going to see a friend.'

'Ah. You be careful, love. Watch yourself on the way back.'

'Don't you worry. I won't be coming through the park again. I just took a notion, you know?'

He pats her arm in approval. 'Aye, best stick to t'main road.'

She watches as he goes back under the over-arching trees. Nice man, though why should she feel she has to answer to him? Somewhere niggling away in her head she can hear Jude teasing her at the demo. 'You're such a people pleaser, Beth. I can't imagine how you've come away against Charles's wishes.'

'I've got a life of my own,' Beth said, stung.

'Of course you do. Good for you for standing up to him, my Bethling.'

'He's not an ogre, Jude.'

'Men are all ogres, darling, even the nice ones like Charles.'

Now Beth wanders down the lane the little fox ran into. It's wide and brightly lit and she can see into people's kitchens. A woman with dark pouches under her eyes wearily lifts dishes from the draining board; next door a teenage boy and girl stand kissing in the half-dark. It's peaceful somehow, seeing other people's lives at one remove, as if the film of glass between you

200

blocks out their passion. The young people's kiss seems chaste, demure, the woman's fatigue manageable.

In one back yard she smells the fragrance of fresh tea, like a camellia she once had in the garden. She pops her head over the wall to see if it's the same one and is met by a barrage of barks from a very small dog. It looks, she realises, like that little lapdog that the woman Maria always carries around. Oh my God, is this her house? She steps back quickly, not wanting to attract her attention. She'd die if that woman came out. What would she say to her? How is she going to react next time they meet?

She walks briskly away from the house, further into the lane, then stops to look back. The little dog is right at the door. Beth's heart is thumping, but she can't see if Myra is there. Why is she so terrified? Myra wouldn't be. She was afraid of nothing as a girl. They said that at home she was afraid of the dark, but you'd never have known it, the way she was outside. Fearless, that's what she was. That's why Beth admired her. She'd take on anyone, lads even, especially anyone who hurt her sister Maureen.

Fearless, fearless Myra. Was that why she was able to do what she did? She wasn't afraid of anything, not blood, not sin, not even death?

Pat is already outside, looking impatiently at her watch, when Jude pulls up to the kerb.

'Sorry, sweetie,' sings Jude. 'You're raring to go, aren't you? I thought you'd wait inside till I came.'

'I should have.' Pat's tone is dry. 'You're never on time. Ever.'

Jude concentrates on pulling out into the fast-moving traffic. 'Hope you don't mind but I thought we'd go a little further afield than planned. I need to do some research.'

'Research? Into what moisturiser to wear when you're power walking? What colour of trainers?'

'Tut tut,' says Jude. 'Tetchy. Why do none of my friends believe I write about serious stuff too?'

'Because you don't,' says Pat flatly.

'Actually I'm well into the book now, the one about serial killers. I've done tons of research.'

'Oh? I didn't think you were serious about that.'

'Well, I am. Charles has been helping me.'

'Beth's Charles?' Pat frowns.

'Yes, Pattikins. Beth's Charles. I told you I was going to ask him.'

'Does she know?'

'I assume so. I imagine Charles tells her what he's up to.'

Pat peers suspiciously at her. 'You haven't mentioned it yourself?'

'Haven't seen her lately. I should have got her to come along today, shouldn't I? She'd enjoy a walk on the moors.'

'What moors?'

'Well, Saddleworth, of course.'

'Oh no,' says Pat. 'You're not serious?'

'Come on darling, this kills two birds with one stone. We have our little exercise session and I get the chance to feel what the moors are like, get a bit of background.'

'Yeah yeah. Make all the excuses you like—you're just doing your usual, making a unilateral decision and expecting everyone else to fall in with it.'

'You don't really mind. You know you don't.'

'Hmm.'

'I do love this motorway,' says Jude. 'It's so dramatic.'

Pat sighs. Typical Jude, to change the subject.

The Saddleworth turn-off, when it comes, makes her shiver. 'I can't see that sign without feeling sick,' she says.

The road crosses vast tracts of bleak moor, featureless and sere, like land blasted by nuclear winter. 'Do you think the end of the world will look like this?' says Jude.

Pat nods. Despite the blue skies and bright sunshine, she feels a sense of foreboding. On they drive, till the town of Oldham is spread out below them. Then the road dips and plunges in and out of a series of little villages, some pretty, some grim. Jude eventually stops the car at the top of a long hill. 'I think this is the place,' she says. 'Look, there's the reservoir down there.'

"Why didn't we go down that way? It looks quite pretty and there's a proper car park.'

Jude walks over to the other side of the road. 'David Smith, you know the brother-in-law who told the police? He posed for pictures where he thought they'd been, and the view is exactly like this spot. Look.' She holds out a book, page open at a photo of a good-looking young man staring into the camera.

Pat shakes her head. 'I'll take your word for it. It gives me the creeps.'

A sheep makes its colicky, cranky cry. Below them a hawk hovers on the air currents, motionless. Has it seen prey? A rabbit shivering in the grass, an adder slithering over the rocks? There are no humans here, no warmth, just the casual cruelty of nature with its unmarked, unmourned deaths.

Jude strides along the road till they reach a stile. 'Come on, let's go back off the road.' They start walking across the hummocky grass but it's rough going and they take a long time to go a short distance. The moors stretch endlessly before them. After only half an hour Jude is tiring. Usually she can walk for hours without difficulty. 'What's wrong,' asks Pat. 'Are you ill?'

'Too many late nights, that's all.'

'That sounds interesting. Spill the beans then.'

'No, it's not what you think. I'm researching the book as well as working every hour that God sends for the newspaper. It's too much, really, but I can't stop now. I'm totally hooked.'

'I don't know how you can do that stuff. These people don't deserve your attention.'

Jude hugs herself against the icy temperature. 'It's depressing. I'm corresponding with Ian Brady and I feel terribly sorry for him. What a wasted life he's had.'

Pat looks at her in astonishment. 'You feel sorry for him?' she explodes. 'At least he's had a life. Don't you mean you feel sorry for his victims?'

'That goes without saying. I think he's a remarkable man in many ways. I just wonder what he could have been if he hadn't made such mistakes in his youth.'

'Mistakes? Is that all his victims were? Little blots on his copybook? These people are dead, Jude.'

'I know. But he's not. He's an intelligent man with a huge amount of self-discipline. Think what he could have made of his life if he'd applied those gifts to something worthwhile.'

'Think of his victims,' says Pat sourly.

203

'It must be nice to live in that black and white world of yours where no-one does anything they regret.'

'I've worked with people like him. You can't believe a word they say. They don't feel for other people the way you and I do and they never will.'

'Well, I feel for *him*. I think of him living in surroundings he hates, not able to choose the simplest thing in his life. No friends, no stimulation, no human touch.' Jude bites her lip, surprised by her own emotion. She must be tired. 'I think he must be the loneliest man in the world.'

'He's manipulating you.'

'He doesn't say any of that. It's what seeps out between the words he writes, not what's in them.'

'You be careful. He'll have you campaigning to get him out next, like dotty old Lord Longford did for Myra Hindley.'

'He knows he'll never be released. Never. And you know what? He wouldn't stoop to ask.'

Pat shakes her head. 'I thought you had more sense.' She holds out a hand to help Jude over the stile. Somewhere on the moor a bird starts squawking frantically, as if chasing a predator away from her nest. The afternoon, which started off clear and cold, is now icy, the skies clouding over. The two women trudge in silence towards the car.

'Let's go back to that last village and see if we can get a coffee in the pub,' suggests Pat.

Jude stops and looks out over the darkening moors, at the rain-battered sheep, the coarse grass that seems to shudder as the wind moves through it. In places the ground has been torn open to reveal damp earth, heavy as blood. How sad life is, in the end. If only humans could be made innocent, but they know too much, want too much. She tries to pull her mind away from the thought of small bodies buried deep underneath the surface, of blood and bone dissolving into the earth. 'Do you think the land retains the memory of what's happened?' she says.

Slowly Pat's gaze sweeps out over the storm-blasted landscape and beyond, to the crabbed grey rocks glowering over the open heath. 'This land does.' She studies Jude's bleak expression and tugs gently at her jacket. 'Come on. You're taking this all far too much to heart.'

'It permeates my whole life. I can't stop thinking about it.'

'But that's madness. You have to learn to be more detached. If I let the prisoners get into my head I'd go right round the twist. I'd never be able to switch off.'

Jude turns and walks to the car. 'It makes you question your whole existence,' she says. 'It makes you want to do something useful, something clean.'

'Jude, what on earth's got into you? Why should some sickos and the horrible things they do affect you? You're not like them.'

Jude starts the car up. 'We're all like them. Which of us gets to go through life without hurting other people?'

'Not like that.'

204

'No, of course not like that. But we all do things we shouldn't. How can any of us sit in judgement on another person?'

'Oh Jude, don't go all bleeding-heart liberal on me. You've worked for the *Daily Mail*, for goodness sake.'

There is a long silence before Jude turns to look at her. 'You're right, of course,' she says, with her most brilliant smile. Strange, how singularly it fails to reassure Pat.

Inside, the jeep is like a pressure cooker, a time machine where all thought has stopped and only heat remains. There is nothing beyond the trickling of sweat down the back of his neck, the discomfort of his heavy camouflage gear weighing on his body.

And the fear.

Will glances across at Kezza. Where he is wet and pink, she looks cool, as if the surface of her skin is made of some magical substance impervious to the sun. What the fuck are they doing here, in this godforsaken country? They should be on a beach somewhere, maybe in Ibiza. She says it's great there though he's never been. His dad's idea of a holiday was always some elegant French resort that had seen better days, like La Baule or Biarritz, some place where you ate Froggy food and drank a lot of wine. He prefers beer.

He should be lying naked in the sun with Kez, brushing the sand from her cleavage, or rolling into the blue surf with her, the waves creaming over them.

'I'm melting. Why do we never get the jeep with air-con?' he says.

They inch forward, eyes roaming, right to left. There's probably Iraqis watching their every move. You can never relax in this damn country, not even in the barracks. He frowns at the thought of Yardley, always trying to brush against Kezza, always sneering when he passes Will. You should be able to trust your fellow soldiers, not feel the skin on your neck bristle when they pass you.

She's promised to take him to Ibiza when their first tour of duty's over. He'll have to go and spend a couple of days with Mum and Dad first but they can't expect him to stop at home after what he'll have been through by then. Mum's bound to be upset but it can't be helped. Maybe he can persuade Kez to come up for a couple of days, though she sniggered when he suggested it.

'Oh yes, I really fit in at your house, posh boy.'

'Don't call me that.'

'Well, you are.'

She's probably right not to come. Dad's attitude was weird the last time. He liked her too much, was too interested in her. Only for one reason. There's no way he'd really like her—she doesn't know anything about literature or Greek mythology or any of the stuff that his dad's into, and anyway, he never approves of anything Will does. If he had his way Will would be stuck in some office toiling away for accountancy exams or some other rubbish.

Still, sometimes he'd give anything just to be back home for Sunday dinner, pulling the cat on to his lap as he watches the football, doing nothing as Mum takes the roast lamb out of the oven. He's lucky. When Kezza talks about her dad, Will's sure the bastard did more than hit her.

'Which way is it now?' asks Jem. They're at a crossroads, tarmacked road in one direction, the other a half-made desert track, dusty and faint.

'Left,' he says. 'The other way's through that place the Yanks trashed last week.'

'Might as well go and see what our brothers in arms have been doing,' says Jem, cheerfully gunning the jeep to the right. Will shrugs as they set off down the track. They drive on through the desert, dust billowing up in front of the windscreen so they can hardly see. Scrubby bits of bush occasionally loom up in front of them, but mostly the sand seems to stretch, featureless, into infinity.

The town is a ghost town, with not a single soul wandering its streets. Many of the buildings are burnt out shells, with blackened walls and people's clothing spilling haphazardly out of doorways like horsehair from a sofa. On one side of the road they can hear the gentle hiss of water or gas escaping. On the other, red cables sprout from every wall, conjuring nests of electric vipers breeding behind them.

'It's creepy,' says Jem.

'Don't be a wimp,' says Kezza. She winks at Will, though he too feels uneasy, as if a thousand unseen eyes are watching them.

'No point in hanging about here,' he says, with the requisite look of contempt for Jem.

They drive smartly through the single street, reluctant to linger if they're being observed. 'What gets into people's heads?' says Will.

'It's just war,' says Kezza flatly.

'Doesn't it bother you?' asks Jem. 'These people didn't do anything, yet here their houses are destroyed, their belongings ruined.'

'Oh boo hoo,' says Kezza.

Jem rolls his eyes.

'What do they expect? Fucking Ali Babas,' she says.

A few miles on they pass a group of small boys, who yell and run down the road away from them. As the jeep pulls past, two of the boys hurl themselves at the vehicle and swing up on to the back. 'Little toerags,' says Jem amiably.

'We used to do that with buses when we were kids,' says Kezza.

The boys laugh and gesticulate, conquering heroes entering their own village. The jeep passes houses with chickens running about in front of them, women hanging out washing, a small herd of goats. An ancient house holds what appears to be the village store, with strings of peppers hanging at the door and cans of olive oil stacked up outside. Just as Jem comes to a halt in the square the youngsters jump off and run away, flicking the finger at the soldiers.

'Charming,' says Will. He gets down from the jeep, pulling out his fags as he does so, and is immediately surrounded by a group of children. 'Mister. Mister soldier.' They rub their stomachs, miming hunger. 'Have we got anything for them?' says Kezza.

'I've got some sweets,' says Will.

'Their mothers will love that,' says Jem.

The harsh sound of a woman scolding sends most of the children scurrying away, but one little girl remains, reluctant to leave. She stares up at Will with solemn eyes, a pretty little thing, her dark hair covered with one of their shawl things, her face beseeching.

He bends to give the child a sweet. She gives him a huge smile, displaying a mouth half full of teeth.

'You're gorgeous, kiddo,' he says, eliciting ecstasy in return. He points to his own chest and says, 'Will.' Then he touches hers and asks, 'What's your name?'

She looks away shyly, casting down her dark eyes. 'Ayesha,' she says, in a whispery little voice.

'Hallo, Ayesha, pleased to meet you.' He shakes her by the hand, causing her to giggle uncontrollably.

He draws the smoke down into his lungs, presses another sweet into the little girl's hand. Jem prods him. 'Come on, Santa Claus—you take that side of the square, I'll take this.' Kezza stands by the jeep, holding her rifle.

Methodically the two men make their way through the buildings lining the square, searching for stores of ammunition, though Will hopes they won't find any. The encounter with the little girl has given him a warm feeling. These people are not the enemy, they're not so different from him after all. Room after dusty room, nothing. In one a shrunken-gummed old man shrinks away as he enters. 'Relax, grandad,' he says, smiling to reassure him, though the old man simply stares at him, expressionless.

He returns to the jeep empty-handed. His little friend is holding Kezza's hand, staring up at her in fascination. 'She's probably never seen a white woman, has she?' he says. Kezza just grins. 'Give 'er some more, then.' He fishes the rest of his toffees out from his pack. 'Here you are, sweetheart.'

Jem returns, empty-handed too, and jumps up into the jeep. 'Yo, troops.' The other two get back into the vehicle, waving at Ayesha, who gives them an enchanting smile in return. Jem starts up the engine, stirring up a maelstrom of dust as they leave.

They clatter and bump along the potholed track. *Every breath you take, every move you make, I'll be watching you*, sings Will. Kezza beats out the rhythm on the dashboard. 'Spooky, wasn't it?' says Jem.

On they drive, passing through villages that are no more than hamlets, mere smatterings of shabby houses littering the desert. At the end of one, the road simply peters out. Jem frowns. 'What do you think, guys?'

'I think if we don't turn back now, we'll miss chowdown,' says Kezza.

'Yeah, I see the hand of Allah in this,' says Will.

Jem turns the jeep and they set back off down the road they came on. Kezza slouches in the front seat now, helmet pulled down over her eyes. Will leans his head against the cool glass of the window, trying to keep awake.

By the time they reach the village where they met Ayesha it is semi-dusk, the sky streaked purple and orange. No small boys come out to jump on their vehicle. No-one comes out to stare at them. The place is eerily silent. Kezza sits bolt upright. 'What's going on here?' she says.

They pass slowly through the long street, rifles held at the ready. Eyes, unseen eyes watching them from all sides. Nothing stirs. Not a hen, not a dog, nothing.

Jem comes to a halt in the village square, just as they did earlier in the day, only now there are no signs of life, as if the whole village has fled or is in mourning.

It is Kezza whose eyes first make out the little body hanging there, from a makeshift wooden cross planted near the mosque. 'Ayesha,' she screams, and runs forward, but the little girl's eyes have rolled up in her head and her swollen tongue lolls from her mouth. Will cannot move. As Kezza cradles the little body, it is Jem who comes forward to cut her down.

'We can't take her away,' he says. 'Her mother will want her.'

Kezza sags as her arms receive the weight of the child. She holds her tightly against her chest, her face numb.

Jem goes back to the jeep and brings out some plastic sheeting. 'This is all we've got,' he says. He walks forward and lays it at the doorway of the mosque. Gently he takes the little girl away from Kezza and places her on the sheeting. Her pink headscarf is lying on the dusty ground and he carefully brushes it off before covering her face with it.

'Come on,' he says, guiding Kezza away.

'Why?' she moans. 'Why?'

'Infidel sweets,' says Jem, his face grim. He touches Will softly on the shoulder. Will's eyes are staring. 'Come on, mate. This isn't your fault.'

'Yeah, I know,' says Will, but as he turns to get into the jeep he catches a glimpse of the little girl's dark, shiny hair above the blanked-out face. 'Bastards,' he screams, his voice emerging from his throat like the eerie ululation made by grieving women here.

Wildly he sprays shot round the square. 'Bastards. Towelhead bastards. Where are you? Too cowardly to come out and face us? Fucking towelhead bastards.'

But there is no sound save the beating of his own heart.

'I'm going to kill him,' Sophie says. She's stomping round looking cross, pulling cupboard doors open and searching through them. M sinks into the chintz sofa, studying the lithe body, the tight straight-leg jeans. It's amazing how often people use those words. They wouldn't if they knew what it took.

'It doesn't matter. Any film'll do. It was just this priest I met over in Manchester was talking about it.' M stretches her legs out on the coffee table, the smoke from her cigarette curling around her.

'Manchester? How did you meet a priest over there?' asks Sophie.

'Same way you meet priests over here, my love. I went to mass in his church.'

'You are good, M. Was that one of the days you went shopping?'

'Yes, but I didn't find what I was looking for and I thought I'd pop into church for a quiet moment.'

Sophie rummages through a pile of DVDs on the floor by the television. 'It's amazing how it de-stresses you, isn't it?'

'Mmm ...' M tweaks her smile into as pious an expression as she can manage. She tries not to think of Aidan's shoulder muscles, the smell of him.

'It's brothers, you know. If they've got sisters they never learn to tidy up after themselves. Well, they didn't in our house. Mummy always favoured the boys. Sometimes I think she'd like to have been a man herself.'

She shrugs her slender shoulders. 'I give up. Bunty's had it.' She collapses back on to the sofa beside M, thigh brushing against hers. 'Oh look, there it is. He's put it in with the books, stupid idiot.' She hauls herself up. '*Natural Born Killers* it is.'

She's just put the DVD in the machine when the doorbell rings. 'Bugger,' she says. 'Back in a mo.' M slides her feet down to the floor. There's a woman's voice and then Sophie walks through the door with Beth. God, this could be disastrous. She'll have to keep a cool head here. She rises, trying to look relaxed. 'Beth, how nice to see you again. You look very pretty in that dress, doesn't she, Sophie?'

'It's such a soft colour,' says Sophie. 'Pistachio, do you call that?'

'Charles gave it to me for Christmas,' says Beth, a faint flush rising to her cheek despite herself. On the television screen the DVD signal is bouncing around on a blue background. 'You were just about to watch something?' she says. What an insipid creature she is, with her pallid frock and her puke-coloured skin. M feels a sudden surge of adrenalin—she might be about to enjoy herself. 'Yes, *Natural Born Killers*. Do you know it? It's an Oliver Stone movie.'

Beth gawps at her. 'I've seen it once, a good while ago now.' She's staring at M as if she can't believe what she's hearing.

'This priest I know was telling me about it,' continues M, eyes not leaving Beth's face. 'He says it's a satire on the way our society makes celebrities out of serial killers.' She can tell Beth is unnerved by her staring. This is going to be too easy, she thinks, but Beth surprises her.

210

'We didn't used to make celebrities out of serial killers,' she says. 'We used to despise them. Like the Moors Murderers, for example. They lived in Gorton, where I grew up. People didn't admire them, they hated them.'

'Really, Beth?' asks Sophie. 'Did you know them?'

'I knew her,' says Beth.

M sits very still. If she moves she'll draw attention to herself.

'I used to see him on his motor bike sometimes. Nobody thought much of him round our way. He was full of himself, God knows why. He was a skinny big drip. And he always had his nose stuck in a book.'

M keeps her face impassive, despite her rage. That stuck up little gobshite. She couldn't have got within yards of Neddy, not unless he was going to strangle whatever life she had out of her pathetic body. She leans forward and stubs her fag end out in the china saucer Sophie lets her use. Daft really. She'd be much better to forget her principles and get a proper ashtray. 'I would have thought,' she says in her creamiest voice, 'that a professor's wife would find that attractive in a man.'

Sophie laughs out loud. 'The pictures make him look as if he had a lot of charisma. All those dandified suits and dark glasses. Don't you think so, M?'

'Not my type, I'm afraid,' she says, relishing Beth's look of outrage.

'What was she really like, Beth?' asks Sophie. 'People are so unfair, the way they hate her much more than him. Why should it be so much worse for a woman to murder a child than it is for a man?'

'Women give birth, that's why,' says Beth. Her voice is trembling, but whether with rage or distress, M can't tell. 'Women are made to bring children into the world, they're soft and squashy so that they can cradle them and nurture them and put their arms round them when they're hurt. Any woman who lets a little girl call her 'Mum' and then allows her to be raped and tortured and murdered is an *abomination*.'

'Is that what happened? Really?' says Sophie.

'You're too young to remember it, I suppose,' says Beth. 'That was little Lesley Ann Downey. Ten years old. Boxing Day, they took her. A day that should be so happy.'

Sophie shudders. 'What a dreadful way for a child to die.'

In the silence that follows M's ears feel assaulted by the sound of the ticking clock. The TV signal bounces wildly back and forward on the blue screen. Then the skin-crawlingly repulsive little worm leans back against the chintzy cushion and says, 'Of course Myra Hindley never had children of her own. She didn't understand what it was to be a real woman.'

M looks at the woman's putty-coloured neck. She'd like to put her two hands round it and throttle her. Was this the sort of rage that drove her Neddy? He didn't seem angry when he talked about it, but underneath maybe he was seething like this? Maybe it's always rage that drives serial killers. She picks her packet of fags up off the table and lights one. 'That's a sadness for any woman, don't you think?' she asks, knowing that her voice is soft and sympathetic.

211

Beth flinches, clearly uncertain how to proceed. No bottle. M leans forward. To the attack then. 'I lost my own baby, you know. She was taken away from me. I was just a girl. They could do things in those days ...'

Sophie leans over and places her hand over M's. 'Don't upset yourself,' she says. 'You don't need to talk about it.'

M can see the snail-trail of doubt creeping across Beth's mind. Good, she's bought herself a reprieve, for a little while at least. Let her work it out.

Sophie stands up. 'I'll make us some coffee, shall I?'

'I should go and leave you to your film,' says Beth. She looks confused.

'Oh stay,' says M, emboldened now. 'I'm just getting a rather belated education. We'd be glad of your opinion.'

'My opinion,' says Beth, 'is that people who murder others and call it love are trashy little scumbags.' Her skin is as vile a green as her stupid dress. She stumbles on her way to the door. 'Sorry,' she tells the table.

M leans her head back on the sofa, relieved that she's going at last. What does that poxy little prat, with her pompous ass of a husband, know about murder? Or love, for that matter?

Empty, empty ... Jude struggles to sit up in the bed. This is no feeling to wake up with. Her head is aching, her throat dry. She leans over for some water from the bedside table and switches the lamp on. Only six o'clock. She must have drifted off after Charles left.

The room is pleasant enough, with its country house chintz and tassels, though not to Jude's taste. Neither, alas, was the sex. Poor Charles was awkward, even shy in bed, as though the spectre of Beth was in the room with him, preventing him from relaxing. Jude fumbles in her handbag for painkillers. He's clearly not used to this kind of thing—there was no need for him to declare his love. Both of them know it's not true.

Well, she does. He probably hasn't admitted it to himself yet.

What a fool she's been. All that discussion at lunch, the elation over the sale of the book, the champagne ... they got carried away, that's all. It mustn't happen again. He's the husband of her oldest friend, for chrissake. Jude lies back on the pillows, feeling sick, the mixture of oysters and beef and alcohol sloshing about inside her like the metronomic waves of nausea she used to get on the cross-Channel Hovercraft.

She is not that kind of person. She's loyal to her friends, supportive, never puts men before them. It's not as if she's ever been short of a partner—she has no need to trail after the married ones. So why, why did she do it? Sweat is trickling down her back and she doesn't feel like herself at all. She must go out and have a walk, otherwise she's in danger of throwing up.

Swiftly she pulls on her clothes and heads for the door. It's already dark outside but she doesn't care. She *must* get some fresh air. Damn, she has no torch, but it doesn't matter—if she sticks to the side of the road she'll be fine. No Army brat like her is going to be put off by a little visual discomfort.

Around her the night air is soft and damp, calming her, settling her stomach. Her legs are a bit shaky but the ground is firm beneath her feet and she sets off up the hill outside the hotel. Occasionally she starts at sudden rustlings in the hedgerow, but for the most part the darkness is peaceful, soothing.

Poor Charles, poor Beth ... how reckless she's been. Isn't that one definition of second degree murder, that you have a reckless indifference to killing? She, with her exuberant happiness, her careless plunging into extremes of sensation, has murdered their marriage. Dear, anxious Beth, always chasing after security and stability as if, coming from some dump in Manchester, she'd decided that safety depended on always having money, a home. Now Jude has shown her that the world is neither secure nor stable. It never can be safe. If only she could roll back time and erase this afternoon, go back to before lunch, insist that Beth come with them.

In the darkness a small unseen animal starts chattering in agitation, threatened by some predator. Why didn't she insist? Why didn't she tell Beth in the first place? She talked about Iraq, so why didn't she mention the book and Charles helping her? Jude stands stock still as the light from a car comes sweeping round the corner towards her. Could it be she intended this all along? With a sinking feeling she realises that at the very least she must have decided to keep her options open.

The car halts beside her and the window rolls down. 'Are you lost, dear?' An elderly woman is leaning out of the car.

'No, I'm just out for a little walk to clear my head. But thank you very much for asking.'

'Be careful, dear. You never know who's lurking about these days.'

'I will,' says Jude automatically, though as the lady drives away it strikes her as ridiculous that some psychopath would be out here in the wilds at this time of night. Or is it? Ian Brady went up to the moors when it was dark, didn't he?

Slowly she turns and starts walking back downhill towards the hotel. The wind is rising and she shivers in her silk blouse, drawing her thin jacket across her chest. Beth must never know. Jude must nip it in the bud now. Charles will surely understand—he clearly felt guilty before they'd even done anything—but he's been too passive, too bowled over by Jude's own excitement to be decisive now. No, it's up to her to take charge of the situation.

Oh Beth, poor Beth. How could she do this to her? An image of Beth on her wedding day flits into Jude's head, of Beth standing there shivering in her white satin mini-dress, skinny shoulders shaking with fright. Beside her, her mother was large and awkward in the too-short dress and jacket that was mother-of-the-bride fashion in those days, while her father's new suit looked cheap and ill-fitting beside Charles's father in his Savile Row morning dress. 'What a mismatch?' Jude heard one of the guests say. 'Isn't the girl just a teensy bit common?' That was the only other time she's betrayed Beth—she said nothing, when really she wanted to biff the guy and shout, *No, my friend is not common. She's gentle and sweet and has more integrity in her big toe than you have in your whole, corpulent body.*

There must be no faltering now. Tomorrow she'll ring that producer and bludgeon him, charm him, bloody well sleep with him if she has to to get the Iraq gig. Why not? She's done worse than that, for nothing, it seems. With the lights of the hotel spooling out before her, she walks past the entrance and into the darkened rose garden. Despite the cold she doesn't want to go inside just yet, needs to think this through.

She will go to Iraq, concentrate on honest reporting again. There will be a war, they all know that. Then let her go there, let her go through what her father and brothers have all gone through. Perhaps by placing her life in danger she will wipe out the harm she's done.

There are still some roses here, she knows. She saw them here this morning before Charles arrived, the palest of pink, their petals curling inwards as if defending themselves from the onset of winter. But it's too cold to catch even the slightest whisper of their scent. Jude closes her eyes, overwhelmed suddenly with the feeling that she has lost something.

214

Somewhere along the corridor they've got the radio on. He lies on his bed, waiting for the rat-turd orderlies to come and subject him to his daily assault. He wants to be still. It would be undignified to struggle, so he concentrates on slowing down his body till he's hardly breathing. Dying could be like this, if they would only let him. Fuckssake, the most irritating song in the universe, *Winchester Cathedral, you're bringing me down. You stood and you watched as my baby left town.* Bloody moronic words. What cretin dreamed them up? Oh, fuck, he can't lie still now.

He sits up. He wouldn't mind but Winchester Cathedral is a place he'd really like to go to. There's a figure in the crypt there, a bronze man standing calf-deep in water—some journalist sent him postcards of Antony Gormley sculptures. In one of them, the arches that hold up the crypt's roof are reflected in the water and there's a soft orange light falling on the white pillars. The man is tall and slender, his head bent over something though Brady can't ever make it out. Perhaps a bowl of water? There's something mysterious about him, something moving in his starkness, though he's only a man.

Brady takes the card from his bedside drawer. His eyes aren't what they were, and he has to hold the thing right up in front of his face to make it out. Ironic really, that after all the Braille books he translated for the blind, he should be going blind himself. It was always an affliction he understood. Wasn't he in darkness himself for many years? He didn't see as other people saw.

He's still in darkness now, a different kind, the darkness of being alone. There's no point in going on. He's never going to have any love or beauty in his life, might as well be dead. Humans need these things. They're like those lab rats that keep pressing the lever to activate the pleasure centre in their brains and end up dying of starvation and exhaustion, tongues lolling out because they'd rather have stimulation than water.

He's starving, starving for laughter, for the touch of another person, for kindness.

Well, no-one's going to care about that. Why would they, when he had no mercy on those children? He's made his bed and will have to lie on it. It's been so long, though. Now that Myra's gone there's not a single human being to think well of him. Not even the Sloans. They're kind, they keep in touch, but they've never understood him and they never will. It's funny to think she's dead. All those years of love, then hate. Over. He'll see her in Hell, no doubt. If there was a God that's the part that would be true, the torments of Hell, not their pisswater Heaven, with its bright lights and soppy angels. If there was a God he'd be the Old Testament Jahweh, inflicting vengeance; he'd be Thor, the god of thunder, hurling his bolts at the pathetic little humans cowering on the earth below him.

Brady flicks on the bedside light so he can see the card better, the patterns of the arches in the water, the unadorned figure. What must it be like to create something like this? He read in the paper that drivers slow down when they approach Gormley's *Angel of the North*, the huge scrap metal angel that hovers over the A1. Now there's what he calls an angel—earthbound, ugly, strong. Some artist, Gormley. How amazing to know that you have that power, that you've forced people to look at what you've made. And what has *he* done? They all accelerate like mad when they see the turn-off for Saddleworth, scurrying away from things they don't understand.

If only his talents had been different ...

There's the expected knock at the door and in they troop, the creatures from the cesspit who have the nerve to call themselves medical staff. He closes his eyes, imagines himself in a long black box unable to move. He will not give them the satisfaction of struggling. Ever since they broke his arm that first time he's known there's no point to it. That was ridiculous, six of them in full riot gear and balaclavas just to move him from one ward to another. What the hell did they think he'd do to them? They looked like the criminals they were, the fucking tossers.

He puts his card in the drawer and makes himself go still, ignoring their pathetic attempts to communicate with him. He hates them and he knows they hate him. Why do these excrescences even bother? *We won't be a minute, Mr Brady.* Simpering bloody woman. What's she doing here with her silly clipboard? If she knew what he thought of her she wouldn't waste her time acting polite.

Weak, all of them. Not one of them would have the willpower to do what he's doing at this moment. Brains stuffed with pigeon droppings. They take their sordid little stacks of money home and slump in front of the telly without a thought or a real desire entering their tiny minds. They have no idea how to live, just wallow in their vomit-filled styes, slurping and slobbering, stuffing their faces with flavoured lard.

One of them takes the narrow tube and approaches the bed. Brady closes his eyes, has no desire to see the grease-clogged pores of the man's skin this close up. The tube slithers into his nasal passage like an earthworm. He tries to relax his body, knows that if he tenses up his nose will start to bleed. Four fucking years of this, why can't these parasites leave him alone? They wouldn't give a toss if he died so who's the pretence for?

The bleeding starts. And the nausea. He has to tune out or he'll be really ill. Even after all these years it never becomes routine. It feels like violation every single time—and they don't even know how to enjoy it. They hate him but they're scared of him, and scared of what others will think of them. None of them have the strength to make him pay for what he did, so they bungle and botch—and bitch afterwards. He took his pleasures without faltering, enjoyed having power over another human being. They don't have the guts even to think about it. He'd respect them more if they did. It's what they want, after all.

The room is stifling and it takes all his willpower to remove himself mentally. There's a purity about being on hunger strike that these imbeciles could never understand. You leave the body behind and they cannot touch you, cannot hurt you. He is a bird, an eagle, soaring on hot air currents, too hot for the golden eagles he's seen in Scotland. A black eagle, black and predatory, an African eagle. The sky is blue and cloudless and below him he sees a small group of humans, gazing upward at him in awe. Herds of antelopes are streaming across the veldt. He slips from one current to the next, knowing he could swoop at any time and carry off one of their little ones, struggling and straggling along at the back. But he doesn't need food. He is strong, free. He flies in the face of the sun.

The plastic tube enters his stomach but his mind takes him far beyond it, far beyond the people in the room. They are worms, maggots, writhing on the ground far below him. He could stab them with his beak, crush them with his talons. They can force their food into his very blood but they'll never control him. A jab of the feeding tube and his body jerks involuntarily. The woman gives the orderly a sharp look. That's what she's here for, is it? As if he needed a woman to protect him.

The idiot's anxious now and proceeds ultra-carefully. The feeding seems interminable today. He's relieved when they're finished, ignores the woman's questions about whether he's in pain. Let her take her made-up eyes and garish mouth elsewhere. He doesn't need her concern.

He's tired when they leave, and sick. He's too old for this, though he'll never give in. The body can be made to do anything. The mind is more intractable. He should have been more alert when that moron jerked the tube. It was a reflex action but if he'd really been paying attention he could have stopped his body moving.

He picks up his card again. Its simple lines of friendship offer him no comfort. This is how human beings like to think of themselves, not how they are. He swings his legs over the side of the bed. He must look at the book he bought about Gormley. There was a picture in there … he works his way slowly through the pages. Yes, there it is, *Field for the British Isles*. That's what human beings really are. He gazes at the image with ferocious attention. A sea of little clay wormheads, with eyes like maws greedy to devour the world. They have no features to distinguish them from each other, are just little maggoty creatures, too many to count or to care about. That Gormley really knew what he was doing in this one.

Yet the longer he stares, the more different each one seems. Some have striving, writhing necks eager to force their way out of the crowd; some are fat, no-neck blobs; some have clever eyes that seem to see you clearly; some are humorous; and some are only eyes, desperate, beseeching.

He has seen that look before.

How could he have been so wrong?

It's Sophie's fault, she made her go to the doctor. If only she hadn't listened, there would be nothing to know now.

It's not fair.

The doctor looks down at his notes. He seems embarrassed at having to give her bad news, as if the social inconvenience of telling her is what concerns him, rather than the shock to her.

'I'm afraid it's a particularly aggressive form of cancer, Miss Spencer,' he's saying. 'What we call small-cell lung cancer.' The room is suddenly too brightly lit. It's hurting her to keep her eyes open. She doesn't want to look at this young idiot. He has everything ahead of him. He will marry, have children, buy a big house in a quiet area—and be careless of all of it—while she, she has never been out of this country, never water-skied, never seen the Mona Lisa, never worn a wedding dress. It's a high price to pay for the immortality of being Myra Hindley.

It's a death sentence.

'Why can't you operate?' she asks.

'I'm afraid the cancer's gone too far for that. You now have secondaries in your lymph nodes and in the brain.'

The brain ... no. 'How long have I got?'

'On average—and this is not to say you will conform to the average, of course—on average, patients with this advanced a form of cancer have around four months. I'm sorry, Miss Spencer.'

She looks straight at him and he flinches. 'Sorry,' he says again. 'Do you have family who can come and pick you up?'

'I didn't want them to worry,' she says. Thank God she didn't tell Sophie about today's appointment. She'd have insisted on coming and now M would have to calm her down when she can hardly take it in herself.

'Well, there's no point in going through radiotherapy or chemotherapy in these circumstances, is there?' she says. She's damned if she's going to use her glamorous wig to cover baldness. It's not a medical tool, it's to have fun in, to make her someone new, not the same old Myra any more.

'You'll need some form of pain control. I suggest you have a word with Sister about that. We'll sort you out with a prescription.'

M needs time to think. Somewhere inside she's known all along. Those bastards at the Home Office, course they wouldn't let her out if they thought she'd have time to enjoy herself. This is almost more cruel than being kept inside all the time.

Amazing how angry she feels, how cheated. She's not afraid, not yet. Somehow dying seems very far away. Grimly she leaves the building, almost clipping the wing of a four wheel drive parked up beside her as she swings the car out. Pity she missed, probably belongs to a consultant or something.

Fuck them all. She revs the engine and shoots out of the car park, past some dozy sod making a meal of reversing out. Why didn't she go to the doctor earlier? That morning with Sophie wasn't the first time she'd coughed up blood. Nothing as spectacular as that day, of course, when the blood was thick as Ribena, but enough to tell her that something was wrong. Stupid, stupid bitch, to think it would go away by itself.

She heads west for the motorway, can't bear to tell Sophie just yet—she'll be too sympathetic, too smothering. That's not what she wants. She wants ... actually, she wants a fuck. A real, honest to goodness fuck with a strong man. She's impatient at the very thought of Sophie's sweetness, her softness. Today she needs Aidan.

The traffic on the M62 moves too slowly for her and she weaves her way through the lanes. She enjoys this part of driving. It takes nerve, decisiveness, and she's good at it. There are so many fucking deadheads out on the motorway, pootling along at sixty miles an hour in the middle lane. She'd like to run them all off the road, just scatter them out of her way like ninepins in a skittle alley. If they can't drive they should take the bloody bus.

As always, she has a real frisson in the blood when she passes the turn-off for Saddleworth. Not going there today, love. Other fish to fry. Was it worth it? was that season of wild, wonderful, crazy insanity worth the years of tedium since? worth being vilified as the most evil woman in Britain? The speedometer's up at ninety. Best watch out or the cops will be down on her like a ton of bricks. She looks back in her mirror at the ordinary people she's passing. Disgusted of Tunbridge Wells—none of them have any idea what it's like to live, really live. They might surprise themselves if they got caught up with someone like Brady. Huh, most of them would be too gutless anyway.

But maybe, maybe some of the more honest ones would admit that there is no excitement that comes close to that of taking a life, to that moment when breath ceases and suddenly the body is just that, a body. Where does the energy go? Sometimes she'd swear you could see it, like a wisp of smoke rising into the darkness. When that Lesley Ann kid died, there was a little puff of sound as if her spirit was escaping from them. But where to? was it still there watching them as they got dressed and went downstairs? or did it just want to get away from that room? Was there a heaven for it to go to? Well, she'll find out for herself soon enough.

She sighs. She doesn't want to die. Life, being free, it's all too exciting right now. Will Sophie and Aidan find out about each other when she dies? Maybe Aidan will say a eulogy for her. How funny would that be, a priest standing up and talking about his lover, the murderer? She'd like a proper funeral, not that hole in the wall affair they had for Myra Hindley. That's why Gran and that friend of hers, Hettie Rafferty, saved up for funeral insurance—you want a decent send-off, don't you? She doesn't want to be like that old man, Old Pebby, the one that died in the workhouse. Comical really, when you think about it, Gran laying out his body herself. Do it yourself funerals. You could write a play about it. The awful smell when M came home from school that day, embalming fluid. Gran put his coffin right next to her bed. *It's not the dead you have to be afraid of, but the living.* Not that she got into bed that night. Neither of them slept. They sat up all night by the coffin with Old Pebby. Who will sit with her body when the time comes?

219

The traffic slows as she comes into Manchester. She's going to be crawling along at slug pace for hours. Don't these arseholes know she's got no time to waste now?

It's after seven by the time she reaches the church and she begins to wonder whether this really is such a good idea. What if there's a service going on? or he's out? or there's another priest at home? What if he's not pleased to see her? She goes to the church first, not the house. No point in giving all the flower-arranging, headscarf-wearing busybodies something to tittle-tattle about.

The church is dark but there's a rib of light coming from the sacristy. Aidan looks shocked when he sees her. 'Maria, what are you doing here?' He pulls her in quickly and shuts the door.

'Should I not have come?'

He takes her hand, looks into her eyes and says, 'Of course. It's wonderful to see you.' That deep Irish voice of his is so soothing.

'But maybe not here?'

'No, no. It's fine. I'm my own boss, you know.'

'I don't want to get you in trouble with the parish gossips.'

He smiles. 'I can give spiritual guidance to a troubled parishioner if I please.'

He takes off his priest's silk stole and kisses it before folding it neatly and placing it in the top drawer of the dresser. 'You look a bit peaky,' he says to her.

She hesitates. 'I had a bit of bad news health-wise, that's all.'

'Is it serious?'

'No,' she says. Now is not the time. She needs to work this out in her head, decide when she'd have the best advantage from talking about it.

He takes her hand. 'I've been thinking about you all week. I can't get you out of my head. It's sacrilegious. I'm there on the altar holding up the host and all I'm thinking about is being in bed with you. You're like no-one I've ever met before.'

There's a smell of incense in here, and freshly ironed robes for Mass. She puts her arms round his neck and presses herself against him. He's excited, she can tell, but he disengages himself from her. 'Not here, my love. Not in the church.'

'Where then?' Her voice has gone hoarse.

'Father Evans is in the house. We can't go there.'

'Let's get in the car,' she says. 'We can drive somewhere out of town.'

The road out of Manchester is clear now. She follows her beloved M62, excitement rising. Why not? Why not take him to the moors? He's not to know. She wishes they had a bottle of white wine with them, the way she and Neddy used to, but he'd probably be horrified at the idea of her drinking and driving.

'You're smiling,' he says. 'That's better. You looked a bit pale when you arrived.'

'It's you, you see. You have this effect on me.'

220

He runs his hand along her thigh, making her skin leap with desire. 'Careful, I'm driving,' she says.

'Ach, you're not as strict as you pretend, you.'

'Wait and see,' she says.

It's dark by the time they reach the moor. Maybe one day she'll bring him in the light, take him to their places—the Eagle's Head, where Ian used to perch and look down on the valley below; Greystones, with its sheer slabs of granite. For now she turns on the car music player. 'Gotterdämmerung?' he says. 'I wouldn't have taken you for a Wagnerian.'

'Always,' she murmurs.

'The Twilight of the Gods …'

She gazes out, thinking of death, thinking of the children. Theirs was a quicker death than hers will be, more traumatic maybe but over in minutes. Less than an hour anyway, most of them … This is a hard way to die, knowing it's coming, afraid it will happen any moment. She turns to Aidan but she has lost all desire, for now. All she wants is to curl up with him and feel his body warm against her own.

It's dark when Beth gets home from choir practice and Charles, as so often these days, is in bed early. *Hope you enjoyed your sing-song - and a noggin or two in the pub afterwards,* says his note. She crushes it in her fist and flicks it in the bin. Does he have to be so arch? A sing-song? When they're doing the Faure Requiem? She loves that piece of music, loved singing it tonight. If ever she got to choose her own funeral music that would be it. It has a quietness, a serenity in the face of death that she finds admirable.

And when did he ever use the word 'noggin?' He knows she drives there anyway. Damn him, he's probably opened some good Burgundy while she's been out. If there's any left she'll ferret it out. She sighs. Who's she kidding? He uses that sort of word all the time, noggin, my lady wife. She never used to mind those things. They seemed funny, endearing. That was when he made her feel he loved her.

When did he stop? When did living with him begin to feel like hard work? When did she begin to be irritated by the pudgy little stomach he's developing, to find his measured way of talking pompous and not soothing? When did she begin to wonder if he was seeing someone?

She finds the wine tucked away right at the back of the counter, behind the bottle of olive oil, Clos de Vougeot 1995. He *has* been treating himself. She considers the bottle, about a glass in there if she's lucky, though she struggles with the fancy stopper he's used to cork it. He knows she can't manage this one, no doubt chose it on purpose.

The wine, when she finally releases it, is dark as old blood. She holds it at the back of her throat, savouring what Charles calls the *peacock's tail* of flavours. If only she still smoked. A cigarette would make this moment not just perfect but absolutely perfect. Can you have gradations of *perfect?* What strange creatures human beings are. Why should she want more than this? this wine, this taste? They will never come again. Open a bottle of the same wine a year from now and it will taste different altogether.

She sits at the kitchen table, staring out into the garden. Charles has left only the side lamps on and the gentleness of the light is soothing. But where is Squeaky? The little cat isn't curled up in her basket. He must have gone off to bed without bothering to call her in. The kitchen feels empty, too quiet. A year ago their marriage tasted different altogether.

Snatches of Will's letter come into her head, setting her nerves buzzing with fear. *These people are animals, Mum, bloody towelheads. Kezza's right. She says someone ought to put the whole mangy lot of them down.* It's hard to imagine her sweet, gentle son going out on patrol in one of the most dangerous countries in the world, marching, wielding a rifle. All that seems a million miles away from her nice safe kitchen. But more than that, it's hard to imagine him using such language. Is she wrong or is this wine starting to taste metallic?

There is a sudden burst of unearthly barking outside the window—a fox, hoarse, half strangulated, as if it's calling from another plane of existence. She must get Squeaky in. They've done such foul things to cats lately, the foxes. Two doors down had her cat's neck snapped by one of them only last week.

She's the coolest girl I've ever met. None of the guys are as brave as her. Kezza was certainly cool when she took Beth's earrings. That was a strange night, that trip to the country club. The cheek of her. You almost had to admire her nerve. Beth couldn't do it, even if she wanted to—walk up someone's stairs, go into their closed bedroom, lift a pair of earrings from their jewellery chest and then have the audacity to wear them in front of her. She must have nipped back to the house when she and Will said they were going to that club, because the earrings were there when Beth got home, back in the little blue velvet box Will gave her. How did Kezza get past him? And how did she explain that she was no longer wearing the same earrings when they went out to the club? Probably she told him they were too valuable to wear in such a crowded place. Or thought he wouldn't notice. Maybe she didn't care? Maybe she just relied on Will supporting her whatever she did?

He probably would. He's susceptible, Will, always ready to do what you ask. She wishes he'd find a decent girl, one they could be proud of. Oops, her glass is empty already—she's drunk the wine awfully quickly. Charles would probably say it was wasted on her. What was he thinking of that night, leching over that little tart and then parading her down the country club? He didn't seem to notice that she didn't fit in. Except with Maria Spencer of course. Beth shivers, though the kitchen is warm. Oh God, what if M really is Myra Hindley? Why would a young girl like Kezza be so pally with her? There seemed to be a real affinity between them. *You wouldn't believe some of the things she does,* he'd written. Yes, she would.

It's late. She'd better get that cat of hers in. As she rises from the table she hears a terrible yowling sound, as if a child or a small animal is being tortured beyond endurance. She runs to the kitchen door, but the key seems jammed in the lock. The noise is unbearable. Calm down, she must calm down. When she finally stumbles into the garden she screams to scare away the fox. Where is it? Where is Squeaky? The security light has come on but the garden beyond is dark and she can't see. She runs up and down, calling, though she knows she sounds hysterical. She'll probably wake half the neighbourhood.

'Beth, Beth. For heaven's sake.'

Charles is standing at the door, his dressing gown open, and wisps of his hair sticking up.

'It's your fault. You didn't bother to get her in at a reasonable time.'

'She's a cat, Beth. They're nocturnal creatures.'

'Not Squeaky. Not if I can help it. There are too many foxes around here these days.'

'Why on earth would a fox attack a cat? That's not exactly their food group, is it?'

'Half-eaten hamburgers and chips aren't either but they eat that. You don't listen to a word I say, do you? Mrs Percy's cat was killed by a fox last week.'

Charles looks irritated. 'It was probably a dog.'

'No it wasn't. Foxes nowadays are lethal. Didn't you hear that terrible noise a few minutes ago?'

Charles viciously tightens the cord of his dressing gown. 'For goodness sake, Beth, it's only a cat.'

'You know what? Just fuck off, Charles.'

He looks astonished. Good, too used to her being namby-pamby around him. Well, if he's got a mistress he can get *her* to play the little woman. Beth's had enough of it. She marches away from him down to the end of the garden, ignores the bang as he slams the door.

It's dark out here, and without a coat she feels cold. Only a cat, only a cat? Damn, she's snagged her tights on some brambles; this is like a wilderness. That's like saying *only a child*. Where is she, where is Squeaky? Warm blood trickles down her leg and the ripped skin is stinging. She feels like a kid again, skinning her knee, only they didn't hurt themselves on brambles back then—it was always on asphalt or some old bit of rubble. She's going to have to go back for a torch. Without light she wouldn't be able to see Squeaky if her little body was laid out on the grass somewhere.

How did this evening turn so bad? She must calm down. Now everything just seems awful—her missing cat, Will and that ghastly Kezza. Could Charles really be having an affair?

And then her, M. Is it really her? Is she still out there? Just thinking about her makes Beth feel afraid.

224

What an idiot. She should have got some Temazepam from the doc. There's no way she's going to be able to sleep properly over the next few months. Months—well, that's what they say. She'll show them.

It's only one o'clock in the morning. She's gone to bed too early, that's all. Why waste time when there's so little left? M climbs out of bed and gets dressed. Tracksuit trousers and a top, no underwear—no point in putting on fresh knickers for half an hour or so. Minim leaps out of his basket and yaps at her, but she shakes her head. 'Shh, lovely. You go back to sleep. It's too cold and wet out there for you.'

She knows where she's going. Once she would have been afraid to go into a park after dark, but now, what does it matter? She's going to die anyway. The park has what she craves, peace and the smell of greenery around her.

It's amazing the way they leave the place open now, probably so they don't have to pay a parky. The gates are black with gold scrollwork, very fancy—that's the sort of stuff they spend money on now, not people. Ahead of her stretches the main avenue, fully lit, but she takes one of the darker paths off it. Once she wouldn't have dared, she was so afraid of the dark, but everything changed when she met Brady. He gave her the darkness, drew her irrevocably into it, drew the black light out of her. *Everybody has it*, he'd say, *but most people are too scared to give themselves up to it*. Those winter nights, when they swooped on someone, when the days were short and the nights filled their world … they made her into someone else. Now she surrenders to the shimmering depths of the darkness, welcomes it, becomes its creature.

It's raining quite heavily and her body is filled with the scent coming off the lime trees. She pulls up the hood of her mac, a much more sensible garment than her black cashmere coat. These credit cards are fantastic, she won't hold back now. Let the government pay it all off when she dies—she'll have fun in the meantime. What will she buy? Maybe some nice jewellery off the shopping channel? a couple of pairs of well-cut trousers? definitely a good dress for when she goes out with Aidan, a proper designer dress, not just Marks and Spencers.

Is that it? Is that the sum total of her desires? She should go to the Ritz, have champagne and afternoon tea in their Palm Court. Or go on holiday somewhere amazing. She's never been out of the country in her life, unless you count Scotland. Where could she go? Brady always wanted to go to New York or New Orleans, but that was because he thought all the criminals hung out there. She'd rather go somewhere like Venice, see all the artworks and the gondolas.

She's almost reached the Victorian bandstand in the centre of the park when she sees the glow of a cigarette and a dark figure standing in the shadows. Her step falters but then she throws her head up and walks as if she owns the place. They always say that predators are more likely to strike if you look like a victim. It's not rocket science, is it? The people she and Brady took were all young, easier to overpower. Well, she's a grown woman now and nobody's pushover. Let the little squirt try.

He's young, she sees when she gets closer to him. Tall and lanky, just like Brady. Not as good looking, mind. She almost laughs out loud. Still, after all these years, she thinks her Neddy was the best looking man she ever saw. God, isn't the mind a funny thing? He's decrepit now, she's seen the photos, but back then ...

'Got a light, missus?'

'You seem to have one already.' She looks directly at him, knowing her frank gaze intimidates most men.

'It's going out, love.'

'You got a fag?'

'Yeah, sure.' He holds out the packet to her. She hesitates, then steps forward, flicking her lighter on for him. She still has a few cigarettes left, but no point in wasting them if she can bum one. Nice looking boy. He gazes into her eyes, no doubt trying to look sexy.

They stand under the trees, smoking in silence. The rain pours down, torrential. She can hear it pounding from one level to the next, tiers of water like a rainwater wedding cake, though somehow it never seems to filter through to them underneath. She draws the nicotine into her lungs. What a pity this is killing her. It's the best taste in the world, a fag in the open air.

It's warm under the trees and she flings back her hood, unbuttons her coat. 'Planning on stopping, then?' says the boy.

'I might.'

He takes a step towards her but halts suddenly, at the sound of a terrible, unearthly scream. It's the sound of torture, of a creature in extremis, the pure sound of pain. The boy stares at her, starts to shake. 'It's just a fox,' she says. 'Nothing to worry about.'

'What's it doing?'

'I don't know. They make such eerie noises, you never know what they're really up to.' She thinks the fox probably has a cat in its clutches but she doesn't want to upset the boy. 'Look, it's on the other side of the park, nowhere near us.'

'Yeah, I s'pose you're right.'

The noise goes on and on, till finally there's a strangled sort of howl, and then silence. She leans back against the trunk of the tree, amused and strangely turned on by the boy's fear. His eyes flick over her. She knows he's seeing someone older than himself, but he could still be attracted to that. Aidan says she's a handsome woman, why shouldn't this one feel the same?

'You're up for it, aren't you?'

She says nothing, simply leans back and smiles. The noise of the rain above them is astounding. Soft water falling on limp leaves, yet it's as loud as a drill pounding through stone. She arches her back against the tree trunk, slowly opens her blouse. The boy looks astonished as she reveals her bare breasts.

'You're wild, man,' he says.

226

Above them the leaves form a dome, the patterns as intricate and beautiful as the roof of a Byzantine basilica. The pungent scent of wet leaves is all around them, strong as incense. She feels wild. She wants to be wild. Here in this public park she remembers what it meant to consecrate herself to the darkness. She hears the boy gasp as she pushes down her trousers. His hands go straight between her legs and she fumbles with his belt. His skin is so soft and young, his bones strong and hard, their kisses smokey. A drop of rain forces its way through the leaves and sets her nipple tingling. The boy is excited, wanting to thrust inside her, not caring whether she's ready or not. A man. This is what she missed during all those years inside. He's big, though she knows she'll never again have the feeling Brady gave her of being pierced, impaled, riven in two with pleasure.

Brady, Brady, her Ian. They were at one with each other and with nature. Now she feels the ridged bark through the folds of her raincoat, feels her very skin quiver with the smell of rain and of wet earth, the smell of leaves, the smell of sex. No-one understood them. No-one knew how much they celebrated life, even as they watched it ooze out of someone else. They had crossed a boundary and entered a new plane of existence, a place of secrecy and blood and their love.

The skin of the stranger is warm against her own, though she can hardly see his face in the darkness. She doesn't need to. In this darkness she can feel the very blood throbbing through his veins, can feel life seething within him. In this darkness
she gives herself utterly to the sensation of being alive. In this darkness she is who she is.

From: "Hal" <wolfman@hotmail.co.uk>
To: lynx1043@hotmail.co.uk
Subject: blue
Date: 10th October 2003 12:05:17

My love, where are you? I've been calling and texting but no answering howl from my lynxwoman.
Am blue tonight - we're in the endgame now and I know it's going to change things for us. Who knows where they'll send me next? She knows about the cancer and seems to have told the girlfriend and the priest. Just her mother now.
From the BlackBerry of Hal Morton

From: La Barbara <lynx1043@hotmail.co.uk>

I couldn't care less whether she dies.
Actually I couldn't care less whether she lives either. All I care about is that you are here with me.
I still hate her but just the way everyone else hates her, not with all my hot-blooded, rank-mouthed lynx-ness.
You see how you've changed me? I can't get so angry any more because I have you to think about.
From the BlackBerry of Pat Shields

From: "Hal" <wolfman@hotmail.co.uk>

I didn't know I was so powerful. That's the thing about us wolves - we're so unused to human society that we don't understand other people.

From: La Barbara <lynx1043@hotmail.co.uk>

Sometimes I think you're the only person who's ever understood me, Hal.

From: "Hal" <wolfman@hotmail.co.uk>

I wish you were here, my darling. Where will we be when this assignment is over? They'll probably send me back to London and we'll be juggling schedules even more than we do now.

From: La Barbara <lynx1043@hotmail.co.uk>

Don't even think about that. I just want to live in the now.

This weekend we'll go away, just the two of us. We'll run right into the mountains and find a lair in the high forest. We'll make love there till the sweat drips from our fur and we're exhausted.

I'll lie along the length of you and lick the salt from your pelt and we'll fall asleep together, satiated by love.

We won't let the world destroy what we have. We'll find a way.

The girl's being awfully stupid today, shoving Nellie's elbow into the cardigan and missing the sleeve entirely. She'll break that bloody arm if she don't watch out. The room is way too hot as usual. Why do they treat old people like battery chicks, sticking them in an incubator and turning the heat up? If it stays this warm she's going to melt. She doesn't need a cardigan as well.

They'll probably go to that nice pub on the outskirts again. She'll have to remember and call her Maria, not Myra. The very thought gives her palpitations. She doesn't want Myra shouting at her, but her memory hasn't been too good lately. No wonder, living in this nuthouse. If you weren't off your trolley when you came in, you would be after a week or two.

By the time she's been trussed up in her coat and manoeuvred into the taxi, she feels as if she's going to have a heart attack. It's Myra's fault, all this secrecy. *Something important to tell you*, what on earth does that mean? She probably just wants more money. It'll be some daft scheme she's cooked up that wants financing. Or maybe she's going to get married. She's never been without someone, not even in prison, from what the papers said. Nellie can't imagine going with another woman, but then Myra's proved there's nothing *she* won't contemplate, nothing that's beyond her.

Nellie stares out as they pass rows of redbrick houses, bleak industrial estates. Lord, she's tired. She should talk to the nice young man who's come to collect her but she can't be bothered. Sometimes she just wants to stay in her own room at the home and never come out. Myra makes everything so difficult. Why did it have to be her who lived and Maureen who died?

She starts to cough, feeling as though she's spewing out the ugly thought. How could a mother think that way?

She doesn't really. She's just tired, that's it.

The pub makes her feel cheerier, with its red lampshades and its smell of beer. Bugger it, she'll have a vodka tonic, even though it's lunchtime. Life would be a lot easier in that bleeding home if they let them get sozzled once in a while.

She's halfway through her drink by the time Myra arrives, late as usual. She suits no-one but herself.

'You've lost a bit of weight,' Nellie says as her daughter leans down to kiss her.

'Great, isn't it?' says Myra. 'I'd put on too much. Plays havoc with the love life. People don't realise you're up for it.'

Cheeky mare. Imagine talking to her mother like that.

'Still vodka tonic, I see,' says Myra, breezing off to the bar.

Good, they'll need strong drink to get through this. It's hard, pretending you're just a nice mother and daughter out for a nice lunch when there's nothing nice about them. Nellie takes a deep breath, anything to stop her heart racing. Most of the time she can forget what Myra's done, but when she's with her, she can't stop wondering, can't stop trying to figure out how her daughter could do the things she did. She always had a strong stomach, did Myra, but the older Nellie gets, the less she understands.

'Now then,' says Myra, plonking the second drink down in front of her. 'I want you just to call me M. Don't start trying to remember the right name. OK?'

'OK,' says Nellie, irritated. She's become the child now, has she? Myra picks up the menu. 'What're you having, then?'

'Just the fish and chips, I suppose. That's about all me store-bought clackers'll manage.'

'There's sausage and mash with onion gravy. That'd be soft for you.'

'All right, I'll have that.'

'You don't have to,' says Myra. 'Have what you want.'

'That'll do. I can't taste owt any more anyway.'

'Only if it comes in alcohol form?'

Nellie tuts. She'd like to clatter her daughter one but she's too old for that. And who knows what she'd do in retaliation? Things were always simpler between her and Maureen. Isn't it strange that both her daughters had summat wrong in the head? Mo with her brain tumour, Myra with whatever it is in her brain that let her do what she did.

'So what did you want to see me for?'

Myra looks annoyed, as if Nellie's spoken out of turn. Probably wants to lead up to whatever big dramatic announcement she's going to make. Hah, that'll stop her gallop. She can bloody well get on wi' it.

Only she doesn't. 'I'll just go and order the food and then I'll tell you,' she says.

'Here, take the money out of there,' says Nellie, handing over her purse. 'There's a twenty quid note there.' Probably a mistake to give her the purse. She's bound to find the other twenty Nellie has tucked away in the inside pocket. Not that it matters really. You can't take it with you. Myra might as well have it as anyone.

As expected, she starts wittering on about nothing when she comes back. Nellie tries hard not to close her eyes. It's all too much, the Turkish bath she went to, her visit to Glasgow with someone called Sophie, her new friends Sue this and Beth that, the priest she's friends with. Friends? Does she really expect Nellie to buy that? Aidan this, Aidan that—she must be bloody joking.

The waitress brings the food. Thank goodness, steam's rising off the plate so it should be good and hot. Nellie can't stand the tepid food they serve at the home. She picks up her cutlery but it's hard to get her knife through the sausage. 'Do you want me to cut it up for you?' asks Myra. Nellie nods mutely. No wonder she's tired. Old age is just a succession of humiliations. She's so feeble that she needs her daughter the child murderer to cut her fucking dinner up for her.

Myra tucks into her roast chicken and chips. Nothing puts her off her food, does it? 'So has someone discovered who you are? Have you got a lynch mob howling outside your door?'

231

Myra looks indignant. 'I spent forty long years inside, even though they knew I was no harm to anyone once I was away from Brady. I've paid for what I did, Mam.'

'Love, you will never ever, not if you lived a thousand years, pay for what you did.'

Myra puts her knife and fork down with a bang. 'You've always hated me, haven't you. It was always Mo, Mo, Mo. I was easy meat for Brady. He was the first person that really loved me.'

'Don't you dare blame me for what you did. I'll never understand how you could do it to them kids. How could you, Myra, eh?'

'It's Maria, you stupid old woman.'

'I'd rather be stupid than what you are. What are you? How could you do it?' Water is collecting in her stupid, teary old eyes. She should never have come. She's not fit for this. Better to let it lie. Does she really need Myra to come up with her half-baked explanations? She probably doesn't know herself. It's beyond explanation, beyond understanding.

'That wasn't me, Mam. That was the woman Brady made me into.'

'But you didn't stop him. All that blood and you put your feet up and had a cup of tea—while that big strong lad David Smith was puking his guts up. It were you who stuffed the gag down that little lass's throat. It *were* a gag, weren't it? Not something worse?'

Myra suddenly looks tired. 'Oh Mam, I was young.' Hettie feels her whole body deflating somehow. This is her daughter. There are times she doesn't like her and times she doesn't even love her, but in the end she is hers, part of her body, part of her blood. And now Myra's all she's got, even though she does nowt for her. Nellie almost puts out a hand to touch her.

'I wanted to meet him, to try and work out how we got to the place we did, but they wouldn't let me.'

'They probably thought you were still in love with him. That it was pleasure for you. They didn't think you deserved that.'

'Someone up there doesn't think I deserve another chance. I may have been let out but I'm still being punished—I've got lung cancer, Mam. I'll be dead before you.'

The gleaming brass pumps, the shiny mirror behind the bar, the lamps with their red shades all start dancing up and down before Nellie's eyes. She feels nauseous. What has she done to deserve this? One daughter dead and the other

dying—it's against nature. She focuses on the dark wood of the table. 'Fags, I suppose?'

'Yes, you know me. One's barely out before the other one's lit.'

'And you're sure?'

'Oh yes. I saw the consultant last week.'

Nellie's stomach is griping away. You can never trust sausages. She doesn't know that she can face this. Why couldn't she just have seen her time out in peace? How could all this happen? how could it happen?

232

'The real secret with these is not the vodka but the balance between the Lee and Perrin's and the chilli,' Aidan says. M watches him in silent astonishment. She's seen all the telly chefs, of course, but she's never had a real man cooking for her before. He's been chopping herbs and capers and God knows what all for the last half hour. He stirs chilli powder into her glass. 'Creole Bloody Mary—most recipes use Worcester sauce and Tabasco. I learned how to make these from the barman at this terrific restaurant in New Orleans.'

'You've been to New Orleans?'

'I've been to a lot of places,' he shrugs, with no trace of boastfulness.

'But how? You're a priest.'

'Well, I could say my lady parishioners have been very kind to me.'

'But you won't.'

He nods. 'Just teasing you. My family are quite well off. In fact my brothers are very relieved I went into the priesthood so they didn't have to. They give me frequent breaks away from it. Not exactly poverty.'

'And you're not keen on chastity either. Not much left of the three priestly vows, is there?' she says.

'Oh, I'm super-obedient.'

He adjusts the temperature of the electric ring. 'I hope you're ready to eat soon.'

'Ready? I'm starving.'

'Good.' He throws some oil into the wok.

'Why did you go into it, Aidan?'

'Every Irish family has to have at least one boy in the priesthood,' he says. 'My mother was very devout. She was getting desperate by the time I came along. Neither of my brothers would go for it, so I was in the seminary by the time I was fourteen.'

'You went away from home?'

'Oh yes,' he says.

Oops, he's going a bit quiet on her, but she needs to know more. 'Didn't she miss you?'

'I felt completely abandoned by her, if you want the truth,' he says.

'I was abandoned by my mother,' she says. 'When my baby sister came along I was sent to live with my grandmother.'

'Didn't she treat you well?'

'Oh yes, I loved my gran, but I always felt I was a second class citizen in our family.'

'I'm the opposite. I definitely became number one son when I became a priest. But I had to go away from her to do it.'

Now he's tossing some grey looking prawns into the wok. Posh people all seem to like prawns—Sophie loves them too—but M's not sure she likes the look of these. Shouldn't they be pink?

'So that's why you went into it.'

233

'You don't think I've got a vocation?'

'I don't know. You take all these vows and yet you seem to ignore them. You've got money in your family so it's not as if you're a poor boy who needs the security. I'm just wondering what the point is now that you're grown up and don't need to please your mother any more.'

'I can see you don't think I'm much of a priest.'

'No, it's not that.'

'There are worse sins than sex, you know.'

'Sex isn't a sin in my book,' she says. The Bloody Mary is piquant and crackles at the back of her throat. She'll have to try making these at home.

He leans over the kitchen counter and kisses her. 'Nor in mine,' he says. 'And this is more than sex, isn't it?'

She nods, unable to speak. He's telling her he loves her, isn't he?

'Anyway, there are much worse things in the world for the Church to get angry about.'

'Like what?'

'Violence. Corruption. War.'

The war again. People are always banging on about it these days. Why can't you just put your vote down and be done with it? She doesn't want to think about politics every minute of the day.

'Worst of all is not feeding your lover properly,' she says, relishing the sound of the word *lover* in her mouth.

He gives her a slow smile, dips one of the prawns into the sauce he's been making. 'This is gorgeous, so it is. See how you like it.' He holds it above her and she hurriedly opens her mouth. The sauce is red and tangy and she licks it off her lips as she eats the prawn.

'What do you call this then?'

'It's cajun remoulade sauce. I got the recipe from the guy in New Orleans.'

'That must be some restaurant.'

'Ah, you'd love it. Arnaud's, they call it. It's a real old-fashioned place with chandeliers and those colonial-type fans. You go there for Sunday brunch and jazz and if you're lucky they'll play a tune just for you.'

She smiles at his enthusiasm, spears a fourth prawn with her fork.

'You're voracious, you are,' he says.

'I have other appetites as well,' she says, smothering the prawn in the sauce. She knows he won't be able to resist her. Sure enough, he comes to stand behind her as she eats the prawn, his hands slipping on to her breasts.

She leans back against him. 'Are we going to do it in the kitchen like that Jessica Lange film?' she asks.

'*The Postman Always Rings Twice*?'

'Yes, that's the one—with Jack Nicholson.'

'I'm not sure I've got that much flour.'

'Actually I didn't like the flour,' she says. 'It reminds me of Dennis Nielsen, you know, the gay serial killer? He used to put talcum on his victims

234

because he was screwed up over seeing his grandfather in his coffin when he was a little boy. He loved his grandfather.'

'You're one fascinating woman, do you know that? You know such strange things, things no-one else would know.'

He puts his hand out to her, pulls her from the chair. At last. After all the blank-faced hotels and motels she's finally going to see his bedroom. She follows him up the mahogany staircase, clutching his hand. Inside, his room is disappointingly devoid of clues to what he's like, with the sort of solid old-fashioned wardrobe and chest of drawers you might have seen in Granny Maybury's house in Bannock Street—she had a few things that were better than Mam and Dad's sticks of furniture. But this room could be a boy's room, with its dark blue carpet and bedspread, its bare white walls broken only by a wooden crucifix above the bed.

M doesn't know whether to be amused or appalled at the idea of the dying Jesus watching her have sex. It certainly doesn't seem to deter Aidan. He pushes her down on the bed, kisses rough and somehow more exciting because he's so impatient. She flings her arms back, abandoning herself to this moment. The gold figure on the crucifix gleams in the half light. Dying ... Jesus ... His arms collapsing under the weight of His body, insides melting, everything falling away ... Aidan ...

Afterwards Aidan seems drained. They lie together, legs entwined. He appears to be half asleep.

'Aidan?'

'Yes?'

'You really don't think that was a sin?'

'Darling, how could something that felt so good be a sin?'

'The Church says it is.'

He smiles wearily. 'The Church doesn't get everything right.'

'Have you ever done anything you do feel ashamed of? A real sin?'

'My, we're in serious mode tonight. You don't feel guilty, do you?'

She laughs out loud. 'Course not. But I'm not a priest.'

'I think that's half the attraction for you.'

'You certainly look very sexy in your cassock.'

He props himself up on his elbow to look at her. 'What's brought all this Catholic guilt on?'

'I don't feel guilty. I'm just curious, that's all. Just because things feel good doesn't mean they are good. Everyone thinks you're one thing when really you're another altogether.'

'I'm a sinner, just like everyone in my congregation. Is that what you mean?'

'I suppose so,' she says. "*Have* you ever done anything you're ashamed of? Something terrible?'

He runs his hand down her flank. 'Yes,' he says. 'When I was younger. I like to make extreme youth my excuse but in my heart of hearts I know there is none. I was about nineteen and I got myself involved with a young married woman one summer when I was home from the seminary. I

235

was delivering groceries from the supermarket to her door. She had a wee baby and she couldn't cope and at first I was just a shoulder for her to cry on—everyone knew I was training for the priesthood so I suppose she thought it was the natural thing to do.'

'Why were you working in a supermarket? I thought you said your family had money.'

'They did, but my dad wanted us all to learn the value of money. D'ye want to hear this story or not.'

'Sorry,' she says, looking up at him mock-penitently.

His face has lost its expression of post-coital well-being and taken on a look of anxiety. 'One day the girl's husband came back from work early. He had a migraine and just wandered straight up to the bedroom. Poor guy, he was really out of it. We were too engrossed to hear him and he came on us in bed together.'

'Oh my God, what did you do?'

'It wasn't what I did, it was what he did.'

'What? What did he do?'

'That day, nothing. He turned and walked out of the bedroom. I thought he'd have a row with her later and that'd be the end of it.'

'But it wasn't.'

'No, he waited till she'd gone to bed that night, then went into the bathroom and slashed his wrists. That was the worst day of my life. I felt like I'd murdered him.'

'Of course you didn't. He did it to himself.'

'I don't kid myself, M. I drained the life out of that man as surely as if I'd held a knife to his throat.'

'You were young, Aidan.'

He glances up at the crucifix above them, quickly crosses himself. 'Now I don't get mixed up with married women. You haven't been kidding me on, have you?'

'I wouldn't lie to you,' she says.

'And have you got a dark secret? Anything you want to confess to your priest?'

She says nothing, till he looks at her too sharply, too curiously. 'You'll hate me if I tell you.'

He takes her hand, strokes the soft skin behind her wrist. 'I won't. Of course I won't.'

'I've done the worst thing a woman can do.'

'Ah, my poor love. I bet it's been eating away at you ever since.'

She nods. He takes her into his arms, cradles her naked body. 'I hear it all the time,' he says. 'Women who can't live with what they've done, women who always miss the child they'll never have.'

'Don't you hate me for it?' she asks. 'A Catholic priest shouldn't be with someone who's done that.'

'You can hate the sin but not the sinner,' he says. 'I know you regret it.'

236

'It made me insane,' she says. 'I was locked up in an institution for years.'

She finds herself sobbing, in great ugly gulps that must be contorting her face. Well, it's the truth, she *was* locked up for years. He strokes her hair. He really is a very gentle man underneath the high voltage exterior. She rubs her face against his chest hair. She loves the feel of him, the smell of him. She wonders if he'll fuck her again.

The dust is relentless, clogging up his nose, his mouth, even his brain. Will dashes grit from his eye, tries to focus. They check the tyres, under the chassis. Nothing. Checkpoint duty's so boring. He should be relieved really. If it wasn't boring there'd be something up.

They walk back and lean on the jeep. 'You wanna watch it, mate. I've told you before, she's really jerking you around,' says Jem.

Will watches as Kezza saunters over from questioning the woman passenger. His stomach is pumping in and out like one of those sea anemones you see on the TV nature programmes. 'What do you mean? Is she mucking about with somebody else?'

'Nah, course not. Who else is there? D'ye think she fancies a towelhead or something? But she blows hot and cold with you all the time so you go panting after her like a little puppy. It's mind control, mate. You know what they say, *Treat 'em mean, keep 'em keen.*'

Will studies Kezza. She's all bundled up in her camouflage gear but he knows what's underneath. He knows those brown, silky legs, the tip-tilted nipples. He wants to be in a proper bedroom with her, lying on fresh cotton sheets with a gentle sea breeze coming through the window. He wants to feel her clean, smooth body rubbing against his own. He doesn't want to feel dirty and tired and dusty.

'I love her, Jem.'

Jem rolls his eyes. ' Doesn't mean you have to be putty in her hands, does it?'

Kezza plants herself in front of Will, her eyes full of mischief. 'Ow'd you fancy me in one of them outfits?' she says.

He looks at the other woman's dusty chador, its heavy folds entombing her in a portable prison. Then he studies Kezza's baggy trousers, the bulletproof vest which makes her chest look like a pouter pigeon's. 'You're almost there, babe. You wouldn't win many fashion contests with that lot.'

'I can still get you hot under the collar, soldier boy,' she says, rubbing herself against him.

'Cut it out,' says Jem sharply. 'D'ya wanna get us all killed? You never know what mad Muslim's watching.'

Kezza perches on the jeep steps. 'Ya gotta have a laugh, Jem.'

The next vehicle they stop is blazoned with BBC stickers. 'Wave 'em through,' says Kezza, but Will walks towards them. 'You never know,' he says. 'They might have been made to carry something.' A well known presenter steps out on one side and on the other a middle-aged blonde whose face looks familiar to Will. He starts to look at the man's documents when the woman calls his name. 'It is you, isn't it, Will? Beth told me to look out for you.'

Oh no, it's Jude, his mother's friend. What on earth is she doing here? No wonder he didn't recognise her—no eye shadow, no red lipstick. She looks distinctly dishevelled. He can't believe she's having an affair with his

238

father, but Kezza saw them sitting engrossed in each other in Jude's sports car that time they were up. 'Jude,' he says. 'What are you doing here?'

She doesn't seem to notice the reserve in his tone. 'I'm on a sabbatical from the paper. I have family connections with the military, you know. Gets me into places other people can't.'

Like his father's bed. 'I'd have thought this was slumming it a bit for you. You're a first class travel kind of bird, aren't you?'

'Only when they're making me do something boring,' she says.

'It's not exactly thrill a minute out here.'

'You've no idea, darling. Everything had got so predictable at home. No harm in shaking your life up a bit, is there?'

'As long as it's just your own life,' he says, giving her a long, hard look.

She stares at him, then he sees the penny drop. 'Did you think you could keep it secret?' he says.

'It's not what you think,' she says, but her flawless skin is flushed.

'It's exactly what I think. You've been friends with my mum for how many years?'

'Please, Will. There's nothing going on, I swear. How can there be when I'm out here.'

'Got too demanding for you, did he, the old man? Don't tell me he fell in love. Is this your idea of reparation or something, coming out here?'

'I'd never hurt your mother, you know that.'

'You're a pair of cheating bastards.'

'That's not fair.'

He shrugs and walks away from her. She was always his favourite of his mum's friends. He thought she was really nice. How could she do it?

The others look at him curiously as he waves the vehicle through.

'What's up, love?' Kezza asks.

'That's that woman my dad's having an affair with—you know, the one you recognised from the picture on the kitchen dresser?'

'I remember. the glamorous blonde sittin' in the car wiv 'im? Doesn't look too hot now, does she?'

'I don't understand how she can do that to her best friend. It sucks.'

'Cool yer jets, love. We don't know for definite.'

'We do now, from the way she reacted.'

He stomps away from her, scuffing the dust up with his boots. He can see Kezza and Jem exchanging surprised looks but he doesn't care. He'd like to sock someone, preferably his dad. What has his mum ever done to hurt anyone? It's not fair.

As the afternoon wears on, fly-ridden and tedious, all he can think of is long cold beers in the mess tent and sex with Kezza, wherever he can manage it. The end of the shift can't come quick enough. But at six o'clock the sergeant drives up. 'Sorry, you guys, but you're going to have to do a stint of guard duty,' he says. Will wants to explode.

'Sir, we've been on duty since 0-600 hours,' says Jem.

'I know, lads, but there's nothing I can do. You know how short we are since everyone ate those kebabs. Not a pleasant thing, dysentery.'

Kezza sighs and swings up into the jeep. 'Oh, let's get it over wiv, then.'

'That's the spirit, Smithy. Look on it as a little exercise in behaviour modification. You can have a bit of fun with those Ali Babas,' he says.

Kezza sleeps with her head on Will's shoulder while Jem drives. The jeep jolts over the potholed track, jarring Will's spine with every rut. He glances down at her peaceful face. Kez the cat, able to sleep through anything. They pass several vehicles going the other way but the dust flies up and obscures them each from the other. It feels as if they're in some landscape of the future, where movement is in slow motion and all communication between people has broken down.

The journey to the barracks takes them an hour, but at least when they get there it's cool inside, cool and restful after the heat of the sun. The outgoing sergeant is brisk. 'Thank goodness you're here. We've been on duty since yesterday.' He gestures to the mini-fridge on his desk. 'There's something in there to help relieve the boredom,' he says. 'Good luck, fellas.'

As soon as he's gone Kez pounces on the fridge. 'Yay, beer. They've left us a six-pack each,' she says.

'Thank God for that,' says Jem. 'Break 'em out then, Kez.'

'Hadn't we better check the prisoners?' asks Will.

'You go,' says Kez. 'We'll keep a can for you.'

'OK.' Will walks down the corridor towards the holding cells. Once through the gate, it's dark, but as he passes, each cell lights up, like the French hotels his father used to take them to on holiday. God, it's primitive, with metal bars for doors, like a kid's idea of prison. Dark-skinned men slump on the floor or on rough wooden benches. A few bow their heads, apparently in prayer; a few stare at him, eyes meeting his as though he is the prisoner. Fucking mad A-rabs. Will wrinkles his nose at the shit-streaked toilet bowls. This place stinks.

He strolls back, relishing their irritation as each light goes on and then off. 'That's a laugh,' he tells Jem and Kezza. 'The lights are on sensors so you walk past and the cells light up for a minute, then go off. You could drive them mad just walking up and down, checking on them.'

'I got better things to do with my time,' says Jem. 'Let's just chill. I'm knackered.' He puts his feet up on the desk and leans back, taking a long pull on his beer.

'You 'eard what the sarge said,' says Kezza. 'It's our patriotic duty to roust 'em up.'

'In a minute, sunshine,' says Will, opening his can. The beer tastes good after the long trials of the day. He better watch out. He could fall asleep in no time if he drinks it too fast. Jem has already drained his can and is lying back with his eyes closed. Kezza grins at Will. 'Come 'ere, soldier boy.'

He slides off his chair, pulls her into the corridor. 'Oh God, Kez, I've been wanting to kiss you all day.'

240

She presses herself against him and laughs. 'Hmm, I can tell. Nothing cool about you, is there, Will?'

'Not where you're concerned.'

His whole body aches for her. God, he's got to control it. The rest of the squad could come through the door any minute.

'Will ...' she draws herself away from him. He can't take his eyes off her. She pushes the heavy camouflage trousers down. He can see a triangle of white lace, then those firm brown legs with their familiar sheen. They're so soft, so shiny. He wants to touch them. He puts out a hand but she's already turned her back on him. She pulls the lace pants down and puts both hands against the wall.

'Kezza, don't.'

She turns and looks over her shoulder at him. 'Chicken?'

There's a crash from the prisoners' corridor as if someone's knocked something over. They stare at each other for a minute. Kezza slowly pulls her trousers up. She seems out of breath. 'Fuck them,' she says.

Will unlocks the gate. 'Let's have a proper look,' he says. He flips the override switch and the corridor surges with light. Slowly they walk down past the cells. He wants to kill these bastards. Why can't they shut up and leave him and Kez in peace? One of the Iraqis, a good looking man whose erect bearing suggests he might be their leader, stares out of the cell, eyes flipping over Kezza with a mixture of contempt and excitement. 'Seen enough?' says Will, jabbing his fist through the bars and grabbing the prisoner by the shirt. Kezza tugs at Will's belt and hauls him back.

'Leave it, babe. I'll sort him.' She stands about a yard away from the bars and slowly unbuttons her shirt. The Iraqi's face flickers with fury but Will can see he has a hard-on. Kezza's white lace bra looks incongruous against the heavy fabric of her camouflage shirt. He wants to touch her little nipples, rub his face against the sheen of sweat on her breasts. He wants to punch the Iraqi for looking at his woman and at the same time he feels as if he will burst with pride at how beautiful she is. Let them all look. She's his.

There's a sound behind them and Jem comes in, looking half-awake. 'What's this?' he asks.

'Just a bit of behaviour modification, like the sarge said,' says Kezza. 'Grab him, Jem.'

Jem looks doubtful. 'Come on, Kez. We don't need to do this.'

She flicks her tongue at the prisoner, who shakes his head in disbelief and spits. 'He needs taught a lesson,' says Kezza.

'I'm out of here,' says Jem. 'Will, if you've got any sense you'll come with me, mate.'

Kezza turns to look at Will. She has the half-smile she always has before they have sex, a secret smile just for him. He wants to walk out but he knows he can't. He looks away as Jem walks back out the gate into the barracks. He is alone with Kez. They are alone. It feels as though he has made a decision though he is not entirely clear what it is.

241

The corridor seems very bright somehow and he hopes he doesn't have a migraine coming on. Kezza is breathing hard. She motions with her gun that the Iraqi should step outside his cell. His companions look down, unwilling to catch Kezza's eye. She steps forward and unzips the man's trousers, yanking them down below his knees. He looks in shock.

'Lady, you do not do this to Muslim man,' shouts one of the other prisoners.

Kezza ignores him. 'Look, Will. D'ya think he fancies me?'

'Looks like it, babe.' Will curses himself for the husky way his voice has come out. Wimp. Despite his disgust he is still turned on. Is he so simple that the mere sight of this woman's flesh is enough to make him forget his whole upbringing, how you treat other human beings?

Kezza moves forward to flip the man's penis. He makes a strange growling sound and lunges at her. Will steps forward and cracks him across the side of the head with his rifle butt. The prisoner topples over, instinctively catching on to Kezza's shirt to prevent himself falling.

'Look what I've got,' she crows. 'A man at my feet.' She hauls his head back by the hair. 'Take my picture, Will. My phone's in my back pocket.'

He holds the phone up, hand shaking with excitement. This is the worst thing he's ever done in his life, so why does he feel so good? The man averts his eyes from the camera, as if by not seeing he will not be seen. Will can tell the other prisoners are mortified for him, but somehow there seems to be no time to feel sorry for the man.

'You little shit,' says Kezza, forcing the Iraqi on to his knees. 'Think you can spit at me?' She bends him forward and starts hitting him with the belt from his own trousers. There is a hiss of disgust—or is it fear?—from the other prisoners. Will watches mesmerised as red marks appear on the man's naked backside. Kezza is panting, whether from exertion or excitement he can't tell.

She pauses, stepping back from the prisoner. The man does not look at her, nor at Will. He lies abject on the ground, dissolved in humiliation. Kezza puts one foot on the small of his back and gives a thumbs-up to the camera. Will wants to fuck her, badly wants to fuck her. For the moment, he takes another picture.

The wind lifts the leaves ahead of her, sending them scurrying and tumbling over each other like a pack of mice swept into orbit. How dry they sound, dice rattling in a cup, bones rattling. And how beautiful their colours—burnished red, bronze, that malevolent poison yellow. In prison she dreamt of walking through autumn leaves, of scuffing them up in front of her like she did as a child. Life is cruel. She has her wish but the dice are rattling out her doom.

'You're struggling today, aren't you?' says Sophie, tucking her arm beneath M's in support.

'I feel I can hardly breathe. I'm on my way out, Sophie.'

'No, you're not. Don't say that,' says Sophie. 'None of us know the minute. Just try not to think about it. There's no point in scaring yourself.'

'Let's sit down for a minute, shall we?' says M, plonking herself down on the nearest bench.

Despite the colder weather, the park is busy, with kids kicking a football around, the occasional jogger, women walking very fast and talking at an equally rapid rate. M studies their curious gait, the swinging arms and barely lifted feet. 'They look like bloody ducks, the way their bums stick out,' she says.

'It's power walking. Nowadays people think jogging's too stressful on the knees.'

M rolls her eyes. 'Sometimes I think the whole world's gone crazy,' she says. 'People walked sensibly in my day.'

Nearby, a small girl falls on the ground and instantly starts caterwauling. 'Oops,' says Sophie. 'Poor little mite.' Privately Myra thinks modern children are encouraged to indulge themselves far too much in public displays of their feelings. Why can't the child put a sock in it?

She shouldn't use that phrase, not even to herself. Brings back too many memories. They never ought to have done that Lesley Ann child. Bad karma. It's haunted them for years. The day that tape was played in court, well, the way people looked at them—no wonder murderers used to be buried in unmarked graves. People would desecrate hers if they knew where it was. She won't give them that satisfaction. Cremation for her, a rush of flames and then nothing but dust. She's going into the fire.

What if it's the fires of Hell? What if it's all true and you really do get sent there? She and Brady escaped execution, they wouldn't escape Hell. Imagine if they'd come to trial just seven months earlier, when the death penalty was still in place, could she have kept her face impassive when they pronounced sentence? Could she, even for Ian?

She must stop thinking about him. He's a wizened old man now, twisted with bitterness. He's not her Ian, slim and elegant in his sharp suit. He might have been just a clerk but he always got his suits tailored for him. He had style. Oh, but he was so cool, even in the dock. She was too—she showed those stuffy judges and lawyers how much she loved him, showed him how controlled she could be. *Never let them see what you feel*, he'd said, and she agreed.

If they had been sentenced to death she'd have stayed impassive because she wouldn't have wanted to embarrass him or herself. She had to hold her head high and show them she wasn't frightened, wasn't ashamed of what they'd done. That's why people were so against her, because she wouldn't put on sackcloth and ashes and pretend to be humble. They can't stand bolshie women and that's all there is to it. Look at what happened with Ruth Ellis—same as M, got her hair all blonded for the trial, made sure she looked good, but it didn't make a good impression. Oh no, they didn't want her to take a pride in herself. They wanted her to creep into court and throw herself on their mercy. Well, Ruth wouldn't do it and neither would she.

On the other side of the park the ducks start squabbling amongst themselves, their squawks carrying clear across the grass to M and Sophie. 'You can't tell whether they're fighting or fucking,' says Sophie.

'Opposite sexes, they're fucking. Same sex, they're fighting over the opposite sex.'

'No gay ducks, then?' laughs Sophie. M smiles back, squeezes Sophie's hand.

Some woman, Ruth Ellis. She held it all together till the very end. One of M's warders was actually there. She said how calm Ellis was, even when they put those awful padded knickers on her. All women being hanged had to wear them after the debacle they had with some woman in the '20s. They had to be sure nothing would come out. Women being such messy creatures, of course.

The long drop, they called it, the trap-door. M's machine was right over it in the Holloway sewing room. They probably thought it was funny to stick her there. She could have been hanged, after all, couldn't she? What a creepy feeling, sewing away, the machine trembling on the floor, and thinking any moment the trap could open and you'd go tumbling down. She used to stand there for minutes at a time sometimes, looking at the square piece of wood on the floor, stomach churning at the thought of it.

What must have it been like, the night before? She'd never have been able to sleep. She'd have stayed calm, though, definitely. She wouldn't have been like that one that went hysterical, screaming and crying for days before— Edith Thompson, that was her name. M would have been like Ruth Ellis, dignified, quiet, not giving them an inch.

Huh, that Thompson one gave them a fright, though. All that blood, blurting out of her in thick, viscous gobbets. Out of her secret places, woman's places. They liked their executions to be nice and tidy but the blood kept coming, streaking Thompson's legs, puddling on the floor. What on earth did all the assembled dignitaries think? They were probably in shock—served them right for thinking you can kill people by a rule book. It's cold that, not the way things really are. You kill in heat, in a fever, and you have to be ready for the blood, prepared mentally. You're not just snuffing out a candle, it's someone's life you're taking. Or two lives with that Edith. They reckoned she haemorrhaged like that because she was pregnant.

244

'Shall we try and walk on a bit?' says Sophie. 'I'm getting cold here. Aren't you?'

They walk past the Victorian bandstand, with its posse of teenagers draped over the fancy wrought-iron balustrade. M feels a queer pity for the yearning girls, the preening boys. They don't know what they're letting themselves in for. They don't know where love could take them.

'I saw Sue yesterday,' says Sophie. 'You know how those lampers put the dead fox on her gatepost?'

'Don't remind me. That was horrible.'

'Well, all it did was drive the foxes underground. She discovered a whole family of them living under her garden shed.'

'How lovely. They're so beautiful. Were there little ones as well?'

'Yes, only it wasn't lovely. One of the cubs had died and the rest of them went on living with the corpse. That was how Sue found out—the smell. Foxes stink anyway so you can imagine the smell of a dead one. Honking! But they didn't seem to notice it.'

M frowns. 'Is that normal, for animals to live alongside a dead body?'

'I don't think so. I haven't heard of it anyway. It's gruesome, don't you think?'

M nods, though she's living with death too, all the time now. If she's honest, she did before. She wasn't like him, though, poring over his book of photographs, staring at the little hummocks of grass that hid the bodies. He must have enjoyed his trip to Saddleworth, knowing that they were looking in the wrong place. Has he got the photographs still? Does he still get off on them?

Sophie tucks her arm under M's. 'Don't tire yourself out,' she says. They walk past the clump of lime trees where M had sex with the boy in the dark; she staved off death that night. She wishes she knew the names of trees. The copper beech is beginning to turn that intense red colour but she doesn't know what the one next to it is, or the one beyond that. Too late now. There are so many things she will never find out, so many places she will never go.

She turns to Sophie, catches her by the hand and gazes at her. 'You know I'm not going to get better, don't you?'

Sophie's eyes well up. 'Please don't say that, Maria. I can't bear it.'

M's hand tightens on her wrist. 'I must be cremated. Make sure they don't bury me,' she says.

Sophie looks bewildered. 'Why ever not, my darling? If there was a grave, I could come and visit.'

'If you want to think of me, think of me when you're walking in the park or on some fine day when you take the car and drive up on to the moors. Think of me then. You don't need some piddling little plot of ground and a twirly headstone to remember me by. This is me, M. I don't want to be cooped up forever in a box. If I'm still out there I'll come back and haunt you, I promise.'

'Don't be morbid. Please.' Sophie's voice is raw, tense. 'You're not dead yet.'

245

'No, not yet.' Her eyes are like black marbles in her gaunt face. 'But we haven't got long. You know that, don't you?'

Sophie stares bleakly at the swans slapping down their webbed feet with as little grace as wet-suited divers. 'They're so clumsy when they're out of their own element, aren't they?'

M stares deep into her eyes. She will not look away first. Sophie is hers, hers. 'Promise you won't leave me,' she says.

A single leaf falls to the ground in front of her, as elegant as if falling of its own volition. 'I promise,' says Sophie.

Thank God for October week and mid-term break. Now Charles has been packed off to work Beth can have some time to herself. She needs to think. Can he really be having an affair? Is he so banal that he must have a mid-life crisis, like all the other men she knows, all her colleagues at school. One day they appear looking self-conscious with a new haircut. Next it's a brightly coloured tie and a younger style of dressing. Before long they're turfed out of their own home and doomed to live in a grotty bedsit, just like they did when they really were young. Could Charles, her clever Charles, be so stupid?

Mechanically, she goes through his pockets, as she's been doing every week for the past few months. He never leaves incriminating receipts or stray phone numbers, never leaves anything. Sometimes she wonders if he knows she's looking because his pockets are suspiciously clean these days … as usual she finds nothing. She sits down on the bed, not knowing whether to be relieved. Her reflection in the wardrobe mirror looks awful, with big dark smudges under the eyes and a complexion the colour of sour milk.

She'd rather know.

But what's the point of torturing herself with these thoughts? She gets up and puts on her coat. No use sitting here brooding—she'll walk across the park into town, maybe treat herself to a couple of drinks in that fun place she went to with Jude. Maybe she'll do what wronged women are supposed to do, hit him where it hurts by taking some money out of the joint account. Well, why shouldn't she? It's her money as well. But what if she's wrong? What if he's completely innocent?

In the park, the grass is lightly touched with dew. The smell of the trees, the dark corridor they create through the park, somehow console her. Autumn is already under way—many of the leaves are tinged with red and yellow. Normally she loves when they change colour, but everything is so ghastly these days that they just seem a harbinger of the colder weather to come. Nothing is fun any more. Charles is remote, her friends always away, the Spencer woman upsets her. And Will, her darling Will is gone and may never come back.

If Maria Spencer really is Myra Hindley, what should she do? Surely she ought to tell Sophie Ferrers? Sophie wouldn't be with the woman if she knew who she was. Would she? You never know with people. They're fascinated by these serial killers. Look at all the women who write to the Yorkshire Ripper.

Beth turns right at the end of the park, away from Myra's lane. Instead she walks along the edge of the grass till she gets to the main road. The town square is still filled with flowers, for all it's so late in the year. There's pale coral astilbe, nebulous as underwater flowers, white gerbera and orange chrysanthemums. The holly berries stand out bright red and cheery against their dark green leaves.

She'll go to that lovely Italian leather shop in the arcade, Bilbo Bags, treat herself to some Penhaligon's. She loves their Victorian Posy soap. Maybe she'll even buy an expensive Italian handbag.

But she quails when she reaches the shop. The prices are absurd. Just the soap then. Maybe some bath oil as well. She's not doing too well spending money. Retail therapy, they call it, but it seems pointless, even in the bookshop. She stares at the rows and rows of bright covers but she doesn't want to think about anyone else's life. She was happy before. How did things get so bad?

By one o'clock she has looked without interest at lingerie, evening wear, cruisewear, office wear. She's rubbed her fingers along silk, leather, viscose and vinyl, and tried on endless tops, dresses and shoes. She's had enough.

She finds her way to the place where she and Jude had their mojitos, hesitates at the entrance. Dare she go in on her own? It was loud, wasn't it? And fashionable? How will it look, for a middle-aged woman to be there alone? To hell with it. She's entitled to go in if she wants.

She pushes open the door. There's a free table in the corner, so she puts her coat and bag of soaps down while she goes to the bar.

'A mojito, please,' she asks the young barman.

The drink is as fragrant as she remembers, with its crushed mint leaves and heady rum. She stirs it with the same cocktail stick, a little monkey climbing up a palm tree. She should have got the jug. Four drinks, wasn't it? That wouldn't be too much. She looks down at the palm tree in her hand. Where is Will? Is he lost in the desert? Why hasn't she heard from him? They'd have told her if he was dead or missing, wouldn't they?

God, she'd better eat something before she gets maudlin. She picks up the menu—skewers of this, tortillas of that.

'Darling, you are going to need *strong* drink today,' says a voice she recognises. 'And oodles of it. I have something to tell you.'

Jude. How lovely. But why has she come home without telling Beth?

'Jude?' she says and turns, to see her friend standing at the bar with Charles. With *her* husband. This can't be real. Jude and Charles blench, spring apart. Beth's whole brain has slowed down. It's as if she can't find a way through the images her eyes are taking in. What can this mean, that Jude and Charles are here? Why are they here, when Jude's supposed to be in Iraq and Charles at university? Why are they here together?

Jude sits down heavily. 'Oh God, this isn't what it looks like,' she says.

'Isn't it?' Beth realises she's whispering. She must make her voice heard.

'I came here to tell Charles something,' says Jude.

'But why would you tell Charles and not me. *I'm* your friend.'

Jude and Charles exchange looks. 'I wanted Charles to tell you,' says Jude. 'You're not going to like it.'

'No,' says Beth. 'No. It's about Will, isn't it?'

'What about Will?' says Charles.

'Let's all just sit down together, shall we?' says Jude.

'I need a whisky,' says Charles.

'One for me too, would you?' says Jude.

She used to be so pretty, so full of energy. Now she looks washed out, old. Can guilt take your looks away? Or stress? Maybe it's stress. Please make it be stress. The service is taking forever. Beth wants to vault the bar and snatch the whisky out of the boy's hand. She knows that whatever Jude is about to tell them is much much worse than the fact that she's having a tawdry little affair with her friend's husband.

Jude takes a sip of her whisky and looks down at the table. 'I'm afraid Will has been mixing with some very unsavoury people in Iraq,' she says.

'It's that Kezza, isn't it? I told you she stole my earrings, didn't I, Charles?'

'Don't be ridiculous,' says Charles.

'She's one of them,' says Jude.

'What have they been doing? Why are *you* telling us this?'

'Because it's going to be in the paper soon.'

'Whose paper, Jude? Is it yours?'

Charles looks at Jude in astonishment. 'Surely not?'

Jude takes a long swallow of her drink. 'You don't understand,' she says. 'This is the sort of thing you can't keep out of the papers. There'll be a court-martial eventually. I've got them to keep it quiet till I could speak to you.'

'What are you saying about my son?' screams Beth.

'Quiet,' says Charles sharply. 'The last thing we need now is a scene.'

'You ... fuck ... off,' says Beth. 'Fuck off with your mistress.' She turns to Jude. 'Tell me what's going on.'

'He's been abusing Iraqi prisoners,' says Jude.

Beth feels a sense of relief sweep over her. 'There must be a mistake. Will wouldn't do that,' she says. 'Will's a gentle boy, a sweet boy.'

Charles looks shocked. 'Will's in the British Army. Of course he wouldn't do such a thing.'

Jude sighs. 'Those days are long gone, I'm afraid.'

His shoulders slump. 'This is going to be plastered everywhere, isn't it? Everyone's going to know.'

'Yes,' says Jude. 'I'm afraid so. Look, the details are pretty sordid and I don't want to be the one to tell you, but they've sexually abused some of the prisoners and beaten them up really badly. They're lucky no-one was killed. They thought they were gods.'

'Will's not like that,' says Beth. She must stop her teeth chattering.

'He clearly is now,' says Charles, his face grey. 'That's what war does to people.'

'And were you the one to get the scoop, Jude?' asks Beth. 'Is this going to get you a press award or something?'

249

'I just wrote about a young boy I know and love who's been corrupted by the experience of war,' says Jude. 'I did the best I could for him, Beth.'

'Saint Jude,' says Beth bitterly. She stands up, feeling the alcohol from her mojito rush to her head. 'You two deserve each other.'

Charles stares morosely at his drink. Beth looks at him. He's lumbered with a tired, clapped-out hack who probably won't stay with him for a week. She almost feels sorry for him but instead walks to the door, turning to look them before she goes. They are sitting a foot away from each other.

'Beth,' says Jude softly. 'I'm sorry.'

'Too late, Jude.' She lets the door swing to behind her. Where can she go now? How can she cope with this? Her blood runs cold. People will know that Will, the fruit of her body, the love of her life, did such a thing. It surprises her that of all the emotions swirling around inside her—fear of the future, disgust at Charles and Jude, anxiety about what will happen to Will, dread of knowing the details—the primary one is shame on her son's behalf. Shame that he's let himself down, that he's behaved like a yob and a bully boy.

The only way this could possibly have happened is through that girl Kezza. How could he ever have fallen for a tramp like that? She passes the town hall, walks back through the municipal garden. The holly berries look like blood now, splashed all over the bushes. He'll go to prison. She'll never see him. As she walks along the side of the park, she suddenly realises where she is heading. Only one person can explain this to her.

By the time she reaches the lane she's almost running. She hammers on the back door. Pray God that Myra's in on her own.

'Who the fuck's making that racket?' The rasping voice grumbles across the kitchen, then the door is yanked open and Myra stands there, frowning. 'Beth? What do you want?' Dark-circled eyes punctuate her pale face. Is she ill?

'I'm sorry. I need to talk. Can I come inside?'

'I don't have anything to say to you.'

Beth is almost sobbing. 'Please. It's about my son.'

'Your son the soldier?'

'Yes.'

She has a strange half-smile on her lips. Her eyes are almost wholly black as she stares at Beth. She's like a snake, eyes unreadable but by definition malevolent. Beth almost recoils but Myra holds the door open.

'What's he done, then?' She smiles as Beth bridles. 'You wouldn't be here unless it was something dreadful. Horror, after all, is what you think I'm an expert on.'

'I know who you are,' says Beth.

'Nobody knows who I am,' she says. 'Not even me, love.'

'I'm not going to say anything, you know.'

'That's smart.' M walks over and switches the kettle on. 'You'd best sit down.'

250

Beth sits at the kitchen table. The whole room is bright and sparklingly clean. She obviously takes a pride in her home. You would, of course, if you'd been in prison all that time. After that it must be amazing to have a space that belongs to you. Beth sips at the hot sweet tea put in front of her.

'He's been abusing prisoners,' she says finally.

'Abusing? What does that mean?' M lights up a cigarette, first emitting a hacking cough.

'Sexual abuse. Beatings.' Beth keeps her eyes on the table; shame is creeping through her whole body. 'Apparently they're lucky they didn't kill someone.'

'They? I take it there's someone else to blame?'

'He was with this girl. Kezza. You met her, don't you remember? I didn't like her but he was obsessed with her.'

'That'll do it every time.'

'Really? How could you be so carried away that you forget your own nature?'

'Maybe your son's nature isn't what you think.'

They stare at each other. 'You've obviously never loved anyone to the point of madness,' says M.

'That seems a good thing, given what it can lead to.'

'Maybe. Or maybe you never see the world fully lit up.'

'I don't want my son to be a sadist,' says Beth.

M's laugh is short and harsh, almost like a bark. 'Better than being a masochist. At least he's not the one getting hurt.'

'Somebody doesn't always have to get hurt.'

'That's not been my experience,' says M. 'Look, I'm not sure I can help you. I don't know anything about this sort of thing.'

Beth looks into her cobra eyes, trying not to be mesmerised by them. She feels weak, as if she could just dissolve, evaporate, the elements of her personality floating off into the atmosphere. Is this how you lose your sense of self, being overpowered by someone stronger? She needs to collect her wits.

'You're obviously a smart woman who knows the world.'

M smiles. 'That's why you came to me, I know.' Her voice is almost soothing. 'Your son is young. His flesh is mixed up in her flesh. His spirit belongs to her. One day he'll come out of it and see what he's done but from the sound of it it'll be too late by then. He'll never go back to being a nice, innocent young man.'

Beth can't help it. She begins to weep. Myra's voice is almost gentle. 'You always were a soft lass, Betty Higginbottom,' she says.

'I'm sorry Soph couldn't come herself, Miss Spencer. The cat's on its last legs, I'm afraid.'

'I am too,' says M, leaning on the arm he offers.

'Not quite yet, I hope,' says Bunty, with that impenetrable politeness that feels as if he's mocking her.

She doesn't answer, is finding it surprisingly difficult to walk to the car. Her breathing comes hard, long, shallow breaths that peter out before the air reaches her lungs. Her little dog scampers ahead of her and leaps straight on to the back seat of the car.

'A well-trained animal, I see,' says Bunty. 'That's the ticket.'

'You like *big* dogs in your family, don't you?'

'Of course. Real chaps don't carry chihuahuas, you know.'

'Heaven forbid. Ghastly little things, aren't they?' says M, though she actually thinks they're cute.

Bunty holds the door open for her and waits while she eases herself in by sliding down the back of the seat. 'That looks painful,' he says.

'I should have got a new hip,' she says. 'But they won't waste NHS money on an old crock like me.'

'It's quite strict nowadays,' he agrees.

They drive the short distance to Sophie's house. He does his best to help her out but he's clumsy and she finds his touch almost painful. God, she's falling apart with alarming rapidity. *She* won't last the weekend at this rate, never mind the cat.

Bunty looks relieved when Sophie comes to the door. 'You are clumsy,' she tells him. 'You were on the verge of hurling Maria to the ground any minute now.'

'Not cut out to be a nurse, Snuffy,' he says. 'Can you take it from here?'

'You're not rushing off already, are you?'

'Sorry, sis. Things to see, people to do. Busy weekend, I'm afraid.'

She looks up at the bleached out sky. 'Be careful driving back, darling. Who knows what it'll be like over the moors?'

M is relieved to have Sophie's arm supporting her. She's gentle, not an oaf like her brother. 'I'm sorry we had to be here this weekend,' says Sophie. 'But I couldn't move Plum.' Her eyes fill with tears. 'She's awfully poorly.'

She leads M into the living room, where a real fire is burning. The flames take her back to her gran's little parlour in Gorton, the smell of coaldust as you walked in the house, the smell of the dirt and the danger that the coal came from. This is sweeter, woodsmoke. She tries to breathe it in, but can't get her breath and starts to cough. 'I'll get you some water,' says Sophie.

The cat is stretched out on that old battered rug of Sophie's. M is shocked at how scrawny she looks. Her bones show through her scraggy fur and you can almost count the nubs on her spine. Minim has always been friends with Plum and goes over to nuzzle her, but he yelps suddenly and darts away, frightened by the death he sees written on her face.

'You and me both, pet,' she says to the cat, and sits down on the sofa. Sophie returns with the water and a fleece rug which she tucks round M. 'She's really gone downhill since last time, love,' says M.

'I know. She was at the vet's all day yesterday. They had her on a drip overnight.' The poor little chick. She looks pale, skinny. It's awful losing an animal. What would M do without Minim? the little warm body to cuddle at night, the devoted eyes looking up at you. She bends to lift the dog on to her knee. 'Come on, you, come and be Mummy's hot water bottle.' He nestles down contentedly on her lap, licking her hands.

Sophie sits cross-legged on the floor, innately graceful as she strokes the sick cat. M's really out of her league, being with Sophie, she's so beautiful. The room is quiet and the cat's wheezing breaths sound very loud. M is sure her own do too.

As the afternoon darkens around them M finds herself drifting off, the faces of the dead floating at the back of her eyelids ... her friend Michael, sliding, sinking, deep beneath the water. That afternoon was one of the worst of her life, the first time she saw death. Poor Michael, he was so proud to be walking in the Whit parade, though he looked awfully small, struggling to carry the big embroidered banner in that heat. If only she'd gone to the reservoir with him after the procession, but they'd been so many times without mishap. She wanted to sip tea wearing her new white frock, not go diving into murky water.

It's dark down there, green and slimy. Strange plants flower into being beside Michael, shooting out seaweedy fronds that entwine themselves round his body, dragging him away from her, pulling him deeper and deeper down. She's seen him going so many times and she wasn't even there. Of all days to decide to be ladylike. They always went together, she should have looked after him. Not that anyone expected her to. Michael's mum was so nice, the way she took Myra on her knee and comforted her. Why *should* she blame herself? She was young then, too young.

And Puppet, darling Puppet, killed by those murdering bastards, the police. They probably thought she'd break then, but she didn't. She was too strong for them. That hardened her heart against them, that they'd use a poor, defenceless dog to get at her.

Her eyes fly open. She doesn't want to think about Puppet. She doesn't want to think about dying, yet here is little Plum fading in front of her eyes. Will M still be here when the cat goes? The poor thing looks very weak. No way she'll last the weekend. What will it be like? Will it be peaceful? Will she just slip away? If she does it will be, M realises, the first time she'll have seen a natural death.

Plum teeters to her feet, legs buckling beneath her. She veers over to one side, head butting against the sofa as if she's going to collapse on the floor again. A little cry escapes Sophie, an involuntary sound almost like a cat's mew. 'Oh sweetie,' she says. There's a terrible smell as the cat opens her bowels. Sophie takes a towel from a basket at the side of the fireplace and gently lays the little animal on it. She pulls on a pair of rubber gloves and wipes her clean. God, almost a whole packet of wet tissues. How could so much shit come out of that little body?

Sophie turns to M and tries to smile. 'Inappropriate defecation, the vet called it. No wonder Bunty hot-footed it out of here today.' She cradles the little creature against her chest, as if she's suckling a baby.

'Has she been eating anything?' asks M.

'She did yesterday, a little, when I brought her back from the vet's, but she hasn't touched a thing today.'

'What did the vet say?'

Sophie half sobs. 'He said it would be kinder to put her to sleep.'

'Oh my God, Sophie, why didn't you?'

'She'd been at the vet's all night. I couldn't do that to her when she'd been in some strange place without me. It would have been too cruel, a terrible betrayal.'

'But surely you wouldn't want to cause a little animal pain?'

'No, of course not. But she's not in pain, is she?'

M peers at the cat, stretched out now on Sophie's knee. 'She looks pretty peaceful,' she admits.

Sophie strokes her fur. 'You're so beautiful,' she croons to the cat. They sit together on the sofa for a long time, Sophie with the dying cat, M with the sleeping dog.

'Darling, Maria. Are you cold? Would you like something to eat?'

'I can't seem to keep much down these days,' says M. 'Maybe just some soup.'

'I could nip out and get us fish and chips if you like.'

'Don't worry on my account, love.'

Sophie looks down at the animal on her lap. 'You think I'm wrong, don't you?'

'No, of course not. She's your cat. It's up to you to say what happens to her.'

'Is it? That seems a terrible responsibility to take on.'

'Don't you think it's kinder to spare her suffering?'

'If she was in pain I would, of course,' says Sophie. 'It's just, maybe I'm more traditional than I thought. It seems a terrible arrogance to take another creature's life.'

She gets up to feed the fire with more logs, laying the cat carefully on the sofa. The animal's eyes follow her as she walks across the room. Plum was such a pretty creature when she was well, a dainty, high-stepping little thing who knew her own beauty. Now she watches Sophie as if to impress every detail on to her mind's eye, as if she wants to remember everything about her. Can it really be true, that an animal loves so completely? M hugs her little dog closer to her. She's frightened suddenly. There's been too much death in her life. She should just go home and get away from all this. And yet there's a terrible fascination in it too. She wants to see what happens. She wants to know how Sophie will be.

Sophie puts on the lamp beside M. 'I'll make you some of that soup now,' she says.

'You should have something proper to eat,' says M, but Sophie shakes her head. 'I feel too sick,' she says.

She brings the soup in mugs and sits holding hers against her chest. Her teeth start chattering. 'Don't, love,' says M. 'Don't.'

'I'm sorry. I've had her for so long …'

'I know.'

M leans her head back on the sofa. She's having trouble swallowing. It's as if she's filling up with water, as if she too is drowning, but in her own body. Sophie looks alarmed and comes over to sit beside her. 'It's all too much for you, my darling, isn't it? Shall I take you home?'

M shakes her head. 'I don't want to be on my own,' she whispers.

Sophie's arms go round her. 'You won't be. I'm here.' There's a softness in her, a sweetness that M has never experienced before. She's not neurotic or damaged like the women in prison; she's not rough in her love, the way they loved you in Gorton, the way Brady loved her. She lifts M's legs on to the sofa and tucks the blanket round her. Maybe, if they'd met early enough in their lives, maybe none of it would have happened. Maybe all M needed was someone to be kind to her.

As the night wears on she drifts in and out of sleep. Sophie puts a duvet down on the floor and lies there with the little cat on top of her. At around two in the morning the animal starts to mew, a terrible sound that cuts through M's dreams. She's heard that sound before, the sound of a creature in distress. She raises her head, her heart pounding. Where's Ian? She can't see Ian … Phlegm rises in her throat and she starts coughing. She feels as if her lungs will burst.

'Maria. Maria.' Sophie is patting her back.

She struggles to sit. 'Sorry. Poor little Plum. What a dreadful noise.'

'I've made an awful mistake, haven't I?' says Sophie.

M stares at the little cat, who is quiet now, her eyes still locked on Sophie as if she doesn't want ever to stop looking at her. M feels a strange excitement rising in her. The animal is so weak. She has very little time left now. Will she just roll over and die? Will she slip away quietly? 'It's too late to get the vet now,' says M.

'I know,' says Sophie. The cat moans. 'I wouldn't have her suffer for anything. What can I do, Maria?' Her face twists in a strange grimace that for a moment makes her look almost ugly. 'I don't want her to be in pain.'

'I don't think it'll be long now,' says M, not taking her eyes off the cat. 'You know, she's very poorly. You'd just have to put that pillow over her face and she'd be gone.'

Sophie's face goes pale. 'No. No, I couldn't.'

'It would be kinder. Would you like me to do it for you? You could go outside. It would all be over in a few seconds.'

255

Sophie takes a deep breath. Then she shakes her head. 'Thank you. It's kind of you, but I couldn't. We've come this far. I think I'll just let nature take its course.'

M takes her hand and squeezes it. 'All right, love,' she says.

They sit in silence. Plum is breathing so quietly now that they strain to tell whether she is alive. Minim slides down off the sofa and lies by the fire on his own. Suddenly the cat's whole body convulses and she yowls, a weird, banshee cry of unbearable pain. Sophie holds her against her chest. 'Oh my little love.'

The cat's eyes stare, sightless now. So this is what a natural death looks
like—it's just as painful and violent as the others. Maybe she and Ian weren't as cruel as everyone said ...

256

'No!' Beth tries to slam the door in Jude's face, but somehow Jude is quicker and blocks it with her foot. 'I suppose this is what you call doorstepping, is it?'

Jude's face is pale, her eyes tired. If Beth didn't know why, she'd feel sorry for her friend. Former friend.

'Please, Beth. I want to explain.'

'Of course you do. That'll make you feel better, but why on earth would it make me feel better?'

'I'm begging you.'

Jude looks so wretched Beth can't help releasing her hold on the door. Hesitantly Jude steps into the house, her whole body proclaiming deference. Well, that's a first for feisty Jude, always ready to take charge of a situation. Of course that's the only way she *can* take charge of this situation.

'I'm going to make some strong coffee. I think I'm going to need it to stomach what you've got to say,' says Beth. Her whole body is trembling as she fills the kettle and lifts the coffee down from the shelf. So many years of friendship down the drain, and for what, a quick shag? She places two china cups on a tray, mind drifting back to the thick Union Jack mugs they had in the flat she and Pat and Jude shared. All those nights of sitting up till three in the morning, agonising about men. Jude was the one who understood when Beth's first year at university went pear-shaped over Ed Maitland. 'Sweetie, he's a competitive swimmer,' Jude told her. 'He's more interested in his body fat ratio than yours. Let him go.'

Letting him go, that was the hard part. Still is. She and Charles are no more than co-existing in the same house at the moment but she can't get up the nerve to kick him out. No, it's not that. She can't make up her mind if it's the right thing to do. The water boils and she pours it over the coffee grounds. Taking a deep breath, she heads for the living room. Let's hear what Jude has to say.

Her friend is standing at the window when she comes through. 'At least sit down,' says Beth, wearily. Suddenly it all seems too much. What does it matter why they did it? They betrayed her, and that's all there is to it. As her eyes follow Jude's progress to the sofa, she realises that her friend too is nervous, not her natural state. They wait for a few minutes in silence while the coffee brews, then Beth releases the cafetière's plunger and pours the coffee.

Jude's voice, when she begins to speak, is surprisingly strong. 'Beth, first of all, I know there are no excuses for what I did. I am so so sorry. I never thought I would ever behave to a friend the way I've done to you.'

Beth is taken aback, expecting excuses, not apologies. 'Are you talking about Charles? Or about Will?'

'I've nothing to apologise for with Will. I used my job to protect him as much as I could, to show the stresses our young soldiers are under, to show the way the people at the top pressurise them into behaving in ways they wouldn't do normally.'

'Oh really, so no personal glory in it for you at all then?'

Jude leans forward as though she is going to lay her hand on Beth's, but stops herself. 'I don't care about that, I really don't. I can't live with what I've done to you—and Charles. I want you to know that there was nothing there to shake your marriage.'

Beth puts her cup down carefully, struggling to control the tremor in her hand. 'Oh Jude, don't be such a hypocrite. How could it not shake my marriage?'

'Men are weak, Beth, you know that. Give them attention, flattery, and they'll do anything you want.'

Jude always had that sense of her own power, could have any man she wanted. Why did she bother with Charles? Isn't he too staid? too pompous, if the truth be told? She's always gone for quick, mercurial men, never looked for the solidity that Beth sought. *There's not many men who can keep me in the style I've become accustomed to,* she used to say, not being entirely accurate. Wealth was the style she grew up with. Did that make her think she was entitled to take what she wanted?

'Why Charles? You've never been short of boyfriends, Jude.'

Jude holds herself so well. Even sitting down she seems erect, but she clearly hasn't had her usual expensive haircut and her nails are bitten to the quick. Only once can Beth remember seeing her so ungroomed, and that was before their final exams, when Jude suddenly realised she had left her revision too late and was cramming into the small hours of the morning. Now she gulps nervously as though she is short of breath.

'I know this sounds weird, but it was an intellectual thing. I was absolutely absorbed in my book and Charles knows so much about the subject. You've no idea what donkeys there are in newsrooms, Beth, people who're sharp at making a buck or stabbing each other in the back but who don't really care about much beyond their next scoop or the pat on the head from the editor or the big bucks in their paycheque. I'd had enough.'

'I thought you liked all the expense account lunches and the freebies.'

Jude nods quickly. Even in her unkempt state she looks exotic against the chintz and chenille of the living room. She is not a domestic creature. 'Yes, yes I did. But there's a terrible price to pay for going for the money. You remember the sort of work I used to do when I started out? I'd forgotten why I went into journalism in the first place. It had all become too easy.'

Despite herself, Beth finds she is amused. So Jude. 'Oh, God forbid things should be too easy.'

Jude gives a small smile. 'Of course, I loved the adventure and the pace and the sheer fun of it. But I've been doing it half a lifetime. I wanted to do something more worthwhile.'

Beth raises an eyebrow. That really takes the cake. 'Congratulations, Jude. You did a fine job of that, very worthwhile to steal someone else's husband.'

Jude's face looks aghast. Then for a moment it's almost as though she might burst out laughing. 'I know, I know, I know. I've made a complete

258

hash of everything. Please, Beth, couldn't we be friends again, pretend this hasn't happened?' With her customary intuition she corrects herself without even looking up at Beth. 'No, I'm sorry, you'll never be able to do that, but couldn't we put it behind us?'

Beth sighs. Poor Charles is distraught, hardly able to look at her; now Jude is abject. Things can't go on like this, but how will it ever be possible to forget, even if one could eventually forgive? Things may limp on, but she's sure she will never feel the same about either of them ever again. She looks at Jude's untouched coffee congealing in the cup.

'I'm not sure I believe in open marriage,' she says.

Jude looks horrified. 'Darling, there's nothing between us. There never really has been. It was the talk, the interesting ideas. You can't *think* there's anything going on now.'

'I wasn't talking about my marriage to Charles,' says Beth. 'I was talking about you and me.'

Beth slouches down in the car, wishing the district nurse would hurry up. It's freezing, far too cold to be hanging around waiting. The woman always comes here at noon so where on earth is she today? Doesn't Myra need things at the same time every day? Beth puffs into the scarf she's wearing, the warmth of her own breath heating her for a moment. If only she wasn't such a coward, she could have done this three days ago.

At last the green Ford Fiesta rolls up and the woman gets out, carrying her bags of medicines and dressings. Beth lets her get into the house. This time she'll do it, she will talk to Myra. Taking a deep breath, she grabs her bunch of flowers and flings the car door open. No going back.

The sky is grey and overcast. She wouldn't be surprised if it snows later, but then it's been threatening for days. She raps sharply on the door. Oops, she should have knocked more quietly. That sounded a bit aggressive.

The nurse looks startled to see her on the doorstep. Myra obviously doesn't have visitors during the day.

'I'm a friend of Maria's. Would it be all right if I came in to see her?'

'She's very weak, I'm afraid.'

'Yes, Sophie told me, so I thought I'd come now, keep her company while Soph's at work.'

The woman stands back to let her in. 'They're lovely,' she says. 'Chrysanths don't half brighten up the place, do they? specially these yellow ones. I'll put them in a vase and you can take them up to her.'

Beth waits in the hall. It's rather overpowering, all yellow and gold stripes. A bit common. 'Just go on up, love,' says the nurse, handing her the chrysanthemums in a clear glass vase. Beth has the same one at home, which makes her smile. So even serial killers shop at Ikea.

She walks up the stairs with a sense of confidence although she hasn't been here before. All these terraced houses have the same layout— Myra will be in the big bedroom at the front. The curtains are drawn and the room is dark, except for the flame from the gas fire. Myra is lying in bed, eyes closed. She wakens as Beth comes in and half smiles when she sees the flowers, eyes fixed on them as if the vivid colour is salvation, will restore her to life. Her eyes drift shut again when she realises who's brought them.

'Have you come to finish me off?' she says, amused, her voice a pallid husk of what it once was.

'I'm sorry, Myra. I don't want to upset you.'

'I'm beyond that now, love.'

Beth sits down by the bed. The darkened room is peaceful, its pale blue walls and old lace creating an unexpected atmosphere of serenity. This isn't how she thought Myra's bedroom would be. She thought it would be more like the hall—gaudy, not quite right.

'How are you feeling?' asks Beth.

Myra sighs. 'You don't care, Betty. What do you want?'

260

Beth looks at her waxen face. She feels guilty being here but if she doesn't speak now it will be too late.

'I need to know,' she says. 'Is my son evil?'

'Like me, you mean?'

Beth says nothing. Is the person evil or just the deed? She's exhausted trying to work it out. The woman on the bed doesn't look evil, doesn't even look like Myra. Invalid skin, dried out and tinged with yellow; dark shadows under her eyes; a short, straight nose much prettier than the beak she had as a child—she must have had surgery before they let her out. She's wan and tired, a spectral echo of the vigorous woman she once was. They may have given her a new outside but could she ever change inside?

'Does it matter what you call it?' says Myra slowly. It seems to be a great effort to her to speak.

'I want my boy back.'

'Mmm ...' Her tongue creeps across dry lips.

'Would you like a drink?'

She nods. Beth pours some water from the jug on the bedside table and holds it out to her but she can barely raise her head. Beth slides on to the bed beside her and puts an arm round her to lift her up. She's so light, like a doll emptied of its stuffing. Her nightdress clings to her corrugated spine. When she tries to drink, a little dribble of liquid trickles out of her mouth and Beth wipes it away with a tissue. The gentleness of the movement feels encoded in her body. From Will, of course. Her son, her darling son—the first time he played rugby and ended up with his nose in the pitch during the scrum, she wiped tears as well as mud from his face that day. He was game as a child, always running after the big boys, always falling and needing to be comforted.

Myra is as vulnerable as a child now. Beth supports her body and plumps the pillow behind her head, finding a tenderness towards her that she did not know she had. Or is it simply that her body, in carrying out these actions, retains the gentleness of the past, that even though they're for someone else, the movements she has made so many times for her son cannot be separated from the feeling she has for him? Myra is so weak, so frail. How little it takes to be a human, just a puff of air, a smattering of bones, a few pints of blood.

'You loved Brady too much, didn't you?' she asks.

'I expect so.' Her head sinks back on the pillow, as if the act of drinking has exhausted her.

'I keep asking myself, was it all the girl's fault? They say love transforms people. Did she change him?'

Myra moves slightly as if she's going to shake her head but can't quite manage it. 'Love doesn't change people,' she says in her raspy voice. 'Love lets people be who they are.'

Beth wonders if her heart will ever stop racing. Oh Will ... she remembers him caring for a sick seagull, crying when his dog died. Never

261

violent, never angry. Cross, maybe, once or twice when Charles nagged him about his schoolwork.

'Will was always a good boy, gentle,' she says.

'He's a human being.'

'Human beings can be compassionate. They have that choice too.'

'Yes—Sophie—she doesn't need to know.'

Beth stares at her, puzzled. She can't be all bad if she cares about Sophie, can she? At school she seemed to care about people. She had that friend Michael, who drowned, and she always stuck up for her sister Maureen, fought her battles for her, though you could say that wasn't about caring, just that she liked fighting. Poor Sophie. She'd be devastated if she ever found out who she'd been having a relationship with.

'She won't hear it from me, you can be sure of that,' she says.

Myra nods with satisfaction. She's not asleep, but looks barely alive. The thought of her imminent death floods Beth with a surge of blood through the body. She has no reason to mourn this woman. Is she mourning the death of her own childhood, the death of her child's lost innocence? Or the fact that we all have to die? Maybe she's just afraid that it will happen while she is here?

'Do you ever look back and regret it, Myra?' she asks.

'Of course,' she says, but Beth can't tell what she regrets.

The longer she stays in this darkened room the more it smells like a sickroom—airless, the wastepaper basket full of used tissues, the table stacked with unfinished drinks. She wants out of here, wants light, life.

'My son's never hurt another person in his life. Why did he have to go along with it?' She can feel her voice rising, so agitated is she, so desperate not to cry in front of this dying woman.

Myra opens her eyes again. She has a familiar expression on her face, one Beth remembers from school, a look of irritation mixed with amusement. 'It's our dirty little secret, Betty,' she says. 'Us humans. You know what? He was having fun.'

262

It's the light that wakens Sophie, a queer, pearlescent light that filters through the cracks in the curtain and casts an eerie pallor on the room. Half past six. There's no point in lying on, she won't sleep now. She pulls on her dressing gown and goes to the window. A thick layer of snow covers the ground, masking the chaos and mess of her garden. Little icicles drip from the garden shed, turning it into a house from a fairytale, while the bare tree branches droop heavily with their white burden. The world is transformed, a spangled stage set glittering under the light of the early morning sun. Pristine, sparkling, its imperfections hidden, yet how can it be beautiful when there is no Maria in it?

Grief sits heavy in Sophie's stomach like a tumour. She takes a long time over her morning tea, just looking out at the snow. 'Oh Minim,' she says, pulling the little dog on to her knee. 'What are we going to do?'

There seem to be so few memories to hold on to. If only they'd had more time together. Not everyone took to Maria—Sophie knows Bunty thought she was mad getting involved. 'She's a hard-faced, middle-aged bitch who looks like a dominatrix,' she heard him say on the phone to Cassandra once. 'God knows what Soph's doing with her. Do you think she likes it rough?'

She did, it turned out, was driven crazy by Maria's strength. Being held down, pinioned, Maria's arms tough as a man's and much more frightening; she felt sometimes like a helpless little doll, unable to resist, unable to fight back. Such an insistent strength, it could overpower you. Why should that excite her? Why be frightened of someone who would never harm you? And being frightened, how could you enjoy it?

Throughout the morning Sophie does the things she needs to do—slowly, doggedly, as if she's living in an underwater world where everything is in danger of floating away. The flotsam and jetsam of a life lived together come drifting back to her, the picnics this summer, lazing up on the moors near Eskdale with a bottle of wine; the concerts they went to in Manchester when Maria would get excited over composers she'd never heard before, Shostakovich, Messaien. Those years in the mental hospital must have been torture for someone so sensitive to art as she was. She wasn't hard-faced—Bunty just brought out the worst in her.

Tissue paper, she needs tissue paper to wrap the jewellery in. *Just pop it in the post, love. She's not well enough to come to the service,* M had said, but it didn't seem right that a mother should find out about her daughter's death in that way. No, going over there is the right thing to do, nothing else for it. She'll take Myra's missal and rosary beads to the priest and then she'll go and see the mum. Fanning out the jewellery in her hand, she considers each piece separately—a few pairs of cheap gold earrings, a ring, a silver locket. A fistful of jewellery, it's not much to leave behind. Sophie puts it all into a carved wooden box she brought back from a holiday in India. That at least makes the sad little legacy look better.

'Come on, Minim. You're going on a trip.' She scoops the dog up and deposits him in the passenger seat. 'Now don't you move—I don't want to be arrested for dangerous driving.' Minim snuggles down as if he's understood, clearly intent on snoozing.

Out on the motorway, the road and the sky are clear. If only there'd been time to have a holiday abroad—Maria had never been out of the country in her life. To the south of France, maybe, where she could feel the warm sun on her skin; or even just a package holiday to Spain, to a hotel with hot pink bougainvillea round its enclosed garden. Towards the end it all seemed to happen so fast, as if they were in a timewarp where events were streaming past like the stars in the Milky Way.

Maria's face keeps swimming into her mind, Maria's body in the funeral parlour, laid out in the open coffin like a doll in its presentation pack, arms straight by her sides. Despite the tasteful makeup her skin looked grey underneath, like putty. It must be a strange job to do—a mortician's beautician, the undertaker called it. Painting the faces of the dead seems surreal, pagan almost, replacing death with this strange facsimile of life, so artificial it's like neither.

There were flowers in the funeral parlour, relieving the pale grey monotony of the decor. The painted doll in its box looked like Maria but wasn't Maria—the beautician had combed her hair differently from normal and she looked older, how she might have looked in twenty years time. Sophie took the doll's hand and it felt plump but awfully cold, as if made of wax. 'My darling,' she'd said, startling herself because she'd said it out loud.

Maria, Maria, putty grey in her lilac suit. She must block the image out and keep her mind on her driving. Halifax, Huddersfield, the road signs pass and she barely notices. Only when she passes the junction for Saddleworth is her memory stirred—that first time she and M drove home for Christmas they hit a real pea-souper of a fog round there. How spooked they were by it, both of them, by the place, by the thought of what had happened there. That was the beginning of her real feelings for Maria. Poor love, she was so upset at the thought of the children who'd been murdered. How sad that she never had any kids of her own. She'd have been a good mother, look how little Emily took to her that Christmas. Too late now.

Once off the motorway Sophie gets lost in the networks of redbrick terraces, modern council flats and bleak stretches of waste ground. The ornate facade of a huge church, a florid confection of redbrick buttresses and honey-coloured embellishment, looms up ahead of her, partially covered in scaffolding. Is this Gorton Monastery, the half-restored friary they're always raising money for? M said she went there as a young girl. Strange to think of a Pugin creation being a local parish church, all that baroque ornament in a Manchester slum.

Father Connor's church, when she eventually finds it, is a modern one, though the house is a shabby Victorian villa with rotting windowframes and a dripping drainpipe. The priest himself answers the door. His handshake is firm and confident and he's surprisingly handsome—rough springy hair, his eyes dark.

'You must be Sophie. Come through to the kitchen—it's the brightest room in the house. Our housekeeper put her foot down—she thought all the Stygian gloom was fine for the likes of us priests, but she didn't fancy working in it herself.'

He reaches into the cupboard for some mugs. The coffee is strong, made in a cafetière. 'I can't stand instant,' he says, seeing her look of surprise. 'It's Fairtrade coffee, so I can feel virtuous about my little luxuries.'

'I'm sure no-one grudges you them, Father.'

'I don't suppose fine coffee comes under anyone's definition of poverty.' He frowns. 'They're always a struggle, these vows.'

Sophie opens her bag and brings out Maria's missal and rosary. 'Maria asked me to give you these.'

He sits in silence, looking at the battered black leather book, the polished rosewood beads. 'Was she peaceful at the end?'

'I wish I could say she was, but she got quite agitated. People don't want to die, no matter that it's in God's plan for them.'

'You're right, of course. We comfort *ourselves* with the myth of the peaceful death.' He runs the rosary beads through his fingers. 'I suppose for most people it's a terrifying moment.'

'She seemed to have very old-fashioned ideas about Hell. I tried to tell her the Church doesn't think like that any more, but it was fixed in her mind that that was where she was going.'

'Ah no, I'm very sad to hear it, though I know why she thought like that.'

'Why? Why would she? She wasn't a bad person.'

'There are some sins the Church finds hard to forgive—or maybe that women find hard to forgive themselves. But God is infinite in his mercy, that is all Maria had to remember.'

The priest's soft Irish accent is somehow comforting, but why is he talking about sins women can't forgive themselves? That can only mean one thing, surely, and that didn't happen. M's baby died. Sophie sips her coffee. She mustn't ask—Father Connor can't break the confidence of the confessional.

Father Connor startles her by leaning over and patting her hand. 'You look done in. You should just have posted the little things. It's too much for you, driving all the way over here at a time like this.'

Sophie sighs. She can feel a headache coming on. 'I had to come over to see Maria's mother. I didn't want to break the news to her over the phone.'

'The poor soul. I didn't know she was still alive.'

'But Maria talked about her all the time? She lives in a nursing home, not too far away from here. I doubt she'll come to the funeral, she's too poorly.'

'Have you met her before?'

'No. No, I haven't. I'm dreading it really.'

'Would you like some moral support? I'd be happy to come with you.'

'Would you? That's ever so kind, Father. I'd really appreciate it.'

'Aidan. Just call me Aidan. I'll go get a coat.'

He returns in a long black wool coat. Really he's a very good looking man, stylish in his black jeans and open-necked shirt. Sophie much prefers a priest to dress informally, no dog collars or cassocks, not like that old Father Murphy at their church. This one seems much more human. It also seems he knows the way, which is a relief—no more wandering the wrong way up one way streets.

The nursing home is a couple of miles away, in a quiet suburban street lined with old trees and new cars. A large redbrick Victorian villa, it could have been a district hospital, or a lunatic asylum. Who knows how many poor people like Maria got stuck in these places for life? At least it looks in good condition, though the girl who answers the door has a slack mouth and stringy hair that make Sophie feel nauseous. How off-putting for the old people.

'I'll just get her. Does she know you're coming?'

Sophie nods, though she hasn't in fact contacted Mrs Moulton. 'How is she today?' she asks.

The girl shrugs. 'Same as ever. You don't get much conversation out of these old ducks.'

'How boring for you,' says Sophie, but the girl fails to realise she's being sarcastic and nods in agreement.

At first sight the residents' lounge seems a fine room, all cornice work and plush upholstery, but there is a smell here, a mixture of warm sweat and cold urine, overlaid with cheap meat stewing, that sickens Sophie. Why did she come? Why this compulsion to meet M's mother? How arrogant of her to think that the news would be better coming from M's friend, rather than the people who look after her all the time and who know her.

'Is there somewhere private we can go?' she asks the girl.

"You could go in the conservatory,' she says. 'It's a bit cold but no-one else'll be in there.'

Sophie and Aidan follow her through a long series of corridors and junctions, past a large lounge with old people nodding and drooling into their cardigans, and finally into the darkened room. The lights switched on, a dank and lugubrious garden is revealed, its trees rendered only marginally less funereal by their coating of snow. Oh dear, not the ideal setting to tell someone their daughter has died. Boom, boom, boom, Sophie's heart is thumping. She puts out a hand to detain the girl. 'Is she really all right? I have some bad news for her.'

The shrug again—the damn girl's shoulders seem the most expressive part of her. 'She's OK,' she says. 'Has one of her friends died? She hasn't got no family left.'

Sophie stares at her in astonishment. 'Her daughter's died.'

266

The girl sniggers. 'Ye-eh.' She looks at Sophie as if she's an idiot. 'Like last year.'

'No, last week.'

The girl lumbers to the door, incurious. 'Nah, you got that wrong. Someone's having you on.'

A few minutes later a middle-aged woman in a smart suit bustles in, a cloud of cheap fragrance in her wake. 'Hallo, I'm Anne-Marie Edwards, the manager. I'm sorry to have to ask you this, but you must understand there are security issues, as there would be with any patient. Could you tell me who you are?'

'I'm Sophie Ferrers, a friend of Nellie Moulton's daughter. This is Father Aidan Connor.'

The woman glances at Aidan, frowning. 'Are you from the press? Because we won't tolerate it, you know.'

'From St Agnes's parish, Mrs Edwards.'

'The press!' says Sophie. 'Why on earth would you think that?'

The woman gives her a very strange look. 'I thought you said you knew Nellie's daughter?'

'Yes.' Sophie is aware she's using her most patrician delivery. 'Indeed I did know her.'

'Well, you know she passed away last year then. Now Jade's telling me you say she died last week.'

'Look, I don't know what this is all about. I've lost my friend and I'm very upset. Could you please just get Mrs Moulton for me?'

Something, whether it be the social advantage implicit in Sophie's tone or simply mistrust of her own employee's reliability, convinces the woman and she nods. 'I'll get Nellie, but she's an old lady. I don't want her upset.'

Aidan Connor steps forward, speaking in his soothing Irish voice. 'Don't you worry. We'll keep Mrs Moulton on an even keel.'

Mrs Edwards relaxes. 'All right, Father. You know best, I'm sure. I'll send in some tea and biscuits.' She fiddles with the radiator. 'I don't want you all to freeze to death in here. We don't use this place much in winter,' she says, before leaving the room.

'A bit odd, all this,' says Sophie.

'Mmmm, I think poor old Jade's got her wires crossed.'

'I think we've come to a madhouse, not an old people's home.'

They hear Nellie Moulton before they see her—she keeps up a steady stream of grumbling as she approaches. 'Who did you say it were? Do I know her? Summat to do with what? Speak up, love. For a young girl you do a lot of mumbling. Why don't you wait till your teeth fall out, see how you get on wi' mumbling then?' Mrs Edwards brings in the old lady in a wheelchair, followed by Jade and a tea tray. 'Nellie, this is Sophie Ferrers and Father Aidan Connor. They've come to see you, dear. Sorry, Father, we have a bit of a crisis on the other wing. I'll have to leave you.'

'That's quite all right, Mrs Edwards. We can see you're a very busy woman.'

He gives an apologetic smile at Sophie as the manager leaves. Really, he's quite charming. He even pours the tea while Sophie pulls her chair closer to the wheelchair. It's hard to see Maria in Nellie Moulton's face. She's not the comfortably plump type of old lady, but one of the scrawny ones, with a long, lined neck and a bony frame. There is natural elegance in her tapering fingers and her carriage, upright despite being in the chair.

A look of fear crosses her face for a moment, followed by an almost pugnacious lift of the chin. 'So, Pinky and Perky. Did my daughter really get two good lookers like you into bed? You're both educated people but I bet she had you dancing to her tune, didn't she?'

Sophie stares at Aidan Connor. The old lady must have a touch of dementia. A flush creeps up his high cheekbones as he stares back at Sophie. Surely not? Perhaps he's just embarrassed at her frankness.

'I'm sure Father Connor wouldn't dream of approaching Maria in such a way. She was a very vulnerable woman.'

Nellie snorts with laughter. The priest's embarrassment is replaced by puzzlement. 'Vulnerable? That wasn't the Maria I knew.'

'What else could she be after the life she'd had? Having to give her baby away ... '

Aidan Connor is stunned. He leans forward and whispers in Sophie's ear. 'She didn't, she had an abortion. That's what she told me.'

They look at each other in astonishment. Who was this woman? Did they know her at all? Sophie can't believe it. Why wouldn't M tell her the truth? After all they'd been through together, what a betrayal. 'She must have trusted you more than she trusted me.'

Nellie shakes her head. 'She lied to both of you, love.'

Sophie's struggles to control the tremor in her voice. 'It wasn't either of us she called for at the end,' she says. 'She went way back to her early years, I think. She was calling for someone named Ian.'

Agitated, Nellie Moulton fidgets with the blanket draped across her lap. 'Is that her dog?' Minim is poking his head up out of Sophie's handbag. 'She always preferred animals to people. Can't say as I blame her. You're a nice little thing, aren't you?' The dog barks and jumps out, eagerly leaping up to lick Nellie's hands. 'Recognises I'm related to her probably.' She looks weary suddenly. 'You've come to tell me she's gone, haven't you?'

Sophie takes her hand. 'I'm so sorry, Mrs Moulton. It was all very peaceful in the end.'

'I shouldn't have had a go at you, love. You looked after her, more than she deserved really. You were very good to her.' She closes her eyes. 'It's not right. A mother shouldn't live longer than her child. I've lost two now. Who'd have thought I'd be the last one left?'

'I didn't know Maria had any brothers or sisters.'

'A sister. She died of a brain tumour, our Mo. Far too young, she were. What with that and the other thing it nearly broke my heart.'

268

'The other …? Maria going into a home, you mean?'

'That weren't a home, love,' she says, rather tartly it seems to Sophie. 'Is that what she told you?'

'Well, not a home, a sort of mental hospital.'

Nellie sighs. 'That's right, it were that,' she says. 'The only place she could be after what she did.'

She looks so sad, Sophie can't stand it; she opens her handbag and pulls out the little box. 'She wanted you to have her jewellery,' she says, pressing it into the old lady's hand. Nellie sits with it, unopened, in her lap. 'You have it, love. There i'n't much call for jewellery in this place.'

'But she told me to give it to you. She wanted you to forgive her.'

'It's not my forgiveness she needs now.' Nellie fumbles with the catch. 'Pretty box,' she says, pushing back the tissue paper. 'That locket's like one my mother had.' She slumps back in the chair. 'Take them, love.'

Sophie looks across at Aidan. 'She's exhausted. We'd better go.'

He nods, and stands up to leave. 'You take care of yourself, Mrs Moulton,' he says.

Nellie looks up at him, a kind of malevolent energy returning to her eyes. 'Hmm, some priest you are. I don't know how the Catholics put up wi' it. Bunch of sodding hypocrites.'

Aidan flinches, while Sophie feels more and more as if she's wandered into some surreal dream. So much doesn't add up here. 'I thought you were a Catholic.'

'Oh no, love. That were one of My … my daughter's affectations. She weren't brought up like that.'

'But you put her in that home the nuns ran, the place for disturbed young mothers.'

Nellie laughs out loud. 'Well, she always had a good imagination, I'll say that for her. She could talk her way out of anything. Well, not quite anything, though she tried that too.'

Sophie bends to take Minim from the folds of Nellie's blanket. 'Mrs Moulton, I don't understand half the things you're saying about Maria. I don't recognise her in them.'

'That's good, love. As well you don't know.'

'Don't know what?'

'Leave it, love. I'm tired now.'

Minim suddenly jumps from Sophie's arms and lands on Nellie's lap, snuggling against her as though he's going to sleep. 'It's the smell, i'n't it? If you've got t'same DNA you've probably got t'same smell.'

Out in the shrubbery slivers of snow slide off the yew trees. 'I expect she told you just to put them things in the post, didn't she? That's what you should have done.'

Sophie bites her lip. 'I thought it better to tell you in person. I didn't think it was right for you to find out in a letter that your daughter had died. '

'My niece, you mean.'

269

Is Sophie going mad or is the old lady quite gaga? Aidan's face reflects the consternation Sophie feels. She leans down and pats the old lady. 'Yes, your niece.'

'You're a lovely girl,' says Nellie. 'You deserve better.'

Aidan moves towards the door. 'I'll go find that girl and see if she can take Mrs Moulton back, will I so?'

As Sophie nods, the door opens and Mrs Edwards clicks in on brisk heels. 'What a cute little dog,' she says, going to pat Minim, though he instantly jumps off Nellie's lap and scampers towards Sophie. 'Such a cheeky little face he has. Well, Father, I hope you've enjoyed your visit.' She turns to Nellie. 'Time for your afternoon nap, dearie. I do hope you'll come again, Father. Some of our old ladies are very religious.'

Nellie makes a curious sound that's suspiciously like a snort. 'Aye, they worship good looking chaps.'

'Oh Nellie,' trills Mrs Edwards. 'You are a cynic. She keeps us all on our toes, Father.'

'I'm sure she does, Mrs Edwards,' he says, falling in beside her. 'Here, let me.' Deftly he takes the wheelchair from her and sets off down the corridor. Sophie follows them, marvelling not only at the constant stream of chatter Mrs Edwards keeps up but at her archly flirtatious manner with the priest. He's probably used to it. No wonder he finds his vows a struggle, with women flinging themselves at him all the time. Would Maria have made the first move? Would she have dared, with a priest? The old woman said so many odd things. What on earth was she talking about?

As they reach the turn-off to the front door, Mrs Edwards simultaneously steers the wheelchair towards a carer coming from one of the rooms and steers Aidan Connor to the right. 'Take Nellie to her room, will you, Janie? Father, why don't you come to my office? It would be so wonderful to be able to contact you in the future. We're desperately in need of a pastor here.'

'I'm not sure ...' He goes on mumbling as he walks away, but is swept along by the sheer force of Mrs Edwards' will. Sophie leans against the radiator, burying her face in Minim's fur. What an exhausting—and confusing—afternoon. The little dog starts yelping. Sophie looks up to see the girl Jade lumbering towards her. A pudgy hand descends on the little dog's head.

'What's he called then?'

'Minim.'

'That's a queer name.'

'Mmm, I suppose it is.'

'Were she all right, then, Nellie?'

'I'm not sure. She's very tired now. Sorry about the mix-up, by the way. It seems it was her niece who died?'

Jade seems startled by the apology. Probably it's a rare occurrence for her—she has the air of someone who would be easily bullied. 'Aye, I knew it couldn't be her daughter. She died last year.'

270

Sophie instinctively hesitates, fearing to put the question. Does she really want to know the answer? 'Who was her daughter?'

A look of satisfaction crosses the girl's face. It's no doubt also a rare occurrence for her to possess knowledge that someone else does not. She lowers her voice dramatically. 'It were Myra Hindley,' she intones.

'Oh my God.' Sophie begins to shake. Her legs give way and she has to hold on to the window sill to keep upright. Minim drops from her hands and starts to run around in circles, barking noisily. Only the arrival of Aidan Connor calms the little dog down. He looks at Sophie's face. 'You look awful. You must sit down.' He turns to Jade, his authority as a priest asserting itself. 'Please, would you bring a chair? And some water.'

She scurries off, shamefaced, returning shortly with the chair. 'Sorry,' says Sophie, sitting down heavily. Jade hovers anxiously until Aidan says sharply, 'Water.' When it comes, Sophie drinks quickly. She must, must collect herself. Clearly, from his calm appearance, Aidan doesn't know. The silly little manageress must have spent the whole time flirting. 'Migraine, I'm afraid. It's been threatening all afternoon.'

'You mustn't drive, not with a migraine.'

'Could you drive us back? Once I get a sleep in the back of the car I'll be right as rain.'

Aidan looks doubtful. 'I *think* my insurance covers me to drive any car, I'm not sure.'

'Let's trust in God, shall we?'

He laughs. 'That's a good idea. Why didn't I think of that?'

Sophie walks towards the back seat and slides in, shutting her eyes immediately.

'You're welcome to a bed in the rectory. I have some house visits to do—you'd be quite alone.'

'I'll be fine in the car,' murmurs Sophie. She doesn't want to talk to him or see him ever again. If only she hadn't told him the time of the funeral. There's only one thing for it—she won't go herself. She'll say she's ill. She is ill.

When the car finally comes to a stop in the church car park she feels more nauseous than she ever has in her life. 'I don't like leaving you like this,' says Aidan Connor.

'Please, I need to be on my own.'

'I'm sorry we've met in these circumstances, Sophie. I had no idea she had a partner. Nor that she was gay.'

'She wasn't. I'm not,' says Sophie flatly. 'I thought we had a special relationship.'

The priest's voice is low and subdued. 'I'm sure you did. You mustn't lose sight of that.'

'I expect you thought you had a special relationship with her too, Father.'

He flushes at her use of his title. 'I don't do this very often, you know.'

271

'No? She was obviously a very special person.'

'Yes, yes, I think so.'

Sophie almost laughs. 'Go, Father.'

'Sure. Sure thing. I'll see you again, Sophie.'

Minim is snuffling in the front seat, eyes blinking as he chases rabbits—or whatever it is that little dogs dream—in his sleep. Sophie curls up in the back, afraid to close her eyes. She mustn't fall asleep, she doesn't want to be here when Aidan Connor comes back. A walk, she'll go for a walk to clear her head, then get back on the motorway as soon as she can.

Snow is turning to slush on the pavements here, but the air feels clean and restores some of her gastric equilibrium. Despite her shock she tries to walks briskly, ignoring a group of teenage boys at the bus stop and striding past a row of shops as if she knows where she's going, though her legs feel heavy and intractable. By the time she gets back to the car the dog is yelping, his little head bobbing at the window as he tries to see where she is. 'Two minutes,' she tells him. 'Do your business and we'll go.' He shivers as soon as he reaches the ground and is back inside within seconds. 'You're a big talker, you,' she tells him, starting up the motor immediately.

The road out of Manchester seems easier to find than the road in and she has no difficulty joining the three lanes of traffic going her way on the M62. Is she angry, that she's driving so fast and so confidently? Despite the dark sky she can see frozen sheets of snow stretching into the distance on either side of the motorway, their reflected light casting a strange glow into the atmosphere. Up the road climbs, the cars ahead edging forward with the regularity of a conveyor belt. Oh no, they'll reach the turn-off for Saddleworth soon and she doesn't want to think of … M? She can't call her Maria now, can't bear to call her Myra, even in her head.

That night they were delayed in the car near Saddleworth Moor, it wasn't the deaths of the children that was upsetting her, it was the thought that she might give herself away to Sophie. How nervous she must have been all the time they were together, and yet she didn't seem on edge, was always in control, not just of herself but of Sophie too. It was she who took charge that first time, in the Turkish baths, she who called the shots, dominating Sophie, just with a gaze, time and time again. Oh God. Sophie's stomach starts to heave. To think of her saliva, her juices mingling with those of the most reviled woman in Britain, her DNA twisting and turning in its chromosomal dance with that of Myra Hindley, her fingers caressing the skin of a child killer. Her lips kissing those of the woman who forced a gag down the throat of a child.

Shivering, she pulls on to the hard shoulder and puts the hazard lights on. Her body goes hot and then cold, convulsing as she tries to expel the disgust inside her. The flickering orange lights, the zooming noise of cars speeding past, combine to disorientate her; she feels as though she's trapped in a nightmarish carnival ride and can't get off. Her stomach aches with the effort of retching—she's eaten too little today, brings up only a black dribble of bile. If there is a Hell, it must feel like this. Teeth chattering, Sophie climbs back into the car and turns the heater full on.

Why her? Is she so obviously prey, so easily manipulated? What a fool, not to know that her lover was betraying her. Yet there were no slips of the tongue, no small nervousnesses when Father Connor's name was mentioned, no blushing or stammering or distracted looks. No guilt, then? Well, why would M feel guilty about such a small sin when she has the dark weight of murder on her soul?

Sophie starts the engine and presses on. Near Saddleworth the sky lightens and the sky is frosted with stars. Once past there she'll feel more relaxed, irrational though that is. She wants to leave it behind her, just get home. The car speeds on through the snowy countryside, as if driven on automatic pilot, a ghost car with no-one at the wheel. By the time Sophie pulls into her street she's exhausted.

She needs to sleep, to blot all this out. First, though, she feeds the little dog. 'It's not your fault, is it, love?' she says, scraping out the tin. She'll go out later to the twenty four hour supermarket, get some bread and milk. But when she lies down, even her bedroom seems a malevolent place, the walls pulsing, the curtains flickering at the window as if spirits are trying to force entrance. Was it all a lie? Was there no love between them?

When she finally drags herself from sleep she realises it's one in the morning. She's been asleep for hours. The room is dark and little Minim is curled up beside her on the bed. Sophie pets the animal, stroking his ears. 'Aren't you lovely?' He snuffles in contentment, but once he realises she's getting dressed again, he leaps from the bed and shoots downstairs as if his life depended on it, rushing to the back door and barking, as he's done repeatedly in the last few days. 'She's not here, petal,' Sophie tells him. 'She won't be coming back.' The thought is as bleak as any she's had in the last few hours.

On the way to the supermarket she rolls the window down so she can feel the night air stinging her skin. Ahead, the lights of a gritting lorry spill an orange glow on to the road. No other cars are around and she drives slowly through the quiet town, its windows dark and dead as those of phantom houses. Snow sparkles on roofs, and roan pipes glint like icy snakes on the sides of the buildings. If it were only a matter of death, only loss, she would be comforted by its prettiness, but the glare off the snow hurts her eyes and her mind crawls with indefinable emotions whose nearest synonyms, *fear* and *repulsion* and *horror,* are only a pale imitation of the reality.

A sign on the side of a factory tells her it's two am and the temperature is minus one. White fields, looming hedgerows and then the supermarket, where lights are blazing into the night though there are only a few cars outside. Sophie turns the headlights off and sits for a moment, with a feeling of exhaustion so absolute she's not sure she can get out of the car.

As she leans her head back, a movement catches her eye. Directly in front of her, two young foxes come running into the car park and start gambolling in the snow. They circle round and round each other, vicious little teeth snapping ineffectually, with no intent to hurt. They are exquisite, with their fine heads, their little white chops, their amber eyes limned in black. She watches them for some minutes, unseen or perhaps just ignored by them. Foxes seem unafraid of human beings nowadays, as if they don't realise they're wild, and animals.

A Landrover drives suddenly into the car park, sweeping into a space and startling them. They stop their play, then turn together and scamper off, tails straight out behind them like flags unfurling, banners, blazoning how beautiful they are and how free ...

Ian ... it was Ian Brady she called for at the end.

Sophie feels sick. How did she not know? Will she ever dare to love anyone again?

He's done with tossing and turning, can't stay in bed a moment more. Goodness knows how he'll have the energy for seven o'clock mass at the convent in the morning, but sleep is impossible tonight. He should have known better than to try, but he craved oblivion, wanted black night to embrace him, blot out this terrible knowledge.

The room is bleak and cold, no comfort in it. No comfort anywhere since Mrs Edwards' call. Flirty Mrs Edwards, calling to say he'd left his scarf, and would he come by and collect it? Gossipy Mrs Edwards, unknowingly firebombing his life. How long did she keep twittering away after he dropped the phone in shock? With a sense of utter weariness, Aidan hauls himself out of bed. No, he won't wear his dressing gown, too cosy. Gloomily he buttons his cassock up to the neck. Some priest he is.

The clock on the kitchen wall says it's two am. He feels sick to his stomach. Outside, the cold wind almost knocks him off his feet. It whistles through the yard, piercing his eardrums and sending snowflakes whirling through the air as he crosses to the church. The door is stiff and he has to tug it closed behind him.

No point in putting on the lights—there are candles in front of the Virgin Mary and anyway, he knows every inch of this place. Slowly he makes his way to the altar and kneels below the red light that burns for the Holy Sacrament. Oh God, oh God. He is not worthy to be here, but where else is he to go? Bowing his head he tries to pray but cannot even approach the inner peace he seeks. What kind of God would send him this as a punishment? This is not the forgiving, loving God he knows. He wants to cry out against Him and yet to abase himself before Him, to flagellate himself like a penitent of old till the blood runs down his back and he passes out from the pain.

This is what comes of going against the Commandments. It wasn't his place to decide what sin is. The arrogance of it. He should fall down dead with shame. Is he so weak that he can't live without the solace of the body? It was enough that his lusts were the cause of a young man's death—that was God's warning, way back then. Why did he not heed it?

He thought he knew better, thought that the women he loved were good women, just weak like him, unable to be without the warmth of another's body beside them. He thought he could love them for a little while and then return to the Lord, that he could be forgiven for being kind to them as they were kind to him.

Was that so wrong? Was it sinful to think that God made the female form beautiful for men to adore, no, *admire*? Only God is to be adored. He closes his eyes, trying to blot out the memories—Katie, the primary school teacher with the pretty nipples; the single mum Siobhan, who loved him too much; Sister Clare ... his heart races at the thought of Sister Clare, her strong thighs and adventurous spirit, the adrenalin rush of seizing stolen moments with her in the convent, in the gardens, in the church.

Maria was older than the women he usually went for, but so passionate ... he thought it was real, this great tornado of feeling that swept them up together. Was it simply that she was good in bed? He closes his eyes, trying not to think of her straddling him, pressing down on him, not to think of the tiny crescent moon scar on her left breast, the teasing tip of her tongue as she leant down to kiss his chest and then ... How could he think that was love?

He was such a fool, falling for that fashionable sixties Hans Küng cant. He disgusts himself ... and yet finds that he is smiling; it's so tricky to say, that. One of the little red votive candles gutters out in front of him, its wick drowning in hot wax. What the hell's wrong with him? How shallow to be smiling at such a time. Is he so easily diverted? Nothing about this is funny. He has followed the wrong doctrine, and why? because it was convenient for him, convenient to think that the sacrament lay in the feeling between people, not the forms of the church; convenient to think that the Church and not God decreed celibacy. Well, that was historically true, of course ...

There's a tight band of pain across his stomach, a sour taste in his mouth. Now God has shown him the truth. Myra Hindley! Myra Hindley is the woman he thought he loved, this excrescence on the face of the earth who wasn't even brave enough to murder adults but hunted down little children, this predatory creature not fit to be called a woman.

How can he ever hope for forgiveness for this? To lie with a woman who has shoved a gag into the mouth of a ten year old girl, who has enticed young boys into her car knowing that the monster beside her will rape and torture them. To lie with a woman who enjoyed watching the life drain out of dying children ... he can't bear it. It's as if he's woken up with the snake-headed Medusa in his bed, or who's that other one? the beautiful queen Lamia, who devours children and whose mask of beauty dissolves to reveal her serpent's body, the corruption and cruelty seething in her scales.

The truth is that not even a woman who is half-serpent could be as foul as Myra Hindley. How did he not recognise those sullen, sensual lips, the blunt jawline? How could he have gazed into those eyes and not seen the hideousness in her soul? That awful mugshot image of her revealed how deep into darkness she had gone, taunted you with its noxious power. So why were there no traces of that brazen malevolence in the middle-aged woman, why no violet smudges below her lashes, no shadow around her? Could she have lived untouched by the weight of her own deeds? Could she? It doesn't seem possible.

Yet that first day they met in the bar, she seemed playful, a woman of unusual confidence and charm. Such a bold look she gave him. He was fed up listening to the young people arguing and boasting, just wanted some warmth for himself, a little flame of human kindness. It was so long since he'd had a woman. That day he wanted to be a man for a while, not a priest.

Is that how Jesus felt? Did He ever want to run away from His destiny, just live the peaceful life of holding a woman's heart in your hands, making a family with her? Is that why He had to be scourged at the pillar, crowned with thorns? Does desire have to be whipped from us, before we can be good?

Aidan raises his eyes to the ornate gold monstrance above him. Sometimes, for all his years of worshipping and serving the Lord, he finds it really hard to believe that this white disc really is the body of Christ. That is his weakness, that his faith is not strong enough to live without the things of this world, that he cannot resign his soul to the future happiness of life after death. He's not even sure he believes that the soul survives.

The wind cries at the window, a high, keening sound like a cat calling for a mate, or a banshee screeching to be let in. That woman—he can't call her Myra—does not deserve to live on after death. He wants her erased from existence, her malign energy extinguished forever. If only he were dead, then he would no longer have to suffer this pain. He would rather be beaten, tortured, than feel such shame.

Yesterday's humiliation is nothing compared to this. Mortifying to discover that the woman he loved was sleeping with someone else, worse that the person was a woman. But this? He almost gags to think of his tongue in Hindley's mouth. His skin creeps at the thought of her reptilian body touching his. No wonder poor Sophie was beside herself. At one point she looked as though she was going to faint. To be with someone for so long and not know … how did she not know? How did *he* not know? Shouldn't they have nosed out the stench of her, the ugly, grave-crawling putridness inside her?

He will ask the Lord for forgiveness. He doesn't deserve it, but God forgives all, will surely give him a sign that he should continue his ministry? He will build a new life for himself, uphold the rules of the Church, not just the ones he wants. He will give everything for others, want nothing for himself. He will work till he drops, till he falls exhausted into bed with no thoughts beyond his night prayers.

In nomine patris et filii, et spiritus sancti. Forgive me, Father, for I have sinned.

He will never, never sleep with a woman again.

277

He can't sleep. The heating pipes are clanking, the wind sighing along their length like a woman whispering to him. He strains but can't hear what she's saying. The words dissolve and disappear before they are formed. If he was superstitious he would think it was the girl calling to him, but it's all nonsense, that beyond the grave stuff. When you're dead you're dead and that's it.

He slides out of bed and opens the curtains, still clutching his hot water bottle to his stomach. Outside the wind is howling, snatching up snowflakes before they fall and sending them whirling into the air again. Even the yard in this godforsaken sumphole looks pretty in the snow.

If only he could get out and walk in it, run in it, rub it on his face like he did when he was a kid. One of the best nights ever was when all the people in the tenement came out for a snowfight in the dark, not just the children but their parents too. Under the orange street lamps they shouted and laughed, the girls squealing when they were hit. The snowballs went flying through the air, often shattering into hundreds of powdery fragments before they reached their target. How innocent it all was. That was living.

This is a living death. He might as well be under the ground with the girl for all the use being alive is to him. He opens his sliver of window to let in air. A cold wind rushes in and he lifts his face towards it, drawing the fresh smell down deep into his lungs. If only he could be out on the moors, walking and walking. When he was young he went for miles without tiring. Out there, the rough grass will be spiked with snow, the peaty smell seeping up from the ground through its white covering. Out there, it will be almost silent, the birds sheltering somewhere, maybe just the call of an occasional unhappy sheep, miserable even in its furry coat.

Out there, there is still one left, one buried too deep for them to find

…

And he, he's stuck here in this snakepit seething with cretinous Neanderthals with no humanity, no honour. They call him a psychopath but these people leave him standing, and are licensed to do it. Who in society cares what's done in their name? None of them. As long as it's out of their sight people don't care, not what happens to the weakest—to the sick, the mentally ill, to prisoners. Not what happens to the poorest—to people skeletal from starvation in Africa, to the poor sods rotting in mediaeval hell-holes in the Middle East. If it makes money for them they don't care.

No wonder the Muslims staged the Twin Towers. Staggering theatre, that. It took creativity, imagination, nerve. To conceive of it—the plane flying right into the building, the flames bellying out, the black pall of smoke sending out a distress signal over the city for miles around. And then to follow it up with a second plane. He laughs out loud. You have to hand it to them. If only he'd had the chance to get involved with people of true vision like that, who knows what kind of legacy he could have left?

No point thinking of that now. He committed the greatest sin in the criminals' rulebook—he got caught. He was weak, succumbing to his own

278

vanity. Myra should have been enough for him. Why did he try to draw in another disciple? Why pick such a worthless specimen as David Smith? It was a risk he should never have taken. In taking it, he ruined his own life—and the girl's.

He lies back down on the bed, eyes closed, listening to the wild wind outside. Somewhere beyond the walls there's an eerie barking noise, a fox lost its way in the snow perhaps? looking for its mate?

The woman in the wind is whispering to him again, calling him, calling ... She is dead and yet she is more alive than he is.

If only ...

THE END

BIOGRAPHY

Jean Rafferty is an award winning journalist who gradually became drawn to darker and darker topics such as prostitution, Satanic ritual abuse, bereavement and rape. She has written two non-fiction books about sport and many short stories and novellas, but *Myra, Beyond Saddleworth* is her first novel. To read more about her, visit her website: www.jeanrafferty.com.

Photograph taken by Mary Rafferty

Lightning Source UK Ltd.
Milton Keynes UK
UKOW032329041012

200011UK00001B/10/P